JULIAN STOCKWIN

BALKAN GLORY

HODDER

First published in Great Britain in 2020 by Hodder & Stoughton
An Hachette UK company

This paperback edition published in 2021

1

Maps by Rodney Paull

A CIP catalogue record for this title is available from the British Library

Paperback ISBN 978 1 473 69880 2

Typeset in Garamond MT by
Palimpsest Book Production Ltd, Falkirk, Stirlingshire

Printed and bound in Great Britain by Clays Ltd, Elcograf S.p.A.

Hodder & Stoughton policy is to use papers that are natural, renewable
and recyclable products and made from wood grown in sustainable forests.
The logging and manufacturing processes are expected to conform to the
environmental regulations of the country of origin.

Hodder & Stoughton Ltd
Carmelite House
50 Victoria Embankment
London EC4Y 0DZ

www.hodder.co.uk

'The trident of Neptune is the sceptre of the world.'
Antoine Lemierre, French revolutionary poet

14°E

16°10'E

French
fleet

wind

43°06'N

Trieste

ISTRIA

BALKANS

British
fleet

ADRIATIC
SEA

Pola

Lookout

Zadar

44°N

Lookout

Šibenik

ADRIATIC

LISSA

Pescano
di Mare

LISSA

Port
St George

0   1

SEA

Ragusa

nautical mile

Cattaro

A
L
Y

Naples

Bari

T
A
L
Y

Messina

TYRRHENIAN
SEA

15°35'E

Pelorus
Tower

Palermo

Messina

Scylla

38°10'N

Punto Pezzo

SICILY

Reggio
Calabria

Syracuse

SICILY

0   10

nautical miles

IONIAN SEA

Dramatis Personae

indicates fictional character

* Sir Thomas Kydd	Captain of HMS *Tyger*, Commodore of the Adriatic Squadron
* Renzi, Nicholas	Earl of Farndon, former confidential secretary to Kydd

Tyger, ship's company

*Bowden	first lieutenant
*Brice	second lieutenant
*Carew	master's mate
*Clinton	captain, Royal Marines; i/c marines aboard *Tyger*
*Dillon	Kydd's confidential secretary
*Doud	petty officer
*Gilmore	temporary gun captain
*Gilpin	senior midshipman
*Halgren	captain's coxswain
*Harman	purser
*Herne	boatswain

*Joyce	sailing master
*Maynard	third lieutenant
*Pinto	quartermaster's mate
*Poulden	petty officer
*Rowan	midshipman
*Scrope	surgeon
*Stirk	gunner's mate
*Tysoe	Kydd's manservant

Others

Amherst, Lord	British minister to Sicilian court
Andréossy, Count	French ambassador to Sicilian court
Bandone	loyalist general at Sicilian court
*Bruni, Cesare	academic of Palermo
Cavaignac	French general
*Cecilia	Kydd's sister, Countess of Farndon, Renzi's wife
*Congalton	high-ranking member of British secret service
Cotton	commander-in-chief, Mediterranean station
*Craddock	merchant of the Balkans
*d'Aubois, Comte Philippe	royalist emigré in Sicily
Dubourdieu	commander of French force sent to destroy Kydd
*Emily	Persephone's cousin and companion
Ferdinand	King Ferdinando III of Sicily and Ferdinando IV of Naples
*Fookes	MP, a.k.a. Prinker
Franz I	Kaiser of Austrian Empire
Gordon	captain, *Active*
Haynes	midshipman, *Active*

*Hetty	companion to Cecilia, Countess of Farndon
Hornby	captain, *Volage*
*Jago	under-steward of Lord Farndon's Eskdale Hall
*Kovacs, Tibor	centurion of Kassa Carpathian Hussars
*Lamb	Agnes, a.k.a. 'lady of the blossoms'
Lewis	captain, *Melampus* 36
Maria Carolina	queen and wife of King Ferdinand
Marie Louise	eldest daughter of Franz I, a.k.a. Archduchess Maria Ludovika
Martin	lieutenant i/c, *Squirrel* cutter
Mazzuoli	general at court of Sicily with French sympathies
Metternich, Count	foreign minister of Austria
Murat	marshal, King of Naples
Pearce	captain, *Redwing*
*Persephone, Lady Kydd	Kydd's wife
*Schönau	Freiherr, Hofmeister; imperial chamberlain
Smith, Sir Sidney	admiral of standing force, Sicily
Stuart	general, notional commander of British forces, Sicily
*Šubić Tvrtkó	youngster, a.k.a. Tomkin Toughknot
*Trautmann	chamberlain assigned to Lord Farndon
*Valois	*général de brigade*, captured by *Tyger*
Vaudrei	colonel, i/c detachment of troops sent against Kydd
Whitby	captain, *Cerberus*
*Willendorf	merchant in Trieste
*Woodhouse, Fanny	wife of Marsala merchant

Chapter 1

Brooks's Club, London, 1811

Captain Sir Thomas Kydd rustled his newspaper in guilty daring but it passed unnoticed, even in the afternoon somnolence of his gentlemen's club. Comfortable in a high-winged leather armchair in the library, he took in remembered odours of polished furniture, the odd whiff of horsehair mustiness and stale cigar smoke.

After his recent time in India and the Orient, he was now back in the civilisation of his birth and looking forward to making its reacquaintance. He'd been in England for some days, posting immediately to the capital to report to the Admiralty after his ship *Tyger* and her convoy of Indiamen had safely arrived after a long but uneventful voyage. While his first lieutenant could be relied on to oversee her docking, his duty was to await their lordships' pleasure in the matter of his future, and on an assurance of enforced idleness for the present, a hurried note to Knowle Manor had brought his wife Persephone flying to his side from their country estate.

'Why, stap me if it isn't Tiger come back to haunt us!' a familiar voice called.

'Prinker, old chap,' Kydd said, with feeling, throwing aside his newspaper. 'Draw up a chair and tell me how you do.'

The plump face of Peregrine Fookes MP, his old friend-about-town, beamed with pleasure. 'As I'd heard you'd long since been shipped out to a land of pagodas and *houris*. Didn't expect you back from such for years.' He signalled a waiter. 'Join me in a snifter?'

'A *burra peg* o' whisky would be prime.'

Fookes blinked in incomprehension but the waiter bowed, with a nod of understanding.

'Not as if there's many pagodas in Madras but as to the other . . .'

'Well—'

'And—'

'You first, old bean,' Fookes prompted.

Kydd realised this worldly man of politics would have heard the news of his successes in the Spice Islands and the Java capitulation. He gave an apologetic smile. 'Prinker, allow that I've been out of the country since . . . for some time. Do tell – what's happened at all while I've been a-cruise?'

'Well, now, rather a lot, I suppose.' He paused and reflected. 'You'll have heard that Portland had to yield the prime minis-tership, stress o' health. We've got a new one, Perceval. A good 'un, I trow, been a dimber hand at the cobbs as chan-cellor of the exchequer for more'n five years. Now fancies to be premier and chancellor both.'

'And who's the—'

'An all-Tory cabinet. Hawkesbury – or should that be Lord Liverpool now? – secretary of state for war, a dry old stick but stands to his guns as he should. Perceval's chum Ryder as home secretary and Wellesley – that's the elder and

2

marquess – in foreign affairs. And as your first lord of the Admiralty we have—'

Kydd gave the ghost of a smile. 'Yorke. I've had the pleasure.' An austere, full-browed man, whose deliberate manner and high voice were unsettling, although as son of an admiral he was no fool in naval affairs.

Kydd's interview had been short with no attempt to draw out first-hand detail of his engagements. This first lord played it by the book. Bluntly, he'd told Kydd that in view of his record he should expect early employment, but whether in continued command of *Tyger* or elevation into a ship-of-the-line was not revealed.

'Talking York, this time the Duke of, did the scandal get out to you in the Indies at all?'

'It did, Prinker.' Kydd sighed at the mention of the hard-living but high-achieving commander-in-chief of the forces brought down for a squalid accusation of the sale of commissions by his mistress. It had prevented him from coming to the fore in the dismal disaster that was the Walcheren expedition when an encouraging thrust against Antwerp was ruined by a combination of indolence and the dreaded Walcheren fever.

'And our famous duel?'

'Castlereagh and Canning? Who would have thought it – our two highest ministers of state on Putney Heath popping away at each other. Yes, Prinker, we did have word of it but you'll tell me more, I'm sanguine.'

'Are we now talking the state o' the world on this side of the planet?'

'Thank you, m' knowing old chap, but my friends in the Admiralty have given me the lay as I need to know. Boney at a stand, can't take an army anywhere without it has dry land to march on, but still owns Europe from Russia to Spain,

Poland to Italy. We rule the sea but are sore pressed in the article of ships and men to keep it. Sweden's declared war on us but their heart isn't in it, and the Baltic's safe. What else? Oh, yes, the tsar is allowing neutrals into Russian ports,' Kydd added.

'Is not that to be celebrated?'

'Why, I'd say it's remarkable. It means he's defying Bonaparte and the tyrant's nose will be put well out of joint. There'll be consequences, my friend.'

Fookes looked grave. 'Don't we get grain and such from there? You should understand that this has been a hard year for the farmers, very hard. Harvests failed for the second time in a row and there's real hunger in the land, Tiger, I'll have you know.'

'I feel for them,' Kydd said sincerely, at the thought of twelve months' labour all for naught.

'This damnable Continental System is making it hellish difficult for the merchantry. Above a dozen banks have failed this year alone and there's manufactories sunk with all hands on every side. It means idleness forced on the northern workers as will see 'em starving soon. And this bullion tiff doesn't help.'

'Oh?'

'Bullion and paper money. Is the tare and tret on redeeming worth the credit advantage?'

Kydd nodded thoughtfully, finished his whisky, then brightened. 'So tell me, dear fellow, what's really been happening in Town? You're not to leave me in ignorance, are you?'

'Ah. Never! Pray do not dare to mention the name of Dolly Witherspoon in the presence of any of our noble families or . . .' With a fruity chortle, Fookes launched into a racy account of the morsels of infamy that had taken his attention, sparing few of the details, until he recollected himself and enquired of Kydd's situation. 'Are you at all in need of an entertainment, Tiger? If so I can—'

'Thank you, Prinker, but I'm being right royally cared for in the townhouse of Lord Farndon, my particular friend – you'll remember he's married to my sister – and I dare to say I'll not be in want of diversion.'

Chapter 2

The London townhouse of the Earl and Countess of Farndon

'He's at his club, Cecilia,' Persephone answered her sister-in-law archly, adding, 'I've no doubt to the vast entertainment of his intimates.' Her tone hinted that his attentions might at this time be more properly bestowed elsewhere.

'Oh, do allow him a mort of leeway, my dear,' the countess responded, with sisterly insight. 'A dash of playtime, as it were. You have him returned safe to you, never taken by the fever and served on a bier as so many are that venture out there.'

'We've a rendezvous at Almack's and I want him on his best behaviour. He's to be a guest of honour and it will be my great pleasure to be led out before the assembly,' Persephone said primly.

Cecilia rolled her eyes at her husband, Nicholas Renzi, Earl of Farndon, who gave a shame-faced grin. He understood perfectly what Kydd was about. A constant round of social performances was the last thing that one who had experienced the loneliness and responsibility of command of a ship-of-war on an independent cruise in distant seas would want on return to his native shore. However much Persephone, who in his absence had been forced to live the life of what amounted to a widow, now wished to flaunt him to the world.

'The fellow has his duties, I'll agree,' Renzi said diplomatically. 'But does this include overmuch the company of women?' he added.

He and Kydd had risen through the ranks as common seamen together until they had parted at Renzi's elevation to the earldom on the death of his father. His taste for danger and adventure had been met by an approach at the highest level of secrecy to undertake clandestine missions of state in the guise of a foppish English aristocrat. After a number of deadly assignments his last had been the successful securing of a large quantity of continental specie to induce the Austrians to rise up in a fifth coalition. But this had been rendered worthless by Bonaparte's subsequent savage victory at Wagram, which had left the Austrians prostrate. He had not been called upon since and was finding it hard to be enthusiastic about yet another rout or ball.

'That's not the point, Nicholas, and well you know it.' When she was cross Persephone could be a formidable woman. 'Thomas is my husband and his place is at my side.'

'Then, sister, I will remonstrate with him,' Renzi said weakly. Under the stern gaze of both women he rose and left the room, reappearing a little later in afternoon promenade garb.

'Shall we know where it is you're visiting without a footman?' Cecilia asked coldly.

'Why, St James's Park, the better to contemplate what cogent persuasion I will bring to bear in the matter.'

He left as decently fast as he could but he had no intention of pacing through the nearby green spaces. He was on another errand entirely, one not connected with Kydd.

His footsteps were taking him towards Whitehall and the centre of power of the kingdom but his destination was a humble windowless building equally close to Horse Guards and the Admiralty. His pace quickened as he drew near and, after observing the usual precautions against watchers, he slipped in through the little door and made his way to the room of his contact in the Foreign Office.

Chapter 3

Congalton rose from his desk and bowed politely. 'Good afternoon to you, m' lord Farndon.'

'As I was passing by I betook it upon myself to pay you a visit, sir.'

The room was, as always, a mass of papers, books and much pencilled-upon wall maps but with only one desk and a single guest chair.

'I stand flattered, m' lord.'

Renzi felt unexpectedly nervous at the crow-like glitter in the man's dark eyes as he asked, 'I presume that affairs across our moat are in a state of quiescence as it were, none daring to defy the Corsican?'

'I will concede that all appears peaceful enough,' replied Congalton, carefully, and paused to adjust a paperweight. 'The Russians have made their gesture but show no inclination to throw off the shackles of Tilsit, and Spain is as quarrelsome and vexatious with their allies as ever they were. Viscount Wellington – General Wellesley that was – sees it as right and proper to sit behind his lines of the Torres Vedras, while the French under Masséna waste their substance against it.'

Renzi took in the studied movements and responses, each word weighed for content and effect before it was uttered. 'Overseas – the Caribbean, perhaps?'

'Every French possession there is now ours.'

'The east?'

'With the reduction of Mauritius and the capture of the entire Dutch East Indies there is now nothing to dismay our shipping in the entirety of their voyage to Canton even.'

'Then . . . ?'

Something in Renzi's tone brought on a slight smile. 'You will know better than to judge by appearances alone, my lord,' Congalton said softly. 'There is one part of the world, not so very far from us, where Bonaparte holds sway and at sea, too.'

Renzi caught the implication and his interest quickened. 'At sea? I cannot imagine where.'

'The Adriatic.' A near-enclosed region of the Mediterranean, it stretched the whole eastern side of Italy from Venice in the north to the Ottoman territories of Greece in the south.

'The French have moved fast. The Austrians, soundly defeated, have lost Trieste and their share of the coast opposite Venice. In fact, the whole of their Adriatic-facing lands. The Austrian Empire is now completely landlocked.'

It was staggering. One of the biggest nations in Europe without access to the sea, their trade highway to the rest of the world.

'Bonaparte has named his new possessions the Illyrian Provinces and, wasting no time, has pushed on further down the coast, taking Dalmatia, with Ragusa and the other ancient trading ports, right down to the Ottoman border.'

'So the devil has his name on both sides of the Adriatic?'

'He has, and proclaims that the Adriatic is a French lake, with his brother King of Italy on the one side, and his troops and ships well able to command the whole Balkan coast on the other – a complete encircling.'

'Surely the Royal Navy has something to say about that?'

'We have individual captains of daring and initiative who penetrate into the forbidden sea to the exceeding annoyance of the French, but because our numbers are stretched so sorely these sallies are infrequent.'

'A military matter, therefore.' Renzi's hopes of employment in a daring exploit were fading fast.

'True, my lord, but there is as well an element of interest that must concern us.'

'Oh?'

'Austria is a proud nation, and three times it's joined a coalition against Bonaparte and in each case has lost the cause, but none as entirely as lately at Wagram. The Schönbrunn treaty for peace terms has robbed and paralysed them, Emperor Franz humbled before all the chancelleries of Europe. Yet with Austria at the very centre of the conti-nent any kind of combined rising to bring down Boney will necessarily depend on their backbone, their willingness to stand up once more against him. Without we can trust they will, how can we attract the rest into any kind of coalition?'

He regarded Renzi for a long moment. 'His Majesty's minister for foreign affairs must make judgement on this very question as central to his decisions on the future course of the war. On what will he base his determination? A dry paper from a book-learned dominie? Or the collective opinions of spies who, for a suitable fee, will always find one? The matter, my lord, is too nice for that, bearing as it does on the fate of Britain and her allies.'

It was a dismaying summary and pointed up the stupefying level of stalemate that the war had reached.

Unexpectedly Congalton broke into a smile. 'My lord, your

presence here today might be considered fortuitous. Indeed it has prompted in me an idea, one that touches on the very essence of this quandary.'

Renzi returned the smile. Something was afoot. Was he about to be rewarded for his less-than-innocent visit?

'Austria, its empire, was not dismembered by Bonaparte after Wagram and remains an untouched sovereign nation under its emperor in Vienna, even if effectively neutralised. It still stands therefore as the most central great power in Europe.'

Congalton continued: 'A thoroughly autocratic court rules, every servant of the state acting in the Emperor's name and not a whiff of the egalitarian. The palace is not merely the seat of the Crown but of the governing apparatus, all found in a monstrous edifice of bumbledom, and set about with the most elaborate ritual and appearance.'

'Your idea, sir?' prompted Renzi, gently.

'Their foreign minister is a wily old bird, one Klemens Wenzel Nepomuk Lothar, otherwise Graf von Metternich-Winneburg zu Beilstein. You may be more comfortable with him known as the Count Metternich.'

'I believe I would.'

'The master of dissembling, the diplomatic manoeuvre, the logical finesse. A gentleman of vast social connections and an uncommonly favoured *élève* of the Kaiser Franz.'

'And so . . . ?'

'My lord, if any may be said to know the mind of the Austrian ruler, it must be he. I wonder – a curious fancy only – that if one were to reach a state of amity approaching the confiding, a more sound and trustworthy picture of the Austrian position might be won? Certainly set against that to be gained from the more usual diplomatic ploys.'

'A reasonable assumption,' Renzi murmured. But was

Congalton suggesting another play at the aristocratic dilettante, opposite a formidable intellect that had no reason to dally with a fop? 'I really cannot see it,' he said abruptly. 'As an Englishman, to appear suddenly in a fiefdom so recently and forcibly drawn into Bonaparte's orbit, then seen to be familiar with its highest functionary would attract attentions of a nature that Count Metternich must find acutely embarrassing.'

A soft but enigmatic smile briefly appeared before Congalton leaned back and responded politely, 'Not if there is a good and valid purpose for your intimate and private converse.'

'What possible reason can be given for such behaviour between us, pray?'

'My lord, what do you know of the *Almanach de Gotha*?'

Taken aback, Renzi replied, 'Why, since the last century this is your directory of royalty and the reigning houses of the civilised world.'

'In which your own lineage is to be found.'

'It is, but hardly notable, being but one entry in above a thousand pages.'

'The volume is regularly consulted upon the continent, much store being set there in ancient bloodlines.'

'So I understand.'

'And none more diligently than in the Imperial Chancellery of Austria. This, my lord, is why you will be allowed, even welcomed, into the country and particularly into private conclave with Count Metternich.'

'Mr Congalton, I fail to see—'

'In England a union between two noble houses through marriage is a weighty matter, never the casual choice of the two principals.' Renzi had the grace to blush as Congalton went on, 'Matters of social standing in polite society, a proper settlement upon the pair and, above all, a satisfaction at the suitability of the match in the affair of birthright and descent are scrupulously examined. How much more, then, in the case of a continental connection where dynasties and crowns pass to the issue of these unions?'

'Such is being contemplated by Austria?'

'The eldest of Emperor Franz the First, Marie Louise, is now of an age. Of the first rank in eligibility she's courted by near every royal house in Europe, not excepting Great Britain, Russia . . . and France. It's to be expected that retainers of the respective courts bearing diplomatic protections will attend on the palace to plead their case to the one Austrian most concerned in the result – their foreign minister. Strict discretion will be observed and no account will be given to the most earnest tête-à-tête for it will be universally assumed that much play will be made with the *Almanach de Gotha* and such in demolishing and vilifying rival claims, with no scandal or canard left unrecruited in the process.'

'So I will be a panderer-in-chief to the Court of St James.'

'Not at all, my lord. We have in place our own man who will in all good faith pursue that goal. Your situation is that of worldly-wise family friend, taking the part of the young and naïve potential groom that he is not pitchforked into an unfortunate foreign marriage.'

'Umm. It does seem possible, Mr Congalton.'

'I believe so, my lord. Dependent as always on your own good self strutting your role upon the stage to satisfaction.'

'Then who do you believe will win the hand of this fair lady?'

'With so many suitors, each the shining ornament of their nation, it would be an invidious choice, accepting one at the certain risk of offending all others. I therefore cannot say, other than that in the end it is the most likely it will be some obscure German principality that will prove fortunate.'

It needed no reply and Renzi waited for the final benediction.

'It really doesn't signify but it does meet the need for an excuse and reason for your presence. I should make mention that there will be one other who must be considered as involved.'

'Oh?'

'The Countess Farndon. For form's sake, she must, of course, accompany you but—'

'No! This is not—'

'My lord, let me assure you that there's no danger to be apprehended. Any untoward incident involving an honoured guest would be intolerable, and I suspect you will be safer in the Hofburg Palace in Vienna than in your own Totnes market of a Wednesday.'

'Then I agree.'

Chapter 4

Kydd strode into the drawing room of the Farndon town-house. 'It's Toulon!' he announced grandly, flinging his coat over the back of a chair and assuming a fine quarterdeck brace. A brief note from Whitehall earlier that day had been a summons from the first lord to learn his fate once *Tyger* had been refitted.

'The Toulon blockade,' Persephone murmured, digesting the news.

'A very important duty, I'm persuaded,' Cecilia said firmly, looking at Renzi as if expecting contradiction.

'What Jack Tar calls the "Toolong Blockade", I seem to remember,' Renzi muttered, 'as being of no sport at all.'

'Then this will suit Thomas admirably,' Persephone pronounced. 'He's lately been called on for more adventuring than is right and proper. The respite will be most welcome.'

At Kydd's rather odd smile, Cecilia broke in, 'Cheer up, Thomas! We're off on an adventure of our own soon. Can I tell them, Nicholas?'

'All the world will know of it before long, I believe, my dear.'

'Well, you'd never guess! Not as if it can stand against your most gallant feats of arms.' She beamed. 'Nicholas and I will be going to Vienna. Hetty has agreed to be my lady companion on the journey and—'

'Vienna?' Persephone gasped. 'Of Herr Beethoven? Of – of Austria and Hungary and the Holy Roman Empire and the three palaces and – and—'

'Just so,' Cecilia said.

'Oh, how I've wished to visit such a monument to the arts in all their glory! You're so fortunate, my dear.' Her eyes shone, then she added in a puzzled voice, 'Um, I thought it had been conquered by Napoleon. How then will you . . .'

Cecilia gave an embarrassed smile. 'Not as if it's so difficult. We sail under cartel to Hamburg, then on to the Danube. You see, the eldest daughter of Emperor Franz is to be married and all Europe contends in providing a match. We're in attendance to press the claim of Viscount Henry Capstock. He's related to Nicholas through his mother and—'

Renzi broke in, 'Yes, my love, but I dare to say your brother can wait to hear the details. He's to prepare *Tyger* for some hard enough sea-time. Wouldn't that be so, old fellow?'

Kydd's wry smile broadened into a grin. 'I would think that probable, given where she'll be venturing.'

'Toulon.'

'Not so, Nicholas. I'm to be sailing under the flag of Admiral Cotton, commander-in-chief of the Mediterranean Fleet before Toulon, true. But as we're sharing confidences, I can tell you that this is a contrivance to keep me from the clutches of the wicked Admiral Sidney Smith, who commands the waters about Sicily.'

'Shall you reveal to us why he shall be cheated of *Tyger*'s presence?' Renzi asked curiously.

'I'm to be given further frigates to make up an independent

17

squadron, which will be charged with giving the lie to Bonaparte's claim that the Adriatic is a French lake!'

Renzi sat bolt upright but said nothing.

'Not in blockade at Toulon?' Persephone said faintly. 'So no rest and reprieve?'

'I fancy not, dearest,' Kydd said gently. 'This is not your daring single frigate making rapid foray and return, it's a proper squadron with a mission to raise havoc in the Adriatic where Boney believes himself secure because he holds both sides of the sea. It'll set his teeth to gnashing, you may trust.'

'So you'll be alone in the middle of the sea, knowing that on every hand there's an enemy who lies in wait, with every port and town closed to your hungry sailors and with danger in every hour.' Her face was pale, her eyes fixed on his.

'Not alone, my dear. A tight ship with as brave a crew as I might desire and others besides to keep me company.'

'The question of a base does arise, old horse,' Renzi added.

'Why, Sicily itself remains to us, Nicholas. And three prime harbours – Messina, Syracuse and, o' course, Palermo.' He grinned boyishly. 'And a rattling fine shame that you won't be with me, as you'll know there's the bones of history on all sides as will forever have your eyes on stalks. I shall probably take shore lodgings at the Syracuse of Archimedes or is it to be the Palermo of the King of the Two Sicilies?'

Cecilia intervened with a frown, 'I've heard that Sicily is not to be thought, who should say, sophisticated in these days,' she said darkly. 'Old ruins to be sure, but . . .'

'Thomas has been in far stranger lands,' Renzi reminded her. 'I'm sanguine he'll know how to endure and take care of himself.'

'He won't have to, in course,' Persephone said firmly. 'I'll be coming with him.'

'You're going to . . . ?'

'My dear, you can't mean it!'

'No!' The voices blended into one but Kydd's sounded above them all. 'No! Seph, thank you for your considering my comfort but this is war and Boney's legions lie only across the Messina Strait, a bare mile or so. I'll not have you thrown into jeopardy just for my convenience.'

'I'm coming, Thomas. If Cecilia can go with Nicholas to exciting places, then so shall I. I'm not content to spend another year or more every day wondering what's become of you so this time I shall be going with you.'

'You'll do no such thing. Whoever heard of wives following their husbands around the world like dogs? As if they didn't trust their men in strange parts.'

'Then you've not heard of Torre Abbey in Torquay?' she answered cuttingly. 'Half a hundred officers' wives of the Brest blockade following their husbands as far as the water's edge, ever ready for when the fleet puts in.'

'This is Sicily, Seph! How will you get there?' Kydd demanded.

'By ship – HMS *Tyger* comes to mind.' There was steel in her voice now.

'Impossible!'

'As does the Admiralty allow a captain, as well you know!'

Cecilia coughed politely and got to her feet. 'Nicholas, can you spare me the time to see my court dresses? I must look my best in Vienna, I believe.'

'Oh? Yes, yes, of course.'

Chapter 5

Tyger, at anchor, Port Mahon, Minorca

Kydd eased into his chair at the head of the table as his officers respectfully rose. 'Do sit, gentlemen.'

The great cabin was dappled with sun patches reflected from the calm of the harbour, its idle gurgle and slap heard through the open stern windows, and there was an elusive fragrance of the land. It was most congenial after weeks at sea.

His officers looked at him expectantly. They had made Minorca and the residence of the commander-in-chief, Mediterranean, with workmanlike dispatch and Kydd had lost no time in making his number with Admiral Cotton. His orders were already prepared and he'd returned aboard his ship without delay.

'For those looking forward to a peaceful time on blockade, I have to disappoint you,' he opened.

There was a rustle of decorous amusement and a general brightening.

Kydd had kept the news of their mission of ravage and despoiling to himself until it had been confirmed by the admiral, and now they had a quite different destiny from that of the fleet at anchor around them. 'We have a cruise. Of a singular character, however. This ship has been given the honour of leading a squadron of frigates into the Adriatic, with the particular purpose of distressing the enemy in his own waters, this to be a planned and deliberate cruise of depredation in lieu of single-ship marauding.'

'Will you fly your pennant, Sir Thomas?' his first lieutenant, Bowden, asked.

'I'm not sure four or five ships is a command as would warrant a commodore, Charles.'

It was rare enough, however, Kydd conceded to himself. British frigates seldom sailed even in pairs, unless scouting, and he was leading four or five in a miniature battle group, a measure of the trust the Admiralty placed in his professional skills as a seaman and leader. A flag of sorts might not be long coming – if he could avoid foolish blunders and make his mark in this post.

'Let us see what we have to contend with, gentlemen. Has any had service in the Adriatic at all?'

It seemed that Brice, his second lieutenant, had once watered in Italy's Pescara in the last war and Maynard, his third, had chased a Moorish *xebec* in a brig-sloop through the Strait of Otranto but none had been further. Kydd kept to himself that he had once been as far as Venice: that had been as a common seaman with very different perspectives.

'Very well, I'll give you the lay.'

It didn't take long to outline. The Adriatic: a cul-de-sac of a sea extending from the heel of the boot of Italy on one side and Ottoman Greece on the other far up to its head. There, Venice and Trieste were to be found. In between, on one shore was Italy, with the major naval port of Ancona, its dockyards and facilities dominating, and further in, the valuable shipbuilding resources of Venice. On the other side, the Balkan shore, with the ports of Ragusa, Fiume and countless others belonging to the antiquated realms of the Dalmatian coast. At its entrance Corfu and the Ionians were gatekeepers to the whole, under the iron rule of Napoleon Bonaparte.

The crucial sea pathway between Gibraltar and entry into the Mediterranean in the west, and the turbulent sprawl of the Levant and Egypt to the east, passed close by in the south. Squarely across this sea lane lay the island of Sicily. If Bonaparte ruled there he could cut the Mediterranean in two.

It was separated from Italy by a mile or so of sea, the Strait of Messina, and where Neptune reigned, Napoleon did not.

'Who then does rule?' Maynard enquired.

'Ferdinando. The Third or Fourth, I can't remember which.'

'Er, both actually, sir,' Dillon interjected apologetically.

'Explain yourself, sir,' Kydd demanded.

'King Ferdinando the Third of Sicily is King Ferdinando the Fourth of Naples as well. You'll no doubt recall, sir, our own Lord Nelson's dramatic rescuing them at cutlass point from Naples when the French swept in from the north. He's been in exile in Palermo since, being deprived of his Neapolitan realm, now ruled by Bonaparte's Marshal Murat, who arrogates to himself the old medieval title of the King of the Two Sicilies.'

'The fellow who turned Madrid into a slaughterhouse when the Spanish rose up?' Bowden asked.

'The very same,' Kydd agreed.

'And who sits opposite us in Messina watching for an excuse to fall upon us?'

'Quite.'

'Then—'

'We maintain a small squadron of ships-of-the-line for the

express purpose of defending Sicily. In addition we've some few thousands of redcoats in fortifications looking across the strait as give pause to Murat's adventuring.'

'To which we are attached.'

'No, sir!' Kydd said firmly. 'That is the command of Admiral Sir Sidney Smith, who would like nothing more than to take us in hand for one of his escapades. He's been bound not to concern himself with the Adriatic in any way, his orders being for the defending of Sicily only. We are our own movers and keepers.'

Bowden gave a puzzled frown. 'Then if the resources of the fleet are denied us, where is our refuge, our stores and dockyard?'

'Ah, yes.' Kydd was unsure on this point, having sensed a certain defensiveness in Cotton's instructions. 'I understand we are to share in the resources afforded the British in Sicily, to be determined on our arriving.'

'A mite irregular, if I may say so, sir,' Bowden murmured.

'Perhaps, but it doesn't alter the circumstances. We accept what we can, make shift for the rest and do our duty. And if it is of any interest to you, may I say that I have the liveliest expectations for the cruise. The French don't know we're coming and will be laid by the lee at our sudden appearance in their sea. If we don't leave with a handsome string of prizes at our tail then I'm a Dutchman.'

Cotton had gone out of his way to impress on Kydd that the seizing of prizes should on no account be neglected for its effect on morale, in addition to its economic impact. Kydd had drily agreed to try his best in the matter.

And then, to his great satisfaction, Kydd heard that he was at liberty to hoist his pennant as commodore. Even if only temporary, for the period of his mission, he'd reached the distinction of flying a distinguishing pennant that placed him above all his fellow officers and captains and elevated *Tyger* to the august situation of pennant-ship to the Adriatic Squadron. If he wished, he was entitled to the uniform of a rear-admiral, and the marks of respect that went with it, even if not the pay: there would be no captain below him in *Tyger* and no staff appointments either.

The move was designed to head off any action by Sidney Smith to interfere with his squadron but Kydd didn't care. He was now one of the select band of captains that had achieved the honour and recognition and would be under eye of the admiralty where it counted from now on. He hugged the thought to himself.

He called for Bowden. 'We sail immediately for Palermo after watering and storing,' he told him. 'There we shall anchor and await our other frigates, which come from other parts to rendezvous on us. Then we make sortie.'

'Sir.'

'And while you're about it, I'd be obliged if you'd bend on and hoist a commodore's broad pennant.'

'Aye aye, sir!' Bowden replied happily.

Chapter 6

A fine ponente wind on her quarter, *Tyger* seethed along to the south-east, deeper into the Mediterranean with its cloudless blue heavens and exuberant white rollers. Kydd automatically cast an eye aloft but the crew bending on the new fore topgallant had the task well in hand, efficiently passing the robands and rousing the long sausage of canvas out to its earrings, thinking nothing of the vertiginous roll and whip at that height.

Satisfied, his gaze lighted on a female figure at the furthest forward, at the root of the soaring bowsprit. In a prettily embroidered muslin gown that billowed in the wind and with a bonnet that was clamped on her head with one hand, she gripped the rope of a stay with the other. The young girl was clearly in thrall to the exhilarating smash and swash of their bow below, as the frigate shouldered aside the seas.

'Mr Rowan,' he snapped.

The midshipman of the watch came smartly over.

'Duck forrard and desire Miss Emily to step aft.' Kydd waited impatiently with his arms folded.

'My dear? Is anything wrong?'

He swung round to find Persephone smiling sweetly up at him. 'Your Emily! How many times must she be told the rules aboard *Tyger*? And here she is again on the fore-deck!'

This was not only a disobedience but was disrespectful to its place of sanctuary for the seamen, who should be able to expect their time-honoured seclusion from the quarterdeck there.

'Don't be hard on the creature, Thomas,' Persephone urged. 'She's still learning her sea manners.'

Kydd snorted. It was tiresome enough giving up part of his living spaces to the pair but the effect of two women, of what must be admitted remarkable comeliness, on *Tyger*'s ship's company was not one he could approve of. The quicker they were bundled ashore, the better for discipline. But he had to admit that having Persephone aboard was pleasing. *Tyger* was now infused with her being, enduringly touched by her presence. From this point forward on an ocean passage, or in the reality of the enemy, he would be seeing her as she was now, a laughing, beautiful, precious creature who was the woman of his heart.

At the same time he was aware that it was a fearsome thing to have her aboard while at sea. A professional sailor who knew the odds in facing the malice of the enemy or a black-hearted storm was one thing: it came with the commitment to follow the sea. Although she was an admiral's daughter, would Persephone really understand that in both cases the ship came first in whatever it faced? It was a grave responsibility that would always be his private anxiety.

The young lady, Emily, was Persephone's choice as travelling companion. Knowing she'd be on her own once they reached Palermo, she'd looked for one who could act as female attendant when in company but as well somebody she could take visiting and exploring. She'd settled on her young cousin, who'd leaped at the chance of foreign travel under

Persephone's wing and had promised anything to be allowed to go. Girlish and naïve, her unclouded freshness of youth and artless enthusiasms would no doubt keep Persephone entertained as she stood ward over her. They made a good pair.

A few days later, they raised Palermo without incident as they entered the broad sweep of the gulf under reduced sail. On *Tyger*'s quarterdeck, telescopes trained on the prospect firming out of the morning mist.

There was no sign of Admiral Sir Sidney Smith's fleet. One solitary frigate was anchored some miles from the harbour, which nestled in the shadow of a single massive brooding mountain. Inland there were more steep, barren ranges that extended as far as the eye could see.

'Moor us clear of the frigate,' Kydd ordered. With no squadron it seemed immodest still to fly a commodore's pennant and it was taken in.

Under the wondering gaze of the two ladies at the ship's side, *Tyger* rounded to and her bower anchor plunged into the sea.

Kydd's orders were vague and, he having no admiral to report to, there was no line of resource for claiming stores. Here, there was no naval base, no comforting presence of dockyard and barracks: who took his courtesy gun salutes? How did he say hello and to whom?

'Sir?' As premier, Bowden had every right to ask about Kydd's intentions. Liberty ashore for which watch? Store and water? The boatswain's party to make good wear and tear in readiness to sail or a less urgent task?

'Secure from sea, stand down sea watches. Hands to clean ship. Before I do anything ashore I'm to pay a visit to the frigate, see what's to do.'

'Aye aye, sir,' Bowden responded.

A small voice began, 'Oh, Captain, can't we just go on the land for—'

'Hush, Emily. We go when the time's right and not before,' Persephone scolded.

Kydd had no need to change into full fig: this was no formal call. Quick work by Maynard had the vessel identified as *Melampus* 36, Captain Lewis and junior to Kydd, and as his barge made for the old frigate he could see a side-party hastily assembling.

'*Tyger*,' Halgren, his coxswain bellowed, in response to the challenge. They would now know formally that the captain of HMS *Tyger* was in the boat about to make visit.

Amid the wail of a boatswain's call Kydd came over the bulwark, removed his hat and was met by Lewis. 'Not a dress call, then, I would hazard, Sir Thomas,' he said, his grey hair and lined features speaking of many years and miles of service.

'Not at all,' Kydd replied genially, shaking his hand. 'I came to beg a steer in foreign parts. Shall we . . . ?'

In his great cabin Lewis took a chair after handing over a bundle. 'The latest *Post* and *Chronicle* from England.'

They were gratefully received, and after refreshments were sent for, Lewis sat back and regarded Kydd with curiosity. 'You're, as it were, passing by, Sir Thomas. I can hardly believe this is an accession to strength of our little band here.'

Briefly, Kydd outlined his position with regard to Sidney Smith, careful to make no judgement of the admiral.

'I do understand, believe me. A controversial fellow is the least of his descriptions. To answer before you ask, I can say that he's not expected here for some time as his practice is to circle the island with his little fleet in watch and patrol,

28

touching at the three main ports in turn – Palermo, Messina and Syracuse.'

'Which one is his base?'

'None. You must understand that, although we are the sure and true defence against the French across the water, we are here on sufferance only. There are sensitivities between us and the King of Sicily and most especially the Queen, Maria Carolina, that makes it impossible for us to establish ashore.'

'He's concerned what Boney will do if he shows too friendly to us as can't be tolerated.'

'Quite. Therefore we have an arrangement. Docking and repair is possible but only on a commercial standing, cash on the nail at the going rate in a local yard, same as any merchant jack. Victualling and else in the same way. Another sherry?'

'No, thanks. So I'm to beg what I can of your sainted admiral.'

'I wouldn't. Whatever you do, keep your yardarm clear of the man. You're directly under the commander-in-chief, you can secure your own necessaries and pay for 'em by a bill on him.'

'I will, thank you for the advice. Um, didn't I hear that we have redcoats here in some quantity? What about them?'

'Ah. We do – but they're all and every one safely at the other end of the island in Messina. General Stuart in command and busy in staring out Murat across the strait. He's notionally commander-in-chief of all British forces but you'll have nothing to do with him. He takes his orders from Amherst – Lord Amherst that is, British minister to the Sicilian court, who tries to balance what's going on in this ragabash kingdom.'

'Then none to salute, to pay mind to?'

'For you, Sir Thomas, I can't think it. You'll be sporting in the Adriatic and have no interest here – although it might be seemly of you to make your number with the King and Queen. They're an odd crew and need cosseting. Did you know this is why a perfectly sound man-o'-war like *Melampus* is sitting here in idleness? Only because their majesties demand to be personally protected from the wrath of Napoleon by Nelson's navy and this they take to be any ship with a row of guns as flies his flag and anchors in full sight. We each take our turn to play the sluggard for a brace of weeks.'

'I see. Er, I've brought my wife out – she's a yen for a foreign shore. The Adriatic is not to be considered but do you think a lodging here in Palermo possible?'

'Why not? There's a quantity of English here, doing well in wines and sulphur – she'll have refined company.'

Chapter 7

The consul was not helpful. 'So you're from the *inglese* frigate. Not a trader, neither a merchantman. A species of traveller, then. My lot is to assist the exporter, the marketer. Your lodgings are not of my concern, sir,' he added, with a shrug of dismissal.

Dillon broke into Italian. 'Signor, these ladies are not asking for charity but information. If you—'

'It remains, I cannot assist, sir,' the man said, somewhat less abruptly at the use of the native language. 'How can I know the state of the common hostelries across Palermo? This is for you to discover.'

'Very well,' Dillon said heavily. 'We shall find our quarters without your help, sir. Come, m' lady.'

'Wait! It springs to mind, you could call on the *signora dei fiori*, she's English and lives in Palermo these many years.'

'Lady of the blossoms?'

'Signora Agnes Lamb. Of a certain age, she knows everyone, everyone knows her. At the end of Via Rizzo, not far from here, on her own. Ask her what you will.'

*   *   *

The donkey's flanks heaved with effort as the tiny, brightly coloured cart, one of the many that plied Palermo's narrow streets, eventually reached the top of a steep rise and a small square of modest residences. At the higher side a flight of stone steps led them up to the summit, where they saw a small but beautifully kept villa looking out to sea. A blaze of flowers on every hand confirmed they had found who they were looking for.

Dillon gave the door knocker two brisk taps, and after a space a diminutive grey-haired woman appeared, a smile of surprise on her face. 'Do come in. I see you're English and you've come to visit and you're welcome for all that.'

'Signora Lamb?' Dillon asked respectfully.

'Miss Agnes Lamb, yes.' Her prim English accent had been charmingly affected by her years in foreign parts.

'May I introduce Persephone, Lady Kydd, new arrived in *Tyger* frigate, which you see in the bay, and her cousin Miss Emily Westerman.'

'So glad to meet you, my dears. We'll have tea directly and you can tell me why you've come.'

The parlour was small but gaily decorated in exuberant Sicilian style, with plain but well-finished traditional furniture displaying small crystal ornaments and other mementos. On the walls strange, almost primeval ceramic masks hung among wistful paintings of the English countryside.

'Shall we go outside?' Miss Lamb invited, leading the way to an airy, balustraded terrace that had a breath-taking view of the lower town out to the shoreline and a wide expanse of sea. *Tyger* lay inshore in full sight, her yards square, every inch one of His Majesty's ships-of-war.

'Ah. Your boat? I don't think I've seen it before.'

Tea arrived and they sat comfortably in rattan easy-chairs, quite taken by the vista.

'Miss Lamb,' Dillon opened. 'Lady Kydd is the captain's wife and I his secretary. I'm asked to stand by his lady, who wishes to take lodgings in Palermo while her husband is on service at sea. We'd be most grateful for any advice you have in this regard.'

'Well, now . . .' She paused to consider. 'There are English here but their residences are near their vineyards and they rarely venture to town, thinking it vulgar and noisy.'

'Do you not, Miss Lamb?' Persephone couldn't help saying.

'Not at all,' she replied firmly. 'The Sicilian character does greatly appeal. Some might term it feckless, others fiery. I think it a noble accepting of life's adversities and, beyond all, a passionate grasping of all that it can offer.'

'You've lived here for some time?'

'Twenty-one years in Palermo and with every intent of staying.' She went on, 'I arrived in brighter times as governess and companion to a family in wine. The gentleman died suddenly and his wife and children returned to England. I did not.'

'I'm so sorry to hear that. You must be—'

'Now, your lodgings, my dear. I may be prejudiced but I find the higher part of the old city in this quarter is of a more salubrious air for one of my years. You could do a lot worse than take up one of the lesser villas. There is no scarcity of staff – of the more humble kind, that is.'

'Can you suggest one at all?'

'The Villa Rossi in the next street below I know is empty these last several months since that nice Signor Brusce left for Genoa. Then again, you may think it too modest for your needs – but it's in the old Sicilian style, which is so warm and friendly. There are others – let me see . . .'

'We'll go to it this minute. Thank you, Miss Lamb, and we'll let you know if we take it.'

In the event Villa Rossi proved most suitable and Persephone didn't hesitate. An equal view to the older lady's, and with a terrace that promised dinners outside in the warmth of the evening. Persephone's artistic sensibility drew her to the house's robust and colourful Sicilian character, and she knew she would be happy there.

'Well, my sweetling, and what can I say?' Kydd gazed in admiration at his wife in a swirl of colour. She was wearing a yellow and green *fadedda*, the traditional long skirt favoured by Sicilian women.

'You like it? When in my villa I shall dress like this, just as our neighbours do.' She twirled again. 'Miss Lamb is a dear. We've got together a household and she says that everyone is proud to be looking after an English lady. She's been telling me something of Sicily and I can't wait to take up my brushes to go forth and paint.'

They sat together on the terrace, hand in hand, in happy contemplation of the view.

'Captain, look at me!' called a small voice. Emily came forward shyly. Also wearing a *fadedda*, hers in muted red tones, she performed a maidenly pirouette.

'Well, what a pair of natives I have to live with.' Kydd chuckled. 'And before you ask, I'm not about to rig out in gear of that sort. What would the Tygers say?'

Kydd had to admit he was delighted that Persephone was taking to the country. And that he was to have her stay by him during his audacious cruise was pleasing beyond belief.

Plates of stuffed sardines, *panelle*, and roast lamb arrived, borne in by beaming ladies chattering together in rapid-fire Italian.

'*Grazie mille, signore*,' Persephone pronounced, with a gracious inclination of the head.

34

'You spoke in . . . ?'

'Why, what did you expect me to do in those tedious hours below deck but make my acquaintance with the dictionary, Thomas?'

They soon did justice to the fine meal and very agreeable Sicilian wine.

Kydd was only now getting used to the idea of having two homes for his heart's repose – the other lay at stately anchor in the bay. He'd sent Dillon and the purser ashore to make arrangements, and now they had a line of credit with the chandlers and provision merchants, who would in addition honour his bills in the matter of funds and therefore he would be able to pay his seamen. There was little he could do until his frigates appeared but it would be a useful time to prepare *Tyger* for whatever she must face.

He raised his glass to Persephone, who wore a faraway smile as she looked out over the vista of ochre and tawny yellow houses down to the sparkling sea. Struggling to think of something to say to match the mood, he took refuge in his Etna *rosso*.

Then, breaking into their enchantment, he heard knocking on the front door, urgent, demanding.

Gilpin, the senior midshipman, looked abashed at finding his captain in domestic serenity. He twisted his hat nervously in his hand.

'What is it, then, younker?' Kydd asked bluntly. Now was not the time to be reporting the ship's state of water or some such.

Before he could speak a figure pushed past. 'L'tenant Martin, *Squirrel* cutter.' The man was edgy and spoke rapidly. 'Sir. I'm standin' off the northern approaches to the strait an' I gets word the Frogs are restless.' There was no need to ask which strait.

'This morning I hears they has their boats out, loadin' and such. Sir – the admiral has his fleet to the suth'ard and it's blowin' from the north, which, together wi' a brisk current, means its dead foul for him to work up to Messina. I came here to tip off *Melampus*, the only one we has this side.'

With Sidney Smith powerless to intervene, Murat, with his forty thousand men and hundreds of boats – and every prospect that the peasant-folk would rise in his support to overthrow the hated Bourbons – had seen his chance . . .

'Aye, sir. The French are invadin' at last!'

Chapter 8

Brandenberg, Prussia

'Darling – how exciting! I can hardly believe we're here on Bonaparte's continent on our way to the wedding of a princess,' Cecilia said, clutching Renzi's arm as their carriage slowed to a walk, a posthorn announcing their arrival to the inn.

'As long as the affair doesn't end as it did in Copenhagen, my love.'

It still burned on his conscience that the only other time he'd allowed her to accompany him on a mission it had ended in deadly danger, the inferno that was the Danish capital under bombardment. This assignment should be safe enough, though, merely the exchange of views with the Austrian foreign minister sufficient for him to make up his mind about the man.

'How can it, sillybilly? No one has designs on Vienna. Or have they?' she added, in sudden misgiving, looking at him closely.

'No, dear,' he answered firmly. If there was any chance of

military adventures he would never have allowed her to leave Eskdale Hall.

They stopped with a jingle of harness and the snorting of horses, the steam of their breath filling the air in the cold autumn mist. A footman appeared, setting down the steps then releasing the door, and Cecilia gracefully alighted, shivering at the sudden chill.

The Brandenburg Inn was warm and welcoming, smelling of bacon fat and beer with a medieval-sized fire shared by half a dozen travellers, who respectfully pulled back to allow them room.

They'd made good time on this first day from Hamburg where they'd been processed with the rest of the cartel, a mixed group of minor diplomats, functionaries and a solitary man of letters. They'd been accorded a private coach, with Jago, Renzi's household under-steward, Hetty, Cecilia's companion, and a small retinue following behind. Jago took matters in hand with the landlord, and after a short while, their baggage was on its way up the broad dark-wood staircase.

The rooms were spacious, the furniture heavy and Teutonic. Renzi guessed that the musty odour probably resulted from these costly chambers being rarely let and kept locked in the meantime.

Cecilia took charge and quickly had their appointments laid out, disappearing into an antechamber with her maid to repair the ravages of the journey while Renzi told Jago to arrange for refreshments to be brought.

The servants retired and the Earl and Countess of Farndon sat in intimate companionship by the fire.

'Tell me about Austria, my love,' Cecilia invited.

'Why, it's the oldest and grandest monarchy in Europe, not discounting our own. Until three or four years ago Kaiser

Franz was Holy Roman Emperor and king of more than a few realms, from Transylvania to Mantua, Venice to Moravia, but since Bonaparte they've been much humbled. His court, though, is maintained to the highest degree imperial and—'

'Not all that, Nicholas. I want to know why we're going – what do we have to do?'

'Ah. Well, the world will know we're attached to the British deputation in support of Viscount Henry Capstock's suit. Viscount Dudley of Leicester will be conducting negotiations while I have been charged by Henry's family to ensure his ancient rights and dignities will be preserved in any agreement.'

'Do you know much of the bride?'

'That is your Archduchess Maria Ludovika, known commonly as Marie Louise, eldest of Kaiser Franz. And accounted a beauty.'

'What chance has Henry got, do you think?'

'Very little, I'm persuaded.'

'Why so?'

'Consider his rivals. They will stop at nothing to secure the prize while for us it does not signify as much. And while you can be sure that the other suitors bring an alliance with royal and ruling ancestry, our own is of a minor noble lineage with no pretensions at a dynastic union. There's always the possibility of a love match but since the principals are made absent that prospect is distant.'

'Oh.'

'The most telling condition against him is that, according to the *Almanach de Gotha*, the court of our King George is not of the highest and purest – it ennobles men of industry and commerce to sully the purity of ancient lines and does not sufficiently value ancestry to the degree of veneration of the German races.'

'So . . .'

Renzi took her hand. 'Trusting your utmost discretion I will allow you to now know that I am present for the one purpose: to make measure of Herr Metternich.'

The journey continued, ever deeper into the heaths and forests of central Europe. From Hanover across Prussia, through Saxony into Bohemia and finally Austria. And with the last of the plains, the foothills of the Alps not so distant, their destination, Vienna.

The carriage rumbled along cobblestoned streets, stern buildings louring as if in defiance of the strangers. Oddly dressed people crowded along their way, and the inevitable reek of horses, with an odour of bakeries and boiled cabbage, hung on the air.

Then, quite abruptly, there was an open avenue and beyond it a bridge across a notable river.

'This must be the Danube,' Renzi breathed, held by the spectacle. A waterway with an immense history that crossed eastward over all of Europe into the Turkish lands before issuing out into the far distant Black Sea at the very doorstep of Russia. He looked again and realised that it was too small to be the great river itself – a tributary perhaps.

Joining the crush of traffic they passed over to the other side, where the city walls proper loomed, high and dusky red. Then it was through the gate and into the old city to sights and sounds that left them enchanted as the carriage progressed through the teeming streets, some narrow, others broad and grand.

The Hofburg Palace was in the opposite quarter and did not disappoint. Less a palace and more a grand imperial complex of vast white edifices and noble squares, it was baroque and ornate. Shimmering gold caught the eye in every direction, and countless liveried servants strutted about their business in an atmosphere that was at the same time imposing and forbidding.

The carriage drew to a stop outside a bluff, square and Germanic-looking building, where a small group waited in front.

A heavy-faced man in old-fashioned breeches and frock-coat came forward and bowed stiffly. 'My lord Farndon?'

'It is.' He returned the bow elegantly. From the man's English accent, he could be only one person. 'And you, sir, must be Viscount Dudley.'

This was answered with a wordless bow and a brief flick of the eyes to Cecilia. 'The Countess Farndon,' Renzi said, in a tone of calculated boredom. 'I do hope our quarters are prepared, sir. It's been an uncommonly tedious journey.'

An earl outranked a viscount and Dudley had no option but to assume the lesser role, clearly put out by Renzi's manner. He gestured behind him to a tall and dignified gentleman in dark green with gold frogging. 'Hofmeister the Freiherr Schönau, imperial chamberlain and responsible for state guests.'

The man had a fierce military bearing and jerked into a bow, clicking his heels in the continental fashion. 'Velcome to Hofburg, Herr der Graf von Farndon.'

'The Freiherr's English may best be described as incomplete, my lord. If necessary, I can communicate your wishes in any matter, as having the German tongue to some degree.'

Renzi raised his eyebrows. 'Have you, indeed? For myself I never had a desire to spend my hours on a foreign cant, but if the need arises I shall call upon you, sir, to be sure.' It would do no harm to have it be known that there would be no danger of his overhearing confidences even if in reality in his youth he'd been captivated by the lyric poetry of Goethe in the original.

They were interrupted by the arrival of Jago, provoking harsh orders from the chamberlain to footmen.

'Carry on, Jago,' Renzi said loftily. 'This is the gentleman in charge,' he added.

Schönau gave a short bow but snapped, 'Trautmann!'

A liveried servant appeared quickly. '*Zis* is your chamberlain, sir!'

'Gunter Trautmann, *Euer Hochgeboren*. It will be my honour to serve you and the *Gräfin*. Shall I . . . ?'

Renzi nodded permission to the man of years, whose lined features held intelligence and humour.

Dudley took the opportunity to draw closer and confided darkly, 'My lord, I feel it of mutual advantage should we discuss our respective positions in this affair as soon as we may. Do you not feel so?'

'If you must, sir,' Renzi said, with a frown, although he could understand the man's agitation. A belted earl with precedence in every ceremony, banquet and circumstance could be an intolerable encumbrance in the delicate manoeuvring ahead. Yet he had to distance himself from this official English representative in order to encourage Metternich to speak freely.

On the pretext of letting the servants get on with preparing the apartment, they strolled together in the immaculate grounds.

Almost immediately Dudley unburdened himself of his concerns. The delicacy of proceedings at this advanced stage, the formidable opposition and the maddening intricacy of the rigid Austrian imperial system. There was also the over-arching need to retain a coherent and credible line of advance, which he'd been working hard to perfect this last half-year. Now that Renzi had arrived, there was the danger of cross-purposes.

With a languid air Renzi eased his fears. Henry Capstock was family and he had an obligation to see the young man was not entangled in a devious foreign match. Therefore his involvement would not even start until the preliminaries of a settlement were in view. Until then he had no interest whatsoever in the tedium of reaching that point and would occupy his time more agreeably in Vienna. As such he would take it as a kindness if Dudley would allow him his liberty from inconvenience in the matter.

Much relieved, as they returned Dudley prattled about the shortcomings of the Austrian imperial court compared to their own of King George and thankfully left Renzi at his chambers.

Cecilia greeted him with a beaming smile. 'Darling, you'll adore our quarters. So ample and generous.'

He pretended to admire the rooms to please her but his mind was on one pressing issue. Just how was he to inveigle himself into the confidence of the highest minister in this near feudal court?

Chapter 9

Villa Rossi, Palermo

At Captain Martin's news of the French invasion, Kydd threw off his comfortable dinner haze and forced his mind into a cold rationality. 'Who've you told?'

'*Melampus* only. They ordered me to find you, being senior, sir. And beggin' your pardon, who else t' tell?'

As far as Kydd knew, the British soldiery were already in Messina and every significant naval unit was with the battle squadron, held to a standoff by foul winds. A full-scale French invasion needed every man and gun available – but where were these coming from?

'They're at sea – that is to say, the Frenchies are on their way across?'

'They will be, sir. My information comes from the Calabrian patriots, who warned me that Murat had massed his troops and brought together more'n five hundred boats in every cove between Reggio and Punta Pezzo opposite. This morning the news was that they'd begun boarding. I thought it m' first duty to report.'

And be relieved of the decision of how to act, Kydd mused. 'Quite right. Your orders are to acquaint the palace with your news, then return to Messina under a press o' sail to observe – not to engage, sir.'

It was a dire situation. Just two frigates to set against the forty thousands by now beginning to flood across, with no hope of reinforcements or succour of any kind. To send to Malta or Minorca was useless: by the time sail arrived they would find it all over by a matter of weeks, the French well established and on the march for Palermo in yet another conquest.

He looked at Persephone, regarding him, troubled and anxious. She must know only too well that this demanded any sacrifice of him and nothing she could say would alter his intentions.

Emily went to her side, clutching her arm, wide-eyed and pale. 'Captain, what's happening? What shall we do?' she said.

'The commodore is not to be disturbed, child. He has to give his orders and then we'll know.'

One thing was certain for Kydd. The longer he delayed, the worse the plight. 'I'm off to *Tyger* and Messina, my dear, and I fear this must be my farewell for now.'

Even as he reached the wharf and his barge, there was a heavy thud out in the bay, a mass of smoke dissipating from *Tyger*'s midships as a flag broke at the fore. Bowden had intelligently anticipated Kydd's decision and hoisted the Blue Peter as a sign to all of her men on liberty that she was about to sail. Instead of the usual light saluting gun accompanying the hoist he'd fired a full-bore eighteen-pounder, its massive concussion sure to draw attention.

'*Melampus*,' Kydd growled, as they drew near the two frigates.

'Aye aye, sir,' Halgren, his coxswain, replied stolidly and put over the tiller.

Lying off her quarterdeck Kydd hailed up. 'Cap'n Lewis, ahoy!'

He responded immediately from the rail. 'Sir Thomas?'

'You've heard the word from Messina concerning the French descent?'

'I have, sir.'

'Then I desire you put to sea this hour to accompany me to—'

'Sir, I'm desolated to advise I cannot..We've a sprung fore topmast and are all ahoo in its replacing. I'll bend every effort to carry through a jury rig and will join you when I can.'

This was a blow. Two sail were greater than the sum of both – by working together in contrasting manoeuvres it was possible to achieve much more than twice that of a single vessel having the undivided attention of all opposing forces. It would leave *Tyger* quite alone in her time of greatest need.

'Very well. I hope to see you before long, sir.'

Tyger was in a ferment of activity, lines stretched along, capstan bars shipped and swifted, fish tackle at the cathead. But one thing would bear vitally on the coming fight. 'Mr Bowden. How many still ashore?'

'Larbowlines on liberty,' his first lieutenant answered at once, then consulted a paper. 'And of them, forty-two not back aboard.'

Nearly half a watch. Guns with gaps in their crews, sail trimmers missing, a thin line only to repel boarders.

'You've until Messina to rework the quarters bill. We sail without a minute's delay.'

He left Bowden to it, going below to shift into sea rig and to brood on the Fates, who had contrived to tilt every circumstance against them.

Chapter 10

Tyger departed within the space of an hour and, in a torrent of emotion, Kydd realised that for the first time he and his ship were sailing to war under the eyes of the one who was dearest to him. His heart beat painfully. Was Persephone seeing him for the last time, a torn and broken body returned to her after the clash, or would he be coming back with a victory?

Every one of *Tyger*'s ship's company would be facing the same odds but without the moral strength and fortitude that a loved one's presence gave. They would see it through to the end. And so, therefore, would he.

They'd raise the north-eastern tip of Sicily and the strait in the morning. He knew from experience how long it took for troops to assemble, then load themselves and their equipment into boats in ordered sequence. The likelihood was that they would not risk a night crossing, timing it for dawn. With luck he would arrive at a critical point as they were putting off and be able to cause mayhem and carnage – if the winds stayed true from the north.

With the quartering wind they made brisk progress, and an hour or two before daybreak they sighted the fishing light of Cape Milazzo under their lee – their timing was perfect.

In the cool dawn, as the grey of first light became infused with the colour of day, *Tyger* stood to her guns, every telescope and eye aboard searching the horizon with tense concentration, but it was as if the sea had been swept clean of sail. Even the usual inshore cluster of fishing boats was nowhere to be seen.

Then, as they approached the tip of Sicily at the northern entrance of the strait, from behind the point first the topsails, then the hull of a man-o'-war emerged – and she flew French colours.

'A gun-brig,' Brice said contemptuously, lowering his telescope. Soon a cutter scurried after it.

'Easy meat,' grunted Maynard, and stood back with folded arms as if to let events take their course.

'Why are they both heading out?' Bowden wondered aloud. 'If the crossing's under way you'd assume they'd want to be with it.'

Impatiently, Kydd watched the low land slip by to starboard. He couldn't see down the length of the strait because for the first two or three miles, at the point of its closest width at the entrance, a dog-leg angle hid the main and ever-widening channel. They had to round the point, ignoring the war vessels, and reach down to where the strait opened up when everything would be revealed.

The trouble was that, with the northerly behind them, it would be easy enough to reach deep into the strait but it would be near impossible to beat out again in the teeth of the same wind. Any move in would be a one-way progress with no return.

Only a mile or so and . . .

The decision was taken out of his hands. The two fleeing craft were stretching out up the Calabrian shore. Firming out of a delicate morning haze was the unmistakable loom of a warship, a frigate. And a big one, broad-beamed and therefore capable of mounting heavy guns. It sent a chill through Kydd.

'She's Venice built,' Brice said decisively, lowering his glass. 'See those hances and galleries.'

It prompted another inspection until Bowden clicked his tongue in sudden remembrance. '*Naval Chronicle*, August last. Made mention that they'd launched a frigate of the newer sort as are being built to make up in weight of metal what they lack in other parts.' This was the seamanship and gunnery skills that the British had won from the countless years of keeping the seas against all their enemies while the French had skulked in harbour.

'What do they call it?'

'Ah, *Venere* if I remember right.'

'So, new, well-found and a bruiser. It'll be a hard day's work to put down the beggar,' Bowden murmured.

Tyger was no longer either youthful or of anything like the latest design. It was going to be a cruel and bloody fight to the finish, and with *Tyger* sadly short-handed.

Kydd knew why the Frenchman was there: the same intelligence that had told them where the main squadron was had also told them of *Melampus*, the only ship of force in a position to interfere with the invasion. Its task was to patrol here to intercept and put down the intruder as quickly as possible. That it was another frigate made little difference – the execution would be the same.

He could ignore the hulking frigate and lunge down into the strait to fall on the troops by now crowding across, but this was no answer. With *Venere* close behind he wouldn't be allowed to close with them and the duel would take place in the cramped confines of the strait itself, which would most certainly tell against *Tyger*.

There was no alternative. 'Lay me alongside the Frenchy,' he ordered.

Obediently the wheel went over and *Tyger*'s bowsprit tracked around until it speared ahead unerringly for the enemy frigate.

There was an hour or more before they would meet and Kydd turned to his first lieutenant. 'Mr Bowden – with me, sir.'

Together they stepped slowly forward, past the men at the conn, who watched them gravely. From the larboard ladderway they went down to the gun-deck to the men who were going to fight the ship for him.

Pleased grins surfaced as Kydd found something to say to each gun crew, some of whom had been with *Tyger* for years, through exploits and adventures without counting. All possessed a fighting spirit that had more than once seen them win through small odds of surviving.

At number-five gun one of the crew stood back at the rear, a young man but already tanned dark and with the deep chest and hard-muscled shoulders of a born mariner. His open face was wreathed with pleasure, and Kydd could guess why.

'Billy Gilmore, rated temporary gun captain,' Bowden confirmed. One of the many shifts he'd had to make in view of their shortage of hands.

'Let's have a look at your match tub if you please, gun captain.'

'Sir!' He whipped off the cover of the conical tub to reveal the perforated head and gently smoking slow-matches hanging down.

'Good. Your sail-trimmers?'

Only two. There would be no swift-footed manoeuvres aloft to fox the enemy in this battle.

'Thank you. Good fortune to you this day, Gilmore.'

An inspection of a gunlock here, a question about sighting on another. Then down into the gloom and stink of the magazines – and the piratical figure of gunner's mate Stirk, whom he'd known from his first days in the navy.

'All square, Mr Stirk?' he asked mildly.

'Sir.' An offended look was all the detail Kydd was going to get.

'It'll be a right grievous mill, I'd have to say.'

'Sir.'

'You've made up extra cartridges, I expect.'

'Enough for yez, sir,' Stirk grunted, his dark eyes gleaming in the dim light of the sconce lanthorns. He and the gunner were even now sewing more to add to the racks of grey-serge tubes. During the battle, unless there was a boarding, they would see none of it, spending their time in this sepulchral gloom, hearing snatches of news only from the powder handlers, and all the time within a fraction of a second of death from the tons of gunpowder stacked around them.

They emerged to the upper deck and three men came sloppily to attention. Kydd didn't mind – this was the cook and his mates, but far from wielding spoons and mess kettles, they bore cutlasses and tomahawks, the picture of resolve for their new tasking of repelling boarders.

And Gilpin, senior of the midshipmen, who was acting as quarter-gunner in charge of the first four guns on each side forward, his set face betraying his inner anxieties. Kydd remembered he'd been in close action before and would have no illusions about what was about to break over them.

Bowden glanced significantly ahead. 'Should we . . . ?' *Venere* was no more than a mile distant, close-hauled and with a swash of white at its bow. At this angle her massively broad beam was visible and it didn't take much imagination to conjure up its other advantages – a considerably larger crew, a new hull clean and fresh-coppered, and with an unknown dominance in guns and thus weight of metal.

They stepped back along the deck and calmly took position on the quarterdeck: it wouldn't be long now.

Kydd watched the ship intently as it drew near. Any clues about its sailing abilities or gunnery he could pick up would pay dividends later.

'He's still got men in the tops,' Bowden said in wonder. To take in sail, set more? It made little sense at the opening of an action. Was this an inexperienced commander?

The final few hundred yards narrowed rapidly, neither ship able to fire in the usual way, facing each other, but when they met it would be cataclysmic.

Not a man moved on *Tyger*'s deck as the onrush approached its climax. Both were close-hauled but on opposite tacks: the one clawing higher could send the other into its lee, steal its wind and smash in its broadside to a naked, rearing hull. Or—

Kydd was ready for the sudden slewing as *Venere*'s helm went hard up, the rapidly wheeling hull rotating to present her entire broadside to face *Tyger*'s unprotected bow in a brutal avalanche of heavy iron shot down her unresisting length.

'Helm down! Hard a-larboard!' Kydd bawled urgently. 'Guns t' starboard only!'

Almost at the same instant *Tyger* surged about likewise in the opposite direction, the two broadsides now facing each other for a split-second before the bellow of guns began, flash and smoke instantly engulfing the space between them before the hammer blows of shot-strike arrived.

A thin cry and a rending crash from forward in the roils

of acrid smoke told of one hit. Another caused furious slatting of severed ropes against taut canvas.

The smoke cleared – the two ships were past each other but *Venere* was continuing its turn in a wide slew around to take the wind now on the other tack, the same as *Tyger*. Kydd could see no sign of crippling damage and went on to give the order to close with the enemy.

Separated by nearly a mile they flew across the sea together, converging, readying. There'd been no betraying sign in the enemy frigate that Kydd could exploit, no fatal flaw in its sailing qualities – but he caught something. They were no longer steadily closing, instead running near parallel. *Venere* was shaping more to the north-east, up the indented coast of Calabria.

Tyger was being lured into some kind of trap, probably a crowding of gunboats out of Palmi to overwhelm him with their numbers.

Did this mean *Venere* was fleeing a further meeting with *Tyger*?

'Put us about, Mr Joyce,' Kydd growled at the sailing master. 'We're going back in against the invasion.'

Tyger was soon on course for her task of destruction.

It brought an instant response. As if anticipating, *Venere* paid off and swung about, now in pursuit of *Tyger* for the threat of the English frigate falling on the invasion could not be ignored.

But time was running out for *Tyger*. All the while she was locked in battle with the Frenchman she was not set loose among the invasion armada – *Venere* was achieving just what it was there to do.

It would be a fight to the finish and Kydd must devise a battle-winning strategy or go down trying.

Hard to windward they slashed on. And very quickly it

became evident that *Venere* was the faster vessel, her far newer build and clean hull telling in the race. *Tyger* was never going to make it into the strait before being hauled in, and the logical outcome was a resuming of the fight to a final conclusion.

Without warning an image of Persephone spread across his vision. Pale-faced and anguished, she was feeling every misfortune and reverse. Despite himself, his heart went out to her. It should have affected him, thrown him off balance, wrenched at him – but it didn't. She was with him as she'd promised and every ounce of his being gloried in it. An undeniable conviction grew and steadied. This day *Tyger* and he would prevail.

'Put about, Mr Joyce. We'll take him bow to bow.'

As before, the two frigates speeded towards each other but this time there was no question of a turn aside and single broadside. There was no trickery to be exploited that would have them wheeling and charging for both craved the same thing – a rapid finish to the game. It was going to be a pitiless close-in brawl that would have only one winner.

The run-in was as before, head to head, but this time Kydd deliberately took the lee position, easing sheets to lessen the heel: there was no need for the last scrap of speed in a pounding match.

Closer and still closer – but *Venere* was keeping her distance. A flinching from what must come?

At the same instant both ships yawed to bring their guns to bear and the mauling began.

The range was a quarter of a mile and the sea between them was torn white with shot, some of which ricocheted into *Tyger*'s hull with a violence that could be felt.

All at once, near Kydd, a quartermaster's mate fell without a sound and lay unmoving in a spreading pool of blood until he was dragged away to the surgeon. Halgren at the wheel didn't so much as glance at the drama, his gaze aloft at the fluttering edge of the sails, skilfully keeping *Tyger* close by the wind, but in no danger of being taken aback.

A marine spun around with a cry as if kicked by a horse, falling to his hands and knees, then crawling away, whimpering.

And a ball that shattered the quarterdeck planksheer into a lethal shower of fragments also ended the life of a seaman. Pierced with innumerable splinters, he died before Kydd's eyes, as though shot through with myriad arrows.

Tyger's captain kept savage reins on his emotions, pacing slowly and watching with ferocious intensity for anything that could offer a scrap of advantage.

The deeper roar in the enemy's fire was certainly from heavier guns. He'd heard that twenty-four-pounders were mounted in these big frigates, which could spell the end for *Tyger* and her fit of eighteen-pounders. They could not withstand such punishment for long and the only question was whether he retreated now . . . or did the honour of his flag demand he go down fighting?

A storm of feeling at the unfairness of his fate coursed through Kydd. Then a last desperate chance offered itself. He peered again through the smoke and fury. Using one enemy gun as a measure he counted the time it took them to reload and it was pitifully long. *Venere* had a competent captain, sailed well and was possessed of many guns but they were served abominably slow. This was its Achilles' heel.

He called Bowden and the master. They looked incredulous as he outlined his idea but obediently went about their tasks.

His plan was unheard of, desperate, but Kydd knew his ship and his men, and if this was a gamble, he was placing all he had on them to win.

Aboard *Venere* they would have seen *Tyger* turn, not away but arrow-straight for them. A suicidal move: she could not fire while bows on to *Venere* but they could thunder in a raking fire from a full broadside.

Kydd had judged well. As his ship under full sail closed in, the enemy gun captains, revealed now to be unskilled, made poor practice at the much-reduced target area. *Tyger* was miraculously spared destruction as she lunged forward.

Venere, unsure of what it meant, shied away, but this played straight into Kydd's hands. At point-blank range *Tyger* rounded on the frigate's bows and opened up with every gun she had in a storm of sound that echoed back from the other's hull with an unholy din.

But it couldn't last and soon *Venere*'s big guns hit back. Working like demons, *Tyger*'s gun crews had their iron beasts in a continual maddening roar, wreaking fearful damage around the fore part of the enemy, gun after gun, shot after shot, driving the Frenchmen from their weapons, which, one by one, fell silent.

Clinton's marines knelt along the bulwarks, plying their musketry at any who showed on the opposite decks. Unchallenged now, *Tyger*'s guns pounded and battered the helpless *Venere* until the inevitable happened and her foremast fell majestically, like a tree in a forest.

Kydd's gamble had worked. His faith and trust in his ship and the men who manned her had not been misplaced. The Tygers had proved to be heroes. Man for man, gun for gun, with superior skills and courage they had outclassed and defeated a greater foe. Now they would see the final act: to lay off and hammer at the helpless ship until its colours were hauled down. It might take time but the end was undeniable.

'Mr Joyce – I'll trouble you to put the barky across the villain's stern.'

To full-throated cheering from all parts of the ship, *Tyger* eased away to begin the wide sweep to take position for the final slaughter – but then Kydd stopped his exhilarated pacing as a cold thought slammed in. There was not enough time. As they circled, the invasion away to the south would see boats landing troops in endless waves unless *Tyger* was there to stop them.

'Belay that,' he shouted hoarsely, the powder-smoke making his throat dry. 'Take us into the strait!'

The cheers died as it became obvious what they were doing but there was no other course, and the reason got around the ship swiftly as they turned to, repairing the ravages of the action. They'd got off remarkably lightly, just one killed and four wounded, with most damage confined to the rigging and sails, to be expected from the French practice of attempting to cripple a vessel to gain ascendancy.

Chapter 11

Ahead, the Pelorus Tower, marking the extreme corner of Sicily, came into view, with the right-hand entrance to the strait and, on the left, the straggling hills and small castle-topped village of Scylla. This was the home of the legendary sea-monster and the point of final turning into the two-mile dog-leg that so effectively hid the crossing point.

Under a press of sail *Tyger* entered the confined and current-dogged Strait of Messina, every man at quarters prepared for the worst.

Kydd quickly had his telescope up, urgently sweeping the Sicilian shoreline for signs of assault and battle. From the Pelorus Tower cape south to Messina on that side was where his army map told him the British fortifications and earth-works were. If the invasion was under way the French, as a prime opening objective, would turn on these to destroy them.

But there was nothing – no firing, columns of advancing troops, artillery on the move. Nothing.

Why was it so quiet? Was there really an invasion? Or might they have been fed false information? Was a massive descent being made elsewhere – Palermo, for instance?

Brice, with his powerful officer-of-the-watch's telescope, made out British colours atop a redoubt, but there was no sign of soldiery taking up position – or any other activity.

It made no sense. Kydd ordered sail to be taken in and, at a cautious pace, they slipped past the empty shore to the point where the dog-leg straightened to the left directly southwards with its unrestricted view. If there was the same unearthly stillness it would be proof they had been comprehensively fooled.

Tense and strained Kydd watched the headland approach, currents curling about it, like a whirlpool, which took *Tyger* in their grip, faster and faster . . . and then they were past.

A flood of boats of all sizes burst into his vision, heading across to Sicily in a swarming mass that stretched from one shore to another.

The invasion was on.

Feverishly Kydd scanned the Sicilian shore and saw that a sizeable quantity of French troops had already established themselves, forming up into their battalions and assembling their artillery. They were too late – Murat had stolen the initiative and was now in the process of the conquest of Sicily.

At the sight a loyal roar rose from *Tyger*'s deck, but Kydd knew there was little he could do. With wind and current against them, he could smash through once and no doubt do grievous harm to their enterprise but after that *Tyger* couldn't turn back into the wind and do more. The French would close up again and continue.

He could see everything. In the far distance was the snow-capped peak of Etna, and nearer to, the rugged coastline and the invasion craft, with brigs and cutters defensively coming together as they streamed across. Then the larger town of Messina, with a deserted coastline up to the fortified British positions.

But why weren't the defending troops marching out to join battle? Why were they staying behind their parapets?

At Messina the invading boats were pouring their troops ashore but on the far side of the town the defenders were not moving. Kydd knew little about the ways of the army and their strategies but could it be that the British general did not believe this was the invasion but a feint designed to lure them out and away to allow the main force to cross at the closest point?

The flood of boats looked impressive in number. More than a hundred were on their way in, but that was far less than the five hundred Murat was known to possess. Where were the others?

Kydd took just seconds to make a decision. 'Helm down, close as she'll lie,' he threw at the startled conn, then to Bowden, 'Clear away the starboard bower and range a kedge aft to anchor by the stern. Hands to moor ship!'

They goggled at him in disbelief until, in mock rage, he repeated the order.

Tyger leaned hard to the northerly but Kydd was satisfied. They would make it.

Several hundred yards off the Sicilian beaches, in front of the British positions, *Tyger*'s bower went down. As her hull rotated to face into the current her stern anchor bit into the sea bed, bringing her to a stop, bowsprit resolutely facing out to sea, ship parallel with the shore.

'Sir, if you'd be kind enough to share your thoughts?' Bowden asked, perplexed.

'You may stand down the men from quarters, if you please.' Kydd enjoyed the effect – it must seem like lunacy. Frantic to disrupt the landing *Tyger* was now ignoring the French flooding ashore and going to anchor and idleness. 'A reasonable thing, I would have thought,' he said lightly. 'What you spy to the suth'ard is a deceit only. They intend to send in their principal force across here. Unfortunately for them they'll find HMS *Tyger* waiting for them, broadside out and loaded. I rather fancy it will take braver men than theirs to suffer an hour or more of pulling into the teeth of a regiment's worth of grape and ball in the open and no cover. Do you not agree?'

Chapter 12

Aboard Tyger *at anchor, Palermo*

'Oh, sweetheart! When I heard . . . and then you return the next day with sails in rags, and holes everywhere in dear *Tyger*, I . . . I didn't know what to expect.' Persephone's eyes glistened and she held him tightly as though he were about to be wrenched from her.

'A mite busy we were, Seph, but I'm doubting we'll encounter the beggars again this age. You should have seen them – when it became comprehensible what we were about, all the decoy force dried up, and before the end of the day they were stretching out for their lives to get back to Calabria and not a peep from Murat's main force.'

She gave a small smile, then smoothed his collar possessively. 'Thomas, I'm so proud of you! To work out what was happening and you not a military man.'

'And when I sent to tell General Stuart what I was doing, he thanked me most generously and sallied immediately to put the decoys to the sword. They surrendered at once, and that includes their commander Cavaignac, who is now a guest of the general, and a thousand or more of his men who are not.'

There was an apologetic knock on the cabin door.

Bowden entered diffidently. 'Boat alongside with an invitation from Lord Amherst when convenient.'

Kydd gave a small smile. The British envoy to the court of His Sicilian Majesty and the direct representative of the Perceval ministry was no doubt considering how to honour the action. About to accept, he had second thoughts. Arriving in days if not hours, Sidney Smith and his squadron had finally won through against wind and current to Messina and the northern entrance to the strait. If he discovered that Kydd had charged ashore first to take honours and distinction for himself, it would earn him hatred and enmity from the ambitious and vainglorious admiral, not something to be looked for in such a small station.

'Tell 'em that I much regret I'm unable to attend just at this moment owing to, um, the ship needing to be taken in hand for damage repair after the battle.'

It would serve to stall the ovations until the squadron arrived. In truth *Tyger* was not sore wounded. No full docking was required for the replacement of the length of rough-tree rail, part of the fore drift and other minor shot-strike, and while her canvas was holed and torn she had her hard-weather suit below to use in an emergency while a new set was sewn.

Later in the day Sidney Smith's little squadron, just three ships-of-the-line, was sighted coming to anchor.

There was no cheer ship, no friendly signal at the flagship's yardarm, never even a casual wave from the quarterdeck: Kydd and *Tyger* were being ignored. Bare minutes later the admiral's barge was seen on its way in. Amherst would probably get a much different story about the action than he would from Kydd but, more important, Cotton off Toulon would hear the full story in due course.

Towards evening a boat came off and delivered a message. It was from Sidney Smith and desired Kydd to make himself available for a royal presentation the following morning. It didn't take much to guess what must have happened – Kydd's true role known, Sidney Smith had been obliged to request him to attend whatever was intended for the victors.

It would be the first time Kydd had seen Sidney Smith since the flight of the Portuguese royal family from Lisbon, and he took delight in reminding Persephone that it was Smith's particular negligence that had left her stranded there as the French Army had stormed in.

Chapter 13

The next day, at eleven precisely, Sir Thomas and Lady Kydd were conveyed to the palace, where they were met by a small group of dignitaries in a luxuriant garden at the rear. Sidney Smith was not among them.

'Amherst,' said a tall, well-built individual, in faultlessly cut court grey. Kydd bowed elegantly and introduced Persephone, who curtsied with charming sweetness, her pale lilac morning dress producing murmurs of admiration. The others appeared to be courtiers and functionaries, who stayed three paces behind as they walked slowly along.

'Your first visit, Sir Thomas?' Amherst asked at once. Kydd admitted that it was, noting the tiredness in his eyes.

'Then be warned, sir.' He dropped his voice as though fearing being overheard. 'Appearances are not as they seem, and our delivering of their kingdom from Bonaparte does not bring with it the applause it so well merits. The court is riven by jealousies, betrayals and rivalries as only Sicily can breed. We are strangers and interlopers, outsiders who cannot be expected to penetrate society. Do, I beg, keep your opinions to yourself, expect nothing, we will both be satisfied.'

Kydd nodded. 'What, then, is our purpose here today?'

'An audience of their Sicilian majesties in honour of your noble action. Possibly an award of some significance or perhaps not. It will be short, Ferdinand being both amiable and indolent but Queen Maria Carolina is a termagant and interferes abominably. Do, pray, render to them both all regal esteem and distinction. You have no idea how difficult my position is at court.'

The little party reached a cloistered passageway and processed along it, their footsteps echoing from immeasurably old walls that were familiarly medieval yet at the same time outlandish and incongruous.

'I'd think this to go back to before our good Queen Bess,' Kydd ventured.

'Oh, far older. It was the seat of King Roger the Norman while we were being subjugated by William the Conqueror, and that set upon an Arab fortress of centuries standing.'

Persephone was thrilled. 'Such ageless majesty! There must have been artists past counting to take its likeness.'

'Not so many,' Amherst said drily. 'Few know of its existence, the exiled queen loathing it so, compared to her Naples palazzo.'

As they passed through, the rooms became ever more palatial, Spanish gold filigree on baroque ornate carvings and ancestral paintings on every side. Finally they arrived at what was clearly a royal presence chamber.

Doors were ceremoniously opened to them and, led by Amherst, Kydd and his lady were ushered in to the audience of King Ferdinando III of Sicily and Queen Maria Carolina.

Amherst bowed deeply and Kydd followed suit, rising to take in the spectacle. And, to his astonishment, there to the side of the Queen lounged Admiral Sir Sidney Smith in a palace chair of not much less grandeur than hers, watching proceedings with a bored expression.

'It is my very great honour, Your Majesty, to be—' Kydd began in French, the usual language of the courts of Europe.

To his astonishment there was a frisson of horror among the courtiers, strained expressions and more than one averted gaze. The Queen thrust to her feet in anger, hurling words at Kydd in impassioned Italian. At a loss, Kydd stood dumbly.

'A fine start you've made, Kydd,' drawled Smith in English. 'There's only Italian spoken in this court unless by special leave, old fellow, for you've entirely forgotten that this is the grieving sister of Marie Antoinette, Queen of France, and she's given orders that the language of the Jacobins will never be heard in her presence.'

'I was not told—'

'A reasonable precaution to find out on learning you're to appear before her, don't you think?'

Burning with annoyance Kydd bowed wordlessly to the Queen, then realised he could say nothing more, having neither Renzi's Italian nor any common language. English did not appear to be one of these, with no one apparently understanding what the admiral was saying.

Amherst came to the rescue. He murmured an apology and, raising his voice, made the requisite address in his stolid Italian.

Kydd's gaze turned to King Ferdinand. A heavy-jowled figure, he had the red-faced looks of a peasant, small eyes and an astonishingly long and ugly nose. He nodded amiably while Amherst spoke and showed a semblance of interest in Kydd.

The Queen resumed her chair, glaring stonily at Kydd, and a footman approached the King with an object on a velvet cushion.

'Move forward and kneel before him,' Amherst whispered. 'You're to be presented with an honour.'

Kydd did so, remembering to keep his face lowered. Above him the King grunted a benediction of some kind, and when it finished, Kydd felt a decoration on a ribbon being fumbled around his neck. He had the wit to stand, bow low and back away to where an enchanted Persephone stood. To his savage delight, he noticed Smith's open admiration for her undoubted elegance and grace, and taking her arm on his, he proudly stood tall.

After more words, it was apparently over. Amherst muttered at him to remember to back from the room.

It seemed there would be no royal occasion to follow, no celebratory dinner or theatre afterwards, for which Kydd was grateful. However, a message was delivered from the admiral, suggesting that a congratulatory entertainment would be in order in his flagship that evening. It was felt that, since the occasion might well involve a degree of professional talk, ladies would perhaps prove out of place.

Kydd knew at once what was in train. He was being appraised, a figure known to the public, honoured by King George and quite able to steal society's adulation if he was so inclined. On an Admiralty mission as a commodore, he stood to make even more of a name for himself while Sidney Smith had been essentially exiled to keep him from rash adventures.

He couldn't sympathise. Since Smith's earlier days, his escape from a death cell in Paris and, above all, his successful defence of Acre against Napoleon Bonaparte, he had sullied his reputation with irresponsible exploits and vain posturing for recognition. On top of this, he had taken his womanising to embarrassing lengths. It was said he'd seduced Princess Caroline, wife of the Prince of Wales – and here it was obvious that he was on intimate terms with Queen Maria Carolina.

Smith needed to snatch martial distinction and where better than in the late repelling of a French invasion? For this he needed a compliant Kydd, who would agree that he was at the time under his orders. If he could establish this, then Kydd's later victories in the Adriatic could be chalked in his log too.

But Kydd was not going to be gulled, and the sooner the whole business was out of the way the better.

Chapter 14

He took boat early in the evening, deliberately wearing his new decoration, a gaudy depiction in gold and green of a lamb being suspended by a tied bow against a background of a pair of crossed trumpets. He also wore his knightly star and ribband, knowing it would irk the man who'd earned the nickname 'The Swedish Knight' for insisting on wearing a foreign order despite lacking the King's permission to do so.

Kydd was not met as he boarded but he remembered Sidney Smith of old and followed the flag-captain below, where he was extravagantly greeted.

The admiral's quarters were decorated in Persian style: a deep carpet and Oriental hangings, a gently smoking incense-burner and a silver-chased hookah coiled up as if in recent use. It was as he remembered from those distant days as a young lieutenant when he'd been under Smith at the near slaughter of the siege of Acre, then witnessed him as the petulant subordinate to Duckworth at the Dardanelles. This theatrical posturing was in keeping.

The eyes slid smoothly from Kydd's decorations – Smith was in a floor-length kaftan embroidered in gold and silver thread, which presumably implied he had no need for the more homely baubles.

'A long time, Kydd, m' friend,' he said, handing him a long-stemmed glass containing a faintly green liquid.

Kydd accepted, sipping cautiously. It was like nothing he'd had before, a little oily and repulsive-tasting. But he wouldn't give Sidney Smith the satisfaction of enlightening him as to what it was. 'It must be, sir. Nigh on to ten years if my recollection holds.'

'Yes. They were the days. Desperate 'n' dangerous. Not like today, Boney driven from the seas, our empire swelling by the day. Do sit, dear chap.'

'It would be a foolish looby who underestimates him, I'd think,' Kydd answered, deliberately relaxing into his winged chair.

'Or who takes fright at his shadow,' was the instant reply. 'It works both ways, as we saw in the recent alarum at Messina. All it needed was for me to show my flag and force in the north, and the mongseers fled like rabbits back to where they'd come from. By the way, I haven't yet commended you for your anticipating my order to place yourself athwart their course until I came up.'

Kydd murmured something but was interrupted.

'But don't worry, I shall be sure to mention it in my dispatches. Rather points up how important it is to work together, don't you think? In fact, if we're to operate in the same seas, doesn't it suggest to you a more orderly arrangement as sees us in regular touch? After all, as admiral-in-command, Central Mediterranean, I am responsible for this area.'

'That could be difficult, given that as a commodore—'

'Come to think of it, the easiest course would be to simply attach you to my squadron for victualling and stores – you could then get on with your tasking without any concern for the papers and funding. Just burning powder and snatching prizes.'

It was smoothly done but Kydd was not to be taken in so easily.

'Sir Sidney, I'm under Admiralty letter through Admiral Cotton for this mission. No deviation from my instructions can be countenanced under any pretext whatsoever.'

'A mere rubbish of words, dear fellow. At this distance from Toulon how can he know the local conditions? Only those in this place can be trusted to judge the situation for what it is. The vital thing is to join forces for the common cause.'

Kydd said nothing, looking at Smith steadily.

'For God's sake, Kydd, think on it,' he said irritably. 'Imagine how it's going to be, completely on your own in Boney's Adriatic. You'll need every scrap of backing you can get from your friends, and here I'm providing a helping hand all the way.'

'I thank you for the offer, sir, but find I must stay by my orders.'

Smith controlled his anger with difficulty. 'You're a man of the world now, Kydd. Be aware then how it will see this – as a barefaced move to seize glory and repute at the cost of your inferior numbers. If I were you—'

'I do thank you for your advice,' Kydd said stiffly, 'and I'll bear it in mind. For now, in view of the urgency, I'm bound to press on to prepare my squadron for their employment. Good evening, sir.'

He rose and bowed politely.

'I'll not forget this jackanapes posturing, Kydd,' he snarled. 'And if ever you come under my command again you'll know what to expect. Go, then, and if you find yourself in a mort of pother don't look to me to come riding to your rescue.'

Returning ashore Kydd felt sadness at what the man had become. And what he could be. The sooner his squadron was made whole and they sailed for the Adriatic, the better he'd like it.

But for now he would take up Persephone's invitation for a rousing Sicilian celebratory dinner to which her friends and his would be invited.

Chapter 15

Aboard Tyger, *Palermo*

'Two sail sighted to the nor'ard,' reported the mate-of-the-watch, his head briefly poking around the cabin door.

'Thank you,' Kydd said, putting down his pen. Could these be his at last? 'I'll be on deck directly.'

Bowden greeted him and pointed to the northern horizon where two pale blobs showed, full-rigged ships still hull-down.

'Deck ho,' piped a voice from the mainmast cross-trees. 'Two frigates standing in, full an' bye.' It was Rowan, the youngest midshipman, legs entwined about the royal mast as he trained and steadied a telescope.

'Hail when you have their colours,' bellowed Kydd. They must be his: precious few frigates were on the loose in this part of the Mediterranean.

Within the hour HM Frigates *Active* and *Volage* had appropriately noticed the admiral's flag but come to their moorings close to *Tyger* with her commodore's pennant.

Shortly afterwards Kydd welcomed their captains on board and took their reports. Both ships were in fine fettle, *Active* lately detached from the Toulon blockade and *Volage* out of Gibraltar. Neither required docking or anything more than storing and watering to fit them for their daring penetration into the Adriatic.

Kydd's squadron was nearly complete, just one frigate, *Cerberus* 32, due from Minorca to make it whole.

Younger than Kydd, Gordon, *Active*'s captain, was alert, intelligent, and showed every enthusiasm for their mission. His ship was of a size with *Tyger* but was a 38-gun vessel, her quarterdeck mounting an impressive four nine-pounders a side in addition to her main battery of eighteen-pounders.

Volage, on the other hand, was not in the same class as the others. Barely half the size of *Tyger*, the sixth rate was armed entirely with carronades, save a pair of diminutive six-pounder chase guns on her fore-deck, twenty-four- and thirty-two-pounder carronades fore and aft. In a pitched battle at sea she would be unable to stand against any opponent armed with long guns unless she closed to a near deadly range. Her even younger captain, Hornby, though, was anything but dismayed and possessed a fierce pride in his first command as a post-captain.

They met again in the morning, braving a cold rain squall to get together in *Tyger*'s great cabin for the first official gathering of captains of the Adriatic marauders.

'Before we begin, might I remark my sensibility of the honour we've been shown in serving under the pennant of the fabled Sir Thomas?' Gordon declared respectfully.

'Hear hear!' Hornby added loudly.

Kydd coloured at the compliment, knowing it was sincerely meant, and from frigate captains who had experienced what it was to stand against a weightier foe. It was still less than half a dozen years since he had stepped aboard his first ship as post-captain, he reflected. 'Thank you, gentlemen,' he said, with feeling, 'and I fear we will have to earn our pay the hard way in this mission.'

Hornby leaned forward intently. 'Sir – what are our orders?'

'In the round, to make life unpleasant for Boney in the Adriatic, which he calls his own. In fine, to harry the sea lanes and bring down our wrath on his ports, Balkan and Italian.'

'Ruination of his trade,' murmured Gordon.

'Quite. Shall we see the charts? . . . The main ports you know,' Kydd said briefly, motioning over the length of the nearly inland sea. Venice, Ragusa, Ancona were major sea havens and heavily defended. But there were, as in Britain, countless smaller trading seaports on both shores that could not be guarded.

'Um, Sir Thomas, may we know your view on prizes?'

Kydd let a broad smile appear. 'Ours for the taking. The commander-in-chief was most insistent we do our duty by him in this, gentlemen.' He cut through the general murmurs of satisfaction, saying, 'As we have a problem there.'

'Prize crews.'

'No, Mr Hornby. The chief complication will be their carrying off. Getting 'em back through a hostile sea to the vice-admiralty court to be condemned – the nearest is Malta.'

'And something else.'

'Mr Gordon?'

'I'm exercised as how we're going to keep the seas for long. Your usual cruise is weeks only and to range north half a thousand miles without we can victual and powder in a friendly harbour, twice that to return and make Sicily or Malta to repair and replenish, why, it leaves precious little time on station to do our business.'

Kydd had already given it some thought. 'All down the Balkan coast there are lonely and forsaken islands by the dozens – scores. We'll find one within the Adriatic as suits us and use it to retire to for victuals and so forth when needed, having stocked it well for this purpose. More than this, it'll possess a hidden harbour where we keep our prizes until it's time to convoy 'em to the Malta prize courts.'

'A secret base? And in the middle of Boney's lake? Could be complicated.'

'Yes, Mr Gordon, but I'm trusting the folk about it will not be his friends and will see it in their interest not to betray us. We'll choose wisely, never fear, sir.'

He went on warmly, 'By my calculations this will cut down our turnabout for re-storing from weeks to a brace o' days only. And you, Mr Hornby, with so few to spare in your smaller barky will find it a mercy to get prize crew back so briskly.'

'Talking of prizes, Sir Thomas, it has been the practice on the Spanish coast that—'

'Yes, I've had service there with Lord Cochrane. I feel we adopt it too – prize money on this commission to be shared among us irrespective of who hauls down the flag. Agreed, gentlemen?'

'This is very generous in you, sir!' Hornby's pinchbeck buckles and epaulette were a brave showing of his impecuniousness.

'Then let it be so. Now, to work. Those charts?'

Chapter 16

Ashore, Palermo

'More tea, my dear?'
'Thank you, Miss Lamb, no,' Persephone answered politely.

'The Sicilians – or should I say "we Sicilians"? – actually do prefer coffee,' the older woman said primly. 'And in the Moorish style – sparing in quantity but bountiful in strength and flavour.'

'I shall try some!'

Pleased, Miss Lamb bustled about, returning with a pair of tiny cups on an equally diminutive tray. 'Here you are. Do be careful as you imbibe. The concoction does go to the head a trifle.'

Persephone obediently sipped, the powerful brew flooding into her being. 'My, such a jounce to the spirits!'

Miss Lamb smiled. 'As I recall, you did mention that it was in your contemplating that you would delight in the painting of a Sicilian perspective.'

'I would adore to do so and—'

'This is not to be encouraged in the usual way, I'm obliged to say.'

'Oh?'

'The countryside is beautiful beyond mortal compare – but infested by *banditti* and for the traveller a trial indeed.'

'I see.'

'So I took a liberty. I asked a friend of mine if he would find it convenient to act the escort in this worthy enterprise and he indicated he would.'

'A friend?'

'Among the many one makes in these tumultuous times. A royalist émigré who must bide his time until he is restored as a faithful Bourbon.'

'I'm not really sure . . .'

'Philippe, Comte d'Aubois. A gifted artist not yet aware of his talents. I'm sure you'll get along well.'

At three precisely the maid announced his arrival.

Persephone greeted him politely. She had an impression of flashing dark eyes in pale features before he swept down in a bow straight from the salons of Paris. When he straightened, it was with a set expression that was suddenly transformed by a dazzling smile.

'M' lady Kydd – *enchanté*.' His voice was low and musical, beautifully pitched. With his down-edged tricorne hat and gold-trimmed shoes, he was dressed in the ornate but elegant style of the past age.

'*Je suis heureux de faire votre connaissance, le comte d'Aubois*,' she replied, in her best schoolgirl French.

'Oh, Philippe, I insist. And if you wish it, shall we make our converse in English? I have been occupying my idle hours here with its learning. How else then shall I exercise it but by your gracious indulgence?'

His manner was both sophisticated yet at ease, his gestures graceful and aristocratic, and Persephone thrilled to think she was addressing a nobleman of the ancien régime. She hoped his time of exile was not proving too oppressive.

'And Persephone, please,' she responded daringly. 'Thank you, Philippe.'

She gave a delighted smile, which was returned with a light laugh. 'Bravo! We shall do well together. Now, Miss Lamb tells me you're an artist? Such a one who is talented is rare indeed to be met with in Sicily. Is this true, Miss Lamb?

I do recall several who've plied their brush here but none as I can positively say are above the common herd.'

Persephone blushed modestly. 'I claim a certain competence, Philippe, but never have I had the chance to try to capture the prodigiously fine light to be had in a sunny clime like this.' Only when she knew him better would she perhaps admit that she'd exhibited at the Royal Academy, if under an assumed name.

'Yes, a difficult affair. The Italian masterworks of centuries past, do they not seem to you to have spurned the bright light of noonday for the unambitious mornings? For myself, I glory in the Romantic, wild and unrestrained, like Nature herself. To daub away how we may, perhaps to bring to the fore the fierce mid-day orb livening all beneath in a blaze of contrasts.' He tailed off, looking down ruefully. 'But your tastes will not be mine, and the Romantic movement is still young, is it not?'

Persephone clapped her hands in glee. 'The Romantic – but yes! We're of like minds, Philippe. Do you prefer to work in oils, or will it be watercolours?'

Their conversation ranged far and wide. Highly educated in the skills of Enlightenment thinking, he was the most intellectually gifted person Persephone felt she had ever met.

Effortlessly discussing Locke and Rousseau in comparison, he cunningly wove in metaphors of art to illustrate his points and listened with touching concentration as she found herself passionately defending some point of view or other.

The count stayed late into the afternoon and she was genuinely sorry when he took his leave. 'Then we shall make up a party of artistic souls who shall venture out into the interior in pursuit of the sublime. We shall be safe, my retainers will accompany us. And you . . . ?'

'My cousin Emily will be gratified beyond measure to be adventuring with us, Philippe.'

'Then I shall bid you adieu, dear lady.'

Chapter 17

Palermo harbour

'Sir! Sir!' The hail from the deck as Kydd took his seat in his barge was excited and breathless. '*Cerberus* in sight standing in from around Priola Point!'

Wasting no time he re-boarded *Tyger*. His evening dinner with Persephone would have to wait. With this last frigate his squadron was complete.

By the time he'd made the deck *Cerberus* was in plain sight, rounding the point under the massive monolith of Mount Pellegrino and smartly coming to a flying moor close to *Tyger*. Her sails vanished together quickly as she swung to her anchor, a display of seamanship that not only reflected credit on her company but probably indicated a full crew. She was an elderly vessel, a 32, like *Tyger*, and somewhat smaller, but Kydd knew she had a fine record dating back to the early days of the war.

In minutes her boat was in the water and headed for *Tyger*, its crew stretching out with a will.

'Welcome aboard, sir. Shall we go below?' Kydd offered warmly to Captain Whitby.

Freshly detailed from the Brest blockade, he'd touched on Minorca to receive orders to join Kydd with all dispatch. But for routine victualling, *Cerberus* was Kydd's to command. A thick-set man of middle years, he had a bear-like growl of a voice and a restless manner, reminding Kydd of his previous first lieutenant, Bray. But for some reason he seemed to be hiding a smile as he accepted an easy-chair near to the stern-windows.

Sitting back he said mysteriously, 'Ah, Sir Thomas. Being as ye're so renowned, not t' say distinguished, by all who ply the seas under our ensign, thought as how ye'd like to know what the mongseers think.' He fumbled in his waistcoat, brought out a neatly folded newspaper and handed it across. '*Moniteur.*'

The propaganda journal of the French state was not to be trusted for news but often provided an insight into the latest postures and moods of Napoleon Bonaparte.

'Page three,' he prompted.

Kydd was intrigued by the headline. '*Le Diable Marin navigue vers son destin,*' it blazed. What was this about – 'The Sea Devil sails to his doom'?

He read on and was dumbfounded to find his own name staring up at him.

We have had intelligence passed to us concerning Sir Thomas Kydd, notoriously known as the Sea Devil for invariably commanding the luck of the devil in his many underhanded actions against the French Empire. Loyal agents have determined that he has recently sailed on a secret mission to fall upon the legitimate trade of the innocent nations bordering on the Adriatic Sea. In his infamous frigate *Tyger* he and several others, including the aged and decrepit *Cerberus* and the near worthless dwarf frigate *Volage*, are contemplating a piratical voyage of pillage among the helpless merchantmen trading with the Balkans, not to be tolerated by all those who cherish the sanctity of the seas.

Emperor Bonaparte, offended at this open insult to his dominions, has therefore determined to put a stop to the Sea Devil's plundering and has decreed that a fleet double the weight of metal be at once prepared under the command of an officer of distinction in order to be certain to bring this about. The honour has been given to Bernard Dubourdieu, victor of Toulon, and who, progressing from humble origins in the navy, has been especially promoted for this particular responsibility.

The Emperor has taken a close interest in the extermination of the Sea Devil and is expecting favourable news before very long . . .

Kydd blinked and handed it back. To be noticed by Bonaparte himself – he didn't know whether to be flattered or intimidated. Either way the mission had now grown more complicated and dangerous. But 'Sea Devil' . . . It had a certain ring.

'I own myself much offended, Sir Thomas,' rumbled Whitby. 'Aged and decrepit indeed!'

'Hah! You'll soon have a chance to give it the lie, sir. This is the bones of my plan,' Kydd said, bringing out the charts and operational orders. 'And we sail for the Adriatic in two days.'

'Then Friday?'

'Meaning Saturday, in course.'

Both men smiled. Friday sail, Friday fail: according to an age-old maritime superstition, to set sail on a Friday was to be avoided at all cost as it would only court disaster.

* * *

84

Kydd hurried up the little street towards his villa, hugging his news to his breast. At the door he rapped twice and waited until the maid came to answer it. 'Oh, Capitano,' she said in confusion, waiting for him to enter.

'Signorina, I desire you not to say who I am but tell Lady Kydd only this: "The devil has come to call!" *Capisco?*

Eyes wide, she looked at him as though he'd lost his senses.

'Go on!' he urged.

After she'd hurried off Kydd overheard the exchange inside.

'M' lady. It . . . it's a gentleman, he say to tell you, "Is the devil come to call on you", m' lady.'

There was a tiny scream, evidently from Emily.

'Nonsense, girl. Go back and ask him his name,' Persephone scolded.

The maid returned to Kydd. 'Capitano, she ask what your name, sir.'

'Tell her – "Napoleon's Devil."'

This brought both ladies to the door, Emily hiding fearfully behind.

'What, Thomas? Whatever do you mean by this?' Persephone demanded.

'If you allow me in you shall find out.' He beamed.

After she had read the *Moniteur* article she looked up at Kydd with mingled wonder and dismay. 'Bonaparte himself knowing you, my love. It . . . It . . .'

'Shows I must be doing my duty that the beggar is annoyed at my existence, don't you think?'

Over a companionable glass, he told Persephone his plans for his little squadron. A stealthy night passage through the Strait of Otranto into the Adriatic. The securing of a secret base from a number of islands that had already been identified as possibilities. A division of the four frigates into two pairs to attend to either side of the semi-enclosed sea simultaneously. Assorted cutters and brigs to discover where Dubourdieu was massing his fleet and report back. And all the while wreaking havoc and despair in the French Lake.

'And you, my darling. What will you do while I'm gone?' he asked.

'Pay no mind to that, dear love. I came to be near you and this is the nearest and I'm content at that. Besides,' she said, brightening, 'I have my painting and a longing to wrestle with the colours this land flaunts under its brazen skies.'

'Pray do.'

'And Miss Lamb is a dear, and good company. With such friends, I'm sure not to lack entertainment.'

'Look after Emily,' Kydd told her.

'I will. When will you leave, Thomas?' she asked, a little too lightly.

'Saturday.'

Her eyes softened. 'Then we must cherish our time together before then.'

Chapter 18

Vienna

The reception had gone well. With impeccable ceremony Kaiser Franz I had made formal acquaintance with the delegations arrayed within the magnificent receiving room in the Hofburg Palace, according strictly equal time to each. Renzi had been standing behind Viscount Dudley but his exquisite court dress and Cecilia's fine gown in shimmering blue, her sparkling tiara and handsome dark features had caught the Emperor's eye and they had been brought forward. Noticed, Renzi could now command attention in any court function, to the blatant pique of Dudley.

It had earned him an early appointment with the elusive Metternich and he now made his way to the Hofkanzlei in the Ballhausplatz, which was separate from but close by the palace. It was from the chancellery there that he ran the Austrian Empire in the name of the Emperor from a vast complex of offices and meeting rooms. It was rumoured that Metternich not only had his quarters in the bluff, square monolith but his family could be found somewhere out of sight in the upper storeys.

Accompanied by guards and discreet attendants, Renzi entered the building. He was shown into the chambers of the chief minister of the kingdom and announced, 'Herr der Graf von Farndon.'

Standing at the bookshelves by the fireplace, a svelte, fashionable figure turned to greet him, the eyes politely amused, the dark hair swept forward in the latest Romantic style.

'Foreign Minister, Count Metternich,' Renzi replied in English, bowing with the easy movement of the drawing room rather than the rigid Austrian genuflection.

'An honour for us all, your presence, Graf von Farndon.'

The reply was heavily accented and on impulse Renzi shifted to the high German of Schiller and Goethe. 'The honour is mine alone, *sehr geehrter Herr.*'

'You have the German, sir,' Metternich said, in polite surprise. 'So unusual in an Englishman, might I remark?'

'My governess was from Hanover, and taught me a proper reverence for the poets. I count Hebel and Müller among my heroes, sir.'

'Then we shall be friends, sir. I own myself in respect of the more bucolic scribes and admire nothing better than a drive in our Prater countryside.'

The room was bright and airy with fresh flowers in three places reflecting his professed love of nature. Renzi tucked away the knowledge and relaxed into one of the comfortable red armchairs.

'Then how might I be of service to you, Graf von Farndon?' Metternich settled decorously in an adjacent chair with an expression of courteous interest.

'No service, my dear sir. Finding myself in Vienna on account of your royal nuptials I merely wished to make your acquaintance.'

'And I would be gratified to make yours. I spent some time in England in earlier times but, curiously, was never introduced or heard you mentioned, sir.'

Renzi snapped to a full alert. He had nothing to fear about being exposed – his accession to the earldom was real and unimpeachable, but he'd spent his youth until then out of sight of polite society. There was a larger issue: his objective was to gain the privileged confiding of this highest power in the land and it was not going to be possible by playing the fop or dilettante aristocrat. His prime purpose was to assess the character of the man, which he could achieve only by making his own persona sufficiently interesting.

'My youth was spent in far wanderings, sir, to the neglect of my duties as son and heir. And when I succeeded to the title I made fortunate investments in the City that have left me free to roam this earth as I desire. You have no idea, my dear Metternich, how wealth can be so liberating as to enable one to stand outside the strivings of the world, making sagacious appraisal with no obligation to enter on the fray.'

Outward appearances would still have him a fop but he hoped Metternich would take him for one whose casual wealth had removed the need for posturing and ambition.

'You are fortunate indeed, sir, and I envy you for it. You'll forgive me then when I enquire of you the real reason for your presence. You are not of the official delegation, I see.'

'Oh, a family matter is all. Young Henry is of my line through my mother and she requires me to sight any agreement before matters reach a public turn.' He smiled engagingly. 'It's not so burdensome for in truth I think it unlikely his will be the suit that prevails, leaving me to the pleasures to be had in the foremost city of literature and music in Europe.'

Renzi saw, by the studied disinterest in the chancellor's expression he'd advanced to an understanding that he was anything but a fop but harmless for all that. Precisely the conditions necessary for a friendliness if not a later intimacy.

'Is this then your conclusion as well?' he essayed, not so much to receive an answer of value but to gauge its warmth, its candour.

'Without he has royal connections I'm grieved to say I must concur.' His smile was beautifully crafted. 'Yet, as we must say, in the last resort it will be the lady who disposes so Cupid may yet come to his rescue.'

Renzi was satisfied. He'd established his value as an acquaintance of unusual independence with no evident agenda of his own and with sufficient intelligence to be worth cultivating. The next move would be to develop a relationship that was open and confiding, a far harder prospect.

Chapter 19

The guests' dining hall, Hofburg Palace

'Do not deny it, sir! You were seen entering the Ballhausplatz in what could only be an unauthorised visit to Foreign Minister Metternich. I will not stand for it, sir!' Dudley said hotly. 'I am head of mission, and all motions towards the Austrians are my responsibility. Negotiations are even now at a delicate stage, which you cannot possibly be expected to fully apprehend. I demand you cease this interference at once!'

Renzi was livid, not so much at Dudley's idea of discretion being a corner of the ornate room after breakfast, within earshot of any passing by, but the insufferable arrogance of the man. One more reasonable would have welcomed the presence and prestige of a full earl in the party and taken advantage of it, but this self-important toad?

'Head of mission? So your enterprise has been elevated to a diplomatic plenipotentiary level. How singular.'

'What? No, of course not, you are mistaken. This remains a detached and private affair on behalf of the supplicant to the hand of the archduchess and—'

'Then, sir, I fail to see the source of any authority you claim over myself. Pray enlighten me on that point, if you will, and I shall consider your request.'

He left the man fuming and spent some time in their apartment absently attending to his morning dress while Cecilia happily chatted about what she'd seen and heard about the palace.

'Darling, did you know there's a gallery open to us in the Gross . . . um . . .'

'Großes Vorzimmer. A species of anteroom.'

'Well, it's been turned over to the hanging of portraits of all the rivals in one place. Shall we visit, do you think?'

It would be less than gallant to refuse her, and later that morning he escorted Cecilia into the lush white and gold of the chamber, lit in respectful dimness to soften the effect on the paintings.

Several others were pondering before the widely spaced likenesses, and eyes slid to the newcomers. Cecilia coolly ignored them, loyally making her way to the English representative's image.

'I really do believe our Henry is much the most handsome of them all, don't you feel, Nicholas?' she said firmly.

Barely audible muttering showed their presence was noted.

'Why, yes, dear, but shouldn't we give fair mind to his rivals?'

They moved across to the most ornate, almost a miniature, of a cavalry officer with supercilious features, gold froggings on scarlet and an enormous silver sabre. 'The son of the tsar, and accounted the leading contender,' Renzi whispered to her.

He became aware that a figure had appeared noiselessly behind him. He turned slowly with a ready prepared smile of greeting but saw a giant of a man with a large and full black beard wearing the gown and cap of a Russian priest.

'An elegant creature,' he said lightly, in French.

'The kin of a tsar — a worthy match for the eldest of a Holy Roman Emperor,' the priest said, in a bear-like rumble, almost as if in challenge.

'But what of the Italian — son of a duke and reputed grandson of the pope?' Renzi replied lazily, gesturing at the magnificent study of what appeared to be a Renaissance duke's son. 'With connections to the Habsburgs through the Medici line, surely—'

'A wastrel and lacking in means,' snarled the priest.

'Then the Frenchman. A duke with estates in Lombardy and now Spain, said to be in favour with the Emperor himself, and who thus may be said to have a shining future.'

'No Austrian would consider allying with the French,' the man spat, with a marked venom. 'Marie Louise has as her grandmother Queen Maria Carolina of Sicily, the much loved sister of Marie Antoinette, who suffered so cruelly at the hands of these vile Jacobins. Do you presume to believe she would stoop to marry into that tribe of regicides?'

'So therefore we are left with our English Henry Capstock, viscount in one of the oldest families in—'

'Ha! A mere Freiherr, no royal connection to be found anywhere in the *Almanach*, bringing nothing to the match. I'm astonished you Englanders think to press your suit with such!'

Renzi recoiled haughtily. 'Sir. When all your suits are dismissed for unresolvable political reasons you will find Kaiser Franz more than happy to place his eldest's hand in that of an English noble for the sake of her happiness.'

Their interchange had stilled all conversation as heads turned in naked interest but the priest snorted and stalked away.

Chapter 20

It wasn't long before Renzi's manoeuvres with Metternich bore fruit. A casual invitation was delivered, hand-written, to attend the Vienna Court Opera expecting he would be accompanied by the countess and offering the use of a carriage.

In the opulence of a private box Cecilia graciously sat on Renzi's right and thus next to Metternich, to whom she paid admiring attention, regaling him with tales of life in aristocratic England, quite untouched by revolution and war.

Renzi was preoccupied. Could he expect to penetrate the impeccably courtly exterior to the man beneath?

Two days later Renzi was returning alone to their apartment, his business with the chamberlain concluded.

It was a bitterly cold evening and his head was bent to the frigid wind, his cloak tugged tight about him. At the corner of the massive white building four figures hurtled out of the bushes and made straight for him, the dull glint of steel in their fists leaving no question of their intent.

Reflexes he'd gained in an early life at sea and later in his covert activities took over. He spun about and ran for his life but not to flee. Before he'd turned the corner he'd noticed a sharp-tined hay fork propped up next to a wheelbarrow by the wall. He snatched it up and swung around, menacing the onrushing figures.

They slid to a stop, one growling something incomprehensible and, with a chill, Renzi saw that none was disguised. Their mission was murder. He was not intended to live to be a witness.

They advanced on him but he jabbed at their faces, quickly, expertly. More than once before, he'd wielded a naval boarding pike in the same way with deadly effect. They jerked back, but one made a lunge at him with his knife. Renzi saw by its grip that it was a feint and so was prepared for the one on the left who barrelled in, his knife expertly low and vicious.

The hay fork shot out and pierced the man's chest, bringing a bubbling cry. Renzi jerked back hard to free it before the dropping corpse could yank it from his grasp then held up the bloody weapon, weaving it from one to another in defiance.

They fell back, broke and ran.

Renzi let the weapon drop, trembling with reaction. This was not his life's calling any more and he'd been taken off guard. Only those far-distant experiences had saved him.

Looking about, he saw no one else in the growing darkness. The guards and sentries would be taking shelter from the icy blasts in their boxes, the inner courtyards of the Imperial Palace hardly the place where deadly knife-play would be expected.

He hesitated, weighing the alternatives. Who had done this? The most likely were the Russians, who had most to lose if their suitor failed. He remembered the peculiar air of malignity in the priest, quite unwarranted if he considered the

English bid as derisory as he'd said, but Renzi must have been seen with Metternich in the private box at the opera. What if they believed he had some sort of hold on the foreign minister that could outflank them?

In a flash of insight he realised that from their point of view he was an outsider, superfluous to the process. What if his attendance had a hidden purpose? The Earl of Farndon was known as a more than usually wealthy aristocrat. Could it be that he was laying out bribes at the highest to put the Englishman to the fore, and he was present simply to ensure due delivery?

On impulse he knelt at the body, pulling back the coat to expose the man's dress. There was little to make an identification but, ignoring the sightless eyes staring up and the blood-soaked chest, he found what he was looking for and snatched it.

His next move should be to hurry to the chamberlain in righteous indignation to make a formal complaint as a guest set upon by brigands in these very grounds. But that would make him the centre of a whirlwind of gossip and conjecture, and he would be kept at arm's length for the rest of his visit. Not what he wanted.

Instead he hurried around the corner and across the short distance to the Ballhausplatz. He called out: '*Der Außenminister – schnell, ist es kritisch!*'

After a small delay Metternich came to the door, a dinner napkin still about his neck. 'Herr der Graf?' he asked, puzzled, taking in Renzi's rumpled appearance.

It took small minutes to explain, still less to dispatch trusted servants to the scene.

'Do come in, *lieber Freund*. A restorative?'

It was left unsaid that, by his action in coming directly to Metternich, Renzi had secured the imperial court from an acute embarrassment. And by it he had achieved what he'd thought impossible – that Metternich was now in obligation to him.

The servants were back quickly and reported that the corpse and all signs of the struggle had been removed.

'No doubt they intended to remove your body in the same way after the deed was done,' Metternich said grimly. 'To make you disappear, as it were.' He muttered an apology as he leaned forward and, with a moistened kerchief, dabbed at some blood spatters on Renzi's clothing.

Renzi saw he had a way to increase his leverage, to draw yet closer.

'Yes, a desperate crew. Have I not told you I know who they were?'

Metternich stiffened. 'Who do you say, sir?'

Renzi felt in his pocket and drew out his evidence. 'I tore this from the neck of the dead one.'

It was a small brass Russian Orthodox crucifix, unmistakable with its three cross pieces.

'I see.' Worry lines formed as Metternich turned it over and over.

Renzi inwardly exulted but said gravely, 'An unpardonable act.'

The foreign minister pretended not to have heard but Renzi pressed on remorselessly: 'And for which they must be condemned.'

'Ah. It would appear . . .'

'Außenminister Metternich. I must formally require you to disbar the Russian delegation from further participation. Their conduct is not that of a civilised nation and I would think thereby brings into question their suitability as a match for an Austrian princess.'

'You ask a great deal,' Metternich said, in a low voice. 'The

97

dismissal of their delegation will demand explanations, reasons, and I must answer for it to my emperor.'

'The alternative is to explain to your only friend and ally why no action has been taken.'

'Should information of the assassination attempt ever leave this room . . .' He looked up steadily to meet Renzi's eyes.

On the assumption that he would now be well guarded, Renzi was satisfied that the Russians would make no further attempt. Nonetheless, he took prudent precautions and made sure Cecilia was discreetly watched over as well.

Chapter 21

Cecilia ran into their private drawing room in great excitement, eyes wide. 'Nicholas! You'd never guess it – everybody's in a tizz. Really, you would never credit it, my love.'

'Pray to what should I never give belief?'

'Which I got from the Gräfin Kellersberg herself.' She drew a deep breath and then announced, 'The French delegation is finished. It's to return to Paris.'

'Oh? A sad end to their mission, then.'

'Wait until you learn the reason!'

'Which is?'

'Nicholas, hear this. None other than Emperor Napoleon Bonaparte himself is to lay suit! He's to divorce his present wife Joséphine, on account she is barren, to make the way clear for the union and desires an early marriage.'

Renzi stood up in shock. This changed everything.

Metternich had now to stand against the might of the Emperor of the French if he wanted to protect Marie Louise from the nightmare prospect, for Bonaparte, having publicly declared himself a suitor, would see a refusal as an unaccept-able insult to his dignity.

It didn't surprise him when he heard that Austria's foreign minister had departed precipitately for an unknown desti-nation, leaving the whole body of delegations and their followers in a state of turmoil. That the most powerful man in the world had thrown his hat into the ring rendered them helpless, unable to compete and without hope or purpose.

They were still in a state of shock when it was learned that Foreign Minister Metternich had returned.

Unreachable by any, within a short space of time he was closely conferring within the imperial apartments with Kaiser Franz, the hours stretching to days. Finally it was proclaimed that the Emperor would be making an announcement at noon of the name and style of the bridegroom chosen by the Archduchess Marie Louise, his eldest daughter.

At a few minutes to midday the magnificent Hall of Ceremonies, packed immovably, resounded to a fanfare of trumpets. An expectant hush descended and, from the lofty door to the left, Kaiser Franz and, on his arm, Archduchess Marie Louise appeared. Processing at a dignified pace, they took position at the centre and turned to face the people. In a spreading rustle the room as one made genuflection.

Silence descended.

In a curiously high voice, he began, 'We, Franz the First, by the Grace of God, Emperor of Austria, King of Jerusalem, Hungary, Bohemia, Dalmatia, Croatia, Slavonia, Galicia and Lodomeria, Archduke of Austria . . .'

Patiently the people waited. Surely, Renzi thought, there could be no alignment with any of the major contenders. It had to be a smaller and inoffensive state, like Mecklenberg or even Hanover. Her arm still in her father's, Marie Louise stood still as a statue, pale-faced and expressionless in her resplendent white court regalia.

Was that the sparkle of tears?

The announcement was duly made. '. . . the hand of my daughter, the dearly beloved Marie Louise, he shall be . . . His Imperial and Royal Majesty Napoleon the First, by the Grace of God and of the Constitutions of the Empire, Emperor of the French.'

A rising gasp of disbelief went up but Renzi had only one thought – that Metternich had failed his sovereign in the most personal way and in this autocratic monarchy was therefore due for dismissal. Renzi's entire reason to be in Vienna had now vanished.

The foreign minister was unapproachable for some time but Renzi was determined to reach out again to this calculating figure, who, he was convinced, would rise again.

His chance came later when Metternich had finally dealt with all the disappointed members of the delegation before they left, shrugging off the accusations and recriminations with a wry aside on the contrariness of the female race.

Choosing his moment, Renzi made his request known and was gratified to be received within the hour. 'Your prophecy was correct, sir,' he said drily. 'We English could never stand against such odds as were here arrayed.'

'Quite.'

'Außenminister, do allow me to be abrupt, if not impolite, if I remark that it would seem you will be made to pay for your failure to derive a form of refusal to the French Emperor. Would it offend if – through bare-faced curiosity – I ask that you throw the light of reason on this lamentable affair?'

'If you desire it, Herr Graf. Simply that man can never be privy to a woman's hopes and desires, still less make disposition on his understanding of them.'

'Forgive my unbelief, but I happen to know that the modest and lamb-like Marie Louise was ever brought up to loathe and despise the French who had dragged her family to the guillotine. Why then should she be joined to the chief of their race?'

'A lady is at liberty to change her mind, particularly when the title of empress comes with the suit.'

Renzi couldn't leave it at that. He shifted in his seat, leaning forward intently. 'Sir. It would not be untrue to say that two of my recent actions have been expedient to you but lie between us unrequited. I do not mean to be ungracious, still less discourteous, but as some measure of return it would gratify me considerably should you open your heart to me on the subject to reveal the true reasons for it.'

Metternich remained still and watchful, in perfect control. Then he looked up, a small smile playing. '*Mein lieber Englischer Freund.* To you I will acknowledge the debt and I believe I will now discharge it as you ask.' He felt around inside his desk and came out with two glasses and a square bottle. 'An Obstler from my home forest in Bad Königswart. You will try some?'

It was a fruit brandy of seductive taste.

'Thank you. Do please go on.'

'You feel a sympathy for me as failing to protect the archduchess. Pray do not, sir. The entire business was in fact my doing, my arranging, and may I admit it, the prolonged labour was mine to bring others to a common view.'

'Your doing!'

'As was patently necessary. Bonaparte was on the point of making a marriage proposal to the tsar's youngest sister, Anna Pavlovna. This cannot be allowed for obvious reasons.'

'Sir?'

'An amicable alliance between the two most dominant powers on the continent would throw into subjection every other nation, an intolerable situation for all proud nations. It had to be prevented.'

'And you put forward Marie Louise, like Marie Antoinette before her.'

'She is beautiful, well-mannered and carries the impeccable ancestry of the oldest dynasty of Europe in her veins, an irresistible lure for a revolutionary upstart desperate for royal legitimacy.'

'Why her, poor soul?'

'For the reason that a Bonaparte marriage carries an even more attractive lure to us.'

'Which would be . . . ?'

'After our crushing defeat at Wagram, and three times before that, the French have beaten us in the field. Now by the simple device of a marriage we have assurance that they will stay their hand against us. Their hated soldiery will not be stationed here and there will be no territorial seizures at our expense.'

'At the sacrifice of your princess.'

'Sacrifice? No more than is to be expected of the soldier with his musket.' He regarded Renzi sardonically. 'Then does this meet your enquiring, Herr Graf?'

Metternich stood revealed as a cold Machiavellian manipulator, but the greater question of how he would act in the event of the offer of a coalition was not evident. What had been established was that to carry Kaiser Franz and all opponents into a course of his devising showed that, as a supreme schemer and diplomat, he could be counted on to remain in his post foreseeably as the man England would have to deal with.

Renzi could not leave Vienna until he'd plumbed Metternich's psyche further to reach the real springs of his motivation.

Chapter 22

Aboard Tyger

From the quarterdeck the spectacle was gratifying. The Adriatic Squadron, Kydd's command all together for the first time, was stretching away under the brisk north-easter, shaping course well to seaward around the heel of Italy and on into the forbidden sea.

Keeping station on *Tyger* were the three frigates, *Cerberus*, *Active* and *Volage*, none daring to fore-reach on their leader and making a fine picture, while ahead, setting the pace for the faster frigates, were his lesser, unrated vessels, three sloops, *Kingfisher*, *Redwing* and *Acorn*. Each mounted sixteen guns, in the fashion of the times all carronades. *Kingfisher* was three-masted and ship-rigged, while the others were brigs with two, but it didn't particularly matter: their primary reason for being was as humble handmaids at the squadron's convenience.

With a twinge Kydd remembered his time in *Teazer*, his first command and a brig-sloop like these. She had sported long sixes, carriage guns of the classic kind. With them she could stand off and defy even a corvette, but he could understand the modern move to larger-bore carronades for the smaller ships. With their short barrels and faster rate of fire, a heavier shot and fewer gun crew were needed. But this was at the cost of accuracy and the imperative to close the range in the teeth of enemy fire. He could remember in *Teazer* more than one hard-fought—

'Night stations, sir?' Bowden asked, clearly reluctant to break in on Kydd's reverie.

Kydd shook off his reminiscences, annoyed that he was doing what old men were said to do. 'Yes,' he replied bluntly, and began to pace again.

The hoist went up: to shorten sail to topsails, the sloops to fall back astern and follow the frigates with their dimmed top-lights.

It felt good – he might not be a grand commodore but this was his squadron and his orders were those that were going out. A warm glow settled in his breast.

Night fell, the wind feeling even chillier, the darkness relieved only by the occasional phosphorescent white flecks that appeared and disappeared in the gloom.

His inner eye told Kydd that slipping invisibly by in the blackness to starboard were the Ionians, with the sizeable French garrison on Corfu acting as turnkey for Bonaparte's Adriatic. To larboard was Otranto and the sentinels of the King of Italy, Bonaparte's place-man Murat.

The ships swashed on in the stillness of the night, the clear *ting-ting* of the bell forward marking the change of watch, the piping down of hammocks and the beginning of the 'silent hours', a comforting sound for its reminder of routine and order in a man-o'-war.

Kydd stayed on deck another half an hour reflecting on their situation. By daybreak they had to be clear of the Strait of Otranto to where the Adriatic widened again and this was all of fifty miles ahead. The north-easter was showing every sign of continuing, and even under their reduced sail they should achieve it.

There was no knowing what they'd come across in their first day at large in the Adriatic – patrolling French frigates, convoys, coastal traders. But if they were seen, the French would know that it was no single daring frigate that had trespassed on their sea but a menacing and powerful squadron. As a priority act, fast light frigates would be sent to dog their heels until Dubourdieu's fleet could come out to challenge them. That would have a serious consequence: there was no way he could establish a secret base with his every motion being tracked.

Kydd's plan was for a rapid establishing of the base followed by the squadron splitting into two, one pair on the Italian coast, the other the Balkan. Then the harrying could commence. The French would be confused, expecting the single Sea Devil expedition their intelligence had told them about. Which should they hunt?

Two separate raiding forces on the high seas would double the fear and despair it was in his orders to spread. And with a clandestine base to keep them supplied, the harassing could go on indefinitely. *If* they could keep the secret of its location.

He turned in, blessing his hard-won ability to banish sleep-destroying fretting.

As hands went to breakfast Kydd was left alone to pace the decks in the tentative morning light. He decided on a round-table discussion with his officers when the men had turned to their part-of-ship at eight. That settled, he would just enjoy the daily miracle of the day's dawning.

*   *   *

'I'd not say there's anywheres on the Italian side,' Joyce, the sailing master, proclaimed. 'As it being so settled an' all.'

The small-scale chart agreed with him, and *Tyger*'s officers set their gaze on the Balkan shore. With none who had sailed in these waters except Kydd, and he never on the lookout for the possible location of a secret base, the charts were all they had to work with.

'But the other side,' said Brice, positively. 'You see? All those islands and inner leads, that's where your coastals will be staying, dodging in among the islands and skerries to keep from being made prize. It means they'll avoid the outer islands as being too much under eye, so these places will be well forsaken.'

'Makes sense,' Kydd muttered. 'And has the advantage that without visitors they'd hold no interest for the French.'

Joyce pulled out a large-scale chart, a Venetian production whose details of harbours, watering, roadsteads and so forth plainly indicated a merchantman origin. The big ports were all there – Cattaro, Ragusa, Trieste and Fiume – and as well a surprising number of lesser. All were on the mainland up and down Dalmatia.

The names meant nothing, the soundings everything. And it was deep water everywhere, first-class navigating and, in the apparent absence of indications of current, all that a master could desire. So which of the outer islands should they look to?

One crucial requirement was concealment. An open roadstead was not what was wanted. In addition, the winds in the Adriatic were legendary in their ferocity. Their haven would need to be at the same time snug and capacious with no local threats of any kind.

'These islands were lairs for sea-robbers for centuries before the Romans,' Dillon said dreamily, his note-taking temporarily suspended. 'Descendants of the Phoenicians, we believe. It would be interesting indeed to compare their linguistic stems with those of—'

'Later, Edward. Your point?'

'It's more than likely we'll find many islands inhabited, and by such fractious tribes as have been driven from the Balkan mainland for unsociable habits. Shall we establish our base on one such I cannot answer to their neighbourliness.'

'All the more reason to, Mr Philology,' Bowden said, with a grin. 'As deterring the French from planting a garrison, which would need defending.'

'Very well. We have to make a start – time's not with us, gentlemen. So how about this one?' Kydd tapped one of the series of long islands trailing out from the coast in the south. Brač, they call it.'

Joyce rubbed his chin. 'I'd think too near Spalato, which the mongseers would be regularly visiting as one of their trade ports, passing by to the nor'ard or suth'ard both.'

'Well, safely further offshore we've got Korčula, here,' offered Maynard.

'All its anchorages to the east 'n' west only, none I can see t' give shelter in a reg'lar-going blow,' said Joyce, after consulting another chart.

'This 'un?' mused Bowden. His eye was on an islet set well out, considerably further than the others, and conveniently at precisely the halfway point into the Adriatic. 'If you were scouting along the Illyrian coast you'd be keeping in with the greater number, and those are along the inshore leads.'

'Um. Has a fine little haven on its north side,' Kydd mused. 'And one more on the other, so whichever the direction of blow we'll have somewhere to lie up.'

'A fishing village in the bay?'

'So tiny as won't worry us.'

'And inland?'

'Looks to be all mountains. I doubt we're to be disturbed from them if we choose the village.'

'Worth investigating, sir?'

'I think so, Mr Bowden. What's it called, by the way?'

'Lissa.'

Chapter 23

The sooner they had their hideaway in this hostile sea the better. On deck Kydd didn't waste time. Altering more to the north-west he ordered each of his squadron to pass within hail and told them their destination.

The following morning, well on their way, the Fates turned against them.

As the early light stole outwards after the impenetrable night, it revealed what they'd dreaded: a French corvette. Studding athwart in a comfortable breeze, by its course it was no doubt headed for the inshore islands.

It soon executed a rapid and courageous wheeling in a wide circle to fall in behind them in an impeccable tracking position, neatly robbing them of any chance at keeping their planned bolt-hole secret.

Kydd knew it had to be eliminated. Merely frightening it off was not enough – it already had their course and it would not take much to work out where the squadron was heading. Staying with them until they arrived would only confirm the assumption.

Their overwhelming numbers would not be an advantage

any more than they would in the case of a British frigate dogging the heels of an evading French battle group. A wise captain of a scouting vessel knew all the tricks and could be relied on to stay on their trail.

Should he scatter and disperse the squadron in different directions? Following any one of them at random would in the end still lead to the secret base and therefore there was no point in it.

'General chase,' Kydd snapped.

The entire squadron turned on the stalker, who instantly wore around in the opposite direction and led off – cheekily on course for Lissa.

Full and bye the frigates complied, leaving the sloops in their wake. There would be no joining battle in any form until they'd overhauled the corvette but that was looking more and more unlikely, the fine-lined Frenchman making excellent sailing in the chill morning breeze while its huskier pursuers wallowed along with all sail set.

After some hours the wind picked up and *Tyger* came into her own, insolently throwing aside the oncoming waves with a crash of spreading white and the lively thrum of a stiff breeze in the rigging. *Cerberus* and *Active* were not far behind but *Volage* was slipping back.

Now the corvette sensed a different mood, particularly when the two bigger frigates spread out on the beam as if to encircle their prey. Abruptly, just before noon, its helm went over and, filling to a useful quarterly wind, it took up on an easterly heading.

'She's making to lose us among the inshore islands,' growled Brice, levelling his telescope at the ship.

Kydd agreed, adding sourly, 'And night coming on makes it a likely thing, too. Mr Joyce, I'll have all sail set conformable to conditions.' His other commands would take the hint and spread their canvas to keep with *Tyger* as they barrelled along. Given the stakes, they had to spare nothing in cracking on to the limit in overhauling the corvette. Taking the risk of crowding sail in these brisk winds, the weakest vessel would fail first but there would always be another two to continue the chase.

This was the only way they could close with the fleeing vessel, which, seeing what was happening, spread as much sail as it could.

'A clever and audacious captain,' acknowledged Kydd, following its movements through his glass. 'And determined.'

The chase was now even, four ships speeding over the sea, their stays and sheets bar-taut, their tracks arrow-straight.

The first island lifted above the horizon. As if choosing another, the corvette shaped course to pass it to starboard while a second, grey-limned, loomed to larboard.

'Mr Joyce?'

'Kopište t' larboard, 'Uble t'other side, sir. An' that's forty-odd miles off the Balkan coast,' he added, seeing Kydd's expression.

The sun was now dipping fast towards a winter darkness. Once lost in the crepuscular shades, the corvette could choose which way to dodge among the denser sprawl of islands further in and could be very quickly lost among them.

'Mr Joyce, can't we find a knot or two more?' Kydd ground out. Any risk to the spars was worth it in this frenzied chase.

But the corvette did the same and, as dusk fell, it became obvious they were not going to land the catch.

A pall of despondency settled over *Tyger* as the last of the daylight saw the straining form of the corvette triumphantly merge with the twilight, then nightfall hid everything.

There was no reason to keep on their breakneck pace and before it became too dark Kydd eased away. For want of a better plan he kept on course to see what the morning would bring. The last he saw of his two frigates, they were extending out even further in a classic search sweep. From what he'd noticed of the corvette's movements during the day, he much doubted the captain would fall in with this manoeuvre.

He stayed a little longer in the bitter wind, then went below to the snug warmth of his cabin where Tysoe had laid out supper.

Kydd had little appetite but took some soup. It was an unfortunate and difficult start to the mission and—

There was the urgent clatter of steps at the main hatchway. Spoon halfway to mouth, Kydd paused.

Brice knocked and leaned in. 'Sir! Rockets and blue lights on the bow. *Active*, we think.'

Kydd's heart leaped. If it was what he thought it could be . . .

Within the hour *Tyger*, with backed topsails, lay off the forlorn sight of the corvette, her foremast a splintered ruin on deck, with *Active*'s boats alongside taking possession. In a cruel reversal of the fortunes of war, the vessel had kept on its wild rush hoping to put distance between them but it had proved too much for the over-strained sparring.

'Knew if we pressed him hard, he'd lose his sticks,' *Active*'s Captain Gordon said smugly. British ships were much superior in deep-sea weatherliness over the slender-sparred Frenchmen. Kydd gave a tight smile, not bothering to point out that it had been his decision in the first place.

'And we've a prize and above a hundred prisoners,' Gordon added, a little less smugly. It was a fine prize but useless until repaired, a lengthy and near impossible business on the open sea. It would have to be destroyed, but there was an even bigger quandary: prisoners.

Hostile seamen in the number of half a ship's company

were a dangerous and man-sapping burden to keep indefinitely under guard. Bonaparte had once solved the problem in an appalling way: after being stranded in the Levant following the battle of the Nile, he'd taken a thousand prisoners down to the beach and had had them bayonetted in cold blood.

The thought still chilled Kydd. 'Share 'em among all of us, keeping them on deck under eye until we've reached Lissa. Then send 'em ashore with the honour of building their own prison, as will keep them well occupied.'

Chapter 24

The squadron approached cautiously. The rugged and irregular coastline of Lissa was less than welcoming, the ridges and peaks forbidding in their darkly wooded covering with no sign of human habitation.

They sailed together along the north side on the lookout for a bay, Porto San Giorgio, which was mentioned in the pilot as having a fine harbour. It was nearly completely concealed from seaward by a convenient islet, which would also double as a breakwater for the bay within. Half a mile across it was twice as long, more than adequate for shelter and a prize anchorage, out of sight of any passing observer.

At its furthest point there was a small and pretty fishing village, and on the opposite shore an even smaller settlement with the prospect of a regular supply of fish and greens. While there didn't appear to be anything like a dockyard, the gently sloping shoreline offered suitable careening in several places. It was perfect.

Kydd turned to his confidential secretary. 'Mr Dillon. Have you the local lingo?'

'As this was Venetian until recently, I believe they'll still speak Italian.'

'Then we go ashore and investigate.'

When Kydd's barge touched the little jetty they found the town deserted. Kydd had expected this and was prepared. No doubt four ocean-going warships appearing out of nowhere to round to brazenly and anchor directly before the village would have been terrifying. As they made their way to the little town square they were accompanied by a splendidly dressed Royal Marine. Kydd and Dillon took their ease on the single public bench and, stiffly at attention, the marine flourished his drumsticks and began a loud tattoo. The sound echoed from all sides of the plaza, volleying and rattling and with contrasting ruffles, intriguing in its exotic sounds.

The first figures emerged on the opposite side, soon joined by others until a small admiring crowd had gathered.

Kydd motioned to the drummer to cease and turned to Dillon. 'Tell 'em I'm here in peace, with a proposing as is intended to please us both. I'd like to talk to the head man to see if—'

'*Il sindaco,*' Dillon offered helpfully.

'Yes, that one. To see if we can come to an arrangement of mutual benefit.'

It seemed that the nearby fishermen's tavern would be available to them, and in great good humour all repaired there to discuss the island's future.

There was much to achieve. Agreement was sought and readily given for men to move freely ashore. For the poverty-ridden island, the possibilities in the steady supply and sale of victuals were compelling.

'I'll have storehouses up behind the dwellings and a small barracks in the village somewhere. We'll have a signal station rigged on that islet we saw at the harbour entrance – that'll be Mr Carew's responsibility,' Kydd added.

'Defences, sir?'

'Not as if we can put up much of a fight if the Frenchies come in force but I think we'll have one or two cannon landed on our islet to give 'em pause about going in.'

'If there's to be a powder store, sir, shouldn't we put it out of the way?'

'The gunner to inspect the fisher-folk's net sheds along the coast and, if suitable, they'll do.'

It was never-ending – the establishing of a base supplying not only four frigates and the sloops but as well prize crews and their prisoners until they were shipped off to their final confinement.

And victuals, watering. If these weren't on hand, their sea raiding would come to a halt until they had sourced supplies from another more distant place.

Powder, shot and a long list of sea stores and spares would be brought in from Malta dockyard by transports and stock-piled for timely use by the squadron in a quick turn-around before they headed back to the hunting grounds.

The management of this very irregular establishment had to be done entirely by themselves. Kydd couldn't afford to lose an officer for a duty watch ashore so it would have to be two midshipmen taking command by rota. Plus enough men to mount guard over the stores and handle the unloading of store-ships and suchlike.

It was a relief when the sloops were sighted, intelligently having assumed the rendezvous point to be Lissa. Without delay the smallest, *Acorn*, was dispatched to let Malta know of the secret base and to redirect all replenishments entitled by the squadron.

For Kydd it was now more than a resupply post. While he

was away on his depredations, orders, dispatches and mail could be left and collected, and he'd need never be out of touch with the bigger picture.

It was a most pleasing start.

Chapter 25

The next day, early in the forenoon, *Active* and *Volage*, under the command of Gordon and accompanied by the ship-sloop *Kingfisher*, put to sea. Their orders were to raise mayhem on the Italian shore and gain intelligence on Bonaparte's challenger to the Sea Devil, Dubourdieu and his fleet.

Kydd, with *Cerberus* and the remaining sloop *Redwing*, shortly made sail in the other direction for the Balkan shore.

There was not much strategy involved. In a sea completely enclosed by the enemy, every port, every ship and every fortification was fair prey. From now on each hail from the masthead was a call to arms, and as for raiding, they could take their choice along the near thousand miles of coastline.

Kydd's thought was to penetrate northwards, deep into the Adriatic, before he unleashed his power.

With *Tyger* in the van leading *Cerberus*, and *Redwing* creaming along in line ahead, a little before noon there was a hail from the masthead that not one but two sail had been seen in the wind's eye to the north-west. Every sail encountered couldn't be anything other than the enemy, and the little band hauled their wind to intercept. As they crossed its track the picture became clearer.

The two sail were conventionally square-rigged but appearing astern of them was a cloud of others in every form of eastern Mediterranean rig, from the twin lug-sails of the *trabàccolo* to the sprit and lateens of the Moorish *felucca*. It was a convoy but apparently this one was expecting nothing more fearful than a privateer as their only escorts were an armed barque and a brig-corvette.

From its course Kydd guessed that they were on their way from Venice to one of the big ports in the south, perhaps Ragusa. Given the presence of so many slow-sailing work-horses, they had probably been at sea for weeks and therefore had not heard of any Sea Devil and his villainous intentions. The fact that they were standing on instead of taking flight supported this, and Kydd almost felt pity for what must happen.

Cerberus knew what to do without being told: she put about close-hauled and worked up one side of the convoy opposite *Tyger* doing the same in order to assume a dominating position upwind. The escorts came out to meet them, unable to make out their colours, which streamed downwind, and confused by their motions came about in a flurry of signals.

It was all too easy. Expecting an officious bracing from some senior officer, they lay quietly under backed topsails until, to their horror, they made out the British ensign. It was too late, and before they got under way *Tyger*'s first balls smashed into the hapless brig-corvette, which fell helplessly off the wind. Kydd closed and lay to weather, *Tyger*'s broadside meaningfully held silent until the inevitable hauling down of its colours. 'Away the starboard cutter, Mr Brice, to take possession.'

The barque, handier in stays, tried manfully to take up on

a track to flee but *Cerberus*, in a languid curve, was there to head it off. It, too, chose prudence over valour, its colours soon coming down.

'Your bird, I think,' Kydd hailed the frigate.

The first fruits of their incursion – a most acceptable start.

With the futility of fleeing a brace of prime frigates, the convoy remained in a close huddle.

With *Redwing* slowly circling, Kydd counted their gains. The brig-corvette was not badly damaged and would be a useful addition to their squadron. The barque, on the other hand, was larger but a sloppily converted merchantman, slow and poorly armed, good enough for convoy work against lesser predators but not much more.

'We keep the corvette,' he pronounced, 'but not the barque. Lay us close aboard *Cerberus* and *Redwing*, if you please.'

Hailing each by turn he gave his orders. The brig-corvette, with a strong prize crew, was to be sent back to Lissa with the men of the barque aboard, the latter ship's fate to be burned. Each of the frigates would send boats to board the ships of the convoy, nine in all, reporting back their flag, destination and cargo.

It did not take long – as suspected all were bound for Ragusa from Venice with variations of the same cargo, stores in some form for the French occupiers in the south. From rope to rations, timber to wine, none of particular value in themselves but all vital necessities to the forward units of the French Army.

Not a day out of Lissa, there were no problems in bringing in the captures. The frigates quickly recovered their men, and the prizes rafted together at their moorings were a sight indeed to behold.

Chapter 26

Kydd took his dinner alone and pondered events. It was a good beginning: the abrupt disappearance of the convoy would begin to spread dismay and alarm but it needed more than that. The risk of being taken on the high seas was one that every merchantman faced as soon as it left safe harbour and put to sea. That was nothing new. What was needed was something to make that safe harbour no more a place of longed-for security but a likely trap.

There were ways to achieve this, the chief one being a surprise cutting-out expedition, but even that would not be enough. There had to be an element of irresistible force, a sense that the British could strike wherever they chose, at random and with the same inevitable result.

Energised, Kydd summoned an officers' meeting. As darkness fell outside and a spiteful autumn blow rattled the stern windows, they bent to their task of bringing terror and ruination to the enemy.

Suggestions were not long in coming, but Kydd was drawn to one in particular, tentatively offered by the most junior, Maynard, the third lieutenant. 'As we put the frighteners on the *crapauds* in St Lucia, four fat sugar droghers sitting under the guns of the Vieux Fort. That night we landed royals and gun crews and took 'em from behind, the guns now ours. We just turned them around and put the beggars under fire from their own, and in a dismal pickle they cuts an' runs out into our welcoming arms.'

It had all the essentials: disagreeable surprise, reversal of the situation, the inexorable climax – and the implied menace that it could happen anywhere at any time.

'Well said, Mr Maynard. So where do we strike?'

Dillon's questioning of their recent Balkan recruits produced the required results, and Kydd could take his choice. Not too sizeable a fortification, a restricted anchorage but free from shoals and skerries. And frequented more by the cross-Adriatic French than the north and south trading Balkan ports.

The nearest possibility on the map meant little to him, other than that the Illyrian Provinces to the north had only recently been annexed by Bonaparte and had the most reason to resent their situation. He looked further, the heathen names not helping, and more or less at random settled on one, Radonice. It was an outlying minor port to the larger Šibenik, which itself was protected within a river system extending well inland. If the outer was set to ruin, the inner would feel the fear for a certainty, two for the price of one.

It was just inside the narrow entrance to the river, which, on Kydd's Ragusan trading chart, was identified as the unpronounceable Krka, and it lay within the protective arm of a small peninsula. It had a fortification marked at its tip, dominating both entry to the river and the sweep of Radonice bay. It seemed ideal for the purpose but it would take more than a little guile and courage to carry the day. On the face of it, there was scant cover in approaching the fort from either side of the little finger of land set out from the shore.

'Ask Mr Clinton to attend on me.'

The captain of marines stepped inside. 'Sir?'

'William, I've a notion to take this fort and turn its guns on any sail sheltering under it in this inner bay. I'm no military man but it seems a tough haul to ask of the men. What do you think?'

The young man studied the chart and its barest of details carefully, then straightened. 'A near impractical objective, sir. If the fort is well mounted and manned with guns of size capable of grape and round-shot, as they would undoubtedly be, they stand to command all approaches. I cannot readily see how even with numbers their fire may be defied without an unhappy result.'

'Impractical' was the closest Kydd would get to an admission of impossibility, he knew. 'A close bombardment?' he asked, then wished he hadn't.

'As would defeat the purpose of turning the guns on your harbour, I'd believe,' Clinton said gently.

'Hmm. Let's see what Mr Bowden has to say.'

The first lieutenant could only agree. 'The fort will be raised on an eminence, and their range will be impressive. And another thing . . .'

'Charles?'

'Even should we succeed, if our intent is to drive them out, what is to prevent them instead fleeing upstream to Šibenik?'

'Well noticed. The answer to that is the wind. Mark the channel width at that point, not more than two or three hundred yards. Should it be anywhere in the north, it will be foul for such. We take care to move on them only under a northerly.'

But how the devil was he to storm and overcome this fiendishly placed redoubt? It would be worse than useless to make the attempt and be bloodily defeated, the vaunted superiority of the Royal Navy being thus shown false. Better to withdraw honourably while there was time.

As if sensing Kydd's misgiving, the marine captain coughed lightly.

'Yes, William?'

'Before we abandon the task, might I make a suggestion?'

'Go on.'

'We make use of the brig-corvette to pass by under French colours to spy out the land. Not for me to cry down a mariner's sea charts, but so often I've observed that the facts on the ground may differ entirely from what I see scratched in on your sea map.'

'And we do not commit ourselves. A good suggestion, William.'

The brig-corvette *Le Coq d'Or* was prepared. With her figurehead of a glinting golden cockerel her new crew immediately dubbed her 'The Dandy Chicken' and she laid course to the north.

The frigates accompanied her to the outer islands, then lay off to seaward while she went on to penetrate the maze of forbiddingly grey overlapping islets to the inner leads along the coast.

Clinton, with his sergeant to make notes, was helped into the vessel's diminutive main-top, where he was provided with the most powerful three-draw glass that could be found. Kydd nestled in the fore-top with his own telescope and a midshipman to take details.

On the deck below, Brice, loosely attired as a *capitaine de frégate*, was stalking to and fro impatiently.

Joyce had his chart spread out with weights on the main-hatch gratings. Beside him were two Lissa crewmen, who claimed knowledge of the region, and Dillon, translating from their coarse Italian.

Above them streamed the pennants of a French National Ship as they closed with the coastline. This was now the mainland of Europe, the famed Balkan shore, which was Bonaparte's conquered territory from Italy to the border with the Ottoman Empire.

'Entry t' the river a mile ahead,' Joyce announced, looking up from the chart. This was relayed up to the tops by a bellowing quartermaster.

To larboard was the rumpled shape of Otok Zlarin, a lengthy island mass that cut off the view out to sea, while to starboard was the well-indented shoreline leading to their objective. If anything happened to them – an abrupt sallying of gunboats from the river, an enemy man-o'-war coming on them from behind one of the suddenly menacing islands – the frigates would not see it before it was too late.

Kydd spotted the fort first: long, prominent and of ghost-grey stone studded with the black menace of gun embrasures. He signalled to Clinton, who hastily trained his telescope on the bearing. He was to concentrate on the close-in details and Kydd would study the bigger picture. It would be their only chance of uncovering some fatal weakness.

In accordance with Kydd's orders, Brice conned the ship within a half-mile of the shore under topsails and brailed courses to slow their progress. But in the cool lighter breezes in the lee of the islands the currents were taking charge, slewing them offshore. He hailed down to Brice to loose the courses, which corrected the tendency at the cost of increasing the speed of passing, and he clamped his eyes fiercely on the fortification.

It took advantage of the narrow, projecting peninsula by having walls of guns along its length with only a narrow side across its width, and all being at a substantial elevation, as Bowden had guessed, its guns having an imperious command of both sides. A large *tricolore* floated above it, a smaller signal staff at the further end.

This was worse than he'd expected. The only cover was a low woodland scrub leading inland directly under the eye of its parapets. Any boat landings were out of the question with every approach dominated by heavy guns raised on high. It was a fortress that was both strong and well placed.

A gun thudded, smoke dissipating from an embrasure, and Kydd's heart skipped a beat. Then at the signal mast a flutter of colour broke out. Their attention was demanded – should they heave to and bluff it out?

But Kydd reasoned the fort commander was insisting on his rights in the article of salutes from this impudent corvette. Relieved, he yelled down, 'Ignore it and press on, Mr Brice.' No doubt indignant letters were being composed at this moment . . .

The peninsula slipped by and, with it, their chances of a spectacular stroke at the enemy. Well past now, Kydd made his way to the deck and all pooled their findings. There was no other conclusion: his plan was simply not possible with what they had at their disposal.

It was a blow. And while Kydd had been intently studying the fort, they'd passed the narrow river entrance and Bowden had glimpsed within the bay a forest of masts of ships kept at anchor by the north-westerly.

Kydd cursed under his breath. Wasn't there some way they could prevail? He had command of two fully armed frigates and another two men-o'-war. Surely he could think of something.

But it was nothing to do with numbers and all to do with the simple facts of the situation. It had been a good idea to reconnoitre first, if only to show them the impossibility and now—

The image of the fort as he'd watched it go by flashed back into his consciousness. Rapidly he brought it to full focus in his mind's eye and, with leaping spirits, saw an answer.

He kept it to himself until 'Dandy' had raised his other frigates, then called a council-of-war in *Tyger*'s great cabin.

The officers barely concealed their interest. They knew the signs when Kydd had something special in mind.

'Gentlemen. I've a device I believe will allow us our way with the fort.'

The silence was complete.

'You'll recall how the fortress stands?'

'Raised up as overlooks all it surveys?' ventured Bowden.

'And there is its fatal weakness.'

'Sir?'

'Its guns are mounted high to give range and dominance. They can't depress worth a damn and therefore we have a dead zone close in to the walls where we can make untroubled escalade.'

'Sir, I cannot believe the French have overlooked this.'

'I'm sanguine you're right – but they'll believe they've little to fear, for their batteries would make short work of any attempt by sea or land from any direction well before this was reached. Not only that but it would take a large and cumbersome ladder to reach a parapet at that height, and I rather fancy in any number these would be seen coming.'

'Are you suggesting . . . ?' Bowden said, with a frown.

'I am. A crew of seamen, not many as we'd find hard to conceal, armed as for boarding and with grapnels. On signal they swarm up together and take the sentries by surprise, a special party detailed off to make for the gate and open it, letting in the marines as will complete the business.'

Bowden hesitated, then said carefully, 'Sir. Might we know

your thoughts on how to get them there without they being discovered?'

'Certainly. This is entirely a matter for the volunteers.'

'Oh?' Bowden asked flatly.

'Indeed. Picked volunteers of the sort that can be wholly relied upon.'

'To do what service, sir?'

'To raise a wind, go on the ran-tan as it were, bowse up the jib, blow out the gaff, sluice one's muns in a bumper.'

'S-sir?'

He had their attention now.

'Surely I don't have to particularise to you gentlemen. A rorty toper, a gage of bowse, the radical moisture – these most jack tars of my familiarity have a close enough acquaintance with, I believe.'

'B-but . . .'

Kydd couldn't help it and burst out laughing, until the sight of their bewildered faces brought him back. 'Here's how it will be. Our seamen assailing will approach under cover of night. The sentries will be on the *qui vive* at this time but their attention will of a sudden be drawn to a most diverting sight. Drifting on the current will be the brig-corvette they saw earlier but this time she'll be flat-aback helpless. Upon her well-lit decks will be seen quantities of *matelots*, who are clearly in uproarious communion with Bacchus, displaying all manner of defiant frolicking.

'These sentries will waken their colleagues, who will crowd the battlements to take sight of the spectacle, while below them our gallant band of seamen stealthily ease themselves into position against the walls. The vessel drifts out of sight and the spectators disperse to their beds, leaving our party below to await the promised dawn at which point they strike. You see?'

A deep intake of breath was his only answer.

'Very well, I take it that you trust we have a plan. Volunteers. A dozen out of each frigate. The shore party of seamen, fifty each, all the royals from both under Captain Clinton in one band.'

He looked around the table. 'Wind from the nor'-east, moon-set a useful two hours before first light – I can't see why we should idle further. Questions? Then, gentlemen, return to your ships and ready yourselves.'

Chapter 27

To Kydd, the slap and gurgle of passing wavelets against the boat's side sounded loud and betraying in the calm night air under the fitful quarter-moon. The shoreline was a contrast of the deep blackness of shadow and the wan luminosity of moonlight, the woodland darkest of all. This was not the usual prelude to a cutting-out expedition. It was an all-or-nothing venture – the plan would work at once or they'd be comprehensively slaughtered.

It had seemed so straightforward as they'd discussed it, but now, with time to reflect, Kydd saw that much could go wrong. They would be landing the seamen nearly two miles down the peninsula in a rock-studded cove to avoid being seen, but then they had to steal along its length in the scrubby woodland to lie in wait for the call. Could they do it without being discovered? And the marines who were to follow: would they manage to keep well out of sight in the background?

Then the drama with the ship of toss-pots. It had seemed convincing when he advanced the idea but would the garrison be taken in? And the timing had to be utterly perfect . . .

A low growl came from the bowman, and the coxswain Halgren put over the helm to avoid a rock ledge as they glided into the Stygian dark of the woods. Then it was over the side, splashing over tumbled rocks to the sandy gravel under the trees.

'Muster the men,' Kydd whispered, stepping cautiously forward, flanked by Halgren and Stirk, indistinct hulks in the gloom.

As he'd reasoned, there was a cart-track running in the middle of the narrow promontory out to the fort. They could either clumsily scramble along over the boulders on the fore-shore out of sight or make fast going along the track with the possibility of discovery. It was not likely, he thought, that any would be out at this hour in the pre-dawn chill and he would take his chances.

Padding softly but urgently forward, the party moved on the fort. Kydd was grateful for the new-pattern pistols that had a long clip on one side allowing them to be securely and handily fastened to the outside of the belt instead of inside, digging into the belly.

Minutes passed, the only sound the soft swish of the night breeze in the leaves and the occasional muttered curse as a man stumbled. The tension grew as they closed with the citadel. If they—

Kydd froze and held up his hand. Something alien had intruded.

He glanced round tensely. His men stood motionless, hard to make out in the blackness.

And then, with a faint squealing and crunching of wheels, a cart came into view from around the bend. A small, one-horsed vehicle with a single driver perched on its seat.

'Sir, should I scrag the bastard?'

'No!' Kydd hissed at Stirk. He'd seen the man's head lolling

– his faithful beast obviously knew the way down the track where it had trodden many times before.

Kydd held up both hands and let them down gently. His men became as still as statues as the cart drew closer.

Soon, without fuss, it was passing, the man's head on his chest, the reins loosely held. The horse's eyes flashed white as it clopped on past the unmoving men, the load in the cart empty wine bottles and wicker demijohns.

Kydd let out his breath as the sounds of its passage faded. 'Move!' he whispered. They resumed their advance.

Then, without warning, the silhouette of the fortification loomed not very far ahead over the tree cover.

It was time for the last act.

Concealed at each side of the trail, Kydd and his party slithered down to the water's edge. His pocket watch was difficult to make out in the shadows but he judged they were in place by the right time and waited with as much patience as he could muster for the brig-corvette. Clinton's marines coming on behind would be slower, confined to the woods each side and held back to positions a quarter-mile in the rear.

And then it happened. On the night air came the faint sounds of revelry, thumping drums and wailing trumpets and into view drifted the impossible sight of a man-o'-war lost to drink and debauchery with lights blazing and colours still a-fly.

Swallowing his excitement, Kydd waited for word to be sent back by the young topman scout.

With Stirk, he was the first to break cover and lope as silently as he could across the untidily cleared turf to the safety of the shadowed wall. One by one the others followed, conscious that on the battlements above a bedlam of voices and laughter was their assurance that they weren't seen.

Kydd had spent some time with the sailing master plotting currents, in the tideless Mediterranean not an easy exercise, but with the breathy wind in the quarter there was a widening southerly exit easing the waters slower. 'Dandy' found herself wafted along at a little more than three knots – some twenty minutes to pass their field of view.

Then, as if but a dream, the vision had moved out of sight and above them the babel of noise fell away as the spectators went down to snatch another hour or two before reveille.

Timing was now all.

The moon had gone down and everything was in complete darkness, which was not what was wanted for a desperate close-quarter fight. Despite the fearful danger of some curious guard peering over the wall and spotting them, Kydd had to hold off the assault to the first glimmerings of daylight. Then he would give the word and hell would break loose for the defenders. After he and his men had secured the upper-works, a rocket would tell Clinton to come at the run.

The informal definition of dawn was whether a grey goose could be made out at a mile, and there were tables for determining 'nautical twilight', but it was Kydd's judgement alone that would send them forward.

Minute by agonising minute, he watched the first hints of daybreak steal in, the nearly imperceptible retreat of the shadows and—

'Tygers, *hoooo!*' he roared and, stepping back, swung his grapnel like the lithe young seaman he'd been. It sailed up to clang and grip at the top. Almost simultaneously he sensed the others hurl theirs and swarm up.

Alarmed and bewildered faces began appearing at the edge of the wall. Some levelled muskets but they were ignored by the mass of seamen, who tumbled over the parapet and, drawing pistols and cutlasses, went for them, snarling and shouting. Few of the enemy's guns spoke – on sentry-go it was a chore to unload a musket at the end of their stint and in their easy security they hadn't bothered to load in the first place.

The gate party flew down the interior steps and, in a trice, had the doors flung wide as the rocket soared away. With a faint roar of triumph, Clinton and the Royal Marines charged out of the scrub.

In a short while it was all over and Kydd stood tall on the battlements in the bitter cold of dawn. 'Mr Stirk, set the gunners to work, if you will,' he ordered.

As the day gradually brightened, it revealed, before the town of Radonice across the bay, more than a dozen sail at anchor, bare of canvas, lying still and somnolent.

The first gun crashed out. Its heavy thirty-six-pound shot arced across and sent up a plume in line but short, the ball skipping on to lose itself among the mass of shipping.

'Take your time,' Kydd admonished with satisfaction.

It wasn't until the seventh gun had spoken that there were visible signs of resolution in the anchored ships. No doubt baffled and infuriated at being fired on by their own side, pale canvas blossomed at the yards and one by one they stood out for the open sea, as Kydd had foreseen, unable to work upriver against the chancy northerly.

'Cease fire,' he ordered. Why damage good prizes as they delivered themselves into his hands?

'And spike those guns. We're leaving.'

The prisoners were left to straggle back to Radonice – no point in adding useless mouths to feed and shelter.

Stirk knew what he had to do and his men, with ringing iron blows, quickly rendered the cannon useless.

The last to leave, the party boarded the boats that would take them back to *Tyger*.

'Where's Mr Stirk?' Kydd demanded.

One of them mutely pointed to the flagstaff towards the end of the citadel. The French flag had been lowered and in its place something was jerking up to the peak. A quick pull and it floated free, revealing a black flag with the unmistakable outline of a rampaging red devil holding Neptune's trident.

Chapter 28

Palermo

'This is Mrs Woodhouse, m'lady,' the Comte d'Aubois said, with a bow, ushering forward a wispy, middle-aged woman. 'Her husband is in Marsala to a large degree.'

Led by the comte and honoured by the presence of Persephone, Lady Kydd, and her companion, the artist party was now complete.

'I'm so delighted to be invited to be with you, m' lady,' Mrs Woodhouse said shyly. 'An artistic expedition to the mountains is so rare, these days, and I've heard you pair are the foremost daubers of the kingdom.'

'Persephone, please. And you . . . ?'

'Fanny, if you will.'

'Then, my ladies, if you're now prepared I have some most tractable beasts for our transporting,' d'Aubois said smoothly, 'for I protest it would be a waste of good horseflesh, the trail being so wretched.'

Outside, the comte's men held their mounts and Persephone had a moment's doubt whether her fashionable English riding habit was quite the thing for the Sicilian high ranges. Fanny's plain and practical tweeds looked more suitable for pack-horses, however amenable.

'We go by the Sentiero del Ladrone – the Way of the Thief – to Altofonte where I promise you a prospect as shall have you reaching for your brushes before you take another pace.'

The early-morning cool warmed as they moved off and headed straight up from the coastal flats into a narrowing pass, which quickly turned into a single stony cart-track winding around the flanks of the first peak. Enchanted, Persephone saw the craggy heights surrounding Palermo cradling the ancient city and pointing up the proximity of the Romantic sublime to the torpor of the centuries of humanity below.

Soon the vista of Palermo spread out beneath disappeared behind an escarpment as they entered the mountains proper. Not a soul intruded. The mountainsides were too rugged and stony for livestock or cultivation, and they were undisturbed to take their fill of the prospect. In rapt silence they plodded on, the vast blue vault of the heavens above, mountaintops far distant and near.

'Shall this be our eyrie?' d'Aubois asked quietly, sweeping his hand to encompass a break in the range that led out to an eminence. He dismounted and walked forward to reach a flat rock where he stood in a contemplative pose.

The ladies drew in breaths of appreciation as they joined him. A great valley spread out below. Away to the left was the tiny sparkle of a river and on the right the distant glitter of a lake, with, far down, the toy-like clustering of dwellings, a small village.

'Perfection!' Persephone whispered, seeing in her mind's eye a canvas of nature overwhelming the insignificant works of man with perhaps themselves as tiny figures in the fore-ground contemplating the whole.

Without a word the expedition unpacked – easels, paint trays, charcoal sticks, water flasks – and set to.

For some reason Persephone couldn't get the conceit to crystallise. Twice she tore up her sketch, the ideas just not coming. Fanny had made a fair hand of a conventional representation, which would be a safe watercolour later, and d'Aubois was executing a bold but confusing piece that involved a thunderstorm and consequent complexity of resulting shadow and piercing light.

Then she had it. 'I haven't the soul of the work yet,' she declared, standing back to appraise her efforts against the grand sweep of scenery spread out before them.

'How do you mean, my dear?' Fanny asked.

'I need to uncover what lies within that of which we are only spectators, so to speak,' she answered, not at all sure herself what she meant. Then it firmed in her mind. 'Should we not go down to the village below and discover who lives there, how they live, what they do – what they dream? That must doubtlessly inform the character of our portraying from on high, don't you feel?'

'An inspiring thought, Persephone! I vote we go – what do you say, Philippe?'

The comte rose from his work, visibly dissatisfied with how his efforts were going. 'Perhaps you are right, Madame. We will go. But be warned that these parts are not, as who might say, appropriate for a lady of quality.'

They picked their way carefully down the steep and winding trail, d'Aubois and his men to the fore.

'He's right, you know,' Fanny said, in a low voice, as they proceeded. 'The Sicilian peasant is not a pleasant creature in his lair. Which is not to say it is his fault entirely, I beg to add.'

'In what sense is this?'

'From my work for my husband I'm in possession of their dialect and hear much. Out of Palermo itself, they're quite ground down by poverty and superstition and, as you can see, without roads to the interior there's little chance for them to learn of the larger world or make possession of its baubles.'

'Miss Lamb makes much of their skills and accomplishments, their sturdy temperament.'

'All I wish to say, my dear, is that you should not be too downcast by what you shall see, that's all.'

Unexpectedly the trail straightened and widened into the approaches to the village leading down towards the river. On each side were modest houses with shuttered windows, one or two with balconies. They stretched down in a straight line past a lofty stone cross with no shops or taverns to be seen.

Down the alleyways away from the single main street there were poor, run-down dwellings, occasionally with an old woman outside preparing vegetables.

D'Aubois seemed to be held in rapture by the spectacle. '*Merveilleux!*' he exclaimed, peering down the length of the street and framing a picture with his fingers.

'How so, Philippe?' Persephone asked, trying to ignore the rustic and pungent odours of the village.

'I have it! You see the light – its angle and quality at this time?'

The early-afternoon sun was behind them and, by chance, was lighting both sides of the street equally. 'There! A fine study of one point of perspective in two frames of reference. I shall start immediately.'

Hastily his easel was set up at the geometric centreline of the downward-sloping street and with strong, confident strokes he began.

Persephone, whose tastes were less technical than passionate, tired of simply watching and wandered about. After a few minutes she returned. 'Philippe, I've a desire to see more of the people. We three will roam down the street a space, perhaps to see inside one of the homes. Do you mind?'

'Oh, er, not at all,' he said distractedly. 'I will send Marcel with you but please to remain on this high road, *mesdames*.'

It was pleasant in the warmth of the sun, sauntering down the coarsely cobbled road. One or two villagers, all of an age, distrustfully stared at the elegant strangers with no business in their world. There were no children to be seen anywhere.

They came to an abode a little larger than the others with its door open to the street. Persephone peered into the darkened interior to the kitchen in the rear where a woman bent over a chopping board, every so often scraping her work into a large earthenware pot.

Impulsively she leaned inside, tapping politely on the door and calling.

The woman whirled about in surprise, which turned swiftly into suspicion. She came out, her kitchen knife still in her hand and angrily threw a stream of Italian at her.

Fanny replied gently in the same dialect and the woman eased, now more puzzled than irate. 'She wonders at our effrontery, interrupting her work at the pot. People of our quality, have we not better things to do?'

'Oh, do apologise and tell her we are English, curious to learn of Sicilian ways.'

The woman's expression tightened. She snapped back a single word.

'She asks why.'

Then Persephone had a flash of inspiration. 'Tell her we'll pay her well if she would be so good as to share her *pranzo* with us.'

'How much?' she demanded.

'Two *tornese*.'

141

'Each person?'

'Certainly.'

This brought a change of expression and animated conversation.

'She is Signora Maria Spadi born here in Altofonte and bids you welcome to her *casa semplice*. Marcel will wait outside for us.'

With a businesslike bustle, she rubbed her hands on her apron and beckoned them into the darkened front room, opening the shutters to let in the daylight. It was small and low-ceilinged, the walls bare stone. The furniture was plain, the chairs upholstered with woven matting. A few brightly coloured trinkets were proudly displayed on a shelf.

'She apologises there is no *cicchetti*, small snacks, as she had no warning of you coming but your *pranzo* will not be long.'

Shortly they were ushered into the kitchen and sat at the table. The food came in brisk succession, Fanny explaining each dish.

Minestra, a hearty vegetable and bean soup, field greens of remarkable succulence and river fish on a bed of pasta. The wine was watered but had a robust appeal and Persephone wondered aloud at its origin.

'Their own,' Fanny said, indicating through the back door. The sloping ground outside had vines, almond trees, and several patches of tomatoes.

Persephone beamed. This was something like the idyllic life she'd hoped to see.

'Do sit with us, Signora,' she invited, 'and tell us something of life in Altofonte.'

Suspiciously the woman complied, drawing up a chair. 'She's married, four sons who work on the land, two more in Catania making tiles and their sister in Palermo in service. What more do you want to know?'

The woman's face was defensive.

'I was, um, just wondering—'

At that moment a child crept into the room. It had a withered arm, which it tried to hide from the strangers as it approached the table warily, eyes wide and hungry.

'Oh, the poor soul – he must be ravenous,' Persephone cried.

It provoked a burst of shouting from Signora Spadi who made to cuff the waif but Persephone hurried to the little boy to shield him. 'Can't you see he's . . . ?'

'She says she knows that, but how can she take him to a doctor without she has means beyond that of a poor *cafone*?'

'But he's so thin, famished.'

'It's because with his arm he's worthless in the fields and workshops both.' Her voice unsteady, Fanny explained, 'As he's a useless mouth, he must learn to be satisfied with less than the others.'

'But surely she can—'

Signora Spadi's eyes blazed and she leaped to her feet, sending her chair crashing, letting fly with a torrent of Italian.

'Do you want to know the truth?' Fanny translated, her face white. 'About Sicily, she means.'

'I do indeed,' Persephone answered strongly.

The woman stalked over to the door, seizing Persephone's arm and dragging her into a mean passageway. Marcel followed awkwardly until they arrived at a tiny courtyard by a church. There, at a number of benches, children were bent in work, listlessly shaping different pieces in wood. A black-robed monk stood among them, looking up in suspicion at their arrival.

'Every one of these children has nowhere else to call home,' Fanny said, in a low voice. 'Some are orphans, others abandoned. Still more are here because their fathers have been conscripted into the army and their mothers can't look after them.'

Signora Spadi hardly paused, taking a sharp corner that led them to the edge of the village. Featureless fields were on either side, barren and stony, but scattered throughout, labourers were hoeing and weeding in a dejected silence, not bothering to look up.

'These are poor but honest folk who've fallen behind with their rent, which they owe to those blood-suckers in the palace.'

The peasant houses there were little more than hovels, some with outhouses and small plots. The *signora* headed straight for one with a pigsty attached and wordlessly pointed into it. Persephone saw an old man in rags lying in the thin straw, snoring loudly and caked with pig slurry. A chipped pottery flagon lay on its side next to him.

'Signor Trapani. His farm was taken in lieu of taxes.'

Persephone's heart wrung with pity. Out here in the interior she'd not seen any sign of the sturdy country life Miss Lamb had spoken of, the blithe revels and colourful costumes. The difference between Palermo and Sicily's interior could not have been more profound.

The day suddenly felt colder, alien and repelling.

As they took their leave she slipped the last of her few coins to the woman, and the group made their way up the street to where d'Aubois was still absorbed in his work.

'Philippe,' she said in a strained voice. 'I'd really like to go back now.'

There were no objections from the others and, having recovered their mounts, they headed back along the trail.

Persephone fell back discreetly to talk with Fanny. 'That was deplorable,' she said quietly. 'Is all of Sicily like it?'

'Most of the country outside the two or three cities of size,' Fanny agreed.

'Why is it so?'

'My dear, you shouldn't ask such questions of someone else's country,' Fanny admonished.

In a state of depression Persephone rode on, d'Aubois picking up on her mood. She tried to explain but he was unsympathetic, contending that it was their own choice, the manner of their living, and it had nothing to do with the court or its governance.

She didn't argue and ended her day despondent and disillusioned.

Chapter 29

After she'd spent a cheerless few days longing for Kydd's presence, Persephone decided to go out and try to lose herself in the company of others.

'Emily, we're off to the market. Please to dress accordingly.' Which meant their colourful Sicilian garments.

There was no need to go herself but in Sicily it was quite understood that the lady of the house would be making it her business to select the freshest and choicest of what was on offer, and she'd noticed more than a few well-dressed matrons on their rounds.

It was always a lively and boisterous experience, discovering new vegetables, like a green radish several feet long, or coming upon the head of a swordfish larger than a pig. She would try out her small Italian on the good-natured hawkers, who always loudly corrected her in the Sicilian dialect. Perhaps the hustle and clamour of the market would dispel her loneliness and melancholy.

Admiring a display of fat nuts of a kind she didn't know in a barrel, she made the mistake of pointing to them to ask. Instantly the man scooped up and wrapped in paper a more than generous helping and held up his fingers impatiently as their price.

'No, no – not want!' she cried and fell back, colliding with someone behind her.

'Oh, I do beg your pardon,' she stammered in English, turning around quickly. 'Oh, er, that is, *mi scusi, signore.*'

'Not at all, madame,' replied a well-groomed gentleman of some years, politely doffing his hat.

'You're English, sir?' she asked in surprise.

He beamed and bowed elegantly. 'You flatter me, madame. My name is Cesare Bruni, a staunch Sicilian, who has the honour to teach language at the Regia Accademia degli Studi here.'

She acknowledged graciously and replied, 'Lady Kydd, wife of Sir Thomas Kydd, of His Majesty's Frigate *Tyger*.'

'Then new arrived in Palermo, m' lady?'

'This is my first season,' she admitted.

'May I know your impressions of our land at all?'

Persephone hesitated, noting the earnestness and sincerity in him, but she'd been affected by what she'd seen more than she was willing to admit to a stranger. 'A fascinating country indeed, but I confess that recent experiences have not disposed me to an unreserved admiration, sir.'

A passing porter jostled her and she smiled her embarrassment, but Bruni seemed concerned by her declaration. 'I'm desolated to hear this, my lady. Should you have the time I'd much like to hear of it. Over there is a bench under the trees. Shall we . . . ?'

They were in the open for all to see and he was undoubtedly a gentleman, so she would indulge him and, in the process, perhaps learn a little more about the reasons for the poverty and distress.

Sitting demurely, while Emily hovered nearby, Persephone opened with an account of her painting expedition and what

147

she'd seen. 'As you can imagine, signore, I'm concerned as to how this state of affairs can be allowed to come about. In England—'

'You cannot compare England with the Kingdom of the Two Sicilies. What can you know of King Ferdinando and his tribe?'

'I have attended at court.'

'Then you know little. I shall tell you a different story in all confidence, for you are not a party to our domestic travails.'

'Your confidence will be respected, sir.'

'Thank you. Then it is very simply thus. The King and his Austrian wife are both Neapolitans in exile. They despise and loathe Sicily and the Sicilians both, and regard their realm as nothing more than a money pit to fund their palaces and multitudes of followers. This is where the proceeds of taxes and impositions go, not to the peasants and needy folk.'

'I had heard something of this,' she murmured.

'Would it then shock you to learn that the Sicilian people are resentful and vocal at their situation?'

'Not at all,' she said sombrely.

He lowered his voice. 'And what if you knew that they are ready to rise up and make demand that they be redressed for the wrong done to them in this way?'

'I could understand it, sir.'

'Of a matter of curiosity only,' he said carefully, 'were you to be one of their number, a Sicilian cruelly ground down, would you see it your duty to stand with them in opposing this foreign king and his consort?'

'I am not a Sicilian, I cannot answer you, signore.'

'Do pardon my impertinence, it's rare indeed for me to be able to talk with an English lady, a woman of breeding.' He smiled winningly.

'Granted then, signore. For what I saw in Altofonte, you are forgiven.'

'Thank you, m' lady. Dare I venture further?'

She sensed his tension, his need for something she could not give, and felt a wash of fear. 'I really must be getting back, signore,' she said briskly. 'Now come along, Emily.'

Chapter 30

Aboard Tyger

As the last of his officers bade Kydd goodnight after a most satisfactory victory dinner, he sat back in the great cabin in lazy contemplation, cradling his cognac. There were now five prizes on their way to Lissa under the watchful eye of *Redwing* – and his commission had only just begun. The action at Radonice had gone well and the object of provoking fear and despondency among Bonaparte's Adriatic possessions was bearing fruit. *Redwing* was carrying his dispatches but he'd been careful not to go into details as to the nature of the distraction 'Dandy' had provided, which had worked so well.

Now it was time to consider his next move. He rather thought Zadar. It was a considerably larger seaport dominating the inner leads that were the highway for the valuable Dalmatian coastal traffic, as well as operating as the receiving port for cross-sea passages from Italy. But if they were going to achieve as much as before, he needed better sources of intelligence than the word of unlettered crew volunteers, who claimed knowledge. This was an increasing problem that had to be met or they could find themselves taken unawares by an unforeseen situation of weather or enemy and fighting for their lives.

An answer suggested itself but, while sure, it was awkward and time-consuming. At each port of significance he would again land Dillon to find the previous English consul and set up a clandestine line of reliable information.

It would be a dangerous mission but Dillon seemed to revel in the evasion and stealth required. And this could be combined with another approach: to make a cast down the length of the coast showing himself and his formidable squadron in order to paralyse Bonaparte's shipping movements and clear the seas. This would have the effect of concentrating the enemy in harbours and save Kydd the effort of hunting them down. On the way, as each seaport was passed, Dillon would be put ashore to do his work overnight.

Relieved, Kydd's mind wandered. What other naval officer was as blessed as he? An independent cruise, a pennant for a squadron of his own, with the express aim of seizing prizes and creating havoc. And Persephone waiting for him, when it was time to rest, safe in the capital city of Sicily and no doubt producing some fine and Romantic paintings. He was certainly a fortunate man.

At first light Kydd's division of the Adriatic Squadron put about for the run up the Illyrian coast. He'd make the first port-of-call Radonice, partly because it was the closest but also to see if ships, thinking the danger was past, were returning to take shelter.

Not long into the crossing, a brig under press of sail was sighted heading towards *Tyger*. It was *Volpe*, an Italian vessel captured by Gordon in the Italian-side division and put to duty as a dispatch vessel. 'Well, L'tenant,' Kydd asked the young man in command, 'what's been happening on your shore?'

He heard how one successful storming of a port near Bari had been followed by the destruction of a convoy of *trabàccoli*, which Gordon had not thought worth the effort of taking prize.

Gordon handed over the dispatches that had sent *Volpe* in search of Kydd. The first he'd ever received in his own name, Kydd noted with secret pleasure. In correct form, they were nevertheless hastily written and dealt mainly with the subject Kydd needed to know about most of all: Dubourdieu.

It seemed he'd arrived with much grandiose acclamation in Venice and, after inspecting the famous shipyards, had made selection of his flagship. Other Italian vessels had been ordered taken up while he left for his base, Ancona, strategically well down Italy's eastern coast and a prime location to cover the most valuable seaports around the upper Adriatic.

His first act was to declare that, in accordance with Napoleon Bonaparte's express orders, his sole objective was to extirpate Le Marin Diable and all his kind from the French Lake, rendering it safe for honest mariners about their lawful business.

The second act was to call down the most stringent penalties on any by land or sea who was seen to be with, to assist, or supply with goods, the ships or men in the charge of the said Sea Devil. On the other hand most generous rewards were on offer for any information that led to the capture or destruction of the sea bandit's fleet.

Gordon had gone to some lengths to find out when Dubourdieu would sail but all he could determine was that he would not consider sallying until the forces under his command exceeded a measure double that of Kydd's – which would be hard for the Frenchman to discover, given their two divisions and random assaults.

One thing was certain: that it was imperative they set about their mission of ruination while they could. Once Dubourdieu pieced together his strength, Kydd could expect to be hunted down like a mad dog. Should he combine their divisions into one in case they met? It would be frigate on frigate and nothing could be taken for granted.

Quickly he scribbled a reply, not forgetting praise where it was due and commending further good work on the Italian coast. *Volpe* put about and disappeared over the western horizon as they took up on their course for the inner leads and Radonice.

Chapter 31

An alert lookout at *Tyger*'s fore-top first saw a spreading cloud of smoke in the calm airs, just inland and lengthening as they neared. It was close to the position of the fort they had so recently sacked.

In keeping with Kydd's orders, *Cerberus* and *Redwing* were following astern, 'Dandy', to preserve her identity, out of sight on the other side of the succession of islands. *Tyger*'s move inshore was followed cautiously, as it became clear that the burning was no freak of nature – it was man-made and was coming from the other side of the bay, the town of Radonice itself.

What was this? An enemy town they'd fired on now being attacked by its own side? It couldn't be a French punishment for they'd been victims of the British, not aided them.

'Clear away the pinnace. I'm going in to see,' Kydd ordered.

'But, sir!' Bowden protested.

'Any that attacks the enemy must be our friend,' Kydd said tightly. 'I don't care who, but the least we can do is see if we can bear a hand.'

In fact he wasn't at all sure that the townsfolk would see

themselves as enemy, given their subjection to Bonaparte, but it needed investigating.

At the fort the red-devil flag had been taken down but it was quite silent while they slipped past into the inner bay. The town on the opposite side lay ahead, the occasional flicker of red and rising smoke appearing among the docks. It would be foolish to attempt a landing there without knowing what they were getting into and Kydd directed Halgren to take the boat to land at the far side of the little town away from the confusion.

There was not a soul about and Kydd felt an air of dread as he stepped on to a small jetty with Dillon, master's mate Carew and four Royal Marines. There was a sea-wall road running the length of the frontage but it wasn't until they reached a sharp corner nearer the harbour and docks that they saw darting figures – and scattered bodies in the cargo working space before the warehouses.

Kydd crouched behind a sack-draped cart and asked the sergeant of marines what he made of it all.

The man scanned the area intently, noting the puffs of gun-smoke, their direction and number. 'Sir. There's a body o' men bailed up in the end warehouse. They's opposed by them in the Customs house and all along the wharf in front. They can't get out or they'd be picked off when they leaves b' the doors so they're stayin' put. Trouble bein' that the warehouse has took fire – probably set off by the attackin' party to force 'em out.'

With an increasing volume of smoke and the occasional flare and crackle in the rear, the fire was taking hold and threatening not only to engulf the wooden storehouses but to spread to other buildings.

'Sergeant. It's important – which ones do you think are the enemy?'

He scratched his head. 'Don't rightly know, sir. Um – the ones on the outside are most all in green. The ones inside when they goes to the window don't seem t' have on a reg'lar-going uniform.'

A flurry of firing broke out and a knot of men raced across, followed by a bellow of encouragement – in French.

This was an uprising being savagely put down. And with the French on the outside it left themselves in deadly danger. At the moment all attention was on the drama taking place in front, but if a flanking troop came across them they would be fallen on mercilessly.

At a small door in what looked like a shoreside residence a figure appeared, hesitated and was instantly struck down by musket fire. Thin cries of defiance came from the upper storeys but died quickly.

Kydd's thoughts whirled. Where did his duty lie? What was the moral issue here? And, more to the point, was there anything that he could do? He was master of near a hundred great guns – but to what end when the enemy was not in plain sight? Prudence dictated he quietly withdrew and left them to it, but that was moral cowardice and he couldn't find it in him to do so.

It would give great heart to the oppressed everywhere on the Balkan coast if the French were seen to have failed – but how? Save the trapped insurgents? Lift the siege to allow them to escape to the hills?

The fire was more visible now. Its rearing flames, vicious crack and roar struck primeval fear deep into him, battering at his reason.

Then he had it. Bluff.

'Mr Carew. Double back to the boat and hang out the blue flag,' he said hoarsely.

'Blue, aye aye, sir.'

There were only two signals agreed for this operation: blue, to mean 'enter harbour, it is safe' and red, 'lay off and await my return'. But by this he was summoning *Tyger* into the bay and potential danger in order to set loose a parcel of rebels. If the bluff failed, attention would inevitably be drawn to themselves and then it would be all over.

Screams and shrieks mingled with the harsh uproar and figures appeared at windows silhouetted against the lurid savagery of the fierce blaze within. To Kydd's revulsion he saw that musket fire was still playing about them, their escape from the fiery horror to certain death by another means.

But then for some reason the musket fire slackened. Soldiers scurried from their hiding places and, goaded by terror-struck shouts, made off down the passages and alleys between the buildings. Were they searching for fleeing victims or was it . . .

He swung round: *Tyger*, under a press of sail, closely followed by *Cerberus* and *Redwing*, was in a pugnacious lunge towards them. Bowden had intelligently interpreted the 'enter harbour' more as an order to come to their aid. And the bluff had worked: the French besiegers were panicking in their rush to flee inland out of sight of the awful threat of those rows of guns.

The entire wharf area was now deserted – but not for long. First one, then several forms lurched out of the buildings, some falling to their knees, others staggering blindly, fleeing as fast as they could, leaving the fire to rage unchecked. Whatever and whoever the insurgents were he'd brought them release and freedom.

'Bring up the boat, we're leaving,' he told Carew, careful to remain hidden in case either side took it into their heads to set upon them. Beside him, Dillon crouched silent, his face set. Kydd could feel his anguish but they could do nothing more and must leave.

The whole row of buildings – warehouses, offices and houses – was now well alight, a stupefying spectacle. No more figures were stumbling from the inferno, and with wrenching pity for the humanity that had met their end in such a horror, he turned away to board the pinnace.

'Sir!' Dillon gasped in a choking voice, pulling at his sleeve. 'Sir – there's . . . there's . . .'

Kydd looked back. Inconceivably, a bent figure, stark against the flames, staggered from the blazing doorway, disoriented and near collapse. It fiercely clutched a bundle in front as though its saving was the last act it could do.

As one, Kydd and Dillon scrambled up the slope, shielding themselves against the ferocious heat.

A blackened face turned to them piteously, the whites of its eyes blinking and rolling, and Kydd saw that it was a man cruelly scorched and the bundle was a wildly struggling child wrapped in a carpet.

'Into the boat,' choked Kydd, and together they dragged the pitiful humanity down to the shore. A shocked seaman reached to haul them in. The child broke free and, howling in fear, tried to run away but Halgren's hand shot out and held its ankle until it, too, could be brought in.

The man in his pain writhed and moaned and couldn't answer Kydd as the boat stroked quickly to *Tyger*, the scrap of a child scrabbling for a hiding place in the bottom of the boat, sobbing inconsolably.

On deck the horrified surgeon cut away the man's clothing and called for help in getting him below. White-faced seamen hastened forward.

'Take the child to my cabin,' Kydd ordered, but when they

tried to separate them it brought a demented shrieking that echoed about the deck with a shocking intensity.

They went below clutched together.

'A terrible business,' Bowden murmured.

Kydd stared forward unseeingly as *Tyger* made for the open sea, reaching out into the clean, limitless ocean immensity.

Chapter 32

Mechanically, the squadron went on with its purpose.
Kydd had the injured man put in his own bed-place.
He slept in the great cabin but it was a trial hearing pitiable
groans, unhinged barks and yelps, and mumbled incoherent
speech as the ordeal was relived.

The child was not so severely hurt but the left-hand side
of his hair was singed and a long burn on one leg told of a
narrow escape. A boy of possibly nine years, stockily built,
his features distorted by grief and torment.

He spent his day cowering in a corner of the cabin, never
speaking, his eyes following everyone. When the surgeon tried
to change his dressings he fought and sobbed under the
restraining of two seamen and left untouched the gruel that
Tysoe patiently brought.

On the third day Kydd, working at his desk, was startled
to hear a voice. Weak but resolute it was coming from the
bed-place and he entered cautiously. The man levered himself
up, his blackened, bandaged figure a pitiable sight.

'Sir – do I address the captain of this ship?'

Prepared for the incomprehensible babble of a foreign

tongue the perfect, even cultured English took him by surprise. Seeing Kydd's mystification he grimaced. 'Do pardon my speech. Your worthy doctor has been lavish with his laudanum.'

'Er, yes, you do, sir. Sir Thomas Kydd, and this is His Majesty's Frigate *Tyger*.'

'My most earnest thanks, Sir Thomas. Words cannot do justice to my sensibility of your action in so taking me from that . . . that Gehenna.'

'I have it from our surgeon that your child is in fine fettle, sir.'

'My child? I have no idea who the urchin might be. In the last moments he clung to me for salvation and . . .' He flopped back in exhaustion, his eyes closed, but then wrenched himself awake. 'I should make myself clearer, sir.' He managed a near sitting position and gave what in other circumstances would have been a courteous smile.

'My name is Craddock, in fine, Lucius Cavendish Henry Craddock, an Englishman resident for many years on this coast in commerce. Being of some utility to the conquerors, I've been largely left to prosper in the late unpleasantness.'

'Go on, sir.'

'Then a day or two ago the outer Fort Pierre was taken and its guns turned on the town, the French fleeing in disorder and dishonour both. Naturally the thunder of the guns gave heart to the patriots in the hills and, thinking it to be the prelude to an invasion, they flocked into Radonice to join in the punishment of the French, but it wasn't to be. Content with the prizes driven out by the cannonade, these aggressors then withdrew, leaving the patriots to the vengeance of the French, who quickly surrounded them where they took refuge in the warehouses. The end was inevitable.'

'You were caught up in this, sir?'

'Early on, all we workaday folk shuttered ourselves in our

161

houses, for the French were shooting down any on the street trying to flee, not knowing or caring who was in arms against them. When the patriots held out they set their hiding place afire. It began spreading promiscuously among the houses and we found ourselves . . . ablaze.'

He looked away, his fists clenching. When he faced Kydd again, his eyes were streaming and his words were lost in a choking hopelessness.

'Shall I return later, Mr Craddock?'

'No, no. For the love of Jesus, hear me, I beg of you, hear me.'

'Of course.'

Gulping, the stricken man continued hoarsely, 'In the inferno perished . . . my dear, dear wife, two children . . . my house and . . . and all I possess in this world. I tried to . . . to save them but the roof came down upon them and . . . and they were lost to me . . .'

Kydd was wrung with pity and tried to reach out to Craddock but he collapsed in a paroxysm of misery. 'Send for the surgeon,' he said softly, to the transfixed door sentry.

It was clear what had so cruelly touched Craddock and it was plain that there was nothing Kydd could do for the man. And that it had been the direct result of his recent triumph was hard to bear.

He left quietly, returning to the quarterdeck where he stood for a long space, letting the episode recede.

There was no question: he could not abandon the cruise to convey Craddock to some form of civilisation for mending in body and soul; neither could he spare one of his minor vessels, which all had vital roles. He could take passage in one of the prizes but that would only be to Lissa, which, with its less than refined circumstances, was hardly a place to heal.

So did this mean he should keep him aboard until they returned to Palermo? In fact both of them, the man sick in mind and the boy child, wrenched from whatever existence he'd now lost.

'Sir Thomas?' It was Dillon, his face drawn and shadowed.

'Edward?'

'You'll be exercised by the presence of our guests.'

'I am.'

'They have to stay on board, I believe.'

'Er, true.'

'This is to say that I do volunteer to take responsibility for them both. Mr Craddock will rally if there is one about him who can talk with him logically and wisely. I stand ready for this, for I've a sense the man's character will respond.'

Dillon had been affected, but his selfless offer had partly lifted the burden from Kydd's conscience. 'Very well, Edward. If you would. You have my permission, knowing you'll always act with discretion.'

'Thank you, Sir Thomas.'

It meant long periods of hearing the drone and mumble of Dillon's gentle coaxing conversations when Kydd was trying to concentrate on his dispatches and orders, but he hadn't the heart to move them elsewhere.

Once, when Dillon was at his dinner and he was taking a turn around the upper deck, a bewildered seaman reported that Craddock was in the orlop, where for some reason he'd wandered and was now curled up outside the after magazine and quietly weeping.

He'd been gently led back and put to bed and Dillon resumed his watch.

There were, mercifully, periods of lucidity and when these happened Craddock was taken up to the sheltered oversway, where the quarterdeck extended a little over the gun-deck. There, tucked away neatly in the after corner, he was placed in a chair under a rug with a view through a gun-port of the grey seas passing by.

'So how is your charge progressing, old fellow?' Kydd asked on one occasion, catching Dillon going out with a clutch of books.

'I'm no physician, neither can I answer to the ailments of the mind, but I'm sanguine this is the best medicine for his ills.'

'Have you an idea how long he must still suffer?'

'He's taken grievous wounds to the mind and soul, the like of which I fancy we cannot conceive. We can only wait and hope for an early restoration of his intellects.'

'Or?'

Dillon looked away. 'Or I fear he will spend the rest of his days in a Bedlam, deranged by reason of war.' He went on, 'Shall you see for yourself? He's in his eyrie on the gun-deck at present.'

Craddock was a much-diminished figure under a rug. The number of bandages had reduced, but his skin was still puckered and swollen, obscenely smooth in places where the hairs had been burned away. His head had been cropped close, bringing the ugliness of the searing of his hair to a uniform sameness. He stared unseeingly out of the gun-port.

'Mr Craddock? How are you feeling today, sir?'

There was no reply. Then, as if suddenly interrupted in a thought, he looked up, confused. He recognised Kydd and his lost features took on a look of pleased animation. 'Oh, good morning, Sir Thomas,' he said, with a civil bow of the head. 'You see I am well cared for by your inestimable Mr Dillon, who plies me with much to occupy my mind.'

'I'm pleased to hear it.' It was all that Kydd could think of to say.

There was an awkward pause. 'Sir Thomas, I'm not unaware that my presence aboard has caused you inconvenience.'

'Not at all, sir. Pray do not think it.'

'I must, for is not this a ship of war, of singular purpose? Surely there is a post or duty I can be put to that assists in some way,' Craddock pleaded. 'Even the bringing of cannon balls to the guns or other, anything but this uselessness.'

'Even suchlike requires a mort of sea proficiency, sir. It would not be an advantage to me to have the action of a gun impeded by a raw hand.'

'I quite understand, Captain,' he said woodenly, and resumed his stare through the gun-port.

Kydd knew what was meant but in a top-rank frigate the crew were a highly trained team and would resent his presence. It was unfortunate, for giving the man an end goal, a reason for being, would be a mercy instead of his aimless existence now.

Struck by a sudden thought he asked, 'Although it does seem that there's a service you're particularly well placed to render *Tyger*.'

'Do ask it, sir.'

'You're a merchant trader in these parts, well-travelled, I believe.'

'That is so.'

'This ship is one of several charged by the Admiralty to enter the Adriatic and cause mischief and destruction to enemy trade in these waters. It would be of signal value to me to secure your advice in respect to specific ports and harbours you can suggest we fall upon to best effect.'

'I can certainly do that for you, sir,' he replied, brightening.

'And possibly something else.'

'Of course.'

'Mr Dillon is being landed in a clandestine manner outside certain ports in order to make contact with the previous British consul, with the object of establishing a channel of intelligence concerning shipping movements. It would hasten the process if you were with him and—'

'No! I – I cannot!' he choked. 'God be my witness, I can't!'

'I'm sorry if I—'

'To go on the land, it's – it's not possible.'

'If it—'

'I cannot yet find it in me to return to walk the land where . . . where . . .' His eyes filled and he twisted away in a nameless pain. 'Only desolation and ruin. It's no longer where my home is, you see.'

'Then, sir, where will that be?'

The eyes were bottomless pits of misery as he turned back to Kydd and whispered, 'As long as I might, it is here, in dear *Tyger* . . .'

Barely in control he was ushered below by Dillon.

Kydd went on ahead to the cabin and froze. 'The child – he's gone! Sentry! Did you see the boy?'

'Er, no, sir.'

'Tysoe?'

It was quickly established that he was nowhere in the great cabin or Kydd's quarters in general.

'Mr Craddock, was the lad upset above the usual?'

'Not that I noticed,' the man replied raggedly. 'I confess I've not paid so much attention.' He sat abruptly. 'I've not been able to speak with him, he's . . . he's gone in on himself. All I know is that his name is Šubić Tvrtkó, he's eight years old and saw his father struck down, his mother lost to the flames. It must be accepted that he's no longer to be accounted responsible for his actions.'

Kydd felt a premonition. It was not impossible that in a

demented state he'd sought some escape in the bowels of the ship, the hold or orlop – or even thrown himself overboard. 'Clear lower deck! All hands to muster – search ship!'

It took several hours with no result. A pall settled over the ship: the only alternative explanation was that the crazed child had taken his own life overside.

Then, in the dog watches, he was found among the captain's cabin stores, in a foetal curl crying softly and hopelessly.

'Edward,' Kydd murmured, as the boy was pulled out and taken back to his cabin. 'The two to be watched by the hour.'

Chapter 33

Vienna

A savage chill set in, rain turning to sleet, the streets an unwelcome grind for carriages among the hurrying winter-clad figures.

Renzi slumped back in the seat. Just what could he at this moment bring back to Whitehall that was insightful enough – proof enough – to formulate policy upon?

Metternich had a deep and shrewd character but, no stranger to the art of guile himself, Renzi had to face that the man's driving principles were as opaque as they'd always been. And now he must return with nothing to show for the effort that had been put into placing him there, itself a unique, rarely occurring coinciding of circumstances.

A spy could, with cunning and duplicity, uncover facts and even embarrassments, but only a confidant could penetrate further and arrive at motivation. Unquestionably he was the only one who stood any chance of getting that close – and if he left, all that would be lost to the British cause.

Should he stay and persevere with the task? On what

pretext? Would he be allowed to? Austria had passed into French suzerainty, despite retaining its own emperor and laws, but as an Englishman he was there only on sufferance on the wording of his one-purpose passport.

But there was really no alternative. He had to try.

The carriage swung into the relative calm of the Ballhausplatz. Descending quickly, he pulled on a padded cloak and braved the stinging sleet the few yards into the Hofkanzlei.

It was a good sign, in fact a trifle puzzling that he'd been given such unstinted respect and time from the chancellor, on the face of it an unlikely thing for such a diligent servant of the Emperor. Most probably it was the heightened trait of deference to aristocracy ingrained so deeply into the Austrian character. He would naturally take shameless advantage of it.

'My dear Graf von Farndon. You have not yet quitted the kingdom?' Metternich enquired in polite surprise, rising and giving a civil bow.

Renzi was not deceived. In this tightly controlled country, all travellers had to register with the border police and he would be well aware of the movements of such a significant visitor.

'Not yet, Herr Außenminister. Which is the chief reason for my trespassing still further upon your time.'

'May I know what troubles my English friend?'

Was that real concern or a conceit on a par with his immaculately casual dress in the fashionable Romantic mode? 'None that might stand beside the adversities that must try the Austrian chancellor so grievously at this time.'

'Thank you. And you . . . ?'

Renzi sighed. 'I will be frank with you, sir. Should I leave at this time I shall be returning to a London out of season and, in these dolorous times of war, not in a mood to make merry in any wise. In fine, *lieber Freund*, after the Vienna I've so lately enjoyed, it will prove a melancholy prospect. I wish that I could find some reason, some pretext, whereby I might delay my return – you do understand me, sir?'

'Why, if that is your difficulty, it is soon dismissed. I have but to append a codicil of extension to your passport and you will be free to remain as long as you wish.'

'That is most kind in you, sir.'

'However, there may be, er, explanations of a kind to be commended to the French, who may find it curious. Your remaining within the Innere Stadt and not noticing those with an undue interest in your movements will go far to ease their misgivings, I believe.'

Renzi grinned broadly. 'That I am not some species of spy?' This was one thing he was completely guiltless of and he could afford to be amused.

'Quite,' Metternich said, his expression not varying.

At their guest quarters in the palace, Renzi went to Cecilia. 'My love, we must talk together.'

Cecilia frowned but continued brushing her hair. 'Is it about your inscrutable Mr Metternich? If so, allow that I find his odious perfection of manners as impervious to amusing conversation as . . . as . . .'

'Not as who should say, dearest. It's I who must get through to the man beneath, God help us, not you. Now, I've secured for us a further stay in Vienna and—'

'Oh, Nicholas! That would be wonderful – but it's getting close to winter and that means my wardrobe must be—'

'Yes, my dear. It's on rather a different tack that I will be desiring your help and understanding.'

'Of course, my love!' She hurried across to him with a smile of adoration. 'Anything!'

Renzi coughed awkwardly. 'In this time I believe we should not be seen over-much together, Cecilia.'

'N-Nicholas?' she said faintly.

'From the outside it would seem we are a happy pair, tight in the bonds of connubial bliss and therefore unassailable by the coils of worldly temptations.'

'But we are!'

'As does not suit my purpose.'

'Nicholas, you don't mean . . .'

'My sweetling, Herr Metternich is no stranger to the ways of the roué, the philanderer. With you so close, this he cannot see in me and it forms a barrier between us. Do allow that this is my primary intent and you will see what I must do.'

'To top it the lecher, the libertine?' she said, in a small voice. Then, recovering quickly, she added, 'Really, Nicholas, I wouldn't have thought it necessary to go quite so far.'

'Nevertheless, do pity me, my love. Tonight I shall be seen in thin disguise at the Roter Hahn – the Red Cockerel – in open admiration of the ladies and strong drink both.'

'Alone?'

'Possibly not. The good Jago may desire an outing, I believe.' If there was going to be anything questionable then his worldly under-steward was the one he wanted about him.

'Then I shall bid you a good night and await your return,' she said frostily.

The evening went well, the discreet Jago easily falling into the character of man-about-town companion, deftly deflecting the more determined of the bawds and loudly making much of the evening's entertainments.

Renzi's dishevelled return was greeted with a cool reserve against which explanations were futile. But then, in following nights, he was more affected than he cared to admit that Cecilia had taken steps of her own. She and Hetty had been seen at soirées and assemblies of the riskier kind, and her outings to town were becoming frequent and lengthy.

And when an invitation to the Court Ball arrived, he was presented with a perplexity: Cecilia loved grand balls and those of Vienna outshone the most splendid in England. He knew she'd been greatly looking forward to her first stepping out in the waltz with him, that daring continental dance that required couples to clasp each other instead of the decorous collective bobbing and curtsying.

With a woman of such striking looks as hers it would have been his delight to show her off before the stately gathering, but to be seen to exult *together* would undo all his mind-numbing forays into the demi-monde.

Kaiser Franz himself was in attendance and it was an affair of the most sumptuous nature. Burnished and decorated to a magnificence that had guests suitably impressed, the Hofburg Palace welcomed them in a flurry of liveried footmen, resplendent guards and blazing illumination.

Renzi and Cecilia entered arm in arm to the snapping of heels and salutes of the imperial guards, acknowledging the respectful bows and taking in the breathless spectacle of silk and flowers, jewels and splendour, all a-glitter under monumental chandeliers.

At eight precisely court trumpeters sounded in a distant room. As one, the body of guests moved forward and gathered in the Ceremonial Salon, their excited conversation now hushed and expectant. With a heavy thud of his golden staff on the floor the Hofmeister gravely announced the Emperor and Empress.

Instantly a silence descended and the assembly parted to

allow the entry of Kaiser Franz of Austria, in the scarlet and white full dress uniform of a *Feldmarschall*, by his side the Kaiserin Maria Beatrix, in an exquisite diadem and ball gown richly embellished with the finest gems obtainable from the imperial treasury.

Later, the requisite ceremonies complete, the regal couple took their place in golden chairs set on a dais and the dancing began, led out by an elderly archduke and his formidable lady.

Renzi covertly scanned the gathering, noting that Metternich was in attendance, standing dutifully in immaculate court dress between the Kaiser and the corpulent French ambassador, Count Andréossy. His gaze also took in the young ladies and their keepers shyly lining the walls, and coldly made his selection. There wasn't going to be a better opportunity to present his other side to Metternich.

His heart shrivelled as he excused himself when the waltz was called and, crossing to the young ladies, bowed extravagantly to the prettiest, then after a breathless consent led her out. As they whirled gaily about he dared a glance at Cecilia, who, he saw, was standing alone, watching him, her fan rigid by her side.

Another glance later revealed a gallant young hussar, red-cheeked and handsome, bowing to kiss her hand and he felt something like grief.

An interval for a sumptuous buffet was announced and he shepherded his lady to the table and furtively looked about for Cecilia. There was no sign anywhere of her.

Then behind him a soft voice asked, 'I see your evening has been blessed, *mein Freund*.'

It was Metternich, accompanied by a woman he did not recognise and who regarded him coolly.

'Life is for the living, I'm told,' Renzi replied smugly, delicately helping his cooing young partner to another sweetmeat.

'Just so.'

At last! He added smoothly, 'And it seems to me that Vienna is where this is best accomplished, my dear sir.'

'For those who know where to find it.'

'True. As always I find myself in a condition of prominence and must exercise a tiresome circumspection in my wanderings.' Would Metternich read this as an opportunity to extend a more risqué social invitation?

'Of course. So you are at liberty in Vienna, the capital of all Europe in the article of pleasures and culture. What now is your desire? Do you wish to make visit upon a theatre — the Hofburgtheater perhaps? I have a trifle of influence and in the matter of seats I believe you may rely on both discretion and indulgence.'

'That would be most kind in you,' Renzi replied but this was not what he wanted. He'd hoped for a shared jaunt, a connection — something like a relationship won from an illicit evening.

His mind raced. 'It would gratify me beyond measure should I be able to return to England boasting of having made acquaintance with your esteemed Herr Beethoven. Should we spend an hour or two with the master I will be more than content. He still resides here?'

He'd heard of the composer's angry discarding of his revolutionary hero Bonaparte as the dedicatee of his latest symphony and suspected that it would extend to the entirety of the French despoilers of his nation. If Metternich fell in with his request and allowed himself to be seen with him and in the company of an Englishman it would say much about his inner views.

'He does. In circumstances that many might consider . . . eccentric, not to say unusual.'

'It does not signify to me, sir.' Renzi sniffed. 'That I spoke to the man is enough.' To converse with the creator of *The Creatures of Prometheus*, the radical string quartets, the Kreutzer violin sonata . . .

'He does not welcome visitors and can be difficult – yet I believe it will be possible.' His woman pouted, urging him away. 'I shall give you the name of his close friend, who shall for my sake allow the introduction.'

Renzi smiled graciously. That the favour had been so readily granted was an act of friendship but this was far from being that of an intimate, which was the only way he would plumb the depths of his disposition. 'You will not accompany me?' he asked.

'The creature claims to be the very antithesis of myself and I very much doubt of a welcome. You shall have your visit, however.'

Even if Metternich didn't come it would not be a wasted experience. If Herr Beethoven was half the character Metternich was hinting at, he would have ample excuse to call again and agreeably debate the foibles of the famed musician. And, in any case, Renzi seemed to have broken through the urbane façade to some extent – there was a chance.

He steered the young lady back to her place and looked about for Cecilia.

She was with the unattached ladies, mechanically chatting with them. She looked up, noticed Renzi and, lifting her head, turned her back on him.

Later, in the carriage, her eyes held the sparkle of tears. Edging away from him, she spoke in a small voice: 'You have to do what you must in this matter, Nicholas, but know you are causing me great hurt. Can you say when it will be past and—'

Renzi said nothing but bleakly pointed upwards to where

the footmen rode outside. The one thing in this business that was certain was that he was being observed night and day, and nothing must be allowed to raise the slightest suspicion of complicity. Even their bedroom quarters would probably have their secret spy-holes and report would be made of their marital relations.

Chapter 34

The Graben, Vienna

Dressed in subdued English clothing, Renzi approached the tavern keeper, 'Herr Ries?' His accent gave pause as the man eyed him. Eventually a flick of the eyes indicated a solitary individual in one corner, a foaming *humpen* untouched in front of him.

'Sir. I am Nicholas Renzi, a visiting Englishman who much desires to meet Herr Beethoven, who I'm told is your especial friend.'

Ries was a young man, prematurely worn, his expression sullen and weary. His dark hair was a mass of closely packed curls and his clothes were cheap and ill-fitting.

'I won't enquire what an Englishman is doing un-hunted in Vienna at this time but this I can say. Louis does not care for guests, still less uninvited intruders. Your errand is worthless.'

Louis – Ludwig. He must be close. 'Sir, I have to tell you that my time in this kingdom is limited and thus I took steps to expedite my quest.' He handed over the note and waited.

Ries slapped it on to the table. 'You have a fiendish taste

in friends, Mr Englishman. And none more calculated to anger the maestro, who I'm sanguine will dismiss you out of hand. What do you think of that?'

'I would take it as an honour were I to be cast out by such a one as Herr Beethoven – I will take my chances, sir.'

There was a twisted smile and a deep pull at the beer before Ries spoke. 'What instrument do you play?'

It caught Renzi off guard but he replied levelly, 'I'm no professional, Mr Ries, but I do hold my Streicher fortepiano dear to me.' As a child he'd been told he was gifted by his piano teacher but, as with so many things, it had been lost to the outer darkness when he'd gone into voluntary exile at sea as expiation for what he considered a family sin.

'Have you touched keys to any of Herr Beethoven's pieces? The sonatas perhaps?'

'Some.' And found them beautiful but impossible to play.

'Hmm. You know that the master is sore afflicted with deafness? If he does see you, it will require the use of a conversation book and much patience.'

'I understand. Then you will take me to him?'

Past the Graben the streets narrowed and the frontage of buildings became mean and drab. This was the boundary between the aristocratic Vienna of the Hofburg and the common folk beyond. Ries walked fast and Renzi soon found himself at the entrance to a three-storey building of no particular character.

From the second floor came the sound of a piano. The playing was masterful, if not miraculous, supernatural. The piece was powerful, driving, and touched on emotions both noble and exhilarating.

'It's like nothing I've heard before,' he breathed, held enraptured by the casual skill so evident.

'And neither could you, *mein Herr*. This is Louis playing to himself the composition he's now working on. We'll go up – now is as good a time as any to break in on his musings.'

The stairs were narrow and cramped but the piano grew clearer and more resounding, and at the top there was a single door with a knocker that dangled askew. Without pausing Ries pushed inside, beckoning Renzi in.

Improbably there were two pianos in the small room and at one was seated a tousle-headed man, whose look of fierce concentration in his dark-complexioned features was near diabolic. The hands had short and stumpy fingers, crashing down flat on the keys with main force instead of the delicate arching movements from above Renzi had so often practised.

He was enthralled. It was no refined sophisticate he was seeing, no salon-gracing servant of the patriciate. Here was raw genius, a daemon of music, who snatched towering beauty from out of the very air he breathed.

Renzi's eyes strayed around the room, even now darkening as the winter evening blustered in.

There was no pretence at tidiness, no evidence of a woman's touch. Both pianos and the cello and viola that carelessly stood against them were dusty and unkempt; the floor was strewn with scribbled paper and scores with angry blotches, and on the only two chairs were the remains of breakfast.

Ries regarded Renzi defensively.

Completely oblivious of them, Beethoven played on, his entire body a coiled spring of energy that would not be repressed, his face sometimes contorted, at others serene, the chords crashing out in glorious succession until, without warning, the fists slammed down on the keys in a discordant crash and he slumped back.

Renzi hesitantly moved closer but Ries restrained him.

Beethoven snatched a rumpled score from the top of the

179

piano and scratched away at it in short, savage jabs, slapping it back with a grunt of satisfaction. Ries stepped forward and, without taking any notice of Renzi, Beethoven barked, 'Who's this, then, Ferdinand? If it's demanding rent, tell it that until the archduke pays me I haven't a *pfennig* to waste on such trifles.' The voice was Norddeutsche, a thick and hard accent after the genteel Viennese, and the words were indistinct, in an odd jumble of mutter and growling.

Deftly extracting a silver-topped pencil from his waistcoat Ries scribbled in a grubby end-bound book and slid it over.

'A visitor? Damn it, you know how I loathe 'em. He's not French, is he?' For the first time he regarded Renzi, squinting in mock rage at him.

Thrilling at the sensation Renzi returned the gaze calmly. The man who glared at him was impressive: lion-headed, a cleft chin in a strong jaw and with eyes of fire that radiated energy. Claiming the conversation book he borrowed Ries's pencil and wrote that he was English and that he'd come to pay homage to the composer of the *Eroica* and he hoped he might live to tell the tale when he returned to speak of his encounter.

'Then what do you think of my third, hey?'

A pencil was passed across while he quickly considered a response. "The key of . . . of E♭ was inspired."

The eyes glittered. 'And what other key could it be?'

It was getting deep waters for Renzi and he tried another tack. Was Beethoven really the radical freedom-lover? He would see – and he scribbled out with a flourish a favourite Goethe quotation: 'None are more hopelessly enslaved than those who falsely believe they are free.'

'Ha! Bravo, Englishman. Your German is prodigious. I've always found only you islanders know the true meaning of valour and sacrifice.'

'Not the French?' Renzi wrote.

'Never!' he spat. 'They cast out their useless aristocrats, then make their hero an emperor! Blood spilled across Europe for an aggrandising tyrant, a despot.'

'Who even now holds Austria under his heel,' Renzi dashed down.

'As destroyed my hearing during Vienna's bombardment,' Beethoven growled fiercely. 'I loathe their very existence on this good earth.'

There was now no mistaking the man's feelings and he had more than enough to take back with him to Metternich to discuss and challenge.

'I can't waste any more words on the vermin, so I'll give you another quote: "With stupidity the gods themselves struggle in vain." Hey?'

This was the prodigy pitted against a world that was leaving him to toil in such squalor, but at the quotation Renzi was obliged to shrug.

'Schiller!' Beethoven roared, then melted. 'One day I'll set him to music, I vow.' He glanced up quizzically. 'Is there a tune in you, Englishman?' Not waiting for a reply he shifted across the broad piano stool and patted it on the left. 'Let's hear you.'

Renzi gestured doubtfully, not sure if he'd understood correctly.

'A big honour,' Ries behind him said quietly. 'Play anything.'

He sat and braced his fingers. It had been a long time but there was a sprightly Purcell piece he'd always enjoyed. The first few notes were hesitant – the instrument seemed tuned a quarter-tone high. He persevered. Then, to his astonishment, Beethoven joined in, at first questing, tentative then boldly, confident – and in perfect imitation of Renzi's prim, classical style.

It didn't stop there. The first subject complete, Beethoven took charge of the keyboard and launched into a series of variations based on it that were both elaborate and inventive. His powerful, Romantic touch was authoritative, almost domineering. One, two, three – more.

It was a virtuoso performance that left Renzi enraptured. And with the certain knowledge that he'd never hear its like again.

Chapter 35

Hofburg Palace

Cecilia sighed, put down her book and crossed to the balcony yet again. From the third floor there was a fine view of royal Vienna and its expanse of manicured parks, and further distant, the close-packed mass of the other parts of the city. But, without a husband, they were firmly out of reach to her. She could visit the nearer shops with Hetty and her Austrian maid, but knowing that she was under a dozen eyes took away much of the pleasure.

Hetty was industriously working on her sampler in the wan winter light, her head down, unusually quiet. She must wonder, Cecilia thought blackly, just what they were doing here so far from their warm and friendly estate and why by now they weren't on their way back. And, more than anything, what was coming between herself and Nicholas that was turning their apartment into a cheerless prison.

The sky was grey and louring, with a dark, impenetrable heart. Snow would be coming soon, and in this central continental country it would then turn bitterly cold.

To pass more of the endless hours she rang for coffee, answering yet again the polite queries on style – cream and cinnamon or chocolate – that was part of the ceremony. Then, picking up her book, she took her chair once more.

Before she could resume reading there was a soft knock.

Hetty went to the door and took a card from the maid. 'Oh, m' lady. It's a Hungarian officer desires to see you.'

'Wait.' Cecilia hastily smoothed down her dress then continued demurely, 'Ask him to come in, Hetty.'

The young man strode in, his green and gold uniform a blaze of splendour. He stopped with a crash before Cecilia and, with a click of his heels and a grand flourish, he presented a posy of flowers to her.

'Why, it's – it's Százados Kovacs!' she exclaimed.

'Tibor! M' lady, to you – Tibor!' For such a young buck his voice held a steely quality of command and, wreathed in smiles, his youthful face with its proud moustache was a picture of vitality.

'Thank you, Tibor. It's very thoughtful of you.' What had he needed to do to find flowers while the world outside froze?

'Your husband? He not here?'

'Um, otherwise engaged,' she said shortly.

Nothing could be detected in his expression as he replied, 'The pity. I come on an errand. To invite you to our *Werbunkosch!*'

'Oh?'

'I am centurion of my regiment, the Kassa Carpathian Hussars. When we recruit, in the village we show we are brave fellows. We dance and feast, and the young men, then they wish be part of us. A grand time you will have.'

'It sounds exciting, Tibor. I really think that—'

In a sudden whirl and energetic bow he threw directly at Hetty, 'And if Mam'selle may be allowed to be with us?'

Almost overcome, Hetty nodded shyly and Cecilia smiled an agreement.

'M' lady will need to dress warm. Her furs, *hein*?'

There couldn't be anything in this that might possibly affect Nicholas's high plotting so she obstinately omitted to tell him of the invitation.

Cecilia was determined to enjoy herself, but when the day came, to her dismay the air was full of the flurry of snow-flakes, at first melting but by late afternoon snow lay over the whole of Vienna. The frowning edifices were transformed into an enchanted fairytale landscape – but what of Tibor's carriage that he'd promised?

Punctually at five Kovacs presented himself. 'We go?'

To her great delight there was no carriage waiting below. Instead there was a sleigh, high-backed and ornamented with the regimental colours. Two cavalrymen on jet-black horses were in position behind, their tall shakoes trimmed in gold, a fur-trimmed pelisse flung carelessly over the shoulder.

After settling the ladies onto their raised bench at the rear, Kovacs added some coverings for their legs, then vaulted into position next to the driver, giving an order that sent the sleigh leaping ahead in a spirited hiss of snow.

It was thrilling, gliding soundlessly through the streets with just muffled hoofbeats, far more comfortable than a carriage on cobblestones.

For near an hour they cantered on, through occasional snow flurries, which drove into their faces in a tingling thrill, and past softly white-shrouded buildings, whose lighted windows made warm splashes of colour. All at once they fell away and she realised they had left the city and were headed out into the country.

The snow lessened, then disappeared, leaving an elfin

landscape of breath-taking enchantment. Ahead, as they emerged from the woods into a clearing, Cecilia saw the blaze of a fire, figures silhouetted all round, its red glare lighting the gathering darkness. Distant sounds of music and revelry floated on the air.

In a showy slewing stop, the sleigh drew up opposite the fire. At first Cecilia couldn't move, transfixed by the sight and sounds.

To one side, a group of gaudily dressed musicians in red headscarves plied tambourines, two violins, a zither, knee-drums, and already some bold souls were capering about to their fiery performance. Long tables to one side were being loaded with steaming dishes of goulash, noodles, and spicy sausages, while on the other old men sat smoking long pipes and women happily gossiped.

In the centre soldiers were gathered together convivially, glasses raised. Shouts of welcome arose when Kovacs stepped down. A trooper with a tray of refreshments hurried across.

'To the devil with care!' he declared, after an impassioned salute in Hungarian. It seemed ungracious to refuse the steaming cup poured from a stone jug and Cecilia cradled the piping hot red wine for a moment before sipping.

An explosion of flavours filled her senses.

'Forralt Bor!' Kovacs exulted. 'Braced with *palinka*!'

An impossibly ornamented officer made his way over and bowed extravagantly, greeting them in excited Hungarian.

'This is Alezredes, my regiment leader. He bids you welcome and wonders why a beautiful woman like you attends here, unless it is to join up to we Magyars.'

Cecilia responded warmly, 'Please convey my pleasure in being invited to witness your leader's recruiting. And tell him pray do not delay on my account.'

The colonel spun on his heels and roared an order. The

band tailed off and, in quick succession, the hussars were gathered and formed a line. Another order went out and five men detached from the line to form a circle while the rest fell back.

The music began again, this time in a loud, compulsive rhythm that had the old men slapping their knees and the women whooping – and a powerfully built man leaped into the centre of the circle.

Kovacs leaned across. 'Sergeant László. He begins with the slow, the officers must return with the quick, then the soldiers the quickest.'

The onlookers watched eagerly as the grizzled sergeant began his dance, arms folded and raised, by turns sinking to his knees followed by a kick to the left and the right and a stupendous bound to full height. It was the signal: energised, Kovacs joined his brother officers in two opposing lines and as the music's tempo increased they began a complex and bewildering but forceful and animated dance. Back and forth, low and leaping in obedience to the driving rhythm, it was an electrifying spectacle.

A shouted command brought the outer circle to life – the cavalrymen themselves.

This was quite another dance – high, twirling, the clink of spurs and heroic leaping that against the outer darkness was wild, unrestrained, from a nameless age of unknown barbarism.

Panting, Kovacs returned to Cecilia. 'See what high blood are our hussars!' he growled proudly.

The Forralt Bor – or was it the *palinka*? – was beginning to have its effect on her and she could only nod enthusiastically. The night was still young and, in this snowy wonderland, magical.

'You will dance?' he demanded, and as the music climaxed

into a frenzy of bounding and cavorting, she was urged into the outer ring of dancing admirers around the furiously gyrating young men in the centre.

Breathless, she had to beg rest, Kovacs solicitously taking her out of the circle. Finding a chair, he shouted loudly, 'Champagne!'

An orderly hurried up with a bottle and glasses and a penknife for the twine yoke.

'*Mais non, mon brave – à sabrage!*'

The man obediently dropped to one knee and held out the bottle. Seizing it by its base, Kovacs drew his heavy cavalry sabre with a hiss of steel and, eyeing his mark, swung it with deadly accuracy, leaving the bottle neatly decapitated and the champagne foaming out.

Cecilia took her glass and gaily acknowledged. Kovacs, with a dazzling smile, bowed and, offering his arm, whirled a bewitched Hetty into the gaiety.

Chapter 36

Wien Hofkanzlei

'Then it may be accounted an interesting visit, Graf von Farndon?'

Metternich's poised and elegant imperturbability concealed everything, but his manner was warm as he passed across a generous glass of Obstler. *'Prost – zum Wohl!'* His eyes met Renzi's over the glass – cool, calculating, without a trace of anything that could be mistaken for fellow-feeling.

'Interesting it was, *mein Freund.*' Renzi replied. 'A gifted man and now a sworn enemy of the French.'

There was not a flicker of emotion even if Metternich had endured the same cruel bombardment that had turned Beethoven implacably against Napoleon Bonaparte. 'Yes, I'd heard. A singular ornament of the musical world but sadly not to be counted in the more ordered ranks of society.'

Renzi was still under the spell of what he'd experienced. 'In a musical genius much might be forgiven, surely,' he countered vigorously. 'I heard that day harmony from the heavens, tenderness and nobility, a perfection of the form.

It was . . . it was . . .' He fumbled for words that could in some way convey what he'd been witness to.

'Like Mozart?'

'Not at all. Beethoven is his own man. He creates for himself, a revolutionary of euphony and discord both, and he suffers for it. A genius, as I said.'

Metternich sat back, regarding Renzi with a speculative eye. At length he spoke. 'Curious.'

Renzi pulled himself together. 'Er, in what way, pray?'

'That one as high-born, wealthy and, dare I say it, free of the common concerns of this world should so care about a musician, however precocious. And in a manner that betrays intelligence, insight and not a little worldly understanding. You are an interesting man, Herr Graf von Farndon.'

'As I do adore fine music,' mumbled Renzi, greatly regretting he'd let his mask slip.

'Yes, a most interesting fellow. This I've known since your acting in the matter of our subvention before the Fifth Coalition.'

'A mere dabbling in finance under advice.'

'Our enquiries do assure us that this is so, but the subterfuge would seem to indicate a closer connection to the Crown than would appear at first sight.'

'The Portland government?'

'Just so. Even a Croesus might balk at the risks involved in a sovereign debt without he has the backing of a government behind him.' Metternich gave a comfortable smile. 'Whatever the truth in the matter, I'm obliged to confess that the combination makes you more than interesting – you are not the man you appear, sir. Another Obstler?'

Renzi felt the walls closing in. The *Außenminister* was at the centre of a network of agents and spies, the notorious Geheime Hofkanzlei, his sources many and verifiable. With his witless blunder over the Beethoven visit, he had now drawn attention to himself. Sooner or later he would be found out, and any thought of reaching a position of confidant was gone.

'I now have to ask myself why you are still here in Vienna. Would it be ungracious of me to agree with my chief of police that it is for the purpose of spying?'

Keeping iron control, Renzi gave an easy smile. 'I trust I don't disappoint, dear fellow, but I'm here only for the reason I gave – to take my enjoyment of Vienna rather than suffer London in this season.'

'Umm. Not spying, I think,' Metternich mused. 'This is better carried out by others not with the impediment of station or wealth. A puzzle – but let us not allow it to intrude into our friendship, so?'

He raised his glass meaningfully and Renzi returned the salutation.

Friendship? So he'd been able to attain the much sought-for status but ironically in quite a different way from how he'd planned. Now it was a genial front for the quiet inquisition, the observing and waiting. But then why was he telling him all this and not keeping it to himself? It made no sense.

In a flash of insight he had it. Metternich was playing a waiting game. His instincts were telling him now that Renzi was no mere foppish earl but in some way had powerful influence where it counted in the court and government of Great Britain, the nature of which he was not in a position to fathom. Renzi was not a diplomat and therefore had no power to enact agreements or debate proposals, still less speak for the reigning government, but if he was not a spy, what was he?

Metternich didn't need to know. From his point of view, all that was certain was that in Renzi he had a priceless channel into the heart of Britain's power structure, free of all the diplomatic baggage of the official apparatus. All he had to do was to make sure Renzi understood a given point and without fail it would arrive at the epicentre of the British government couched faithfully as he wanted it.

With a wash of relief Renzi sat back, stunned at the scale of the achievement however it was arrived at. For if Metternich was going to use him in such a manner he would first have to explain himself, his reasons, his motivation. Which was all that he was here to uncover.

It certainly made sense, but for it to function the man had to get closer, much closer.

If there was any approach along these lines he would have the proof that his notion was correct and he could abandon all else.

Chapter 37

Aboard HMS Tyger

'A good morning to you, Mr Craddock,' Kydd said pleasantly. It was a promising sign that the man was now to be seen on deck, walking a deliberate and considered measure along one side and back the other, occasionally looking up at the fine sight of the lofty sails, straining taut and trim. His hair was now a strong stubble, the bandages over his burns far fewer and his eyes no longer haunted and desperate.

'Oh, er, and the same to you – to a sailor doubly so, I'd think it.'

'Not always the case, sir,' Kydd replied gently. 'Take today, fine and sunny, a soft breeze only, what a landman would say is a perfect day but to us a sad hindrance.'

'Why so, Captain?'

'As we desire to make our northing to the head of the Adriatic as quickly as we must and this slight wind conveys us only at a walking pace, you see.'

Kydd wanted to make his presence felt in the far north

where the rich land made its curve up from Italy over and down to Dalmatia, Venice to Fiume, and thereby force the enemy to deploy valuable assets in defending it against another visitation from him.

'Quite. I see your point and I do beg your pardon – your good ship is a stout friend to me now in my healing and I do not look forward to my leaving her. Long may the voyage continue, sir!'

Kydd said nothing for soon the dispatch cutter from Lissa would be making rendezvous and, by rights, he should transfer Craddock aboard. Instead he pointed to the islands they were passing as they threaded through the leads. 'These islands, Mr Craddock. I'm noticing their curious appearance that I hope you'll explain to me.'

'What's that, sir?'

'I've noted that in these waters they're all bare of vegetation on their northern faces. Is this the work of man or Nature?'

It was indeed strange, one side of the islands pale bald rock, the other green with thickets of brush and undergrowth.

'Nature, sir, Nature. This is from their continual inundation by waves, the salt poisoning all roots.'

'Waves?' Kydd said in disbelief. 'Those islands are hundreds of feet high. I've never seen a wave that can overtop my masthead, stand fast those islands.'

'I'm no sailor, sir, but those here who are tell of the dreadful Bora, a wind only to be found in these parts. Out of a clear blue sky without warning it descends in a fierce shriek to lash the seas to a frenzy and always from the north-east. A wicked wind, the Bora.'

'That could come upon us here and now?'

'I conceive it possible. Mariners know to take care on sighting these bare islands, for they're a sure omen that the Bora often visits.'

'Thank you, Mr Craddock. I shall take due precautions.'

Waves that could break over the top of a whole island? With a fetch of small miles only? It was nonsense, of course. Probably a peasant fable of some kind.

'And on another matter. The child – how does he?'

'Difficult. Not to say rebellious but speaks not a word, hides when he can. I cannot help him. He'll not listen to a soul and lives inside himself, if you understand me.'

Kydd could think of nothing to say. The sooner the boy was off the ship the better for him and those who had to care for him. He had other things on his mind.

Soon after the men were piped to their midday meal the wind picked up, ironically from the north-east. Under its thrust *Tyger*'s sails bellied and the welcome sound of the thump and swash of an eager bow-wave was heard.

Their objective was Fiume, tucked away securely at the end of the long string of islands before the massive finality of the Istrian peninsula and the head of the Adriatic. Craddock had spent some time with the sailing master discussing their route but, not being a sailor, could speak only of places and destinations.

In the end it was decided to go east to enter the long Velebitski channel fringing the mainland. This would take them in full intimidating sight of the Balkan shore to break into the Gulf of Fiume when, after a hoped-for brisk gun action, they could then wheel about to round Istria, away into the obscurity of the wider Adriatic.

The north-easterly was fair for Otok Krk, the seaward guardian of the channel, and Kydd had a feeling that once in the final lead their haul of prizes would increase.

The breeze strengthening by the hour, *Tyger* leaned happily into it.

'How's the glass?' Kydd demanded, of the officer-of-the-watch. There was no harm in keeping a weather eye open just in case Craddock's Bora should prove a reality.

'Naught but a quarter-inch drop in the last three hours,' Maynard answered indifferently. Nothing at all, really, and with clear skies and no dirty weather looming, the chances of one of his monster blows was vanishingly remote.

They passed the tip of the island and into the channel but were then met with a wind that was increasingly flat and hard yet still out of the north-east. It made the necessary change of tack a tense business, sail cracking and banging, lines squealing through their blocks and the ship going about in an alarming bucking motion.

'Odd sort of blow, wouldn't you say, sir?' Maynard seemed to be looking for reassurance in this freakish turn of weather.

'It'll pass,' Kydd said stubbornly. Before very long they'd be entering the channel proper and sighting the ancient town of Senj, which they'd 'salute' appropriately as they passed, and he didn't want to waste the good northing they were making.

The sky was still winter bright, with only a few distant tufts of white cloud and not a trace of black building, scud overhead or other dire forerunners of any storm that Kydd knew. With the glass steady, he believed it would settle in due course, as quickly past as it had come.

Then he was struck by something so ominous it froze him to the spot: there was not a single sail of any kind anywhere. This was a major inshore passage and should have quite a number, coastal and sea-going. Where were they?

'Sir, shorten sail?' Maynard said anxiously, thumping a line from aloft. It was bar taut.

Kydd responded quickly. 'I don't like this. Up helm and take us out again, Mr Joyce.'

'You have the ship, sir,' Maynard said thankfully. Kydd hadn't intended to relieve him but in the circumstances it was the prudent thing to do.

Hands hurried to the braces and the frigate fell off the wind, taking up with it coming in hard on *Tyger*'s quarter. They were now on their way in a direct slant before the wind between the islands to the open sea where they'd been before, to the blessed sea-room that every mariner craved.

'I don't like 'un either,' Joyce said, stroking his chin, his face grave. 'Look at that'n,' he said, indicating the seas in general about *Tyger*. 'Never seen it like that anywheres.'

Kydd hadn't either.

The wind was hammering in but, extraordinarily, the sea surface remained calm and smooth, even if plucked and lacerated by what must now be considered a gale into short, angry white crests. The consequence was that there was no pitching and rolling to mountainous seas, no heaving and tossing, simply a steady, straining drive forwards.

'We'll triple reef the courses, two in the topsails.' Better now than when whatever was coming arrived.

Even with all hands on deck, by the time the last sailor was down from aloft the gale had increased to a relentless, roaring blow that had every man reaching for a rope to hold himself against the punishing blast. There were now combers, vicious and disorderly, crowding on each other, their tops torn and shredded into stinging spume.

And all the time a beneficent sun smiled down on them.

It was unnerving in its incomprehensible meaninglessness, and Kydd felt the clutch of primeval fear.

'All hands. Take in every piece o' canvas.'

For the fore topsail it was not necessary. With a report like a gun over the noise of the gale, it blew out, leaving canvas strips streaming and whipping out to leeward. For the rest it was a near-run thing, with men clawing their way out on the yards to fist in the furiously banging canvas, then make the deck again with ballooning oilskins.

There was a rising shriek in the wind above its growing roar. Aloft, purposeless rigging was enduring the merciless blast while the torn crests were growing from inches to feet in height, their tops snatched away in a sea-smoke that filled the air. Through it, just visible, were the two islands on either bow. And, terrifyingly, *Tyger* was now drifting aimlessly before the wind.

Kydd hauled his way over to Maynard as the wind battered him mercilessly. 'We lie a-try!' he shouted hoarsely. It was the only course left to them. 'Get a sea-anchor over each bow. Go!'

It was difficult to stand upright on deck. The wind hammered at the body, like a prize-fighter in the ring, but Maynard knew what to do and bawling for the boatswain they fought their way forward, nearly hidden in the driving spume.

Forcing his eyes off the indistinct activity on the fore-deck Kydd tried to make sense of what was going on. Without doubt they'd been caught by Craddock's Bora – but what of the tales of waves overwhelming islands? Were they going to be swamped, engulfed and overcome?

In this madness there was no knowing. Mindlessly he hung on, waiting for news from forward. Then there was a sudden jibbing and slewing round. *Tyger* was answering the urgent tug of the invisible sea-anchors and coming round to face into the furious winds.

His ship seemed to know what was asked of her. Nobly she rose to each wave, now of considerable size, arrogantly shouldering aside the assaults on her bow with a heavy thump and explosion that sent cold spray lashing aft.

At last the two islands were on either side and they were being driven bodily downwind and out to the open sea.

Maynard suddenly appeared, a dark figure at first, then the white of a wide grin showed. 'Streamed 'em both, sir.'

'Well done,' Kydd told him. 'Anchor watch forward and two lookouts. For the rest get everyone below.' There was no point in having men on deck to be pummelled by the gale to no purpose.

Kydd stayed for Maynard's report but his eyes were red and stinging with salt and he was grateful when the bulk of his third lieutenant reappeared. He did not speak but pointed a finger towards the main-chains. Kydd made his way there hand over hand and recoiled in shock to see a small ragged scrap clinging to the lower shrouds, its arms locked into the tarry ropes, its face staring out into the chaos.

'Our little rapscallion,' Maynard shouted. 'Won't go below.'

Kydd turned the little body to face him, wanting to explain that the deck of a ship in this insanity was not the place for a small boy, however deranged by his experiences – but then he stopped. The child had a joyous, exhilarated grin. He seemed not at all terrified by the storm but energised by it, glorying in it.

And in an instant Kydd was transported back to himself as an impressed man condemned to servitude. In the old *Duke William* one night he had experienced just what the young lad was feeling at that moment. The sea was appalling in its savagery but at the same time magnificent in its oceanic majesty, holding the soul in thrall while the intoxicating grandeur raged everywhere about him.

The boy looked up at him, struggling to say something but failing. One hand went out, seeking Kydd's. He grasped it firmly. But it wasn't for comfort or support: to his wonder and tender delight the child drew it close to him – and kissed it, the only release the little fellow knew for the emotions coursing through.

Touched, Kydd gently detached the entwining arms from the shrouds and carried the boy on his back below and into his cabin, where a white-faced Craddock sat wedged into a chair.

'I think we've turned a corner,' he said, pushing the lad forward.

His face shining, a joyous babble in some barbarian tongue burst out and he ran to Craddock, who flinched and held him at arm's length. 'It would seem so,' the man said woodenly.

Kydd needed Craddock to take some sort of parental charge of the boy now he was on the mend, but then, with a stab of guilty insight, he knew the reason for his reaction. Craddock's own child had been lost to him in a most cruel way and it had been with an unthinking heartlessness that they'd expected him to act as some kind of father figure to the boy.

'Well, now,' he said brightly, taking the child back. 'We'll have to think what to do with him.'

Quite unconcerned with the squeal and cacophony of timbers as the ship worked in the storm, the boy contentedly took his hand again.

At that moment Dillon came into the cabin. 'Sir, I'd heard that—'

He broke off at seeing the captain hand in hand with a trustful, happy boy and beamed with delight. 'So Neptune worked a miracle where we could not.' He chuckled.

'Ah, but we have a mort of difficulty,' Kydd said, with a glance down at the child. 'Where does this rascal berth? Who's to take charge of him?'

Dillon came back immediately. 'Why, that's no puzzle. We rate him volunteer on the books and ask Mr Stirk to look out for him.'

Kydd readily agreed. 'Pass the word for the gunner's mate to lay aft.'

Chapter 38

As if in salute to the gladdening scenes unfolding in *Tyger*, the winds took pity, eased and, well before nightfall, sail was loosed for the north.

And the mystery of the island-overwhelming waves became clear. It was not gigantic billows devastating the high-sided islands, it was sea-smoke, fine mist driven from the sea surface to soak the windward side in an all-poisoning salt.

Some days later, coming up to the next of Dillon's stealthy landings, Kydd shared the deck with his confidential secretary. 'Edward, is our younker enduring at all?'

'I've every hope,' Dillon said with confidence. 'Shall we see how he fares?'

Passing down the aft ladderway to the lower deck, Kydd removed his hat to show his unofficial visiting status. Past the forward bulkhead of the boatswain's cabin was the senior petty officers' berth. An enclosed space decorated with mermaids and battle scenes, it was a snug and comfortable refuge in a frigate without the hulking great guns to share their being.

Dillon scratched on the canvas hanging and a head thrust

out. 'Yes, cully? Oh, it's Mr Dillon. And the cap'n, b' gob!' The head abruptly disappeared and there were hoarse whispers inside before it poked out again.

'Well, er, come in, sir. We's just a-learnin' young Tomkin his sea savvy, like.'

'Er, who?'

'As we gives him a purser's name t' put on the muster-roll. His own ain't Christian, like.'

'Šubić Tvrtkó,' muttered Dillon, 'who henceforth rejoices under the name "Tomkin Toughknot" as is now in the books, sir.'

Tomkin, Little Tom. It was a rough sailor's compliment.

Further in, Stirk looked up, embarrassed, as he coiled the lanyards of a laid-out hammock. Beside him, eyes wide and shining, the youngster was doing the same with a miniature hammock half the size, but complete in all its fitments and with its lines immaculately pointed and grafted. 'Needs to sling his mick like a good 'un, don't he?' he huffed.

'Just so. Carry on, please.'

Kydd watched as Stirk deftly folded his canvas into the requisite precursor to a well-rolled hammock, to be secured with the seven turns of line said to be in respect for the seven seas.

'You makee do?' He indicated. The youngster nodded vigorously and after two tries succeeded.

'Now yez finish the job, compree?' After neat and dexterous work he had it done and dramatically flourished an iron ring. 'Goes through here,' Stirk said loudly, pointing. 'An' if it don't, y' starts again!' When hammocks were piped up they had to be a standard fit for the nettings that lined the deckside where they acted as barricades against musket balls in action. A quartermaster with a hoop would be on hand to see that it was done properly.

It seemed that the universals of the sea profession could well overcome the absence of English. Little Tom was in good hands.

Kydd left the boy to it, protectively surrounded by a circle of gnarled senior petty officers. Was it right, though? He'd be leaving the ship before long and would then have no use for sea lore of any kind. But on the other hand it was occupying an active mind, which otherwise would fret and grieve. And it were better for the youngling that he learned his sea savvy from the likes of Toby Stirk rather than among the careless immaturity of the midshipmen's berth.

Chapter 39

To make Fiume after their untimely interruption, the sailing master took a chance on a route to the opposite side of Otok Krk directly into the broad seas of the gulf. It could be done in just a brace of tacks if the final headland was shaved particularly close, and on the last run each officer-of-the-watch vied with the other to claw every foot to windward that was possible.

Tyger responded and, taking advantage of the bold-to mountainous coast with its two-hundred-foot depths only a quarter-mile offshore, the taut-rigged frigate made it with yards to spare.

There, readying to round the same headland from the opposite direction towards them, was a ship, not the usual small handy *trabàccolo* but a sizeable brig.

'French colours!' rapped Brice, quicker off the mark than the others.

Clearly outward bound, probably from Fiume, it would be carrying valuable cargo to rate a such-sized vessel but not important enough to warrant an escort – and it was unarguably fair prize. Perhaps they hadn't heard in these parts of the Sea Devil on the loose.

It was trivially easy to take. With *Tyger* oncoming already close, close-hauled under full sail, the victim's larboard side was blocked from turning by the rocky coast and it could only try to wheel about under frantic bracing for the open sea. There was never really any hope and, within the hour and to the cost of His Majesty of just one six-pounder charge and shot, the brig lay sullenly hove to under *Tyger*'s guns to await boarding.

'Mr Bowden – if you please.'

The launch returned quickly under the host of interested eyes along the lined decks of the conquering frigate. In its stern sheets a single figure was arrayed in some degree of pomp.

Bowden lay off and hailed. 'Captain, I have a prisoner. His name is Général de Brigade Édouard Valois.'

It was Kydd's prerogative to decide how he brought the man aboard – anywhere from the honours of war to in chains. 'Assemble a side-party,' he snapped. He'd settled on a simple piping aboard to receive the general.

The boatswain had to moisten his lips several times as he waited ready to pipe. No doubt the general was finding the side-steps and man-rope a little out of his experience, Kydd thought drily.

Eventually a tall cocked hat became visible and Kydd nodded to the boatswain, whose pipe pealed out the traditional wail while the rest of the person of the general awkwardly made its way over the bulwark.

He was an elderly individual, his pale face set. Attired in full dress uniform, dark blue crossed with a red sash and what appeared to be solid gold epaulettes and elaborately gold-worked high collar, he also wore an ornate gold cummerbund and spotless white breeches. He removed his ridiculously tall cocked hat in respect, hesitating at the beginning of the double line of sailors until Kydd encouraged him forward.

Ramrod stiff, his expression a blend of outrage and humiliation, he stalked forward, ignored Kydd's outstretched hand and gave a curt bow.

'Commodore Sir Thomas Kydd. My commiserations to you, sir, at the hand the gods of war have dealt you,' Kydd said pleasantly.

'If my fool of a ship commander had taken my advice to sail the longer way we would not have met,' Valois said acidly. 'As it is, I'm obliged to yield to the greater force. I take it that I am your guest for the moment?'

'You are my prisoner, sir.'

'Then it seems I must send for my baggage and servants.' He sniffed, looking about him disdainfully.

'Baggage to the first lieutenant's discretion, servants – one,' Kydd retorted.

'Sir! Are you aware who you're addressing?'

'I am,' Kydd replied, and without waiting, said sharply, 'Mr Brice. Kindly escort the general down to my cabin for now.'

'Aye aye, sir.'

'And make sure he's locked in,' he added quietly.

'Carry on, the side-party,' he called, after the pair had left the deck.

It didn't take long to deal with the boat, a brig-of-war, the smallest class and often used for such missions as this. In itself it was not of great value to Kydd, but he detailed off a prize crew to send it to his secret base at Lissa to lie up until ready to be convoyed to the prize courts with the others. And he knew how he'd get rid of the French general at no trouble to himself. When they reached the routine rendezvous he'd hand the whole thing over to the dispatch cutter commander to carry into Lissa.

Bowden reported briefly that the brig had indeed left Fiume and had been bound for Ancona and Dubourdieu's headquarters with the general. He'd searched the vessel but his intelligence haul was not great, for the papers and codes had been dumped over the side. But there were several charts of the upper Adriatic, which could prove useful.

As soon as the prize crew had taken stations, the prisoners had been transferred and gear checked, they would get under way for the rendezvous off Istria, at Rabac, reputedly a tiny fishing village, well hidden and sheltered with—

A sudden burst of urgent shouting broke out at the base of the ladderway and Kydd recognised the voice of Tysoe, his servant. He hurried to the breast-rail and looked down. Tysoe was pleading with a boatswain's mate and, seeing Kydd, cried, 'Sir! Sir! Come quick, it's murder! Murder!'

Kydd raced down the ladder to the closed door to his cabin. The frightened sentry outside was doing all he could, scrabbling to open the door as maddened howls and outraged screams came from inside.

'It's locked, you fool! Someone get the key!'

A white-faced Brice came at the run, proffering the key. 'Sorry, sir, I hadn't yet returned them and—'

'Get the door open!'

Inside, Kydd struggled to make sense of what he saw. Two figures grappled on the deck before the stern windows, one unmistakably the French general and the other Craddock, whose upraised arm was seized where it held a paper knife ready to plunge down. There was blood, a great deal of it.

'Get 'em apart,' Kydd growled, as the cabin quickly filled with horrified onlookers.

'This – this lunatic!' gasped Valois, who was bodily manhandled into one of Kydd's chairs. 'Comes out of there –' he pointed at the bed-place door '– and falls on me! With a knife!'

Craddock, near demented with pain, was not in any state to be questioned and was bundled back into Kydd's bed-place.

'Take this officer to the first lieutenant's cabin to be cleaned up.' He flashed an apologetic look at Bowden who, catching on, firmly took the general in tow. It was unfortunate that the journey to Bowden's cabin required the blood-smeared officer to be escorted there in full view of a goggling ship's company.

It was not hard to work out what had happened. Craddock, obediently staying out of the way when the ship went to quarters, had chosen to be in the bed-place until he'd heard French spoken. Entering the great cabin, he'd been confronted with the unexpected sight of a French Army general and, after no doubt arrogant words had been exchanged, he'd snapped and seized the nearest offensive weapon to lunge at the mocking vision. Valois had snatched and torn at Craddock's bandages, hence the blood.

Kydd sighed. There was neither point nor justice in disciplining the suffering Craddock but Valois would need careful handling. His humiliation would not be forgiven lightly and the two would be in the same ship until he could get the general off at the rendezvous.

When his long-suffering first lieutenant had finished with the general, he issued his orders. Craddock would be moved forward to the mess-deck where he'd temporarily berth with the seamen. Under no circumstance might he venture a single inch abaft the mainmast. The general would stay where he was with a similar restriction: not one inch afore the same mast.

It would have to do.

Chapter 40

Rabac

To Kydd's great satisfaction, a vessel at anchor lay in the harbour. It was the brig-sloop *Redwing*, obediently attending at the rendezvous. 'Ah, so pleased to see you, Mr Pearce,' he greeted the youthful commander. 'Dispatches?'

A satchel was handed over, which Kydd passed to Dillon. Lissa was already proving its worth as a home for their prizes and a penitentiary for the prisoners, but more importantly as an exchange for dispatches.

'I have a task for you. On board I have a *général de brigade*, one Édouard Valois. I'd be obliged should you relieve me of his presence this hour.'

'Sir.'

'He'll be boarding directly but I shall not be standing on ceremony in the article of farewells.'

'Sir.'

'You'll have my dispatches as well so you may weigh anchor when able and God speed.'

It was a relief to have the pompous French officer out of

the ship but Craddock was still in no fit shape to be taken to Lissa and would remain aboard for now. And it would not be a mercy to part the child from his new friends so Little Tom would stay in *Tyger* as well.

It gave a chance to get on with fettling the ship for their next exploit while the two brigs sailed for Lissa. Their prize crew would return by the first available means, giving them some small days to see to *Tyger*.

First, there was wooding and watering to attend to. The ship's galley consumed a prodigious amount of firewood, for sea-coals were not readily to be had in foreign parts. And the wood had to be the right kind, spark-free, not common brush-wood but stout trimmed and dry saplings that would lie tightly together in their stowage. No wood – no boiling coppers – no hot meals for two hundred and eighty odd men.

Whenever a far-cruising frigate found herself running dry of water in enemy seas like these, there was no other recourse than to land men under a midshipman with barrels to find an innocent spring on a hostile shore. The enemy was aware of the well-known watering places and often a vulnerable party would find itself caught unawares, to be at best captured, at worst slain. It was a slow business, too, for the full man-sized barrels were extraordinarily heavy, needing to be floated out to the ship one by one, fresh water slightly less dense than salt.

For the ship herself there was much to do. As stores and water were consumed the hold emptied unevenly. The ship's waterline varied its angle as more or less weight was removed from either end and then its trim changed. If as a result the ship's bow rose further out of the water, it was less able to resist being pressured downwind when close-hauled and could not keep tight up to the wind. If the bow dipped down she was said to gripe, where her forefoot bit deep into the seas and allowed tracking a point or two closer to the wind but at the cost of a fury of swearing when attempting to tack about in a stubborn vessel.

At rest, *Tyger* could be re-stowed under the eye of the master and his mates until her marks fore and aft observed from a boat were back in alignment.

The boatswain would then be able to seize the opportunity to get work done that was impossible when the ship was at sea. Generally the first task was to rattle down the rigging. Across the inch-or-two-thick shrouds were secured the ratlines, thinner rope crossing the shrouds horizontally that formed a ladder aloft for the seamen. If this was out of kilter with respect to the waterline, it sent the men to one side and slowed the response to the 'topmen lay aloft' order. Hog's lard and tallow were well smeared into the lanyards of the shrouds to let them each take up an equal strain after which the shrouds themselves, with the mighty tension of drawing sails relieved, were set up correctly: hemp rope had the habit of shrinking when wet and hanging limp when dry.

On this occasion the boatswain Herne and his mates were also being exercised, discovering the multitude of scars left by the Bora. Parted lines left spars free to play and had to be repaired. Blown-out sails needed to be unbent and sent down to the sailmaker. Strained masts and spars required close inspection for the tell-tale signs of sprung timbers, dark fissures in the wood that would later result in a splintering crack and toppling canvas.

For the rest of the Tygers, there was endless painting and polishing, and the usual gunner's duties – flinting pistols, checking gun-locks for a fat spark and ensuring the shot-garlands were filled with rounded, scaled and rust-free balls.

But then, after a good swabbing fore and aft, *Tyger* was ready for anything.

Chapter 41

Their prize crew returned in good time and course was laid to land Dillon surreptitiously to make his dispositions for intelligence out of Fiume.

Craddock advised the best location, and after dark the courageous secretary was put ashore. *Tyger* stood out to sea.

The following evening he was picked up and immediately demanded to see Kydd. 'Sir. Grave news as I believe must affect your cruise. May we talk alone?'

'Why, yes. Clear the cabin, if you please, Mr Craddock, Tysoe.'

'So what is this news?' Kydd asked calmly, when they'd left, but saw Dillon was in a state of suppressed excitement and his pulse quickened.

'I found my retired captain quickly enough and he was pleased to act as we ask and all arrangements are now made. It was what he said later as an after-thought that shocked me.'

'Go on, please, Edward.'

'In view of our arrangements he wanted to know what to do in the event that the fleet sails.'

Kydd was taken aback. 'The fleet sails? What fleet?'

'He seemed surprised we didn't know and told me that in Trieste, well-guarded in the Porto Vecchio – what they call the old port – there is at this moment a force of no less than four ships-of-the-line and another four frigates.'

'Good God!' Kydd said faintly.

'Sir, you'll want to know how reliable the information is. Well, the captain is not the kind to be given to vapours and is well experienced but, seeing my uncertainty, called in an assistant and asked him if the fleet had sailed yet. Without hesitation the fellow replied that it had not and was still in Trieste.'

This was earth-shaking news. In Minorca no mention of this vitally important factor in the Adriatic balance of power had been made. Neither was there any reference in the routine dispatch he'd just been given. And, to his knowledge, no one in his squadron had heard of such a powerful assembly of might, quite able to dominate the whole eastern Mediterranean.

'Ah, what colours did they fly?' Kydd wanted to know. If it was not a hidden French fleet the dire urgency would instantly fall away. A Turkish squadron?

'They were flying none.'

That was odd but it changed little. There was now an overwhelming need to verify its existence and, if true, report back with the utmost speed.

Within the hour *Tyger* had shaken down sail and was stretching out to round Istria on her way to Trieste, until recently Austria's only access to the seas and beyond. If there was indeed a fleet ready to emerge, the Adriatic was as good as lost to the British.

Kydd's chart of Trieste was a merchantman's and detailed so he had no difficulty in placing things in perspective. The harbour was little more than a lengthy shoreline with piers, jetties and moles set out from it for the working of cargoes. Beside the biggest mole there was an enclosed docking area. With the ten-fathom line less than a mile offshore, a flying reconnaissance was more than possible. He would time it for dawn the next day.

As the sky paled above the mountains in the interior, *Tyger* was ready, sweeping in from the south and closing swiftly with the grand prospect of the prosperous city. In her tops every telescope the ship possessed was trained on the land. Kydd himself was in the main-top scanning every inch of the seafront for a clue to the hidden fleet.

Ashore, there was little activity so early in the morning and the two forts in view didn't have colours raised yet. The last appearance of a sizeable unit of the Royal Navy hereabouts would have been some time ago, and there were evidently no precautions mounted against them.

It took only some twenty minutes to pass by the entire sea frontage of the city and, to Kydd's immense relief, there were no sudden hails or shouts of alarm to make the fleet a reality. It had been a false report.

'Deck there – put about and we'll go back to make sure.'

An answering hail saw *Tyger* fall off the wind for a return pass, which placed them nearer to the shore and this time the fort at the end of the big mole opened up with one or two badly aimed shots before lapsing into silence.

The frigate surged on and the enclosed dock area opened up for a short time, a quite substantial reach but all set about with obscuring tall warehouses – and then Kydd's glass leaped to his eye for he'd glimpsed not one but several stumpy black poles at different places as the view changed. Then they were gone but it didn't matter. He knew what they were. Masts.

There were ships inside with their topmasts sent down, leaving just the lower masts in place and, by their forbidding size, probably belonging to battleships. The hidden fleet had been found – and the hideous threat revealed.

Kydd descended slowly, leaving disconcerted men watching him.

It was now decision time. His urgent and overriding duty was to get the dread news back to Cotton off Toulon but that alone was not enough. If it were at all possible, he must find out all he could of interest to the admiral in drawing up his plans. What were its true colours? Was it readying for sea? Were troops massing to board? And, importantly, were the ships in a good enough condition to put to sea at any time?

In the privacy of his cabin he held his head in his hands. The answer to all this was simple but deadly dangerous: send ashore men who, at great risk, could be relied on to find out.

With the urgency of the situation there was no alternative. And, given this same imperative, was it a matter not of calling for volunteers but being prepared brutally to order the best men in? Only he, the captain, could make the decision.

He needed reliable and level-headed sailors, who knew intimately ships and their affairs to interpret what they were seeing. These would necessarily be the invaluable older hands, the most irreplaceable. And they would be more than aware of the fearful danger they were being sent into.

'Sir?' Dillon let himself in, bearing a generous whisky, and Kydd knew the signs. He'd recognised that Kydd was in some sort of mortal dilemma and was quietly offering himself up to talk it over, something a captain could never ask of his lieutenants.

'Oh, Edward – come in, old fellow. Sit down, I've a lot on my mind.'

Dillon had already reasoned what it would be about and it took only a few minutes to lay out the essentials.

'So it reduces to the single question: do I make an order as it being in the line of duty or will it be volunteers?'

'In logic I believe you have no choice,' Dillon answered slowly. 'None. The weight of consequence of any discovery must always overshadow all other considerations. You must give the orders to those best placed to carry them out.'

Kydd knew in his heart that Dillon was right. If he raced back with the bare news of the sighting of an unknown number of masts it wouldn't be enough to cause the commander-in-chief to strip the Toulon blockade of perhaps half of its sorely needed ships-of-the-line. Any risk was worth taking to settle the issue.

Just who would he send? He had the rest of the day to decide, for *Tyger* would reverse course at noon to arrive off Trieste at—

A firm knock at the door interrupted his thoughts.

Stirk stepped in, shapeless cap in hand, an obstinate look on his weather-beaten face. 'Cap'n – heard yez wants a crew to take a sightin' of them maulers in dock.'

'Well—'

'Has t' be a parcel o' the right sort, none o' yer hellfire jacks as wants a fight only.'

'Um, yes, but—'

'I'd be right scunnered if it ain't given t' me to muster a party fer the job. Sir.'

'That's very handsome in you, Toby,' Kydd said, the years from when they'd been shipmates before the mast together quickly falling away. 'But I have to warn you, the risks are great.'

'Risks?' Stirk threw off scornfully. 'As we was a-runnin' brandy 'n' baccy on Romney Marsh we didn't reckon on risks then, why now?'

Dillon hid a smile. 'You'll be sure to include in your men

one who knows Italian, French and, especially, Austro-German? Could be sticky going without one to hear what's being said.' At Stirk's stubborn silence he added, 'So you'll be obliged to include myself, I believe.'

'Not you, Edward,' Kydd intervened. 'You've done enough already. I can't allow it.'

'With Mr Stirk and friends to look after me? Do rest your worries, sir.'

It was unanswerable. His dilemma had been settled in the noblest way but there was one detail that still had to be faced.

Any high-level intelligence said to come from a foremast hand was given little credence. That from an officer was another matter. He had now to find his officer to lead the mission.

This time he had no choice at all. He himself could not land for, if he was killed or taken, the entire squadron would be left leaderless.

His first lieutenant was a deputy captain and too valuable to hazard. The third lieutenant was too junior for such a vital task leaving his second lieutenant the only remaining officer. The man was cool and collected under fire, very experienced in matters nautical, and senior enough for the duty.

'Desire Mr Brice to attend on me,' Kydd ordered quietly.

He appeared promptly. 'Sir?'

'There's no other way for me to put this, but—'

'I understand, sir. You need an officer – the first lieutenant is required and our third too junior, therefore it must needs be me. I'll go, sir.'

Chapter 42

There could be little in the way of planning. The objective was simple – to get ashore unseen and be close enough to satisfy themselves on the details, then return safely. That the ships could be fully manned and operational, with sentries and guard barracks, had to be expected. And the biggest threat lay at the end of the big mole in front of the docks, the fort.

It was not a huge structure, more a squat, rounded building with cannon embrasures positioned to take any assault from either side of the mole and larger ones facing out to sea. If this was a garrison outwork it could well be heavily manned by soldiers, and even half-awake sentries would make it impossible to land for, with the whole waterfront open and flat, there was no hiding place until the set-back docking area with its tall surrounding warehouses.

This was looking impossible – but the stakes were worth anything.

'Sir – Mr Craddock?' Bowden suggested.

He knew the port well and confirmed all that they feared

about the open ground but did mention that the fort was not heavily manned and had rarely fired its cannon in anger.

He also pointed out that there might be activity on the waterfront until nine at night, after which time it would be shortly deserted. At the sound of a gun the curfew would come into force, and any caught out on the streets or docks would be summarily arrested. Before the curfew, to be seen as strangers and reported, or after, to be taken up on sight by gendarmes. It was passing from hopeless to desperate. A despondent quiet descended as each took in the futility of going much further with their intentions.

'Thank you, gentlemen,' Kydd, said with a sigh. 'Carry on about your duties and if you think of anything . . .'

He was left alone in the cabin and slumped back wearily in his chair. It was now afternoon, *Tyger* had put about and was on her way back inshore to be in position to make a landing but without any kind of plan.

What were the options? Swimmers? In these frigid waters they'd never last the distance. Send in the child to ask questions innocently? As a native he would not be spotted for what he was but, being ignorant of what he'd see, it would be meaningless to let him go. Blaze away from *Tyger* as a distraction? At night, close enough inshore to range the guns, it would be firing blind with about as much chance of hitting friend as foe.

The crowning frustration was the curfew, making movements after this time out of the question.

He'd known curfews in seaports from all parts and could imagine what it would be like here, too. Just as soon as the evening gun thudded, the taverns would start to empty and topers would slowly stream off home and . . . and . . .

That was it! He saw an answer. There was a small window of time – but enough to see it through. They would blend into the homeward crowd and, at the right moment, fade into the shadows closest to the dock and complete the assignment.

The rest was details. Borrow a fishing boat and with it a set of ready-made disguises. Use it to deliver the party and take them off afterwards – if all went to plan this would offer the most rapid exit. And *Tyger* would be ready to intervene if it fell under chase.

The fishing boat was easy. They quickly found a craft down on its luck returning to harbour and a foreigner willing to pay for a night's hire with no questions asked.

One by one the shore party boarded the boat – Stirk, shipmates Pinto and Doud, Dillon and, last, Lieutenant Brice. He took the tiller and, with a brief wave, gave his orders and cast off. With the sincerest best wishes of *Tyger*'s company ringing in his ears, he set course for Trieste.

This was not the sort of adventure he relished: a dashing cutting-out expedition was more to his taste, with blood-stirring excitement, storming action and the chance of distinction and prize-money. This was a stealthy, dangerous and nerve-freezing assignment where success would be measured not by prizes taken but by their survival alone.

Given the stakes it had to be done. But, like so many before him, he took strength from the sight of the unruffled bulk of the gunner's mate, Stirk, at his ease with his back against the bulwark and comfortably yarning with his crewmates. How could he fail with men like that beside him?

In the clamping darkness of the evening Dillon emerged from the tiny deck-house with an expression of disgust on his face. 'Not as if I'm staying below another minute.' He took position next to Brice and continued light-heartedly, 'An interesting place, Trieste. The name's Roman – Tergeste, of an Illyrian root probably.'

'I see,' Brice said, not in the mood for a history lesson but he guessed this was Dillon's way of coping with the tension. He relented. 'What lingo do they speak now?'

'Austrian persists, along with Italian – and Slovene, Croat, Hungarian—'

'Still!' Brice growled, cupping his hand to his ear. 'Something's out there.'

On the air he heard the creak and swash of another vessel under sail and a vague shape appeared to starboard. If it was the coastguard or its equivalent they were in trouble – but as it sheered closer they saw it was another fishing boat much the same as theirs.

There was a derisory wave and shouted insults before it made off again.

Brice consulted his watch. 'Ease sail,' he ordered. There was no point in arriving early.

It was becoming fully dark but lights were perceptible along the horizon – Trieste.

'Ready the gear,' he grunted. Stirk broke off his tale and got the others to their feet, feeling about for their tools of trade.

As they approached, Brice scanned the shore for memo-rised landmarks and was able to fix his position, the enclosed inner dock area handily indicated by the shadowed mass of the fort on the largest mole. This meant that their chosen objective, a humble jetty of the kind favoured by lowly fish-er-folk, lay a few hundred yards before it.

Nearer, he saw that Kydd had been right: under the fitful full moon the waterfront was filling with figures trudging along, some merry with drink, others head down on their way home. Dousing sail he conned the little craft to a neat alongside. Doud leaped ashore to take their lines.

Brice glanced about – not a soul was taking any notice of them. 'Get the gear ashore, lively now,' he snapped.

Pinto lumbered a wheelbarrow down a makeshift gang-plank. It was bundled full of a coarse net and any who saw it would hopefully believe that the fishermen were on their way to the barking shed to have it routinely preserved in a solution of tree-bark. What they would not know was that under it lay grapnels, rope ladders and a dark-lanthorn.

'Dillon – you lead, Doud and Stirk each side, you're telling a yarn to 'em in some heathen tongue. Touch your ear when you want 'em to laugh. Pinto and myself will follow behind.' Dressed in their foetid fishing clothes Brice didn't expect friendly approaches.

They progressed along the seafront, weaving among the thickening swarm and edging over to pass close to the docking area to the right. Furtively he observed the fort on the mole, opposite and to the left. There were lights in some of the casement windows and an occasional bored sentry wandered along the parapets, no doubt waiting for the horde to lessen.

Heart thudding, Brice saw the tall, shadowed warehouses draw close, not a light visible in any of them, but that was expected for it was never the practice to work cargo or stow holds at night. On the other hand, there was no sign of sailors under curfew returning to the battleships: hundreds should have been making their way back.

It had to be very soon that they made their move. The moon, thankfully full and occasionally obscured, would make it possible to see all they had to, but at the price of putting themselves in plain sight. They would have to keep to the shadows.

'Stand by!' Brice warned. 'On my word, into the passage

between the end two warehouses.' This was a narrow pathway that led to the docks and was impenetrably dark.

He stopped and bent over, fiddling with his shoe-strings and taking a furtive look around. 'Move!' he hissed.

In the passageway they regrouped. 'Stirk – get a grapnel up to the first storey, another to the top.'

For first-rate seamen it was a trivial exercise to swarm up the ropes to emerge on to the flat roof, and within small minutes they were mustered there together. Dillon was hauled up with a bowline stirrup, his face shining with excitement in the moonlight.

'Keep down!' Brice whispered. 'I'm going for a look-see.'

There was a small but handy fringing raised wall overlooking the dockside interior and, bent double, he hurried over to it. Carefully easing above its top, in one quick glance he took in what they had come so far to see. Along one side of the long dock were no less than four line-of-battle ships and around the head and down the other side were four frigates, more than Brice had seen anywhere at the same time.

His gasp of dismay brought Stirk loping to his side. 'The fleet!' he whispered harshly. 'It's real.'

As if on cue, clouds drew away from the full moon and its cold light threw the row of ships into pitiless relief.

Topmasts had been sent down and lay tidily on the dock-side beside each vessel but all the lower rigging was in place, spars trim and square.

'Well, I'll be buggered!' Stirk chuckled, shifting to get a better view.

'Yes. An awful sight, I'll agree.'

'Sir?'

'Well, we've nothing in this half of the Mediterranean to match this Frenchy fleet, and—'

'We don't have to.'

'What are you saying?'

'Cos they ain't French. These 'ere are Ruskies – remember 'em from after we comes down the Dardynells. See the scroll-work on their stern-quarters?'

Brice bridled, put out that he'd not seen it himself. 'If they're Russians they're still allies with the French, and these—'

'I don't reckon on it. Know what I think? If these are the same, they've been here fer years. These are laid up, no crew aboard, fit fer nothin' but slow rot.'

'You can't be sure.'

'See them shrouds? Slack an' a rubbish o' working. Lines fr'm aloft – hanging in bights they're so ill used.' He peered more closely. 'That there fleet ain't about to put to sea this age.'

Taking out his night-glass Brice carefully inspected the nearest ship-of-the-line from stem to stern. Stirk was right. All the ship's gear was in place but it was shamefully set up. And there was hardly a light showing from any of the massive hulks, certainly nothing like the row of dim lower-deck lights to be expected of a fully manned warship, or the cluster of lanthorns about the ship's corporal at the head of the brow.

'We've got to be sure,' Brice muttered uneasily. Proof was needed, not simply reports of bad seamanship and ship-keeping.

How the devil . . . ?

Dillon squirmed up. 'There is one sure way.'

'Oh?'

'Slip into the dock, swim to an open gun-port and look inside.'

'Who's a swimmer here?' Brice demanded.

'There's some steps at this end by the passageway,' Dillon

came in. 'I'll enter there, and it's only twenty yards across to that nearest two-decker.'

'You?'

'I'm a good swimmer and I believe I may be counted upon to know the difference between a stoutly crewed man-o'-war and a rotting hulk.'

They descended to the ground and gathered in the shadows. Dillon stripped off his shoes and coat, his face expressionless.

'Wait.' Brice checked carefully and saw that there was a ship-keeper of sorts on the upper deck of the next along but, apart from that, no one else in sight. 'Go!'

Dillon ran across the dockside road in stockinged feet and disappeared down the steps. After a short time he was seen stroking strongly across to the big ship-of-the-line. When he reached the side he edged along to the nearest open port and, hauling himself carefully up, peered inside. After a few moments he slithered through the gun-port and was lost to view.

'The looby!' Brice whispered, at the same time in awe at the man's courage.

Some long minutes later Dillon reappeared, lowered himself silently into the water and swam back.

'No d-doubt about it,' he gasped, shuddering uncontrollably. 'Th-they've kept up a-appearances on the outside but within is a sh-shambles. G-grass growing i-in the m-messdecks.' His shivering lessened as he added, 'And I s-saw its name across the stern. *Yaroslav*, after the g-grand prince of Russia at the time of—'

Brice let out a long sigh. 'Well done. We've our proof, now let's be back to the boat. Here's your coat and shoes, Mr Dillon.'

'No! One m-might be accounted ch-chance. I'll visit one of the f-frigates as well.'

'You've done enough this night, Mr Dillon. We can't tempt Fate further, sir.'

But Dillon was already returning to the icy dock waters. This time it was a harder matter, for there were no gun-ports that let into the interior of a frigate. His barely seen figure vanished around the stem of the frigate and all Brice could do was wait in the snapping tension with the others in the shadows of the passage.

'Sir!' Raising a hand for silence, Stirk cocked his head. There were voices and the sound of tramping feet away to the left.

With a sickening sense of inevitability they saw it all play out. At the very moment that Dillon came up the steps an armed party swung into view from around the corner, marching at ease along the dockside. The patrol came to a stop in confusion. Quickly Dillon dived back into the dock and began desperately swimming for a gap between two ships.

At shouted orders from the officer the patrol parted, half of them doubling around the dock one way, the remainder heading in the opposite direction.

The exhausted Dillon had no chance. Hauled out, dripping and slumping, he was roughly dragged away.

'We go 'em!' Stirk urged tightly.

'No,' Brice countered. Besides having no weapons, they had a far higher responsibility – safeguarding their precious intelligence and getting it back to Kydd.

'Pinto, Doud. Follow 'em and see where they put him, then get back to the boat.'

The homeward tide was thinning fast. They had to merge with them but without Dillon's convincing jocular banter to keep suspicion at bay.

'Keep close with me,' Brice muttered and, head down, he strode out.

They were not troubled on the short distance to the old

jetty and boarded the rank-smelling boat, singling up their lines ready for a sudden departure.

After only a few minutes Pinto and Doud appeared out of the dark. 'In the fort,' Doud said breathlessly, pointing to the one on the mole.

Brice nodded and wasted no time in getting the boat out to the enfolding safety of the outer darkness.

Chapter 43

Kydd was waiting at the top of the side-steps, his face worn and haggard.

Brice quickly gave his report. 'They're Russians, laid up and rotting. No threat to anybody. We need do nothing more.'

'Thank God for that. Er, where's Mr Dillon, pray?' he added gravely.

'Taken, I much regret to say.'

Brice told him how it had happened. 'A braver man I never met,' he finished simply.

Kydd grimaced. Dillon knew intimately all the confidential matters concerning *Tyger* and her mission, and if the French ever discovered his position in Kydd's – the commodore's – flagship, they would make it very uncomfortable for him.

And the thought of the intelligent and resourceful young man being held idle in the tedium of a French gaol was near unbearable. In a wash of pity for his closest friend aboard *Tyger* Kydd's heart went out to him. 'We have to do something,' he muttered.

After more questioning of Brice it became no clearer just what could be done. Kydd wanted to mount a rescue, but how was this practicable with Dillon being held in a fortress?

Then he remembered Craddock mentioning that the fort was not strongly manned and seldom had recourse to its heavy guns. An assault from the sea? But it would be a bloody affair, the open ground of the seafront making an attack into the teeth of the guns one of suicidal desperation.

And behind it all was the need for an explanation to the admiral of why he'd risk his ship and spend the lives of men in rescuing a lone prisoner when capture was the gamble every man took who went into battle.

But to sail away and blithely continue their cruise, leaving Dillon to rot, was galling.

'Oh, I didn't notice you there, Mr Craddock.'

'Do you mind if I stay with you for a space, Captain? Edward is my friend, too,' he added, in an affected tone.

'Of course. How are you feeling now?'

'My physical hurts are healing fast, sir. And my inner wounds are no longer tormenting me, I'm happy to say.'

'This is good news, Mr Craddock,' Kydd said sincerely. 'And you shall be found a place in the next ship I can discover that will take you home.'

He regretted what he'd said as soon as it came out.

'Home? I know that was kindly said but it has no meaning for me, sir.' This time there were no tears or choking grief, only an infinitely sad calm. 'Oh, do forgive me, sir. I hadn't thought – you are speaking of my departure, my quitting your cabin, the inconvenience of my presence. Then naturally I will take ship when asked.'

'Not at all, sir. You have a welcome in *Tyger* for as long as—'

'Captain. Allow I have a modicum of pride left in me, sir. I shall quit your cabin as of this hour, begging only I might be found a place to rest my head until this cruise is over.'

Kydd suppressed a guilty swell of satisfaction that at last his cabin would be his once more. 'That should be possible.' *Tyger* carried a captain of marines and therefore the cabin of the non-existent lieutenant of marines should be available, even if at the moment it was being used as an officers' baggage store.

'And while I'm in the posture of begging, I do sincerely crave any kind of employment that will justify my existence, even in the most humble of situations. You may be assured of my total and utter loyalty in the matter, even as I pray it in some way contributes to the smiting of the tyrant.' There was strength in the voice now, together with a hint of dry humour.

'Well, as I said before, a sailor's life in a frigate is for the skilled and dedicated, and I really cannot readily see you buckling down to learn your ropes as an ordinary seaman.'

'Anything.'

'I rather think you are of far more use to me as a species of counsellor in matters trade and custom in these parts, which are unknown to us. Yes – to continue to advise how best to annoy the enemy, to hurt him in the particulars. In fact I do believe that you shall appear at every council-of-war I shall hold to contribute your piece. Will this satisfy?'

Craddock's eyes glowed. 'Sir – it will!'

'Then your first appearing shall be this forenoon at our next colloquy.'

'Oh?'

'What to do about Mr Dillon.'

The officers filed into the great cabin and assumed their places.

Kydd took in their long faces. 'Gentlemen. As of this point on I'm asking Mr Craddock to attend these meetings. I recognise that this is, as to say, irregular but his knowledge of the Adriatic is great and should not be overlooked by us.'

There was a slight stirring but no comment.

'Now, to Mr Dillon. We know he was taken acting in the most gallant manner and in the best traditions of *Tyger* and her company. I'm sure you join with me in desiring to achieve something to remedy his situation.'

'Sir. Am I to understand you are contemplating some form of extrication or release?' Bowden said.

'A rescue? If that's at all possible.'

None of them met his eye. It was clear they knew the practical unlikelihood of anything of the kind suggesting itself.

Kydd let it hang.

After a long pause Bowden spoke again. 'He's being held in the fort on the mole. This has an unobstructed field of fire making a direct assault impractical. Am I right, Mr Clinton?'

The long-experienced captain of marines gave a tight smile. 'You are indeed, sir.'

'Then how else shall we get entry without we knock on the door?' said Maynard. No one laughed.

A discussion followed with the conclusion that there was no easy way to achieve what they wanted, all delicately not mentioning the fact that in any operation against the fort there would be unavoidable casualties not to be justified by reason of rescuing the captain's friend.

The meeting lapsed into silence.

Kydd saw that Craddock wished to speak but was hesitant. 'Yes, Mr Craddock?'

'Do forgive me if I make a suggestion, touching as it does

on matters military, which I'm not in a position to comment upon.'

'Carry on, please.'

'Trieste. A port of many nationalities, lately Austrians, now Croats, Slovenes. Of these none love the French, the conquerors and despoilers of their land.' He hesitated, looking at Kydd.

'Please continue, sir.'

'Then it is this. The garrison manning the fort will therefore be conscripts of this ilk, obeying orders reluctantly. Could I make a suggestion?'

'Do so, sir. You are entitled as a member of this meeting.'

'Thank you, Captain. Then it is this. Should your grand and fearsome man-o'-war make sally against the fort, its mighty cannon firing as it comes on with bloody intent, then I've not the slightest doubt that its inhabitants will not calculate Mr Bonaparte worth throwing their life away and will flee promiscuously.'

'Well said, Mr Craddock,' growled Brice in respect. 'A worthy contribution.'

'It is,' agreed Kydd, warmly. 'With our gun captains advised not to be too nice in their shooting as will touch the fort to the hazard of Mr Dillon inside.'

'And *Tyger* tows her boats astern,' Clinton added, 'manned with a party ready to land and enter the fort.'

Kydd beamed. 'I do believe we have a plan.' And, he reasoned, he was only doing his duty by the orders he'd been given, which were to harry and unnerve the enemy along the Balkan shore. That he was landing and taking a fort was a vital move – who knew what secrets might fall into his hands?

Chapter 44

There was no need to wait for dark, which would be a disadvantage in gun-aiming. They did not have to take notice of tides in the Mediterranean, and the steady offshore north-easterly would ensure a prompt retreat in case of difficulty.

Kydd had taken charge of the shore party and, in pale afternoon sunshine, as they hauled closer to Trieste he mustered his men.

'Barkers and slashers' were all that were needed, flintlocks and blades. But they must be ready to go in and come out in minutes, for who knew if the fleeing men could be rallied or reinforcements hastily summoned? But that should be all the time they needed to free Dillon.

A mile offshore the boats were lowered, manned and taken under tow astern. With Bowden in command, *Tyger* laid course as straight as an arrow for the mole and its fort. At half a mile distant it would have penetrated in the fort that the warship was in deadly earnest and they were the target for a vicious cannonading.

The frigate didn't deviate from her course, a chilling lunge, like a spear thrown directly at them. Then the helm went hard over and, with her broadside presented, *Tyger* erupted in a thunder of guns. One gun followed the previous down the length of the vessel, keeping up an appalling roar of sound and a continual roil of gun-smoke.

In the smoke and clamour the boats were cast off and started for the mole. All about the fort, heavy eighteen-pound iron shot tore into the sea-wall, splintering stone bollards into a thousand fragments and howling past the defenders in an unholy din.

As they stroked hard for the landing steps Kydd exulted. Dillon would know by now that his incarceration was only minutes away from ending and he'd every chance to be back aboard for a good dinner.

The firing stopped but this was only while *Tyger* wore about to give her other side of guns their turn.

It was just as Craddock had predicted. In the lull in the cannonade, the doors at the rear of the fort were thrown open and out burst the defenders, racing away for their lives.

Roaring like a madman, Kydd urged his rowers on, and when they closed with the steps he stood in the bows with blade aloft and leaped ashore. 'With me, the Tygers!' he bawled, and ran for the back of the fort.

The doors were still wide open and the few that had not yet fled threw down their weapons.

But they didn't have long to find Dillon, and Kydd wasted no time. Leaving Clinton and the marines on guard facing inland he took in the layout of the fort. It made sense that the cells were in the lowest part, probably underground, and there were two doorways that led down out of sight.

'Take that one,' he ordered Carew, pointing to the smaller of the two. With a naked blade and with Halgren close by him, Kydd ran down the steps, blinking at the sudden drop in light levels. There was muffled shouting coming from around a corner, and they came upon four cells, with prisoners yelling and whooping.

'Dillon!' Kydd called above the noise but there was too much of a riot.

The keys were still on the peg where they'd been abandoned. 'Release 'em all,' he told Halgren, and in a general frenzy of jubilation the inmates flooded out.

But there was no sign of Dillon. Kydd was unable to question any of them for there was no one who could speak the local languages. And time was running out.

Back on the upper level Carew had returned with no news of Dillon, and others who'd been sent out came back empty-handed as well.

Kydd bit his lip – this was an ordinary enough fort, with now-deserted casemates and bastions, the usual sleeping accommodation in the floor above. There had to be an administrative quarter of some sort – was Dillon being kept away from the others? 'This way!' he snapped, taking the passage up, which led to a pair of windowless offices, still with lanterns a-gleam, but no sign of holding cells. A chill of foreboding clamped in.

In the smaller office a figure sat calmly at a table. He looked up as Kydd entered and greeted him languidly in French.

'This is your doing, this unpleasantness, m'sieur?' he asked.

'Captain Sir Thomas Kydd. And you . . . ?'

'Does it signify?'

Kydd couldn't help asking, 'Why have you not retreated with your men, sir?'

With a rueful smile the man flicked aside the tablecloth to reveal a leg in plaster.

There was no time for pleasantries. Minutes counted. 'Sir, I demand to know the present whereabouts of one Edward Dillon, my servant.'

The expression changed from one of amazement to calculation. 'Are you saying then that this descent on our little fort is in the pursuit of his liberty?'

'I asked you a question, sir, and will not be denied an answer.'

'Ah. Then our esteemed commandant was right. He is not your common . . . What do you say? . . . prigger.'

'I warn you, sir, that—'

'Calm yourself, m'sieur. I will tell you what you want to know.' He felt about under the table and extracted a wine bottle. 'This, while I can.' Pouring himself a glass he mock-toasted Kydd, who smouldered.

'Very well,' the Frenchman continued. 'This gentleman was taken in chains early this morning to Ancona to explain to Admiral Dubourdieu why he is not to be accounted a spy of the vilest kind.'

His lazy smile infuriated Kydd, who grabbed the table and overturned it in one savage movement, leaving the man prostrate on the floor as he stormed out.

Regaining *Tyger*, Kydd calmed under the urgent need for answers. Did he trust the truth of what the Frenchman had said? Or was Dillon in some inland prison? Had the cunning rogue achieved both confirmation of Dillon's importance and, at the same time, sent *Tyger* off on a wild-goose chase that would save Trieste from destruction?

Colder reasoning suggested that, with the dispatch vessel for Ancona having left well before, there was every motivation to crow over Kydd's discomfiting and so it was the more likely to be true.

His first thought was to order an instant chase but with

more than half a day's start and no idea of the course taken? Or to give up without an effort? No.

'Mr Joyce – a course for Ancona, the most direct,' he told the master.

With the same north-easterly it was a stern chase, sailing large – downwind. This was not *Tyger*'s best point of sailing but it would not be much better for the fore-and-aft-rigged aviso, which could not carry stun-sails. If he took risks, there was a not inconceivable chance he could fore-reach on the smaller craft and head it off at the Ancona harbour entrance.

But what was he thinking of? There could be no excuse for abandoning his overriding mission to fly off to the other side of the Adriatic and one of the most heavily defended naval bases in Bonaparte's kingdom of Italy for the sake of a single captive.

He glanced up at the boom-tricers at their perilous work in the brisk wind at the outer extremities of the yards. They were doing it for their shipmate Dillon. How could he let them all down by calling it off?

Stubbornly, he paced on along the deck, poignantly reminded of Dillon's presence, which he'd taken for granted just hours before.

It had now turned deadly serious for his friend. Taken in the most compromising of circumstances he would most likely be accused of spying, which, of course, was precisely what he had been doing. And if Dubourdieu had the slightest inkling that he was in any way connected with the Sea Devil he'd been sent to crush it would go very hard for him.

The hours passed in leaden succession. He should be at his desk, getting together orders for when his two divisions of raiders met at the head of the Adriatic to prepare for a devastating second pass down the coast. But his heart wasn't in it, and, besides, he reflected bitterly, he didn't have a confidential secretary now to assist him.

Then he was aware that someone was walking with him, silently joining his vigil. 'Mr Craddock?' he said in surprise.

'Captain.' The voice was soft but with a strangely compelling calmness, like that of an older man in counsel to a younger. 'There's no point in my offering to do anything to relieve your travails. It's not within my power. Yet might I be so bold as to mention that in my life I've been faced with a great deal that has tempered me and fitted me to understand much of the human condition? What is in my gift is this well of experience, which is yours to plumb as you will.'

Kydd stopped. Craddock was revealing a side of himself that he found both steadying and appealing in its strength, insight and intelligence. If things turned out for the worst in the next few days, he would need every morsel of those qualities. 'That's most kind in you, sir,' he said, with a little bow. 'I believe I may soon need to take advantage of your offer.'

Craddock's features eased, then a deep smile broke through that left Kydd in no doubt about his faithfulness to his words.

As the light of daybreak stole over the cold grey seas, and the customary readiness at quarters had been stood down on finding a clear horizon, Bowden joined Kydd before they went below.

'Sir, I confess myself troubled.' He rubbed his chin, a sure sign of uneasiness in the first lieutenant.

'Why is this, Charles?'

'I cannot rightly see that we've a way forward in any wise. Ancona is a formidable naval presence, dockyards, citadel, all manner of military. And we've no idea where Mr Dillon is being held.'

'And you fear we've no chance against these odds. I agree, old fellow.'

'And you're going on?'

Kydd sighed. 'I have to. In the naval service I've learned that no battle is won by any who yields and withdraws before all avenues are explored. We keep a weather eye lifted for any chance – any chance at all – that offers.'

Chapter 45

It seemed so natural to have Craddock sitting down to breakfast with him.

'I must act,' Kydd said, with gravity.

'You have a plan of sorts?'

'Not as if I can call it by such an elevated term.'

'Then . . . ?'

'I rather thought I'd first give you the chance to offer recommendation,' Kydd said lightly.

'An advising or an opinion?'

'Either, sir.'

'Very well. Then for an advising I will commend lying offshore well out of sight, for your Italian sailing master is exceeding nervous of any known as the Sea Devil. Not only that but your presence will animate the coast to a degree.'

'So how will we close with Ancona?'

'By way of an opinion I would not think it prudent. Together with it revealing your presence to Dubourdieu it as well presents him with the priceless gift of the sight before all the world of the Sea Devil lying helpless under his guns.'

'So what would you have me do?'

'To my infinite regret this is a matter I cannot comment upon,' Craddock said gently.

So this was going to be the nature of his contribution: the play of cool rationality and perspectives on a hot-blooded warrior's schemes.

Kydd paused, then put down his coffee cup. 'Very well. This is what I will do. Before all, I need to know if Mr Dillon is indeed there. The next is to discover the character of his holding that will then inform my plans for his liberating. So first I must set someone on shore to gain intelligence from Ancona for this purpose.'

It was easily said but, without the services of one of Dillon's calibre whom could he send? He frowned. 'Excepting I've no one on board who's able to perform the task.' Even if Craddock volunteered he'd not allow it.

The man's face lightened. 'If this knowledge is the requirement then there's no need to send anyone into danger,' he said briskly.

'I can't see any other way, sir.'

'We do as the natives do, Captain. The biggest business by far on this coast is octopus catching.'

'Octopus?'

'That and smuggling,' Craddock said, with a dry smile. 'One feeds the other. The octopus fisherman takes out his pots in his perfectly legitimate pursuit of the cephalopod, baits them and casts them into the deep with a flag to mark their position. Later he returns but he is not looking to hauling in his harvest. He is there to see if he's caught a much bigger fish – a boat sent in by a smuggler staying well offshore. If he has, the arrangement is that he accepts a list of goods the smuggler is offering or wishes to buy and takes it in to his receiving friends ashore who will bid on prices, the highest winning the contraband and ensuring the fisherman is suitably recompensed.'

'Then—'

'Yes. We become a smuggler who desires to buy a certain commodity – information.'

'With a premium on the quality, and no goods to trans-ship. As will be an attractive proposition to any. The only difficulty I have is that—'

'That you have none to make communication with these gentlemen. Captain, this does not require me to set foot on a Frenchman's soil so I will be available to you.'

Safely out of sight, *Tyger* lay to while she sent away her gig. It carried three seamen and a midshipman – and Craddock, tranquil and untroubled in the stern sheets. Despite his air of confidence Kydd knew they were heading into an unknown and dangerous situation and his respect for the man increased.

They were back just as the evening was darkling the calm sea, much to Kydd's relief.

Craddock heaved himself aboard and went up to Kydd. 'I have here a list of those willing to do this service for us. One stands out – a Greek, Yanis, whom I've had occasion to do business with before now. He's not only a successful smuggler but has wisely diversified his dealings into many and various, always careful to be known as a man of his word.'

'Very well – we will do our business with him.'

'Yes. Then, as is the usual practice, we will meet him at the octopus catcher's grounds at first light to negotiate.'

It was a rapid sail in the gig to pick up on the dirty yellow and red flag of the octopus catcher. Sail was taken in and they gently bobbed to the waves.

Almost immediately a boat appeared from the mouth of a small creek nearly hidden by a twist of sand. It stood out towards them, a grubby craft with a high red-painted stem under a single lateen sail and with two figures aboard.

An indistinct hail came, to which Craddock replied, and very soon the boats were alongside each other.

Yanis was powerfully built and sun-darkened but his face was twisted with suspicion. 'You I knows, Craddock. Who's he?'

'His name is Kydd and he has gold in his ship that goes to he who satisfies him in the article of news.'

The scowl did not ease as the man's eyes swept over the gig. 'This is navy. Which one?'

'The Royal Navy – British. Why should you care if you're paid?'

'Not here. We go to the ship.'

They left the fisherman hauling in his terracotta pots, extracting the occupants with a deft twist and flinging them into a basket without a single glance at the strangers.

If Yanis was impressed by the powerful frigate he showed no sign as he was quickly taken below.

'So. What you want to know?'

'Is there word of a British spy being brought here from Trieste?'

'Word? The whole town knows. The *francese* admiral makes sure of that. An agent of the Sea Devil himself, he say.'

'Where is he kept at all?'

'We're told that too. Double guards, and he say any who come near are arrest and sent to join him.'

'Where?'

'La Fortezza – the Cittadella Monte Astagno.'

'Above the harbour,' murmured Craddock. 'Massive fortress from the 1500s and impregnable.'

So the secret was out. By whatever means, Dillon was now revealed to be one of his own, and a spy. And he was being held in the unassailable fastness of Dubourdieu's headquarters. No brazen frontal storming could be expected to succeed, but what else was there?

A black despair began to descend.

Kydd slipped several gold coins on to the table. 'Yanis. You're a man to trust. What do you say to my chances of bribing the sentries to let him escape?'

It brought a cynical smile. 'These are not common Italian *milizia*. They are French posted by Dubourdieu himself.' He shrugged, at the same time contriving to cause the gold to disappear into his pocket. '*Capitano*, your man, understand – he is lost to you.'

'Yes,' Kydd said woodenly.

'Any more you want?'

He could ask for a detailed account of the forces at Dubourdieu's command, the location of his perimeter defences and so forth, but to what end? He had neither the military weight nor even the authorisation to carry out a major assault on such a stronghold. Would he ever see Dillon again?

'Thank you, Yanis. Mr Brice, do please see that he's returned safely, would you?' He got up, mechanically shook hands and watched them leave.

At the door Yanis paused, remembering. 'I have today newspaper for you. Says about your agent.'

He felt in his waistcoat and brought out a folded paper, handed it over and with a wave was gone.

Morosely Kydd found a chair. 'No, do stay, Mr Craddock,' he said, at the man's tactful withdrawing. 'I've a notion I'll need to talk.'

Craddock sat down next to him. 'I fear we must give best to Dubourdieu,' he allowed delicately, after Kydd had made no attempt at conversation.

'Without we can reach Edward in any way I fear we must.'

Kydd opened the newspaper. It was the *Moniteur*, the French state propaganda sheet. On the front page, the article immediately caught his eye. '*The Sea Devil thwarted*,' ran the headline. In larger print than normal it went on to glory in the bravery of the Trieste garrison who at grave peril to their lives had laid a dangerous agent by the heels in a dramatic chase after catching him spying for the Sea Devil's intended attack on the town, later easily beaten off.

Kydd snorted and went on:

Commodore Dubourdieu personally congratulated the courageous soldiers, and assured citizens of the Adriatic that such treacherous acts in furtherance of the English objective of ruining their trade would not be tolerated.

The next words shocked him rigid and he re-read them very slowly.

In view of the disgraceful nature of the crime and the need to set a stern precedent, the spy Dillon is sentenced to be shot at dawn one week hence against the walls of the Fortezza before witnesses.

'Captain? Is something wrong?'

'Edward is to be shot as a spy in seven days.' Kydd swallowed. 'Here – look.'

Craddock took it. Only a slight trembling at the edge of the paper betrayed any emotion as he read on carefully to the end. Then he handed it back and said calmly, pointing to the last paragraph. 'There is more.'

Kydd took it and read:

Our correspondent understands however that clemency might be shown in this case, should Dillon be made the subject of an exchange with Général de Brigade Édouard Valois, previously captured at sea in a treacherous deception by British forces.

Craddock brightened, 'Dubourdieu is using the *Moniteur* for his own purposes, it having the ability to dangle an offer before you wherever in these regions you may be.'

'An exchange! I do believe I'll do it,' Kydd breathed, in a gust of relief. 'A neutral ship, that sort of thing.'

'And no requirement to show yourself or have direct dealings with the villain.'

It was as if the sun had come out after a storm. It shouldn't take long and—

But as quickly as it had come, hope vanished, leaving nothing but blackness.

An unanswerable reason had just hammered in why it could never be. The French general was at this moment in Lissa. If he was released into Dubourdieu's hands the secret of Kydd's operational base would be out and, without delay, Dubourdieu would get together an invasion fleet to take Lissa, driving him and his squadron from the Adriatic.

Had he the right to sacrifice his mission to save Dillon? Holding his head in his hands he bludgeoned his brain for an answer.

'God help me,' he croaked, 'But I've a deciding to make that's set to break me. What should I do?'

Chapter 46

Metternich's private apartment in the Hofkanzlei

The billiard room was broad but low-ceilinged with an eye-height cluster of lights over the table throwing the rest of the room into shadow.

A spotted canine, which Renzi recognised as a Dalmatian Coach Dog, lay on the floor. The irony of its origin in the lost lands of Austria in the Adriatic brought a subdued smile to his face.

'Shall we say three hundred?' Metternich murmured, taking down a cue.

So this was going to be a game played under traditional English rules, with the number of points agreed beforehand for a win. Renzi eased a little.

A butler hovered while the chancellor raised an eyebrow interrogatively.

'Oh, I'll stay with your very acceptable champagne,' Renzi replied airily, inspecting his cue.

The servant departed and they were left alone.

For some reason Renzi felt that the very near future was

going to be a turning point, a decisive moment in their relationship, and who knew what lay ahead? He'd succeeded far beyond what he'd hoped, piquing the interest of the most powerful man in Austria, opening a channel of understanding that seemed to indicate he was perceived as a carelessly wealthy individual, whose friends must include the highest in the land.

They set to, the noiseless travel of the ivory balls and their discreet clicking in some way soothing to the ear.

'Did you remark the *jungfrau* in the black pearls, Farndon?' Metternich unexpectedly dropped into the silence. 'A pullet as ripe for plucking as any, if I be the judge.'

Renzi had not got used to the easy familiarity he'd experienced only that evening at the modish gathering they'd deserted for Metternich's suggested respite at billiards.

'But a knowing eye, that one, Klemens,' he replied lazily. 'As will warn the prudent.'

Nothing further was said until a clumsy attempt at a cannon by Metternich ended in ignominy.

'*Verdammt!*' He straightened, resting his cue at a careless angle.

Renzi was not fooled. 'Bad luck, old fellow,' he said, and waited.

'It's just that – well, we all have our distractions as haunt us unduly. I won't bore you with mine.'

'Dear chap, if there's anything I can do for my friend? A mort of philosophising?'

Metternich looked at him with a wry smile. 'Thank you, Farndon. Your offer is well taken, but in this world the philosopher may say what he will, but the statesman will be judged most sternly by what he does.'

Renzi tensed. It was happening! 'A perplexity of a politicking nature?' he asked, as casually as he could. If Metternich was going to allow him to share in his deepest reasoning on a point of statecraft, this was all of what he'd been sent here to discover.

'Of nations, not polities,' Metternich replied, then gave a disarming smile. 'Not to trouble us on this night of entertainment, *nicht wahr?*'

'If it causes my friend to miss his shot, this becomes a serious matter. Do trot it out, Klemens. At the least you'll get my views, for what they're worth.'

Metternich said nothing but bent to sight down at his cue ball and the awkwardly placed red. There was a moment's hesitation. Then he straightened and glanced at Renzi as if to make up his mind.

'I know you'll not betray my confidences,' he said quietly, 'and in the course of things the world will learn of my deciding in all good time.'

Renzi continued to chalk his cue, a look of concern wrinkling his brow.

'Austria is not in a fortunate position at this time,' Metternich began, putting down his cue and pacing slowly around the room, 'laid prostrate by events and powerless to prevent them, locked in on all sides and dependent on others for her existence. True?'

'Unhappily, it seems so,' Renzi answered. 'Go on.'

'Yet still a central European power – some might say the chief about which all of Europe orbits, and therefore, by its very existence, of weighty significance to the continent.'

'I would think most would agree with you there, Klemens.'

'Then as her ruling minister I must face a profound and unspeakably harsh destiny in store for my country.'

'Say away, old fellow.'

'It is this. The continent is riven in contention by ferociously ambitious emperors, who must inescapably come to grapple together for mastery of the whole. Austria has survived so far as a neutral not to be feared or despised but, caught in the midst between the striving forces, will be ground to a desolation, a wasteland until at last the victor seizes his spoils.'

'It can't be as bad as—'

'A fate which is as certain as death itself.'

Was this Metternich reaching for an answer, some way out? No, that would be preposterous! If it was, Renzi was not the one he should be talking with. But had the man made up his mind what course he would take and was passing it by him for reaction?

'A hard thing to take, my friend.'

'Unless I make a bold move that would in one erect invisible battlements about the entire country.' He turned and stopped, looking for a response from Renzi.

'Do tell, Klemens,' he encouraged.

There was the briefest of hesitations, then Metternich said flatly, 'An alliance.'

Renzi caught his breath, unable to think of a reply to match the gravity of the announcement.

Metternich continued, 'An alliance that must deter a third party from trespass on the soil of Austria but not one that will irrevocably bind me into a course of action I may regret at a later date.'

Surely he couldn't mean . . . Renzi's pulse raced. The last alignment of any form Austria had made with Great Britain had been the Fifth Coalition, involving, on the Austrian side, the raising of an army in concert with other nations, and on the British side, a heavy sum in financial subventions. The whole thing had ended miserably at Wagram.

Was Metternich floating before him the possibility of a formal alliance, a very different matter from a coalition? If so, the implications were breath-taking and he had no business even venturing an opinion.

'Old chap,' he said, a little unsteadily, 'should this not be left to the ambassadors, envoys and such of that stripe?'

'My dear Farndon, this goes far above their petty concerns, their task merely to take care of details in the wake of events. In your charming innocence you believe them to be masters of strategy, minds above the sordid minutiae of existence, thinkers of sapience and resolve. They are not! Each will pursue the selfish interests of not only their nation but the wretched dictates of the politics of the day in that realm. How can any shining settlement be arrived at between them when minds never rise above mortal cupidity?'

He paused significantly. 'This is why I value your thoughts, my friend. You are above it all, yet have the intelligence and perspectives to perceive the higher purpose, and most invaluable is that there will be no need for tedious documenting and justifying.'

Renzi reached for sanity. Did Metternich ascribe to him some sort of wisdom and sagacity beyond the actual? Did he really believe that he was above acknowledging the primacy of England, the country of his birth and the fount of the honours he held?

It was getting out of hand and he was fast losing grip on where things stood.

'I'll do my best, Klemens,' he replied humbly.

'Is all I ask,' Metternich said, with evident relief. 'Now, shall I rehearse to you my reasoning?'

At that moment, nothing could have been more desirable to Renzi.

'Very well. My greatest belief is that, *au fond*, peace and stability in Europe may only prevail if there is a balance. A balance of powers, military and economic, that leaves no single nation in domination of the others, for there lie resentments, revolt and intolerant patriotism.'

'France – Bonaparte,' Renzi put in.

It seemed not to have been heard. Metternich continued, 'A superior being would surmount petty strivings to seek this balance, even as he rises above the natural clamours of his own country, as I must.'

'If we're talking alliances this will be a difficult objective, I'm persuaded,' Renzi said delicately.

'Just so.'

Metternich selected two chairs from the back of the room and brought them into the pool of light, inviting Renzi to sit with him. 'It may surprise you to learn that for some months I've been pressed hard by Tsar Alexander to ally with him. What do you think of that?'

Renzi deflected the question. 'Klemens, my views are of little account. I'd much rather hear yours and then give opinion on them.'

'So. It's been said by others that Russia is a land of barbarians led by one civilised, while France is a land of the civilised led by a barbarian. I can only agree.'

'And I.'

'Then you'll understand if I reject the alliance out of hand. For the sake of administering the quietus to one who must inevitably fall to his own hubris, the price is too high.'

'Price?'

'To admit a barbarous horde beyond counting into the very heart of Europe, never to be rid of them.'

'The balance for ever a-kilter.'

'*Genau richtig*, my friend.'

'Then . . . ?'

'We must examine who is left with the requisite puissance to deter but at the same time will make no territorial demands on me.'

Renzi inwardly thrilled – Castlereagh wanted an appreciation of the man and instead was being handed an alliance. 'One with a world view,' he agreed, 'whose interests are not bounded by petty conquests. With the resources to stand by its friends.'

'Why, yes. With Russia not in question there are precious few who can meet that requirement. In fact I believe only the one,' Metternich said, with a decisive finality.

'Oh?'

'It can only stand to reason.'

'Which is?' Renzi wanted him to say it.

Like a physical blow, the single word slammed in. 'France.'

'An alliance with Napoleon Bonaparte?' Renzi managed. The consequences of an open alliance with England's deadliest enemy was too much to take in all at once.

'Whatever my feelings as an Austrian – one who suffered in the bombardment by the same, whose country's slain made hills in the snows of Austerlitz, whose Adriatic lands have been wantonly seized – logic and the higher purpose demands I must.'

'Why? For the love of God, why?'

'You do not see it? The Emperor gains much by an alliance, the first and most important of which is that by so doing no other power might steal one. No longer need he fear a sudden irruption in the centre of his empire, no more the need to tie down his valuable *soldat* thousands in idleness. These are now released for further adventures. And he can point to an ally, a great power of Europe, that chose him as the eventual victor in this great war.'

It left Renzi speechless until he found tongue enough to blurt, 'And you – that is, Austria – what do you stand to gain by this?'

'Only one thing.'

'Yes?'

'Existence.'

'Er . . .'

'Bonaparte prowls Europe like a beast at the water's edge, denied further conquests by your Royal Navy. It would take little to provoke his seizing upon this fallen kingdom for his own vainglory. An alliance has advantages that make this inadvisable, so by just this we may sleep soundly in our beds. And of other predators, not even the Russians dare fall on a declared brother-in-arms of the greatest military presence in the continent.'

It was unanswerable.

'As for any other demands he might make – there will be no territorial confiscating, for one does not make such claims on one's alliance partner. Austria will remain sacrosanct. And any other exactions are impossible on a nation so recently crushed and impoverished by war. An alliance will therefore cost us nothing.'

He gave a small smile. 'How say you to this reasoning, Farndon? Should I make alliance with the French?'

Renzi struggled to find a reply but the logic was faultless. He was witless to have thought that maritime England could do anything to stand by a friend in the very core of Bonaparte's land empire but it had gone well past that. Was he being put in the impossible situation of being the only one in any kind of position able to dissuade Metternich from such a fatal move?

There was no conceivable argument he could bring to bear against the move, and that being so, it had to be accepted that Metternich would go ahead with it anyway. Any weak and pathetic protestations would only demean him in the chancellor's eyes, and if there was anything to be salvaged from this situation it had to be his hard-won friendship.

'Yes. You should, I believe, Klemens. The rationality of your argument cannot be denied.' Oddly, he knew he was being sincere as he uttered the words.

Metternich regarded him steadily, then said softly, 'I would sign the alliance tomorrow were it not for one thing.'

'Oh?'

'I'm exercised by what England, our steadfast friend of years, would construe from the tidings of a formal alliance with its direst enemy.'

In a flash, it all fell into place and became crystal clear. The decision had already been taken – Metternich was going to do it but first he wanted his reasons known in full in Whitehall, and Renzi was to be the conduit. Why did he need this? Because he had every intention of casting aside the alliance when circumstances allowed, presumably at some point in the future when Bonaparte had been beaten and in retreat.

Smothering a heaving sigh of relief, Renzi gave a half-smile. 'Dear friend, I've a feeling they'll uncover your reasoning by some means. Shall we finish the game?'

Chapter 47

Guest quarters, Hofburg Palace

Cecilia stood pale-faced as Renzi briskly entered and crossed to her as if to give her a peck of greeting on the cheek. 'Go to the kitchen,' he whispered urgently in her ear, 'and turn away the cook.'

He picked up a newspaper, then with a bored expression flung it down and wandered towards the kitchen.

She was waiting alone for him there, stiff and defensive.

He suspected that the kitchen was the only room not worth mounting spy-holes and, without a moment's hesitation, he went to her, crushing her in a long and passionate kiss. He felt her body loosen, melt and return the ardour. Then came her muffled and broken plea: 'Nicholas – why?'

'Cec – it's over!' he breathed. 'I have it – I have it all and there's no need to play the abandoned wife any more!'

'Oh, my darling,' she said, her voice breaking. 'Do you mean it?'

Only another kiss could convince her.

'Now, sweetling, we must still keep up appearances for a few days. I've this minute to get word to London to satisfy them in the particulars as will allow them to release us to go home. Home, my dearest!'

It was essential to get his priceless haul to Whitehall before the bombshell of an alliance became known with the risk of a savage and inappropriate official response being made in ignorance. He'd been scrupulously careful about keeping his distance from any functionary, open or covert, that could in any way be taken as an association with the British powers-that-be. But Congalton had made provision for emergencies: a cipher secured on the text of a mutually agreed book and a signal based on flower vases in a window.

The substance of his intelligence he phrased rapidly and pithily. That there was about to be an alliance, with France, and for compelling reasons. Metternich was to be understood as an overarching European, not simply as an Austrian, whose driving principle was maintaining a power balance on the continent. It was to be expected that, given a decline in French influence and pressures occasioned by military reverses, a different alignment would be in contemplation at some point in the future.

The cyphering was lengthy and tedious but well before dawn it was complete. The message was folded many times and sealed, then placed under the left-hand vase, his workings safely consigned to the kitchen fire.

By evening the order of the two vases had been changed and the message removed – the signal had been seen and his intelligence was on its way by the most urgent means possible, presumably imperial post to Hamburg and an overnight voyage to England, a matter of small days only. If he didn't get a reply within a week or two, he'd take it he should return.

* * *

Then, one morning, he discovered the order of the vases was restored. Concealed in the base of one was a tiny many-creased scrap of paper, carefully sealed. Minute examination failed to turn up the betraying hair-line of an intercepting blade. He held it before him, heart hammering.

Chapter 48

Aboard Tyger

It was no use agonising. What Dillon needed now was for Kydd to keep a cool head and come up with something that would see him safely restored to *Tyger*. If it wasn't an exchange, then what? But with the situation loaded so unequally against him nothing resembled a workable plan for rescue and time was running out fast.

There was always the same unbreakable logic: an exchange was impossible, for the secret of his covert base would be betrayed and he could never explain his action for the sake of a single man before a commander-in-chief. On the other hand neither could he justify casualties in a vain attempt to storm a major military stronghold.

Through the rest of the day he wrestled with the quandary, aware that a more stern commander would never allow himself to be delayed in his main mission by such a concern. Yet here he was anchored, with the rest of his squadron close by, all idle, their purpose laid aside.

But this was Dillon, the young man recommended by Lord

Farndon who'd elected to go to sea to seek adventure and found it with *Tyger*. Whose intelligence and resource had resonated with Kydd to the point of exchanging personal confidences and who had eventually become his closest friend aboard.

And he was now in a death cell.

The following days brought no sudden insight, no wash of relief at the arrival of a cunning plan.

But then came news. On the front page of the *Moniteur* a black-edged announcement was short and to the point.

In the absence of any approach from Captain Sir Thomas Kydd in the matter of an exchange, the sentence on the spy Edward Dillon will be carried out at dawn on the twenty-first of this month. Death by firing squad at the walls of the Fortezza Monte Astagno. By order, Bernard Dubourdieu, Contre-amiral.

The next morning! Kydd knew he'd run out of time.

He took to the deck and the peculiar solitude granted a captain as he paced slowly up and down the weather side, traditionally never to suffer intrusion by any save those whose duty required it, but no answer came. He'd been over the options so often his mind was frozen. And ever louder sounded the grim drumbeat of time, marking the last hours of Dillon's life – unless he obeyed the siren call to fall in with Dubourdieu's offer of exchange. It was not too late: a last-minute dash by the cutter under white flag and . . . He crushed the thought and blackly resumed his pacing.

As dusk drew in he reluctantly went below. There were papers for his attention thick on his desk but he hadn't the heart even to begin to deal with them without Dillon at his right hand.

He sat in his armchair by the stern windows, unseeingly staring out into the black night. This was now a vigil and he the supplicatory vigilant.

Tysoe appeared, bearing a tray with a glass and a bottle of whisky. 'Sir. I . . . I thought you might wish . . .'

'Why, thank you, Tysoe. That's thoughtful in you.' It was placed tenderly on the little Turkish table.

'Sir Thomas, I . . . I . . . that is,' he gulped, 'we all . . . it's a terrible thing, and . . . and . . .'

Kydd felt his eyes sting. 'Yes, a grievous time. You carry on, Tysoe. I shan't need you further tonight.' He splashed himself a generous measure of whisky.

At this very moment that fine mind and youthful energy were trapped in a French cell reflecting on the fate and circumstances that had put him there. Would he be sunk in misery and terror or stoutly trusting in a gallant rescue at the last minute? He knew the answer: Dillon would never allow the French the satisfaction of seeing fear and would take things as they came with the calm certitude of logic right to the end.

The whisky burned a path of fire to his stomach and his heart cried out at the unfairness of it all.

He lifted the bottle for another but at a soft knock on the door he put it down. 'Come!'

Craddock entered, his face ashen. 'I thought as if you . . . you wanted a mort of company, Captain,' he said thickly.

Kydd glanced across at the other armchair, now empty and poignantly with a book left on it by Dillon the last time he'd sat there. It had a scrap of torn paper marking his place, now never to be taken up and resumed by the one who'd put it there. 'Come in, please do, Mr Craddock.'

Sensing something, the man went to the desk and retrieved a chair instead, leaving the armchair empty. 'A dreadful, insane and cruel business, war,' Craddock began, in a voice that was barely audible. 'What place does it find for reason, pity, humanity?'

Kydd had no desire to debate the ethics of war and reached for the bottle. 'A whisky?'

'I'd rather not,' he murmured. 'It seems . . . wrong, at this time.'

This brought Kydd up sharply. To honour a brave man in his last hours in a maudlin, liquor-fuelled huddle was not how it should be done. But the strong bite of the liquor was spreading in his vitals and the thoughts raged on unchecked and unsaid.

Then suddenly the pricking in his eyes was overtaken by a flooding tide of grief and anguish, and Commodore Sir Thomas Kydd dropped his head and wept.

After he came to himself he looked up to see Craddock regarding him gravely with infinite sadness.

'I – I'm sorry,' Kydd managed, but it was waved aside.

'Edward is your dearest friend and I honour you for your feelings, sir.' Only his whitened knuckles betrayed any emotion as he went on, 'But do reflect that for me he is even more – he's the one who saved my life, who pulled me through my vale of tears and anguish. I can only . . . only . . .' He broke off, choking back what he was going to say.

After a time they both steadied. Conversation was resumed, calm and gentlemanly, and later, in the small hours before dawn, Kydd doused all lamps save one and they sat in silence together until the day had come.

In an eerie silence the ship lay at anchor, waiting for word. It came in the late afternoon, a *Moniteur* handed over by an expressionless fisherman.

Kydd's eyes took in only one thing: 'Sentence of death was

carried out on the spy Dillon . . . who it is my duty to report died well . . .'

Without a word he went to his cabin. A tidal wave of desolation nearly unmanned him, the reality too much to bear that never more would he hear his cheerful greeting, see him with a bundle of work or join him at the backgammon board.

Craddock arrived but, overcome, shortly excused himself to his own private grief and Kydd was left on his own.

An hour later, Bowden diffidently put his head around the door. 'Sir. The gunroom asks if there's anything they can do for you.'

'No – thank you, Charles, no.'

Hesitating, the first lieutenant seemed reluctant to leave. 'It's not my place to make comment on your grief, sir, but I beg leave to say something.'

'Say away, old fellow.'

'Do you remember Mr Beekman?'

Sunk in misery, Kydd shook his head. 'No, Charles, I don't,' he said wearily.

'Sir, a midshipman in our flying *L'Aurore*.'

'If you say so.'

'Lost to us most gallantly in an action near Buenos Aires.'

'I have a vague remembrance.'

'What I want to point out is that he and Mr Dillon share something in common.'

'Oh?'

'Both of them were shot in the performance of their duty. If you openly grieve for one why do you not for the other?'

It came back to him: the plucky lad slithering out on a cutter's bowsprit to pull away a snaring grapnel and taking a musket shot that left him gasping his life away on its fore-deck.

'You're quite right, Charles.' Dillon was in the line of duty when he lost his life just as much as Beekman. Both should be mourned as was the way of it in the navy – quietly, without drama, all who knew them in their little company sharing their sadness in unspoken communion.

Kydd took a deep breath and added, 'And I humbly apologise for appearances. I shall be on deck presently.'

The deck watch in sombre respect crossed to the leeward side of the quarterdeck and all conversation ceased.

For some minutes Kydd gazed out over the chill grey-green seas, then abruptly turned on the officer-of-the-watch. 'Where's the squadron?' he asked bluntly.

'Standing to seaward, in accordance with your orders, Sir Thomas,' Brice said uneasily.

'Very well.'

At that moment Bowden came up and doffed his hat formally. 'This morning *Redwing* reported intelligence of a convoy from the north.' He handed over a folded sheet of paper.

It tersely stated that her commander had had contact with the shore near Venice and his reliable informant had supplied details of a large escorted convoy about to sail thence to Ancona with military stores and troop reinforcements for onward dispatch across the Adriatic to Corfu in the Ionians. So important was it considered that Admiral Dubourdieu was himself taking personal direction of its safe arrival.

'Why wasn't I given this before?' he demanded, a sudden charge of excitement sweeping away his low spirits. 'No, never mind. Tell *Redwing* to find the frigates and desire them to close with *Tyger* tomorrow forenoon for a conference.'

From out of the blue here was a chance for deadly action directly against the one Kydd most wanted to hurt. It was a prey worthy of his squadron and the outcome would not be in doubt, but only if it was played out well, and he would make damned sure of that.

A small voice at the back of his mind added that intelligence demanding his presence there provided a good excuse for his headlong dash across to Ancona after Dillon. Another reason to ensure that the Sea Devil prevailed.

Chapter 49

The captains of the Adriatic Squadron entered the flagship cabin warily, taking their seats quietly.

'On behalf of my fellow captains, may I say how deeply we sympathise in the grievous loss of your secretary and friend,' the senior, Whitby of *Cerberus,* opened ponderously.

'Thank you, Mr Whitby. I believe that Lord Nelson mourned likewise the loss of his Mr Scott.'

'Quite so, Sir Thomas.'

'And now we have urgent business as I believe will honour his name. The extirpation of an entire convoy.'

There were raised eyebrows and exchanged glances but Kydd affected not to notice. He outlined the intelligence from *Redwing,* emphasising the strategic importance of cutting the flow of military supplies to the chief gatekeeper of the Adriatic. It was taken in quickly, and when he threw open the meeting to suggestions, there were more than a few.

He'd taken a close look at the charts and had his own ideas but wanted to hear theirs. When they'd finished he knew his was the most workable. 'Gentlemen. I rather think that a meeting at sea with the convoy with but four frigates would certainly dispose of any escorts but would sadly limit our prize-taking to some three or four, the remaining making their escape while a victim apiece was boarded and possessed.'

It would be a handsome enough day's work but was not what Kydd wanted. To utterly destroy and ruin every one of Dubourdieu's convoy needed a different strategy. 'The chart, please, Mr Joyce.'

It was a large-scale one of the east coast of Italy, Venice in the north, Ancona a third the way down.

'Here,' he pronounced, stabbing a finger at a medium-sized port on the coast not far short of Ancona, Pescano di Mare.

'This is what we shall do. The convoy will be inshore on its way to Ancona and therefore passing close by. Just at that very position they spy ahead of them the Sea Devil and his squadron but, fortunately for them, Pescano is under their lee and they waste no time in making harbour and the shelter of its considerable number of guns.'

He watched their faces – this was routine. What he was about to announce was not.

With a bleak smile he continued, 'Lamentably for them, on the previous day the Sea Devil has come a-visiting Pescano, landing in the overwhelming force that all of four frigates can provide. They take the fortifications and then man the guns so thoughtfully provided, being sure to keep out of sight and maintaining the requisite flags and banners flying.'

'A nice intrigue,' Whitby chuckled, 'allowing them only the choice of being pounded to pieces by their own guns or putting back to sea where they'll receive a right royal welcome!'

Gordon of *Active* leaned back in open admiration.

'Every one a prize!' gloated Hornby, of the diminutive *Volage*, not normally able to look forward to a shower of gold. 'And when I bear mind to the poor beggars on blockade at Toulon, why, my heart bleeds.'

The whole thing was only possible because of their unique numbers – a frigate squadron that was capable of feats of arms denied to the lone marauders of before.

Kydd's grim smile widened. 'There's only one thing can scupper the plan.'

There was instant concern.

'That we miss the convoy as being too laggardly. Gentlemen, my information is that it sails in three days. Unless we make our descent on Pescano tomorrow it will escape us.'

Their chart was not forthcoming about military hazards but Mr Craddock was able to enlighten them. 'Think of Falmouth. A small entrance with Pendennis Castle on the left and St Mawes to the right, their heavy guns facing each other from atop a rocky headland and quite capable of commanding entry into the harbour. Falmouth, our Pescano, lies out of sight around the Pendennis foreland within a spacious harbour but there the resemblance ends. There's no mighty Carrick Roads or a great river extending inland, but in truth the town of Pescano di Mare is a well enough used port having much profited out of this war in trans-shipments and smuggling.'

'Does it have a stronghold in the town, a fortress of note?'

'There is nothing of real value, military or otherwise, save the shipping that is to be found there from time to time. All military resources are in the two castles.'

'I don't suppose . . .'

'I do apologise but, they being immured out of sight in the castles, their numbers are unknown to me,' Craddock admitted.

'So. A tough nut to crack, I believe.'

'Not so much, I'm persuaded,' Clinton offered. 'Should we reduce one, then the threat of turning its guns on the other will give pause even to the stoutest heart.'

'And with the threat multiplied by four hostile ships of heavy metal jockeying to be first to join the merciless mauling then what follows could be interesting,' Whitby mused.

Kydd harrumphed. 'We've yet to seize our first, gentlemen. Shall we get to work?'

His time with Cochrane on the Spanish coast wreaking mayhem had not been wasted: he had a notion how they could achieve the same dramatic results and quickly laid it before them.

'A petard. Placed up against the weakest place of the outer wall.' This was an explosive device that could blow a breach in the defences.

But how was this to be achieved in the teeth of concentrated fire from the fortress?

'Boats,' Kydd said briefly. 'Boats with carronades charged with grape as will continuously sweep the battlements and parapets.'

'Sir? Boats will be under fire from—'

'The boats will be overshot by a frigate in turn, whose target will be the casemates at point-blank range, dismaying the gunners to a degree.'

'So we have—'

Kydd cut through Whitby's assessment. 'Two frigates will appear out of the dawn opposite the left-hand, larger fortification and open a fierce bombardment. While this keeps the defenders from their guns, a boat lands with the petard party. At the same time half a dozen boats will manoeuvre such that, at very close range and protected by the overshooting, they will train their carronades loaded with grape and canister on the battlements above, and any defender who disputes their work will be discouraged with an instant blast of shot.'

Smiles were now general. This was something like the Kydd

of old and there was every reason to think that in short minutes, with a practicable breach, the castle would be theirs.

'In the confusion of the blast and the continued bombardment the remaining boats will land marines and seamen on the landward side to storm the objective.'

Boats. It entirely depended on them but that was what a squadron was all about: between them they could muster numbers in the dozens, an extravagance Kydd couldn't recall seeing in action together before.

'Questions?'

'Who shall provide the petard and its party?' Hornby enquired delicately.

'*Tyger.*'

'And the Jollies?'

'Marines will be contributed by each ship and under the overall command of Captain Clinton, who, I believe, is the squadron's senior commissioned officer, Royal Marines.'

Chapter 50

With the cutters and brigs to seaward on watch, *Tyger* and *Cerberus* glided shore-wards in the last of the night, the darker mass of land below, only a very few lights abroad. Launched and manned, the designated boats were towed astern, their occupants huddled and shivering in the numbing pre-dawn cold.

Active and *Volage* lay off out to sea, ready to add their weight, and when the shadows retreated, details of the shore firmed and they moved in.

Never had Kydd felt so certain of victory. Beneath his professional manner roared a fierce rage that could be satisfied only with a crushing strike-back against the one who'd removed Edward Dillon from the ranks of the living. He was going to make it so, whatever it took.

'Signal close action,' he ordered. This was the command to begin the bombardment and the two frigates shortened in and set their bowsprits directly for the fortress.

He wondered fleetingly what was going through the mind of the commandant of this minor redoubt, whose usual work was to bring in suspected contraband. His guns would not be primed, with all the inconvenience in the unloading at the end of the day. In the usual way of things, they'd have been warned well in advance by sloops and cutters but those small craft would have fled before the awesome power of a frigate squadron.

There was no reply from ashore after the first broadsides from *Cerberus*, the gunners no doubt bleary and disbelieving, and keeping well out of sight. Then *Tyger* added the thunder of her eighteen-pounders, some three times the size of any artillery that the French could bring into the field.

'Away the red cutter.' The petard party cast off and headed inshore.

'Away the launch and both cutters.' The carronade party was on its way.

Kydd gave a savage smile. 'You have the ship, Mr Bowden!' he grated, and bounded down to where his gig was secured. His fighting sword was handed to him.

'Stretch out, lads!' he roared, against the blast of *Tyger*'s guns overhead. 'There's a purse of cobbs waiting for every man!'

They laid out with a will and, as the light strengthened and the detail of raw gun-smoke and rising masonry dust became evident, so did the drama of the petard party.

The landing, below the overhang of a small escarpment not far from the walls of the citadel, was unopposed. No doubt the defenders had been puzzled by why so few were in on the assault. As they ran towards the walls, dragging their improvised framework petard it became clear, however, and marksmen appeared on the parapet as the bombardment lifted. The nearest boat's carronade spoke and a storm of canister swept them from sight. When a few brave souls tried to replace them, they, too, were instantly cleared by the next boat's gun.

Timing was crucial, and with the frigate cannonade ceasing as the petard was set, the boats furiously served their bow carronades until a sullen thump and rising coil of dirty smoke told of the successful detonation of the infernal device, the signal Kydd had waited for.

A massive cheer came from every boat as the real assault began.

Nosing into the shallows, the gig grounded on a spit of gravel and Kydd leaped ashore with ferocious elation, his blade drawn as he bounded up to join the mêlée.

It was almost an anti-climax. The massive oaken doors of the fortress hung askew, still smoking, an entry to the fortress for the cheering attackers, who lost no time in flooding in.

Briefly, Kydd felt sorry for the dusty and grimed commandant standing shaking and staring before him, offering his sword to the fierce and vengeful Sea Devil.

And all before breakfast.

Chapter 51

As Kydd tucked into his toast and marmalade, news came that, on seeing the larger stronghold reduced to capitulation so quickly and the frigates turning on them, the opposite citadel had chosen to yield without a fight.

With a pang, Kydd realised he now felt at a remove from his grief. Dillon was not forgotten but he was inhabiting a part of his life that was receding into the past.

They had all day to enter the harbour, make it theirs and prepare for the next day's events. Preparations were complete well before dusk. As they'd approached that morning, it had been the duty of two midshipmen to take note of every flag, banner and mark that in any way indicated French or Italian occupation and they had all been faithfully restored. At the wharves a covering gun battery received its new owners, and in the two entrance forts, guns were levered around and trained ready on the anchorage.

The four frigates slipped out to sea to take up their position just to the south of Pescano.

The next day they were in classic search formation: strung out in a broad front with a frigate on the beam only just at masthead visibility, the four together able to cast an eye over nearly a hundred sea miles.

Hove to, they lay in wait, lookouts straining to the north for the first signs of a mass of ships. If the convoy passed their watchfulness the chance of prizes beyond counting would be lost.

It was uncannily quiet on deck, no usual creaks and squeals of timbers or the steady swash of a vessel under way. The speaker of any unnecessary word was glared at, and the cook roundly cursed for allowing a pot to bang in the galley. All heads were turning up to the cross-trees to catch the first hail to the deck that would herald their golden destiny.

Several individual ships passed through but were ignored, unknowing that below the horizon was a second frigate and beyond her a third and fourth.

And then as the afternoon wore on a hail came, '*Deck hoooo! Red flag in Volage!*'

Kydd's instructions were that only in the event multiple ships in company were sighted was the immense distant-signal flag, which could be seen over many miles of sea, to be flown. Course was to be altered directly towards and the signal repeated by all others so there would be a general convergence on the sighting.

Excitement was impossible to quell, and the decks crowded with seamen noisily waiting for the convoy to lift into view over the horizon.

Kydd knew that for the unknown convoy escort commander a single small frigate had been sighted ahead. He would 'whip in' the convoy members and post any other escorts to the fore to join him – and then would come the awful realisation that the enemy was not alone. First another would appear and then more until, unbelievably, four full-blooded frigates were closing in on him.

Kydd's orders were strict. Suppressing every instinct to clap on all sail for the foe, matters had to take their course as planned, economical sail only loosed while the escort came to its senses.

Well before they came up with the convoy it had put about and begun to claw its way to Pescano.

Kydd took report of its size from eager onlookers. Nineteen fair-sized brigs and barques, one or two Italian lateen-rigged craft and a substantial full-rigged merchantman, not dissimilar to a Calcutta Indiaman. The three brig-rig and one ship-rig corvette escort hadn't a chance against the squadron and were soon cravenly in the lead of the slower merchantman in crowding on for the safety of Pescano.

The four frigates heaved to at the harbour entrance to watch the show, allowing time for the convoy to make harbour and anchor in the roadstead opposite. Taking in their sail they were no doubt thankful for their lucky escape, but then both forts unbelievably opened up on them.

With one or two token rounds from the gun battery on the wharves, the situation must have dawned on the luckless escort commander that Pescano was no longer a welcoming sanctuary but an enemy-held territory. In angry jerks his flag came down in submission.

The four frigates entered, taking position in an outer ring about the convoy.

'Mr Bowden, you know what to do. Any trouble will be answered from a provost cutter, and I give you joy of our capture.'

It was gratifying as a commodore to hand over to a junior, even if this was his own first lieutenant. It would spare Kydd the painstaking seizing of each prize by turn, the examination of papers and the securing under a skeleton prize crew. Then on to the next, all under the helpless and enraged eye of the escorts.

He received the escort commander, red-faced and sputtering, on the quarterdeck of *Tyger*, pointing out that it was not Kydd's decision that had led the convoy into a harbour that just happened to be occupied by his forces and urged him to accept the fortunes of war, which could turn at any moment.

Duty done, he could retire to his cabin to write an account of the day to Persephone, a letter that would be on its way the next time he touched at Lissa. Which would be . . . soon. So many prizes would need a convoy of their own to bring them safely to his base, and what better time than now?

He bent to his task but was soon interrupted.

'Sir?'

It was Bowden.

He wore an odd smile as he handed across a letter. 'Found in the effects of a certain Colonel Vaudrei, taking passage in the *Ville de Lyon* – the sizeable ship-rigged one.'

If this was not personal mail Kydd felt no compunction in reading it.

'Have you read this, Charles?' he asked in astonishment.

'I did, sir. A letter from the Emperor himself. It instructs Vaudrei to take a stiffening of men to Dubourdieu and demands his immediate steps to obey his orders to rid the Adriatic of the insolent Sea Devil, he being increasingly impatient at the delay in the face of other strategic imperatives.'

Kydd grinned delightedly. 'And now he is my prisoner . . .'

They chuckled. 'So how many in this colonel's band?'

'Some one hundred, sir, but be advised they are of a quite different sort – some kind of ornamental breed from Napoleon's own stable used to enforce his particular will, hard men all.'

The convoy had been of routine military stores, not troop

reinforcements, so these must now be under special guard away from the rest.

'I do believe I'll make my number with our guest. See how he does, that kind of thing.'

'Aye aye, sir.'

'Sir – Colonel de Groupement Auguste Vaudrei.' There was a subdued clinking of accoutrements outside, which told Kydd he'd been under heavy guard.

'Do I address Sir Thomas Kydd?' he demanded. The French was not that of the salons and polite society that Kydd had so diligently learned from Renzi, it was flat, uncompromising and smacked of the field encampment.

'You do, sir.'

Vaudrei's eyes were of an unsettling colourlessness that, with his iron-hard features and the build of a long-service foot-soldier, must have terrified many he'd been sent to deal with.

'You have my letter and know why I'm here. This is not the act of a gentleman.'

Kydd gave a dry smile. 'I'm obliged to seek intelligence from wherever it offers itself, as well you know, sir.'

There was a smouldering malice in the man but also a glimmering of respect. Well into his forties, he was speaking to one ten years or more his junior, one whose sea skills had made him a feared foe, so much so that he'd attracted the personal animosity of Emperor Bonaparte himself.

'You have twenty prizes and must lose many of your men in crews for them,' he said evenly. 'And more for the guarding of my men, who are hardened veterans of the Imperial Service.'

An intelligent deduction from an army officer and one that Kydd had to deal with now. If his men were as dangerous as he, this would be a challenging task, but what was disquieting was the thought of such a number of formidable men sent to join the prisoners in Lissa. Unless he greatly increased his watch and guard they would undoubtedly incite a rising.

'Thank you for your concern, Colonel. Do tell, why do you mention this?' he replied mildly.

'We are each commanders, you on the sea, I on the land, and we both know that there is a simple answer to your dilemma.'

Kydd tensed. There was something repellent in the man's arrogance, his immediate assumption of the superior position. 'What is that, pray?'

'Set myself and my men on shore and you will be free to sail away.'

Kydd was lost for words at the brazen effrontery, but then a sudden and alluring picture burst into view and he saw how to grant that wish. This officer would never respect an oath of parole but with what he had in mind he didn't need to.

'Very well. I see your logic and am minded to agree. Tomorrow you shall be landed before we set sail.'

A flash of triumph was briefly visible. Then, without a change in the even tone of his voice, Vaudrei added, 'And with the honours of war, of course.'

Pavillons, banners, drums beating and bearing arms? Kydd nearly choked at the presumption. 'It will be considered. Mr Bowden!' he called.

When his first lieutenant appeared, he announced loudly, 'The colonel and I have agreed that when we sail tomorrow he and his men will be released ashore. Make all arrangements necessary.'

Bowden started in surprise but refrained from protesting, and left quietly.

Kydd dismissed Vaudrei. 'Thank you, Colonel. The rest you may leave to us.'

In the morning, when the squadron and its prizes were made ready for sea, Kydd kept his promise to Vaudrei. He boarded *Ville de Lyon* himself to ensure it was carried out to satisfaction.

'Bring Colonel Vaudrei and his men on deck. They're going ashore,' he ordered the prize captain.

Vaudrei stood next to him as the men filed up into ranks, affecting to look bored and disinterested, shuffling into line. They made an impressive sight, their uniforms, with copious amounts of gold lace, glittering in the early sun, silk cravats and peeping lace evidence of their status in Bonaparte's great military machine.

'The honours of war?'

'Oh. In this case I regret not, as I find I'm greatly offended by the tone the Emperor used when discussing me in your letter, Colonel.'

The man's face darkened but eased a little as Kydd went on, 'However, I've taken the liberty of circulating the towns and villages you must pass through on your way to Ancona, warning them that part of a regiment of Napoleon Bonaparte's finest will be marching through and a lining of the streets for cheering would not be taken amiss.'

Craddock's skill at wording the circular in official form, as both advice and a decree, was masterly.

'Your attentions are appreciated, Sir Thomas, and I assure you will never be forgotten.'

This, the colonel would find shortly, was only too true, Kydd mused.

'Boats ready for boarding, sir.'

'One by one into the boats, if you please.'

The first man strode to the side but was stopped by a burly boatswain's mate. 'Off!' he growled.

Not understanding, the man appealed to Vaudrei, who looked back at Kydd, puzzled.

'He means the man must strip to his small clothes,' Kydd replied helpfully.

'Y-you mean . . . ?'

'Yes. Their magnificent uniforms. These are my spoils of war, Colonel.'

It took three large marines to restrain the enraged colonel, who seemed not to understand the meaning of plunder and, in the course of things, was divested of his own apparel. In a gesture of magnanimity Kydd had ensured that each would carry away a coarse grey blanket to wrap around himself.

In less than an hour a disconsolate, huddled group were trudging on their way to Ancona.

The great cabin of *Tyger*, the flagship of the Adriatic Squadron, rang with merriment. And not only at the knowledge that under their lee, as they sailed on for Lissa, were two whole columns of prizes on their way to be justly condemned, but at the stroke Kydd had pulled that, even now, must be resounding among the gunrooms and mess-decks of every ship that wore the ensign of the Royal Navy in the Sea Devil's command.

'And a bumper, three times three!' roared Brice, quite overcome by these twin boons and not a little excellent cognac that had so lately been bound for Admiral Dubourdieu's table.

'When they hear of this in England, why, they'll fall about in the streets, laughing,' spluttered Maynard, whose own purse was set to be swollen with the equivalent of quite some years' pay.

'Well, it was the attitude of the villain that decided me,' Kydd responded playfully, smiling at the memory. 'He brought it on himself.'

Chapter 52

Kydd was aware that he had created a bitter enemy in both Dubourdieu and Bonaparte. The shame and ridicule experienced by those released would resound about the world and he'd never be forgiven. Events in the future would be steeped in an intimate malignity.

The unfettered release of high-value prisoners was easy enough to justify. In accordance with his orders he'd spread alarm and dismay on the coast, and if that had turned to mirth at the sight of the humbled regiment, what better indication of the helplessness of Bonaparte to defend his dominions?

But now there was the need to shore up the gap left by the loss of his confidential secretary. Dillon had known the background, the paper trail, the implications of every event, and his mastery of languages had proved invaluable.

There was no easy solution. Another secretary of his skills and qualities could only be obtained in England, an impossible distance away.

There was only one way to deal with it: the officers of *Tyger* must shoulder the burden.

Cyphering and dispatches: that would be the doctor.

Newspapers: it would arbitrarily be the junior, Maynard, assisted by Craddock, perhaps.

Written orders: Brice, with help from the morose ship's clerk.

Confidential matters: Bowden, with help from . . . Craddock? Possibly not – the man would be perfectly capable but soon he would be fully recovered and resuming his life as a well-placed man of business. Kydd couldn't possibly ask him to demean himself in taking on a secretarial role.

But expecting his officers to assume the burden demanded a harsh sacrifice from them. As each came off watch, exhausted, he could be faced with a demanding assignment requiring a delicacy of judgement and tact as to whether he brought it to the attention of a distracted Kydd. But it was all he could do until he could sign up another Dillon.

The passage to Lissa was rapid and uneventful.

In a short while, and to the joy of the watch and guard remaining there, the bay was filled end to end with prizes, an eye-watering haul.

Kydd ordered away his gig and stepped ashore into a storm of rejoicing, pausing only to wave his cocked hat in acknowledgement to a three times three.

His visit would be short – the Sea Devil must wreak havoc while he could – and he stepped out briskly with Bowden by his side.

'The prisoners, sir?' he asked, as they passed one of four stockades, their gaunt wooden huts filled with sullen inmates. 'Above two hundred in all and twice that number in the convoy.'

Kydd knew that for them to be fed, housed, guarded was well beyond the pitiful resources he could afford to leave with the two midshipmen in charge, who had nevertheless manfully risen to the challenge. He took pride in what they'd achieved. The secret of his base had been preserved: the stockades had been erected well out of sight in the centre of vineyards, the storehouses within the town market and the powder stores in the fields, underground. From seaward, the impression was of a minor fishing village with the usual vegetable plots and grape terracing, nothing to reveal that this was a vital naval base.

For the watch ashore there was immediate relief. Kydd detailed *Volage* and *Active* to be escorts for the onward voyage of delivery of prizes and prisoners to Malta and the prize courts. The hapless General Valois would not be joining them, remaining on Lissa to keep the secret of the base's location. The other prisoners would no doubt be incarcerated on one of the outer islands of Malta, such as Gozo, where they would have no chance to pass on their knowledge.

To hasten matters, he dispatched *Kingfisher* and *Acorn* to the north to ports along the Balkan coast to gather up the latest harvest of intelligence planted by Dillon's seeds. When they returned he and Bowden would distil their meaning into further strikes against Bonaparte's empire.

In a brace of days Kydd wanted *Cerberus* and *Tyger* to put to sea to resume their depredations while they could. Such a feat could never be achieved without a base like Lissa, a turn-around of a few days instead of weeks of sailing to a distant naval port and back, let alone the boon of swift recovery of prize crews.

Kydd saw off young Rowan – the midshipmen in charge ashore would be changed and Rowan would relieve an older lad, who'd return thankfully to his rightful place in *Cerberus*, a junior from *Active* accompanying him. Clinton assured him that the small detachment of marines under Sergeant Dodd could be relied on to protect and assist the midshipmen's working party of seamen as they unloaded supply ships and went to market for fresh produce.

The frigates took their fill of powder and shot, along with stores and provisions from Sicily and Malta that had been carefully stockpiled.

And there was mail. In a haze of happiness he learned that Persephone was creating images of the ancient island of Sicily, which she smugly informed him was the home of Persephone, daughter of the Greek god Zeus and his wife the goddess Demeter. Her symbols were flowers, the deer and the pomegranate; her chief employment as queen of the Underworld was to carry out the curses of men on the souls of the dead.

His Persephone would be spared the dangers of the conflict in the Adriatic as it intensified, but he hoped she would not be cast into boredom by the inanity of King Ferdinand's court. At least she had her cousin to keep her amused.

And there was a short but querulous demand from the commander-in-chief requiring him to explain himself in respect to his dealings with Vice Admiral Sidney Smith, whom he'd been ordered to avoid at all costs. The reply would cost him the rest of the morning but his good humour after Persephone's letters stayed with him.

When the intelligence came it was a mixed bag. The entire Adriatic was in a ferment of anxiety and dismay at the reign of the Sea Devil, throwing into doubt much of the value of ship-sailing times and destinations but also providing compelling evidence of the effectiveness of their campaign. It would seem that just flaunting themselves along the coast would be sufficient to bring paralysis to all sea movements.

Craddock passed across a crumpled paper. 'This one,

Captain?' In fractured English it disclosed that a certain Slovenian merchant was recalling his ships to be laid up in Spalato until the Sea Devil had been put down.

Kydd gave a wintry smile. 'So?'

'From the north he must pass them through the Trogir narrows. I dare to say a welcome might be arranged for them as they emerge?'

'To lay up – this means ships in ballast, empty ships.' In prizes, the richest part of its value was in the cargo.

'Not if I know Josip Pavelić. He'll have them stuffed with his own goods – anything that has a price in Spalato.'

Chapter 53

To Kydd, the chill grey of the sea as they left seemed to be a symbol of the waste and destruction he was being commanded to inflict on these age-old lands. Britain's quarrel was with the tyrant Bonaparte and his ambitions, not the Balkan folk, who'd now been caught up in the titanic fray to the hazard of their lives and trade. Craddock was only one of the many guiltless innocents in Napoleon's sea war.

Their appearance at the eastern exit of the Trogir cleared the seas rapidly. Sails taken in, they lay to a single anchor until first one, then a gaggle of six of the common Mediterranean trading brigs sailed out. *Tyger* eased herself in behind the last while *Cerberus* lay ahead in their path downwind.

It was trivially easy. Under the threat of the guns of a pair of wickedly large frigates there was no resistance.

'You are taken in prize, sir,' Kydd told the grey-haired master of the biggest. 'You and the others.'

'We are neutral Ragusans,' he protested.

'You are employed by Mr Josip Pavelić and your registry is in Spalato,' Kydd replied remorselessly. 'If your cargo is

French goods in any wise then I'm duty bound to condemn you, sir.'

The crestfallen look was all the evidence he needed that Craddock's guess had been right. He gestured to Brice, who entered the hold, reporting shortly afterwards, expressionless, 'French goods, sir. The usual – brandy and lace, wine and porcelain.' All exports that Bonaparte was having the greatest difficulty getting out of the country because of Britain's supremacy at sea and which the Slovenian merchant had thought to consign in a last illicit cargo run.

For some reason the sight of the man's crushed and devastated features reached out to Kydd. In a short while, and almost within sight of his home port, his ship would be taken from him and with it his living and being, with no prospect of further employment. But *Tyger*'s captain had his duty.

Kydd stayed in the background as the ship's papers were collected, examined and the required interrogatories applied. With such a cargo it was only a formality and the waiting prize crew quickly took charge. Six more prizes – even spread across the entire squadron and including the admiral's share, it was a handsome return.

And now word had come from an observer in Pola that an artillery train was on its way by ship from Trieste to Corfu. From a seamanlike deduction of its movements, it could be expected to make use of the inner leads off Zadar where Kydd could play the same kind of trick.

This was a prime target – not in terms of setting a price on it, but on its value to the Corfu garrison, who otherwise would need to haul it bodily over the wild roads flanking the coastline of Dalmatia.

Kydd set their bows northwards and put in motion their

snare. By now the Adriatic would be in an uproar, and he could no longer expect straightforward captures.

Sail was reported above the low tip of the final cape. It turned out to be a leading pair of brig-corvettes, two military transports and a further two corvettes and five gunboats.

In the workmanlike north-easter the gunboats stood no chance against the frigates seething along at speed, and even for the four corvettes the sight of the two frigates bearing down on them was too much: they hauled their wind and fled.

The deserted transports soon gave up and Kydd took possession, this time feeling little compassion for the young man in charge. Proud and aloof, he seemed not to care that he and the guns were going to quite another place, but was taken by surprise to learn that none other than the infamous Sea Devil had been responsible for his situation.

He gave a grim smile. 'Enseigne de Vaisseau Crozier – it is my honour to make your acquaintance, Monsieur' Le Diable. Particularly as it seems you are not long for this world.'

'Do make clear what you mean, *mon brave*,' Kydd replied.

'*Certainement*. My commandant tells me that l'Amiral Dubourdieu has at last been given the full weight of metal he asked for, and three days ago he put to sea, with orders from the Emperor himself to bring your pillage and destruction finally to an end.'

'Thank you for your warning.'

'So, even as we speak together, the admiral is hunting you down to the ends of the earth, like a mad dog.'

'Or even the Adriatic.'

'As you will, Sir Thomas.'

So the game had tightened. This was where everything had

been heading ever since the English squadron had first challenged and violated the French Lake.

And at this moment Dubourdieu, driven by hatred, was actively combing the seas with his powerful fleet, double that of Kydd's own, and willing to stop at nothing to triumph.

Sooner or later they would cross wakes. From now on, at any time of the day or night, Dubourdieu might appear from behind one of the long Balkan islands, trapping him against the inner shore, and then a momentous engagement would take place. Kydd had to be prepared for this everywhere they went. Without question the Frenchman would keep his fleet together, while Kydd's squadron was parted in two divisions of just two frigates, easy meat were he to come across them. Should he bring them together as one? They'd have a fighting chance then. But on the other hand it would halve their effectiveness in distributing dread and anxiety randomly across the Adriatic.

He didn't want a battle. His task was to lay waste to the French Lake to the prejudice of his commerce and reputation, and damage of any kind to Kydd's precious assets would not help in this. At all costs he should avoid a meeting – not only was he badly outclassed but if he lost the fight, however heroically, the hard-won name and reputation of the Royal Navy would suffer a stinging reverse that would reverberate around the world.

Lissa was still concealed from the French, the precious hideaway that enabled him to keep the seas to strike without warning in any direction. As long as he had this, and the intelligence contributions from Dillon's network legacy, he could keep up the pressure on the Adriatic, raiding and capturing every few days. But he would have to keep his squadron together. His Italian division was only three days away, which gave him time to consider where best to flourish the full squadron.

He decided they'd head south, towards the entrance of the Adriatic and the powerful strategic French stronghold of Corfu. But not in direct challenge, more as a frightener – at Cattaro, a large trading port a day's sail to its north, then afterwards a lunge across the strait to Brindisi.

He wooded and watered *Tyger* and *Cerberus* at an offshore island, which he had set as the rendezvous. There he awaited his squadron to be made whole again.

Chapter 54

Ancona naval base, five days earlier

'*Mon amiral?*' the aide said cautiously. It never did to interrupt Contre-amiral Dubourdieu while he meditated at his desk but this was crucially important.

Dubourdieu swung around with a snarl, his tight-mouthed features ruthless. '*Qu'est-ce que tu veux, imbécile?*' he snarled.

The commodore was one of the very few in the Marine de la République to have bested the Royal Navy at sea, capturing one of their frigates off Toulon earlier in the war and, like his sworn enemy and rival, had clawed his way up through the ranks. Twice captured, he had escaped both times from the prison hulks to resume a career of daring and initiative against the English. Decrès, the minister of marine, had proffered his name before Napoleon Bonaparte as being the only one sure of putting an end to Le Diable Marin.

'Sir, might I present—'

'You may not, damn your insolence! Can't you see I'm occupied?'

'—who brings information of the location of the Sea Devil's secret lair.'

Dubourdieu shot out of his chair. 'Did you say . . . ?'

'Enseigne de Vaisseau Crozier. This hour arrived in Ancona and demands a hearing.'

'Send him in!' he barked.

Still in a ragged, stained sea uniform, the young man was brought into his presence, wide-eyed but determined. 'Sir. I've the honour to report—'

'Never mind that. Why do you say you know for certain where Le Diable Marin has his den?'

'Sir, because I heard it from the mouths of their seamen.'

'Explain!'

'I was taken in prize off Zadar. It's the practice of the Englishmen to carry all captures to their hideaway, there to be concentrated before being convoyed on. Sir, as they prepared my ship I overheard some seamen, who'd noticed our lading of wine, suggest that some few bottles would not be missed, their refuge of Lissa being so poorly served in the article of entertainment.'

'Lissa! Impossible, damn it. I've had ships pass by several times and no sign of a barracks, storehouses or any other buildings of significance.'

Crozier swallowed. 'A chart was brought aboard for the prize-master, who left it unattended with his course marked. Sir, it is Lissa.'

Dubourdieu's eyes glowed, then his face darkened. 'So how is it you're now here instead of Lissa?'

'That night I went silently over the bows and, being a strong swimmer since a child, I struck out for the island where I found a neutral ship, who for a promised sum agreed to bring me here – he's alongside below, sir.'

295

'He'll get his due, leave that to me,' Dubourdieu snapped. 'As for you, Lieutenant Crozier . . .'

'Sir?'

He brightened. 'Acting Lieutenant Crozier, as of this hour – and nobly deserved, sir!'

Ancona plunged into activity, the admiral's frenzied orders leaving none untouched for within hours, if not days, he would have settled his score and won unmatched glory.

The squadron completed for sea, as it had done before, but now with a grim purpose. Soldiers of the Milan Guard regiment marched to the docks and embarked, six pieces of field artillery were swayed aboard and, with every expression of pomp and glory, the squadron put out into the Adriatic.

Chapter 55

Tyger *at anchor*

Before the other division had arrived to restore the squadron a small cutter rounded the point, its sails board-taut to the wind, clearly in a desperate hurry. It made for *Tyger* and rounded to at her stern. Her boat was in the water in seconds.

'L'tenant Grove, and with the most lamentable tidings for Commodore Kydd.'

In his cabin Kydd took the dreadful news with as much composure as he could find.

The cutter was, as far as could be told, the only naval survivor from an invasion in force of Lissa by a large French squadron, which, even as he fled, was landing its troops in their thousands. There was no sign of the shore watch-party under the two midshipmen, except for distant figures frantically scrabbling up the craggy heights inland while twisting smoke and flames roiled above storehouses and sheds.

Gripped by anguish at the thought of what was going on even as they spoke, Kydd was on the point of roaring orders to put to sea instantly for Lissa but stopped at the realisation that this would be playing directly into the Frenchman's hands. The onslaught would certainly be covered by the full strength of Dubourdieu's frigate squadron, and he would like nothing better than to crush the Sea Devil in the same action. And while Kydd would take savage delight in facing him, he had only half of his own squadron. The odds were too high. Consumed with impatience he waited, knowing that their secret base had been betrayed and Dubourdieu was wasting no time in wreaking his vengeance.

Chapter 56

Lissa, three days earlier

'Guilty as charged!'

Midshipman Rowan straightened importantly from his improvised lectern. Where the devil these seamen were getting their liquor from was a baffling mystery but it had to be stopped. Who knew when the next batch of prizes would be sent in or a frigate would arrive for urgent replenishment?

'Ten days number nines,' he intoned, in as close to Captain Kydd's manner as he could manage. A period of mucking out the chickens before breakfast was all he, officer-in-charge, Lissa, could award. As a lowly midshipman, flogging or tricing up in the shrouds was not open to him.

The man shuffled off and Rowan packed up his gear. It was going to be like this for another two- or three-week stint.

Haynes, the midshipman from *Active* with him, was a jolly sort but didn't seem to realise the perilous situation they were in. There were no defences to speak of on Lissa, their only shield the secret of their whereabouts and if that should get out . . .

He'd done what he could. It wasn't only the seamen and marines that constituted his little command but the local townsfolk, who, the French would assume, had aided the enemy, (which they were doing wholeheartedly).

Once or twice the French had sailed past, no doubt looking for a sign of some kind of base, but they had not spotted anything and there was every reason to think they could get away with it as long as—

A distant pop sounded and a wisp of smoke rose from the lookout post on the crest of the central spine of rock that marked off the interior.

A sighting – ships! On the stumpy flag-staff rose a hoist of three black balls – a fleet of sorts. Then a red flag that remained fluttering urgently.

'Sound the alarm!' Rowan bellowed, pink with embarrassment when his voice tailed off in a squeak.

But his precautions were now paying off. The six-pounder at the edge of the town gave tongue, its warning heard everywhere, and was soon taken up by church bells sounding an urgent tocsin.

His seamen mustered at the run, abandoning what they were doing, and Sergeant Dodd reported his Royal Marines present and accounted for. What happened next depended on the intruders.

It didn't take long: one by one frigates and others rounded the small wooded islet at the entrance to the harbour and from where he stood he could see British colours at every masthead.

A babble of reassurance rose from the onlookers. They must indeed be the Royal Navy for how else would they know to enter boldly down the length of the main cove to the hidden prize anchorage at its end?

Rowan did not share their relief. The signal of a red flag

indicated that a satisfactory reply had not been received by the lookout station at their challenge, and if they *had* been betrayed, the details of the harbour would have been passed on.

The little bay was soon filled with ships taking in sail, giving every sign of preparing to stay and anchor – and then a sharp-eyed seaman spotted uniforms beginning to crowd the deck and they were not redcoats.

Rowan's worst fears had been confirmed. They were under false colours and this was an enemy invasion fleet preparing to make a landing.

To stand and fight, or run? What would Captain Kydd do?

He knew as soon as the thought formed. There was no chance they could prevail against an invading force of possibly thousands – it would be a waste of life, a futile gesture.

'Sar'nt!'

Dodd came at the double. 'Mr Rowan?'

'Can you, who should say, discourage 'em as they land? I've got to get the people away.' He trailed off, eyeing the tiny handful of Royal Marines doubtfully.

'Do m' best. Give 'em a welcome from the houses. They dursn't like fightin' among houses, they don't.'

His heart went out to the seamed, homely soldier, who was taking it all as just part of the day's duties, and reluctantly he turned away.

There must be other things he should be doing and he racked his brain. After all, he was the officer-in-charge, even if he'd been only a Guildford schoolboy not so very long ago. He had to get word to the commodore.

How? The dispatch cutter moored on the opposite side of the harbour, he forgot its name.

'Mr Haynes. Get to the cutter and desire it to acquaint Commodore Kydd at his earliest convenience' – he was a midshipman ordering its acting lieutenant-in-command to obey him – 'of the turn of events in Lissa.'

What else?

The enemy ships were halfway down the bay, and every deck was now swarming with uniformed figures impatient to get ashore. It was a mind-freezing sight but he forced himself to coolness. 'We withdraw now,' he announced. 'Lecky, you know what to do,' he called, to the duty boatswain's mate, who went off bellowing for the shore watch of seamen to muster.

Flanking the harbour on all sides were steep hills of thick scrub, near impenetrable for those who didn't know the tracks. But, thanks to local market traders, Rowan did. 'This way!' he shouted to the townsfolk, now milling about in terror. 'You men, with 'em!' The seamen needed no urging and made for the upward track followed by the people.

They moved hurriedly through the vineyards behind the town and then it was a frightened, breathless scramble over loose stony tracks to the spiny summit. Rowan let the local folk rush on down the other side towards another small fishing village, while he stopped to look back.

Below him, in the curve of the bay before the town, the drama unfolded.

Troops flooded ashore – more and more of them, spreading out along the deserted waterfront, guns and equipment landed in an unstoppable tide. At points among the town buildings the first curls of smoke rose as the destruction began. Parties of soldiers marched in every direction towards suspected supply sheds and repair forges and to the inner stockades where they released the prisoners. The two prizes remaining after the convoy to Malta were boarded but all their prize crew were safe in the hills.

The last of the fleeing individuals puffed their way over the hill path but below the French were destroying their snug lair, heart-breaking to see. Were they going to occupy and garrison the island? It was not as if it mattered, Rowan mused bitterly. The secret was out and Lissa was lost to them as a hideaway for ever.

He'd done all he could . . . or had he? There was something – and he'd thought of it all on his own, he realised proudly.

He wheeled on Haynes. 'Where's Doggo?' he demanded, calling for the unsightly old seaman who was acting as interpreter for him.

Rowan told him to go down the track to the fishing village and promise Spanish dollars to the fisherman who sailed around and entered Port St George. He was to inform the French admiral that he'd been stopped not so far away by the Sea Devil, who was asking where the French were that he could fall on them with all his squadron.

Doggo seemed to think it a good joke and set off willingly. Now it was just a matter of patience.

Dubourdieu's squadron and his expeditionary force were anchored in the deepest reaches of the cove as they had to be to land at the town. If Kydd came upon them now they'd be completely trapped. As each ship of the French squadron emerged singly through the narrow entrance they would be set upon and annihilated, one by one.

It couldn't be risked. Dubourdieu would have to get his ships to the open sea as soon as he could.

For an hour or two there was no indication that the information had been passed, but then chaos broke out. Trumpets wailed, mingling with frantic shouts, and men broke into a run as they converged on the ships from every direction.

It was fear and panic. Fighting broke out at the gangways as frightened soldiers demanded to be taken aboard. They were not going to be left on Lissa to be foully done away with by Le Diable Marin.

Around him seamen convulsed at the ludicrous scenes below and Rowan allowed himself a stab of pride. As a future officer he'd seen that battles were not only won by powder and shot but by intelligence, artfully applied. The captain would be proud of him.

Chapter 57

The Adriatic Squadron, just outside Lissa

The squadron stood to its guns as two cutters entered the harbour. In a ferment of anxiety Kydd paced up and down until they returned. They came with a report of fired stores, released prizes and destruction everywhere, but otherwise a deserted anchorage.

Dubourdieu had come and destroyed but, for some reason, had not stayed. In any event he'd prevailed: he'd won – and Kydd had lost.

It was no use grieving. The base was known, so even if the French had left, it was unusable. His squadron cruise was, to all intents and purposes, over.

As soon as *Tyger*'s anchor touched bottom he sent Clinton ashore for news of the watch party and, as he bleakly watched the boats head in, he became aware of Bowden by his side.

'A hard thing, Sir Thomas.'

'Yes.'

'To end our fine expedition.'

'We've as much sea endurance as we've victuals and water

aboard, Charles, some days yet before we have to quit the Adriatic.'

'Or . . .'

'No. To go in deliberate search of Dubourdieu at twice my force gives no advantage and would leave me with a string of much-injured ships. A frigate is a precious thing in this part of the world and shouldn't be thrown away on some kind of revenge. In any case, I'd wager that having achieved this advantage he's this hour making for Ancona and a hero's welcome.'

'Can we not—'

'I fear not. It has to be accepted that this is a hostile sea and we have no business in it without we fight for the privilege. At half the clout I'm not about to dispute for possession of the whole Adriatic. We withdraw, Charles, and that's as it has to be.'

'Retreat.'

'Retire. Fight again another day with greater forces.'

'Sir.'

Chapter 58

Palermo

There was no question about it, this was good work. Persephone took another of her charcoal impressions and laid it by the first. The light was not good, the lantern guttering in the evening breeze through the open window and another night drawing in, but in a way it added to the drama of her study of a market contretemps. Many great artists used charcoal in the composition of a grander oil and seldom took pains in its execution, but she enjoyed the bold strokes and subtle suggestive teasing that went with the cruder medium.

'Have a look at these, Emily,' she called to her cousin. 'Tell me what you think – really, now.'

Still cross after her rebuke for being late back yet again from running an errand, she took her time in laying down her embroidery with a sigh. 'Quite good, I suppose,' she said off-handedly.

'Oh? Why, I do feel these are my—'

A sudden tattoo of soft knocks at the door interrupted

her, unexpected at this hour. It was followed by another flurry, louder, more urgent.

The maid had been dismissed for the night so there was no other course than for Persephone to answer the door herself.

'Who is it at this hour?' she called nervously.

'Madame – let me in, I beg of you! It's Cesare Bruni.'

For a brief moment she couldn't remember who this was, then recalled the gentlemanly scholar she'd met at the market, and hesitantly opened the door to him.

To her surprise he thrust past her and closed the door swiftly.

His face was drawn and ashen. 'Forgive me, please – but I don't know any else I might trust at this hour.' Without waiting for an answer he peered intently around the room and spotted Emily, standing petrified.

'My cousin, whom you have met,' Persephone said coolly. 'There is no one else here. And I believe you owe us an explanation of your conduct, sir.'

Bruni held absolutely still, listening intently, then eased. 'Certainly, my lady.'

He went to an armchair and said, 'May I? I'm much fatigued.'

Persephone nodded cautiously.

'You see, I'm being hunted,' Bruni continued. 'For my life, I believe.'

'You came to me, sir. What can you want from a lady alone in her house?'

'I can only beg it of you – hide me! Just for a day or so until they believe me fled.'

There was something in his manner, a noble decency that steadied her.

'Before I answer, Signor Bruni, I would rather you told me why you are being pursued and by whom.' Any story of being wrongly accused of a crime or even a chase by an outraged husband would lose her sympathy, but neither seemed to fit his character.

'You are English, m' lady. As you said before, any Sicilian matter of unrest or plotting cannot concern you.' He regarded her gravely, as though unsure whether he could go on.

'This is so,' she answered firmly.

'Then I pray for your indulgence as I disclose to you a plot to which I'm just this day made privy that directly threatens the British and their entire existence in the Mediterrancan.'

'You're being chased because you know of this plot?'

'Just so,' he said, with a polite inclination of his head. 'It being within a very short while of coming to fruition.'

'And you're telling me? Why?'

'Should you be so kind as to offer me sanctuary you shall be amply rewarded by the knowledge.'

'You shall have it – providing it is as you say.'

'Very well. I will tell you.'

In dry, factual phrases Bruni set out the essence.

It shocked Persephone to the core. The King and Queen of Sicily had before been King and Queen of Naples. Driven from their thrones by French victories, they had been exiled to Sicily, taken there by Nelson himself. Pining for the richer, more cosmopolitan kingdom, they had resented their banishment but at least here they were safe with the British offering their protection.

The plot was as simple as it was extraordinary. Through an unknown intermediary, Queen Maria Carolina had made contact with Murat, Bonaparte's placeman as King of Italy. A secret offer had been made and accepted that, should she persuade her husband King Ferdinando to declare for the French and turn over the kingdom, they would be restored in full to the far greater throne of Naples.

For the British this would be an unimaginable catastrophe. A French Sicily sitting at the exact centre of the Mediterranean would dominate and control all seaborne traffic east and west. The British would lose their trade in the entire eastern Mediterranean – the Middle East, Turkey, Russia, Greece and even the lands flanking the Adriatic. And, further, Bonaparte would have safe passage for his troops to the Levant and then India.

It would seem that the sister of Marie Antoinette had lost her hatred of the French at the prospect of a crown, and her granddaughter in Vienna had recently given her hand to Bonaparte.

Shakily, Persephone asked, 'You say it is near to culmination, Mr Bruni?'

'The French are sending a fleet of occupation. When it appears around the headland this is the signal for the King to appear on the palace balcony to make declaration in the French interest. General Mazzuoli, who is head of the pro-French faction at court, will disarm and arrest the opposition and thereby show to the world that the French are welcome. All will be over in hours.'

Persephone turned away for a moment, trying to collect her wits. 'Mr Bruni, where is your proof? That a queen will betray her own kingdom for the sake of a larger crown – it's hard to believe.'

He shook his head slowly. 'It is true, dear lady, believe me. As to the proof, it would take too long to explain without you have the Sicilian tongue.'

The implications crowded in, but one thing was of paramount importance. She had to tell somebody, one who had the authority to bring forces to bear to stop it happening.

If only she had angel's wings that she could fly to Kydd in *Tyger* and let him take swift and decisive action.

But she hadn't and time was running out.

If she somehow got word to General Stuart, head of the British military in Sicily, it would be of no use – they were all far to the east around Messina, days' march away with no fighting troops anywhere close to Palermo.

On the other hand Amherst, the British minister, was to her certain knowledge attending at court. That was it. She'd tell him and he would know what to do.

'Mr Bruni, I'm to find Lord Amherst, our minister, and acquaint him of your plot. Will you come with me?'

The three emerged from Amherst's study together, the minister's long face even more dolorous than usual.

'Lady Kydd, I can only thank you for your action in bringing this to my attention. There have been rumours, true, however nothing to indicate how close the coup was to reality, but this gentleman has satisfied me that it is very near.'

'Sir, what might be done? If the French—'

'My hands at this time are largely tied, I fear. In truth I have no authority to interfere in another nation's actions, however inimical to our interests. If the King declares for the French we have no recourse but to accept his decision and leave.'

'No!' she gasped, appalled. 'We must do something, or . . . or . . .'

'Besides,' Amherst continued gravely, 'I have no forces of my own to call upon.'

'None?' Persephone replied, disbelieving.

'Madam, I understand your dismay at the situation but you must know that I am a minister of the Crown, not in the line of military command, and have no authority of any kind over them. I can appeal for assistance – what we call "aid to the civil power" – but the decisions are entirely with the military commander. Who in this instance might well conclude that the whole business is a ruse to decoy our redcoats away from Messina in order to effect a crossing.'

'The French are sending a fleet of occupation. Then surely Admiral Sir Sidney Smith needs to know, to place his ships across their path. Can you not—'

A long sigh escaped Amherst. 'Would that I could summon his fleet, as you rightly point out, but there are even more difficulties in his case. First, he is, as he should be, on continual circumnavigation of this island and I have no knowledge of where he might be found.'

'Wasn't he in Syracuse earlier?' Persephone asked.

'Yes, but how does that—'

'The prevailing winds are in the north-east, sir. Married as I am to a gentleman mariner, I've an understanding that he will be taking advantage of these to sail to the west – from Messina towards here.'

'Lady Kydd, that places him as far out of reach as General Stuart.'

She frowned. 'Send a fast aviso to the east and he will assuredly be met within half a day or so.'

His grey head shook slowly. 'Much as I'd wish it, dear lady, this is not a course I'm able to take. Our admiral is a difficult creature. He believes he has a discreet *entrée* into the Sicilian court through the Queen and will not hear of others claiming knowledge he does not have. Further, he distances himself from the chain of military command, including, I believe, his own commander-in-chief, in the self-centred belief that in any successful action within his area all glory must accrue to him alone.'

'I've heard something of this,' Persephone murmured.

'He will of a surety scorn any orders or directions I might issue and therefore I shall send an urgent intelligence to

Admiral Cotton off Toulon and, of course, your own good husband in the Adriatic.'

'Thomas will come, of that you may be sure.'

'Ah, if he receives word. At the present, as you must know, he's engaged in clandestine activities taking him all over the Adriatic with no means of contact beyond the leaving of messages at his base. I rather fear that in both cases, while I hope we're in time, we will be too late.'

She bit her lip in vexation. Was there nothing that could be done to head off the looming catastrophe? If Thomas were here before her, what would he advise?

Navy.

Therefore Sidney Smith it had to be. Amherst was not going to move on it . . . but she would.

'Sir. I cannot stand by meekly. I'm going to your admiral myself and shall make it plain what he risks by hanging back.'

'You? Madam, you cannot—'

'I can – and I will.'

Amherst hesitated, then said quietly. 'If you do manage to cozen the man, it occurs to me that there's a sovereign advantage to be gained by his early arrival off Palermo.'

'Oh?'

'If he can be persuaded to abstain from flaunting his colours, he might very well be mistaken by the uninformed for the French fleet.'

'But they'll then rise up.'

'Quite. With the happy effect that all those part of the plot must thereby unmask themselves.'

'To no purpose! A formidable result indeed. Leave it to me, my lord. I'll find him and oblige him to move on Palermo.'

'Madam, your transporting is—'

But she'd already left him with Bruni and made her own way out, her head full of half-thought plans.

Chapter 59

In a cold dawn the next morning Persephone hurried down the hill past the market, starting its day, and on to the waterfront. Turning left towards the violet grey mass of Mount Pellegrino, she sought out the rickety jetties of the old port.

Ignoring the astonished stares, to her great satisfaction she saw alongside a colourful open-decked craft about the same length as a naval launch. It was a Maltese *speronara*, pointed out to her once by Kydd as the fastest thing under sail in the southern Mediterranean.

A sailor half beneath a tarpaulin in its bottom boards snored loudly.

She roused the man and thrust a paper at him. It promised a substantial sum for an immediate passage east along the coast no further than Messina.

Groggily, he rubbed his eyes and squinted up at her. 'You?' he mimed.

She nodded vigorously and put a Venetian ducat into his hand.

In a short space of time two other crew members were found, oars shipped, and the boat propelled to the open sea where the morning breeze was beginning to ruffle the waters. Swiftly they boated their oars and raised sail, an odd combination of diagonal and bellying sail forward, with a peculiar horizontal jib raised above the others.

The boat gathered speed at a run. Very light and low in the water, all the sail was in the fore part and seemed to lift the bows in an urging thrust that had the coastline fast sliding away. It was not comfortable even with the rolled bolsters of canvas pressed on her, but Persephone was grateful for the chance to do something. Who knew but that there were hours left to them?

They sighted Sidney Smith in the early dog-watches, a little beyond Cape Milazzo, not far from Messina and bound towards them.

'There – that one.' She pointed eagerly.

It took some miming to put across that she wanted to be laid alongside the flagship, the lordly ship-of-the-line in the centre of the loose cluster of warships.

Off the ship's quarter, with every eye aboard on her in curiosity, she stood up clutching the mast and hailed the quarterdeck. 'Flag ahoy! This is Persephone, Lady Kydd with secret intelligence for the admiral. I desire you let me aboard.'

There was an astonished discussion around the officer-of-the-watch, who eventually came to the ship's side. 'Who did you say?'

'Lady Kydd, sir. Any delay in allowing me on board to transmit my intelligence will have damaging consequences. And these will be laid entirely upon you, sir.' Her voice broke off.

'Very well, er, my lady. Pray wait for a chair to—'

She didn't want to waste any time and nimbly transferred to the side-steps and up to the bulwark. 'The admiral?' she demanded, as soon as she made the deck.

Smith's astonishment at her arrival made her hide a smile. 'So kind in you to receive me, Sir Sidney.'

'Hmmph. More than a trifle irregular, I'd have thought, Lady Kydd. Your errand must be of some significance, I'm persuaded. You spoke of secret intelligence to my officer-of-the-watch. How can this be?'

'You are right, sir. Of the utmost moment in which the fate of the British in the eastern Mediterranean hangs in the balance.'

'Pray be clearer, madam.'

'Certainly, Sir Sidney. Not occasioned by any act on my part, I've been unavoidably made privy to a species of plot at the very highest levels in the kingdom. For reasons that will become clear I could not go to the palace with the details and instead went directly to Lord Amherst.'

'What is this to me?'

'This gentleman was shocked and discommoded by my information but unhappily he could not see how he should act in the matter. Greatly dismayed, I didn't know to whom I should turn, then remembered that we have one of the most distinguished naval officers of the age in the offing. One who can be relied upon in the matter of placing himself across the bows of a French fleet whatever its menace.'

'French fleet?' His eyes glowed with naked anticipation. 'Lady Kydd, I rather think you'd better tell me your intelligence and allow me to make my dispositions accordingly.'

She played it well, emphasising the distinction he could win on putting down a villainous French plot. And there was also the prospect of an action on the scale of the meeting of fleets that could only thrust him into the public eye. If he moved rapidly he would be ahead of any military interference and might then claim undisputed credit for all.

Clearly interested, Smith allowed Persephone to put the

suggestion that an advance without colours a-fly would serve to unmask the plotters and put them ready for arrest by the Royal Marines, whom he'd no doubt wish to put ashore.

'As we have no idea of the force of the French fleet, I shall summon every vessel under my command, then descend on the rogues. Do you desire passage back to Palermo, my dear? I have an entire admiral's quarters open to me.'

Persephone declined his invitation politely and rejoined her humble transport. With the breeze on her quarter, the little *speronara* flew back even more swiftly than she'd come, and she soon found herself ashore in a gathering Sicilian dusk. To her immense relief, there was no sign of the occupation fleet.

Admiral Smith would delay his arrival until he'd brought up all his ships into the most formidable mass he could contrive but it wouldn't be very long. Then there would be the dreadful prospect of the two fleets confronting each other off Palermo, their great guns firing in every direction. Perhaps it would be prudent to slip away into the countryside until it was all over.

Chapter 60

Early the next morning she and her little household prepared to leave for five days or so at a country *podere* the housekeeper knew, well away from the coast. They should be safe there.

Then a thought struck. She'd forgotten all about Miss Lamb, the kind old soul who'd taken her under her wing in this most treacherous of foreign shores. She should know what evil was threatening and be taken inland with them. With violent factions on the streets it would be dangerous to be in the capital at this time.

The morning was chasing away the night shadows and promising a fine day when she mounted the steps to the villa's door, the dusky fragrance of the garden lying charmingly on the air.

'Why, my dear! What a pleasant surprise. Do come in – we were just taking tea.'

A shadowy figure materialised behind her, startling Persephone. It resolved by the light of the new day and she calmed when she saw it was only the royalist French nobleman, the Comte d'Aubois, who had been her painting companion.

'Oh, Comte! You did frighten me.' She laughed. For some reason he was dressed in an ornate uniform, complete with an elegant rapier. To her puzzlement, there was no humorous response, not even a word of greeting. And Miss Lamb seemed a little out of sorts, somewhat flustered. 'I'm so sorry to intrude, but there's a matter of great urgency I must tell you.'

'What is that, dear?'

'Only yesterday I was made aware of a dreadful plot involving the palace. I could hardly credit it, Miss Lamb.'

'Go on,' the older woman said, in an odd voice.

'Would you believe it? The King and Queen are themselves conspiring to declare Sicily for the French! In return for the throne of Naples! And very soon there'll be—'

'I see.' Miss Lamb and d'Aubois exchanged glances. 'Then I believe we must do something about it.' Her tone had hardened, her eyes now steely, a disconcerting change that made Persephone uneasy.

'Oh, yes,' she replied uncertainly, 'I came to invite you to fly with us into the country for a few days until it blows over.' She heard her own voice grow thin with apprehension – something here was definitely not right.

'I rather think the palace.'

'But . . . but that's where—'

'We go to the palace if Miss Lamb wishes it,' d'Aubois said quietly, and eased himself to the door, a hand dropping pointedly to his sword.

She sat between them in d'Aubois' carriage, the two unspeaking and rigid until at last they passed within the massive gate at the rear of the palace into the courtyard. Miss Lamb was handed down and began striding towards the gloomy interior staircase off to the side, Persephone following, and d'Aubois taking up the rear, his hand still on the hilt of his sword.

Climbing two floors, they moved at a pace along a servant's access before emerging into a brightly lit passage clearly leading to a royal apartment.

Miss Lamb strode along to the far door, which was flanked by two halberd-clutching guardsmen. She pushed past them and stormed into the chamber.

From inside came voices, defensive and raised in anger, screaming, hectoring, rising to a crescendo and then lapsing into silence.

She burst through the doors, her expression ugly. 'Stupid woman! She hasn't even begun on the King and time's nearly upon us.'

To Persephone, she snapped, 'And you – stay with me or . . .' D'Aubois closed with her threateningly, as Miss Lamb hurried to a small flight of stairs that led up to a door and then to daylight – a balustraded roof balcony with a spectacular view in both directions of the glittering expanse of the Gulf of Palermo.

'We sit and wait for our friends to make their appearance,' she said acidly, occupying one of the elaborately ornate recliner chairs and gesturing impatiently for Persephone to take the one next to her. D'Aubois sat behind, out of sight.

'Miss Lamb, I'd be obliged should you explain to me what is happening,' Persephone ventured, already guessing at the answer.

'I don't see why not. It'll all be over soon.' She closed her eyes wearily for a long moment. 'I'm part of a circle of agents connected directly to Murat, King of Naples. Knowing how these two Neapolitans so detest the Sicilians, we contrived a plot that gives their cherished Naples back to them in return for the cession of Sicily to Murat. All that foolish queen has to do is persuade her doltish husband to make public declaration of the change of allegiance at the right time.'

'How could you? You're English and—'

'Half an Englishwoman, my dear. Born here of a French mother and English father but decided not to return when my merchant father quit his vineyards. Then I was deceived by a worthless wretch of an Englishman and left here, abandoned.' She paused reflectively. 'But I like it here. If these blood-sucking Bourbons can be induced to depart the realm for good, to be replaced by incorruptible French rule, then I'll do whatever is necessary.'

'But—'

'That useless king, by making his declaration, will ensure that the whole business will be concluded without undue bloodshed. *Force majeure* comes to mind, and you should be thankful for it.'

She glanced at Persephone with a brief smile. 'Have no concerns about yourself, my dear. I can assure you that, like all the English here, you'll be bundled out in a civilised manner, no prisons or detention. You'll be on your way home shortly.'

Closing her eyes again, she settled back into the cushions.

Persephone tried to calm herself but it was no good: the nervous tension was too much. Around the far headland would appear either the French fleet or Sir Sidney Smith, and her own fate – and that of Sicily – would depend on which it was.

An hour or so later a door crashed open and in strode a red-faced officer, by his attire of some high degree of rank.

'Is he ready?' he snarled at Miss Lamb in French. 'I've a whole regiment standing idle below and they're getting hard to restrain.'

'General Mazzuoli, when I know, you'll be the next to do

so,' she answered irritably. 'Understand that these things aren't to be commanded, like a line of soldiers. His Majesty has to compose his speech and then write it. The Queen is encouraging him and he'll step out before the crowd just as soon as the fleet makes its appearance. Then you can move against the loyalists. Until then, please don't bother us.'

He stalked off, and as soon as he had gone Miss Lamb stormed below. After some muffled shouts she reappeared. 'That idiot!' she fulminated, as she took her chair again. 'Can't make up his mind – dithers, claims he's sore puzzled by it all. Although we'll see what happens when the fleet arrives.'

Refreshments came mid-morning, shortly followed by a distraught Queen Maria Carolina, wringing her hands.

Persephone scrambled to her feet but it was as if she wasn't present. She heard Miss Lamb scold the Queen, urging her to go back and make the King see sense.

A roar of voices from below interrupted the charade. She edged discreetly to the balustrade and looked over. Officials and servants were spilling out of the palace, pointing and shouting in great excitement at the headland across the bay where ships were emerging one by one – three, five, a dozen, more!

The breeze was not strong and they came on at a maddeningly languid pace. At this distance it was not possible to see what colours were hoisted and she'd never been able to tell the difference between French and British men-o'-war. Her heart bumped painfully as they crept along. The swelling crowd cheering below, however, seemed in no doubt – did they know something?

'Get that swine-faced loon out on the balcony!' General Mazzuoli roared, from behind. 'We've work to do!'

'He's still composing his speech,' Miss Lamb said coldly. 'Kindly allow him to finish.'

The general glared venomously at her, then shouted, 'For the love of Christ, it has to begin! I'm going down to fling that *furfante* Bandone into the cells – someone has to.'

'What you do with the loyalists later will be your business,' she said crossly. 'For now, have patience, General.'

'The old goat, if he's not done in one minute I'll—'

'General Mazzuoli. Should you perform any act of open military violence in Palermo before the King has declared for the French, you will be guilty of sedition. Hold yourself in check for a little longer, if you please, sir.' She snapped to the Queen, 'Tell King Ferdinando that if he's not out in five minutes, speech or no speech, I'll have him dragged here. Go!'

The armada was now fully in view: it was a horde that crowded into the bay, dozens – scores – of ships of every kind she'd ever seen, heading slowly and purposefully towards the anchorage off Palermo. Persephone strained to see the flags they flew but couldn't make out any. The largest, the flagship, reminded her of Smith's, but was it him? Then she remembered his big ship had been originally captured from the French.

Not far now. With a stab of anguish she thought of Kydd, urgently called from wherever he had been. If he with his three ships threw himself against this huge assembly he would go down gloriously, but go down he must.

A tear pricked but she would not let it be seen and proudly stood erect, ready to face events.

Along the waterfront and into the town confused and riotous mobs were beginning to form. Were they going to resist?

'That's close enough. Get that fool up here, no excuses. Now!'

In short minutes, King Ferdinando III of Sicily stood gabbling incoherently before them.

In front of the palace it was as if the entire royal household had turned out, some fighting others, most looking up in wonder and bewilderment.

'Pull yourself together!' the Queen muttered spitefully to her husband. 'Tell 'em anything but say how you're going back to Naples and the French will look after Sicily now.'

'No! No! I'm not ready, Maria,' he quavered. 'Say I'm ill or . . .'

'Show yourself, you craven cur!' She pushed him towards the balustrade. At his appearance a loyal clamour rose up while, weakly, he bowed this way and that.

Mazzuoli thrust forward and bellowed, 'Silence, you Sicilian rabble! Hear your king, what he's going to say . . . Go to it, Your Majesty,' he growled.

The crowd subsided and Ferdinando began. 'M-my f-faithful s-subjects,' he called, in a thin, wavering voice, 'this day I'm here to proclaim . . . um, to declare that is, er, that . . .'

Astonishingly he was drowned out by a chanting roar carrying up from the town.

Seeing the sudden shock and dismay on the faces of those with her, Persephone tried to make it out.

Then she took it in: *'l'inglese, i'inglese, l'inglese!'* The English!

Unbelieving she strained to see – and there on the flagship, and on every one of the warships as they anchored off Palermo, now flew the ensign of the Royal Navy. It was Sir Sidney Smith.

Nearly overcome with relief she kept still. Who knew what would happen, with the plot fraying so dramatically?

Mazzuoli bolted for a door, followed by his aides, and with a wild look back at Persephone, Miss Lamb hobbled as fast as she could the same way.

Then came shouts and the jingling of weapons. It was Amherst and, with him, presumably the loyalist General

Bandone, stripped to his shirt. A dozen *moschettiere* in palace livery followed.

Miss Lamb, then Mazzuoli, reappeared, their escape having been stolidly barred by a detachment of halberd-bearing guards.

Bandone swaggered up to Mazzuoli and slowly and deliberately spat at him. 'You pig! Take 'em both away,' he ordered.

'Lady Kydd!' Amherst managed, on catching sight of her.

'My lord?' Persephone answered primly.

'B-but why are you in this place?' he asked.

'As a spectator only,' she answered. 'With an imperishable subject for a painting, don't you think?'

Chapter 61

Vienna

Renzi carefully smoothed out the message with its rows of meaningless five-letter groups that had been hidden in the base of the vase. Swift work at the cypher-text soon had its meaning – and he sat back in dismay. 'Well done. C satisfied. Asks you stay for passover.' Meaning Austria's transition from neutral to full French ally and ostensible adversary to Great Britain.

He winced. Did Congalton know what he was asking? The French would be installing themselves in the Austrian capital shortly and he'd run out of credible excuses as an Englishman for staying on. The city was heaving with spies and, without doubt, his presence and location would be known. And, from now on, Metternich couldn't claim him as a friend so how would they hold converse?

The reason for his presence here was nullified. Should he go back now, before the French came?

Perhaps Congalton meant him simply to remain in case

the chancellor had a need to let the British know his reasons for some act. Whatever, the game had just turned deadly.

It was Cecilia who came up with the answer. One evening a certain English nobleman leaving a notorious hostelry on the Wollzeil, slipped on the ice in his befuddlement and broke his leg. A doctor happening by took charge and he was returned to his apartment where the leg was splinted and the patient consigned to bed.

For the cost of a modicum in bribes to the physician, Renzi had a reason for delay in returning to England. Now it was only the tedium of what amounted to a house arrest.

Day followed day in wearisome succession and then, in extravagant pomp and style, the new French minister arrived and presented his credentials to the Kaiser in a grand ceremony. In a way it was a relief, for the charade couldn't be maintained for long now.

Renzi had taken to being propped up in a Bath chair on a sheltered balcony to read, grateful for the keen air riffling his hair and the sanctuary it gave for quiet thinking.

One morning as he was gently dozing he was disturbed by three men. They gagged him and dragged him away suspended between two of them, the third holding up his splinted leg.

Hurriedly taken down a passage and away, he found himself lying in the well of a coach as it crunched and swayed. It had to be the French making their move and, with a lurch to the heart, he realised that he was not visible from the street. There would be no witness to his disappearance.

He heard the sudden thunderous echoing of an enclosed space and then the carriage came to a stop. Deftly extracted, he looked rapidly about. He was in a bare grey basement without a window. His gag was released and from behind him he heard a well-known voice.

'I do apologise for the abrupt manner of your coming here, Graf von Farndon,' Metternich said softly, 'and I can only plead the urgency of the case.'

'But neatly done, Klemens,' Renzi said, with a half-smile.

There was no need of the pretence of a broken leg as they went to a nearby room, also without a window, and he guessed they were in the heart of the Geheime Hofkanzlei, the secret chancellery.

'You mentioned an urgency?' Renzi prompted.

'Of a surety,' Metternich muttered, his distracted gaze unsettling.

'How so, old fellow?' Renzi tried to keep his tone light and friendly but there was no change in the chancellor's expression.

'Hard though it is for me to admit it, but I've been played for a fool, deceived if you will.'

'This is difficult to credit, Klemens. What is it that has you so exercised?'

'The Emperor of the French has demanded we as an ally furnish him with no less than one hundred thousand first-class troops.'

For a few seconds Renzi thought he'd misheard. 'Doesn't your alliance detail that this wasn't to be expected of Austria?'

'Each party has claim on the other if they are attacked. This is the essence of the treaty. And on these grounds he now claims that he is threatened by Russia.'

At this scale of numbers Whitehall could never tolerate an intervention to assist Bonaparte in any way and would react strenuously. Austria would slide from being a theoretical adversary into a situation of active hostility. 'The British would never accept this, I fear.'

'So I imagine,' Metternich answered readily. 'Which is why he shall not get them.'

'Ah.'

'I can rightly claim that, since Wagram, our army is derisory in numbers and sadly ill-equipped. I shall protest my willingness to supply him, but first he must find me the means to pay and fit them out.' He gave a brief smile. 'You'll see that in this way, although at the moment I haven't an army worth the name, I soon will have. And it will be paid for and trained by the French themselves.'

To be turned against them at the appropriate time and place? Renzi mused silently.

'He has to be satisfied by token thousands now, no more than, say, ten or twenty at the most.'

Renzi knew there was more to it than that. This was the typical deviousness of the man, but the urgency didn't fit. 'You have more to tell me, Klemens.'

'Yes.' Metternich took a deep breath and let it out raggedly, so uncharacteristically that Renzi felt a stab of foreboding. 'There is more . . .' He paused abruptly and his eyes met Renzi's. 'You must accept that my sources are unimpeachable, that the information is very recent.'

'I will.'

'Then I have to tell you that I've uncovered the reason why these troops are being demanded of me.'

'Yes?'

'Napoleon Bonaparte is very soon about to embark on a sinister adventure of incalculable significance to the world. This is why the issue is so pressing – and why now I would be obliged for your views in an area I freely admit is outside my competence, and the small time left does not allow more leisured attention.'

Renzi tensed. This was another matter entirely. He knew as much as any educated man of the world and in certain areas more, but to have the chancellor of Austria openly solicit his opinion was a responsibility beyond his desiring. Metternich must be in a serious dilemma.

'You will have my most sincere contribution, Klemens,' he answered gravely.

'Then this is the nature of the intrigue. Bonaparte is abandoning Europe.'

'Good God – why?'

'It's too small for a world-striding colossus.'

'What, then, is left to him?'

'He's found a way to march an army of half a million or more to India and Asia, dry-shod all the way, no seas for the Royal Navy to bar his way, and he intends to launch this enterprise in the very near future. The consequences will be monumentally disastrous. Once well on his way, nothing can stop a horde of that immensity, and we can therefore safely assume he will be triumphant. India and Persia will be his and, with it, a sovereign highway to the rest of the world.'

Renzi sat rigid, mesmerised with horror.

'My own instincts are in helpless rebellion at the end result, for instead of the balance-at-war we now have, Bonaparte will have destroyed Britain's richest trade in one blow and she must sue for peace, unable to fund herself or a coalition of the opposition. The world will be utterly deranged, with one power wholly dominant over all others and able to impose anything it desires on the rest.'

'A disaster for mankind, indeed.' What else could he say?

'The most galling for me, Farndon, is that I know of this but am completely unable to affect its course. Either diplomatically or by subterfuge. I'm helpless in truth.'

'Tell me, how will he achieve this?'

'He now possesses and occupies the entire Balkan coast down to Albania and the border of the Ottoman lands. To him it's merely a matter of assembling his army in the north, then a rapid march down its length, some hundreds of miles, which for Napoleon will be days only. With his vast army, he demands of the Turks they let him pass. He then overawes the Shah of Persia in the same way. In India, with limitless well-trained European troops, he is everywhere victorious, and he secures the prize he's been lusting after for so long.'

It was all too plausible.

'Dear fellow,' Renzi began hesitantly, 'you ask me for advice and I have none. If this is being contemplated then—'

'I shall be clearer, Farndon. I said that I was helpless to affect events but that is not to say you are, and this is why we are talking this hour.'

'So . . . ?'

'Bonaparte has one Achilles' heel. All land movement down the Balkans must take place not far from the coast, the interior being so mountainous. After Spain he has a dread of coast roads being attacked from the sea and in this case he has more than the usual cause for fear. A great army such as his must be supplied on a daily basis. Either by sea or by wagon along the same road. If the British were to send in even a small expeditionary force that is landed in his rear, this flow would be cut off and his army starves.'

He paused for Renzi to digest the implications, then went on, 'I can tell you he's already taken steps to clear the Adriatic of the Royal Navy by sending in a special squadron twice the size of any the British have, with the excuse that it's intended to put down raiders and privateers. The real reason for it is to provide him with his safe transit of the Balkan coast.'

'And you say I can do something about this?' Renzi asked incredulously.

'Quite. If the British can prevail in the Adriatic, Bonaparte will not move for dread that they will cut his lines behind him. His adventure will stop at that point.'

Renzi thought immediately of Kydd. Sent to cause mayhem in the French Lake, he was now caught up in far greater stakes. 'There is a British squadron in the Adriatic at the moment,' he said quietly. 'And its commander is the most valiant and resourceful I know.'

'Yes. I've heard of this gentleman but know as well that his squadron is composed only of two or three frigates, hardly fitted to stand against Bonaparte's full might. And only yesterday I received information that the French special squadron has found and destroyed his base. Without supplies, no doubt he must quit the Adriatic.

'This would be a grievous blow to one attempting to maintain his ships in the face of an enemy sea, bordered on all sides by hostile coasts, and he must now withdraw, leaving the Adriatic to Bonaparte.'

'I wasn't aware of this,' Renzi replied uneasily, 'but do tell what part you wish me to play.'

'We must cause a great fleet to be sent into the Adriatic, its purpose to wrest control from the French and prevent this frightful movement. Sir, whom do we call upon, given that time is of critical importance?'

Renzi couldn't say that, with his background as a seaman and officer, he was well placed to answer. Ironically, for the same reason, it was also next to impossible to reply.

The most powerful fleet in the Mediterranean was with the commander-in-chief off Toulon. But without Admiralty approval he could not detach forces from the most important station there was. At the same time the nearest, Sir Sidney Smith, couldn't be spared from the vital task of preserving Sicily. Malta had only paltry forces, which left Gibraltar and whatever naval ships were there by chance.

But all paled into insignificance compared to the crushing time problem. A full dispatch and reply with orders from the

Admiralty would take all of six weeks at best. And, given that it would be based on unverifiable foreign intelligence, this would be optimistic. Bonaparte would be on the march and far south by the time a response was received.

'Klemens. I have to tell you – there are no naval fleets within call in the time we have.'

Metternich sagged visibly. 'Reinforcements to what you already have?'

'I'm sorry.'

He held his head in his hands for a long minute, then looked up. 'So, we might say that the only thing at this moment standing between Bonaparte and his destiny is your Adriatic squadron commander. His name is Kitt, I believe.'

'Kydd.'

'If we're not too late a message has to be conveyed to him, telling him of the terrible situation that's developed and . . . well, leaving it to him to act as he thinks proper. To find reinforcements as we're not in a position to know of, to send a flying dispatch to another commander we've overlooked, or . . .'

Renzi went cold. He knew exactly what Kydd would do. Given the stakes, he'd fling himself at the enemy in a fight to the finish. Whoever gave him the message was sending him to a sea grave – and there was only one who was in a position to know the facts that would persuade him to do so. 'I will leave tonight,' he said, rising reluctantly.

'I rather think not,' Metternich said immediately.

'Oh?'

'The French undoubtedly have you closely watched. Should you quit Vienna in haste the worst will be assumed.'

He was right, of course.

'A great pity, for Kydd is a close friend of mine as would listen to what I have to say – in fact, his sister is married to me, now my countess.'

333

And therefore the deadly message would be passed to him by a stranger.

Metternich brightened. 'Ah, but this is by way of a stroke of fortune.'

'How can it be so?'

'Should the Gräfin von Farndon be the one to convey the intelligence then she is her own authentication, that what she says is to be believed by her brother, she need never carry incriminating documents.'

'Cecilia? This I really can't allow, Klemens. Why, the travel alone is beyond what a lady might be expected to endure at this time of the year! From Vienna to the sea – won't this include a crossing of the Alps through snow-choked passes and so forth?'

'It will.'

'On her own.'

'Perhaps not.'

'You're being a mite obscure, Klemens.'

'You cannot venture abroad without the French will take a close interest – but not in the Countess Cecilia, for it will be discovered by you that she has run away with a lover and you will stop at nothing to bring her back. The French will chuckle behind their hands and do anything but assist in tracking her down.'

Renzi was struck speechless.

'She will, of course, take her lady companion with her, the three in a carriage together, and it will be given out that they are headed to Bohemia, well to the east.' He coughed slightly. 'Er, at this point it has to be said that it's needful you suggest a lover, one of credible qualities. Who do you believe will best suit the part?'

Cecilia – a lover? And he to name him? 'Will this really be necessary, old fellow?'

'Only if we desire to convince.'

'Then . . . then . . .'

'Very well, allow me to make a suggestion – the centurion of Carpathian Hussars, Százados Kovacs.'

'I'm not sure I . . . ?'

'Your wife has been seen in his company, sir.'

'How, er, reliable is he, this centurion?'

'His loyalty to the Kaiser is unquestioned, to me he owes his advancement – you may trust him in the pretence, I believe.'

Cecilia heard him through with growing incredulity. 'You're saying you wish me to flee with a lover across the Alps to the other side?'

'With Hetty, naturally,' Renzi added lamely.

'Just to pass Thomas a message?'

To make sure she'd heard aright, and to give herself time to think, she made him spell out the plan again. Of course she would do anything he really wanted, but this was a terrifying prospect. She'd seen Alpine paintings by the new wave of Romantic artists. They'd delighted in sepulchral razor-sharp peaks streaked in snow above vertiginous valley floors with tiny figures standing in awe, dressed in mountain boots with crampons and carrying crooks.

While Renzi patiently went over it again she glanced discreetly at Hetty. She didn't seem worried, her hands clasped and her eyes shining, no doubt seeing them released from their wearisome confinement, their prison, to go on an adventure a well-brought-up lass from Guildford could only have dreamed of. Or was it that the 'lover' accompanying them was the handsome Tibor?

Cecilia shuddered. 'It's just that I've always hated wolves. Nasty, wicked creatures.'

'I rather fancy you'd be very lucky to sight one, my dear.'

'Oh, and don't forget the bears!' Hetty came in. 'Great big black ones they are – I saw one in a circus in chains and here we are trespassing on their home.'

'You'll be in a coach – just keep the door closed.' Renzi grinned.

Cecilia felt a rush of annoyance. It was all very well for Nicholas – it wasn't him braving the wilderness, and there was the weather: it was winter. Did people really make the crossing at this time of the year?

'What about all the snow and ice? If we get trapped no one will find us until the summer melts it all,' she said, in a small voice.

'Think on this, dearest. The extraordinary Punic Hannibal did cross the Alps burdened by many elephants and his thousands, yet was able to burst in on the Romans the other side like an avenging angel.'

'I will think on it, Nicholas. But he had many men to protect him and probably rode in comfort on one of his elephants.'

'You'll ride in comfort too – the chancellor is providing a coach and four, with an experienced driver. I'm sanguine he'll navigate your craft to a successful conclusion.

'Now, if you are leaving tomorrow I do commend an early packing.'

'So soon!'

'Time is pressing – in fact is overbearing in its insistence.'

Chapter 62

Pre-dawn the following day

A fearful icy blast from across the Hungarian plains met them as Cecilia and Hetty scuttled out to a plain imperial carriage. Tibor was waiting and flashed a wide grin as he helped them in, as bundled up as they. He rapped an order to the caped driver, and the coach ground off into the empty streets. Quickly they passed out of the Vienna of high and noble buildings into the Vienna of industry and commerce and, as the city began to stir, into drab grey suburbs, then winter-bleached countryside.

'What are you doing, Tibor?' Cecilia hid her annoyance but it was getting tiresome as every so often he opened a window and looked out.

'I do beg your pardon, lady,' he said apologetically. 'I see behind if there are any who follow.'

With a lurch she realised that more than a few parties would be interested in her departure. And if any had it in mind to move against them, this was the time to do it.

They stretched out to the east in slush and mud in a dull

and wearisome rattle until, after one of his checks, Tibor stiffened. 'A carriage following,' he hissed.

He shouted orders to the driver and drew back in.

After a mile or two they rounded a bend. The coach swerved off the road and, in a sweep around, disappeared behind a large farmhouse. They could just see the road through a gap between two outbuildings, and about twenty minutes later a carriage as plain as theirs sped past, no clue about its origin.

They lingered some minutes, then moved out cautiously and a little further on struck out down a side road to the right. 'On our way to the Alps now,' Tibor declared.

If the pursuing carriage reported back it would say that they'd been lost after having been seen rushing headlong towards the Carpathians, precisely what Tibor wished, and as of this hour they were on their way to the south.

In the distance there was a serrated chain of white-topped peaks, getting ever nearer as they rumbled on. Then, without warning, they came upon an upward incline. The coach bumped and ground over frost-fractured stones as they climbed into the first mountain range. Their passage was along an acute V-shaped valley that wound ever upward, no longer the monotony of the ruler-straight roads of the plains.

Cecilia clutched her warm coverlet against the piercing cold, her gaze held in awed fascination. Fierce, jagged, dark-blotched ranges ahead thrust up from pure sparkling white with, on steep slopes, the black band of an Alpine forest.

On the opposite seat Tibor bounced and swayed. He flashed an engaging smile, which she returned primly, then stared determinedly through her window.

Higher still, the light seemed to change. Now a harsher, brittle brightness, it picked out everything with a pitiless clarity. Then snow began falling gently, and without a sound. Soon they were slowing as the world outside began to transform into one of enfolding softly whirling flakes that blotted out the passing view.

'He knows where to go?' Cecilia asked nervously.

'Perfectly,' Tibor answered, with a laugh. 'He's a Slovenian and wants to get home.'

The snowfall increased and muffled curses came from the driver. Their grinding progress softened to a squeaking as the wheels met the fluffiness of snow.

Later in the afternoon the snow relented, turning to wisps, then disappearing to leave a glistening, pristine landscape cloaked in white, the horses making hard work of the tortuously winding road.

The worst happened. With the road almost impossible to make out under a foot or more of snow, the coach struck an unyielding rock on one side and the wheel gave way in a splintering crash, sending it toppling into the hidden roadside gully. The driver was thrown clear and the ladies found themselves in a terrified tangle inside. Tibor clambered out, and pulled them into a chill snow-flecked wind, leaving them there while he helped the driver subdue the horses.

A quick inspection of the wheel showed there was no hope of repair, and in the silent desolation of the mountains they considered their situation.

'We can't stay here, we'd soon freeze,' Cecilia said, shivering in the bluster and spite of the wind. 'We have to find someone to help.'

'The driver says few are out on the roads at this season and we shouldn't expect anyone to pass by.'

'Then we walk to the next village,' Cecilia told him.

'In those shoes? And what if the snow returns?' There was nothing jovial about Tibor any more and his manner dismayed her.

'Someone must get help.'

'I cannot leave you ladies out here alone.' Tibor reached into the coach, retrieved his sword belt and buckled it on. 'The driver will go – he knows the way and he can ride one of the horses.'

'I-I'm c-cold,' Hetty said, in a small voice.

'You ladies will shelter back in the carriage.'

Cecilia shivered in the crazily tilted vehicle, fears of bears and wolves haunting her, then another: were there high-waymen and footpads in the Alps? And what if the driver cravenly left them there and never came back?

The snow returned. The windows quickly became opaque, then dimmed and darkened. Her worst fear was upon them – that they'd be covered over into another anonymous mound in the snow, never to be found until the thaw. She fought down a growing hysteria. Tibor gallantly remained outside, brushing the snow away as best he could.

After what seemed an unbearably long time, there was a muffled shouting and the whinny of horses, and in the gathering dusk a drab covered cart and the unmistakable figure of a blacksmith and his assistant came into view. Clearly accustomed to being called out for such accidents, he set up and within the hour had fitted a wheel and hauled them out.

In the early evening the weary horses drew into the warm, pungent stable-yard of their accommodation for the night and they could find surcease at last.

It was a charming inn, built of wood, with a steeply gabled roof and a large fire that filled the air with the fragrance of spruce smoke. It was all but empty and the innkeeper fussed about. Over piping hot *glühwein* he was asked for his opinion of the road ahead. Without hesitation he confessed that if it were himself, there was no question, he'd try again, but not for a month.

It was not what they wanted to hear but with so much riding on the mission there was no alternative but to press on in the morning.

The journey continued.

On bright clear days it was sparkling snowscapes, picturesque montane pastures, the distant glitter of a glacier, and once a skittering flock of chamois.

On grey, windswept days it was a trial: the snow came and went with always the threat of snow-drifts and hidden danger.

The most perilous time came when they were passing through a steep snow-sided valley on a deceptively calm, quiet and sun-touched day. Halfway along, the entire slope gently detached and began to slip downwards in a distant low rumble.

With an anxious shout the driver lashed the horses, the coach gathering speed and flying ahead.

'Avalanche!' croaked Tibor, staring at the gathering fury descending on them at an impossible velocity and gripping the leather seat until the white of his knuckles showed.

But with only an occasional thud of outlying clods of frozen snow flung at them, they pulled clear and the frenzied horses could be spared. The coach slowed and stopped and Cecilia looked back, trembling, on the vast, still-shifting mass that had nearly taken their lives.

Several days later the snow cover thinned, turned to slush and then it was gone. They had penetrated through the snow-line and were descending the southern slope towards the sea.

The coach jingled and rattled on joyously, eating up the miles. Then the edge of a limestone massif the colour of bleached bones intruded from the right, and soon after, the road fell away in a steep drop down to Trieste – and the delirious sight of the sea.

They had done it!

The sea was the Adriatic, and somewhere upon it was her brother, to whom she would shortly hand over her vital intelligence.

They were back in the world of houses and shops, churches and fish markets, and all the subtle difference in smells that distinguished a Mediterranean seaport from a northern European. They progressed lower and lower, the road winding and steep until they levelled in the busy town among grand houses and squares.

Cecilia found the precious letter of introduction she'd been given and showed it to Tibor, who relayed the address to the driver. He nodded wearily, and tooled the vehicle through the traffic to the eastern end of the seafront, stopping before a dignified but faded building.

'Your letter, m' lady,' Tibor asked, looking peculiarly excited. 'Do stay within the coach. Trieste is French, these days, not any more Austrian.'

He returned quickly, accompanied by a fussy servant in a state of anxiety. 'You are my lady countess?' he asked in English. 'We didn't expect you, so nothing is prepared. No matter, do come in.' He scuttled back inside.

Cecilia was helped out, her baggage taken by a footman. 'Come along, Hetty, quickly, now. Time is pressing,' she urged, but the girl didn't move, sitting rigid, her face set.

Something was odd, very odd. Cecilia became aware of Tibor standing to one side, wordless and frowning, waiting.

'M' lady, I've something to tell you,' Hetty said, in a small voice.

Cecilia checked her impatience. 'What is it, then, my dear?'

'Er, Tibor and I . . . that is, the centurion and I, well, we want to go to Hungary – together, that is. To live at his estate as man and wife.' She stole a quick glance at Tibor, then dropped her eyes, blushing.

It rocked Cecilia that the homely and unworldly soul from Guildford Town could dream of eloping to a life in the wilds of central Europe, of Bohemia, Transylvania – but she had, and the two had hidden it from her the entire journey.

Recovering a little, she said, 'You must allow me a moment to gather my thoughts.' But, looking at them both, she realised that nothing she could say could alter the inexorable flow of destiny and an impulsive surge of joy took its place.

'I'm very happy for you, Hetty, very happy, although what I'm going to tell your parents I'm sure I don't know.'

'Really? I thought you'd be so angry! And . . . and I'm so sorry I must leave you now, but the coach has to go back.'

'You'll write to me, please?'

'When we're settled in, my lady,' she said happily.

The fussy servant came out to see what was keeping them, and abruptly Cecilia found herself kissing Hetty goodbye and acknowledging a sweeping bow from Tibor. Then they were off, and soon disappeared around the corner.

In a sudden wash of loneliness Cecilia turned and went inside.

It was an old-fashioned merchant house, all dark polished wood with a wide staircase from the working ground floor to the upper levels to which she was diffidently ushered. In a small but tastefully furnished room a large man in well-tailored attire stood, bowing respectfully as she entered.

'My lady,' he greeted, his features expressionless. 'I am your Hans Willendorf.' The name on the letter.

Cecilia drew herself up. 'For reasons that it is not necessary for me to explain, it's my purpose to contact a British ship-of-war at the earliest opportunity.'

'And, from the letter, your friend Hofkanzler Metternich believes me best placed to effect this.'

She tensed, aware that after her epic journey from Vienna she was now quite alone and essentially at his mercy. If he was unable to help, she would be left with nothing – and the fate of half the world in her hands.

She'd been led to believe that Willendorf was a respected merchant, long established, and would therefore know the complexity of sea lanes of the Balkans, but in all the hurry and impatience they hadn't given thought to just how they'd track down a pack of frigates once she'd arrived in far-off Trieste. And it seemed now it was this man – or none.

In a reaction to the stress and anxiety of the past days, a wave of despair and desolation threatened to overcome her. A lump in her throat turned to a sob and she broke into helpless weeping, angry at her weakness in front of him.

Willendorf recoiled in astonishment but recovered quickly. 'My dear lady, forgive me. An expedition over the Alps is not to be undertaken lightly and at this time of the year . . .'

He offered a kerchief and she made a supreme effort to compose herself. 'It is vital, Mr Willendorf, that I find a British man-o'-war, believe me.'

'Yes, I understand. And so you shall.' He broke off to call for a restorative, then added ruefully, 'If you were here only recently you would have had the opportunity when the Sea Devil himself visited us – with all guns blazing, that is.'

She gave a small smile.

'You will be on your own, my lady?' he asked softly.

'As I must,' she answered, with as much spirit as she could.

'That is not to be contemplated,' he replied kindly. 'I shall accompany you.'

'It will not be necessary.'

'No, but nevertheless I shall do so.'

His smile was genuine, and she responded gratefully, 'That is very kind in you, Mr Willendorf.'

'I should make mention for your ears only that the Count Metternich knows me to be a friend to the English through my merchantry. If this business requires an early conclusion we shall leave in the morning – but tonight you shall be our honoured guest, Countess.'

Chapter 63

The fishing boat rounded to the raw north-easterly, its lengthy lateen boom lowering quickly to lie triced to the rails on deck while nets were shot into the cold grey depths. In the stuffy deckhouse Cecilia looked out, queasy but excited.

'To your left is Istria,' Willendorf confided, his large frame looking peculiar under his grubby fisherman's smock. 'And half a day further is Fiume.'

'I see,' she said, taking his word that this was important.

Picking up on her mystification, he added, 'Which is to say we are in a fine position to see the English brig-sloop that regularly passes up the Balkan coast in order, I believe, to collect intelligence from the shore.'

And which would take her to see her brother who, she had learned, was the Sea Devil himself. She hugged herself with anticipation, the hard times of the last days falling away at last.

There was nothing that could be done until it showed and the hours passed slowly until late in the afternoon when the topsails of a brig appeared from the direction of Fiume. It drew closer, and at the wonderful sight of an ensign of the Royal Navy, Cecilia clapped her hands in glee.

Willendorf was not so convinced and watched it carefully. 'I rather fear . . . yes, it's seen us but doesn't care to make our acquaintance . . . Ah, there it goes and it's not coming our way.'

'What's happening?' Cecilia wailed, seeing the shape of the brig foreshortening as it bore away to the south.

'It's not going to Trieste, it's heading back down the Adriatic, probably to its base to report.'

'But it can't!' she burst out, in a frenzy of anxiety. 'Signal it to come back!'

'We haven't such flags, I do regret, my lady.'

'Then – then we must do something!'

She was wearing a white shawl and wrenched it off. 'Hoist this!' she demanded.

With a wry smile Willendorf gave it to a deck-hand to raise. It soared to the top of the stumpy mast, flapping joyfully in the cold breeze.

There was no sign that it had been noticed.

'Jerk it up and down!' she shouted. The deck-hand didn't understand so she thrust him aside and feverishly hauled it down, then back up. Despite the biting cold, this was her last chance so she dipped and raised it, again and again.

And miraculously – wonderfully – it was seen.

The brig backed its foresail and she could see figures bunching on its quarterdeck. She jumped and waved and, caught up in the drama, all aboard did the same until the sloop braced around and made its way to them.

'L'tenant Pearce.' The hailing officer's eyes turned to the remarkable sight of a lady of quality on the deck of a Dalmatian squid boat. 'What do you wish, madam?'

'Cecilia, Countess of Farndon, and I desire to come aboard and speak with you.'

In a very short time it was established that not only did

the lieutenant know of Commodore Kydd but was under his command. 'You are more fortunate than you know, m' lady,' he told her. 'After his base had been betrayed he was obliged to quit the Adriatic. In this, my last duty here, I'm to inform his friends up and down the coast that we will no longer visit these waters.'

'Quit the Adriatic?' she gasped. If he had, then her mission was, at a stroke, rendered useless.

'I believe he has no alternative, m' lady.' Then, quite without realising what he'd said, he added, 'You may ask him yourself – I'm to rendezvous at Lissa with the squadron before they leave.'

Chapter 64

Aboard Tyger, *at anchor, Lissa*

Kydd could see the men ashore piling up the few stores and timber that had survived the French descent, what remained of the victuals and anything else valuable enough to take away with them. Through the salt-encrusted stern windows he could tell by their lackadaisical movements that not only were they downhearted that their successful – and profitable – harrying and prize-chasing was at an end, but that his decision not to seek revenge against the enemy was unpopular.

But the string of captures the squadron had made, even when shared out equally as agreed, translated to a considerable award of prize money – when it eventually made its way through the courts – and Persephone would put it to good use at Knowle Manor. He brightened at the thought: he'd be calling in at Palermo on the way back to the Toulon fleet at Minorca and, over a fine dinner, they'd exchange news and take the utmost pleasure in each other's company.

She would shyly take out the paintings she'd executed while

he was away; they would be good, strong and bold in the Romantic style, reflecting, as nothing else could, her essential character. Then they'd—

'Sir. *Redwing*, coming to rendezvous per your orders.'

He looked up at the duty master's mate. 'Er, thank you. Require the captain to report to me.'

Collecting up the notes that would later become his orders concerning their passage to Minorca, he became aware that, strangely, the ship had fallen quiet.

'Sir – you have a visitor,' the master's mate announced, in an odd voice, stepping aside to allow a figure to enter.

Kydd put down his papers and stood up in shock and confusion.

'Thomas! My dear Thomas!' Cecilia ran to him and threw her arms around him, just one sob escaping her. 'Oh, how I've longed for this moment, you've no idea!'

'Cec! What the devil—'

'So much to tell, Thomas. And I must – right away!' she blurted, falling into an armchair.

As if on cue Tysoe arrived, bearing a hot negus, which she took gratefully.

'You see, Nicholas was sent to Vienna for a very good reason and . . .' It all came out. Metternich. Napoleon's marriage. The shock of the French alliance. Then the final thunderbolt of the plot to march to India dry-shod and its appalling threat to the entire world.

And the only one in a position to stop the tyrant's passage along the Balkan shore was Kydd, who could deny the Adriatic Sea to the French.

'Thank you, Cec. You've made it very clear to me,' Kydd said quietly. 'I need to think on it.'

He handed her over to Tysoe and paced the cabin. There was only one way to secure the Adriatic for the British and deny it to the French – to take on Dubourdieu and win, sweeping him from the seas. Bonaparte would never attempt a march within striking distance of the sea over such a distance and the danger would be past.

But against such odds? He had no qualms about throwing himself at Dubourdieu but if it was at the cost of defeat and failure it would be disastrous for the cause of England in both senses.

Should he seek urgent reinforcement from Sir Sidney Smith? He could imagine the admiral's reaction when asked to contribute forces in response to a flimsy tale brought by a mere woman. Let alone the task of finding him.

There were no others closer than the Toulon blockade and time was against this. That left only the first alternative. He had to put to sea immediately and hunt down Dubourdieu, fighting to a finish, a Nelsonian clash of annihilation.

He had one advantage. He'd been able to acquire valuable intelligence from *Redwing* and others concerning the extent and power of the forces opposing him – the forty-four-gun flagship *Favorite* with *Flore*, *Danae* and *Corona* the same impressive potency, each of which outgunned *Tyger*. And as well there were two more of the same rate and guns as herself. Could he hope to win against these and the *xebecs*, schooners and gunboats accompanying them?

He had to. No matter the odds, he had to.

Finding a sheet of paper he noted a few ideas.

It was unusual to the point of incredible that such a number of frigates would meet in battle together on the open sea, almost like miniature fleets, and the usual conventions didn't apply.

Kydd had to keep his squadron together or the French with their numbers could individually crush them. This sounded very like a fleet in action wielded by one man. Would

Dubourdieu do the same? If they were not in formation but a cloud of individuals, the boot would be on the other foot and Kydd would have a chance at Dubourdieu's destruction, ship by ship.

One thing he kept closest to his heart: when at last they met he would make the man pay for his vile extinguishing of Dillon's life. Whatever it took, he wanted to end the day standing over Dubourdieu's corpse with bloodied sword or, better yet, have him dangling at *Tyger's* fore yardarm.

Still burning with the fire of his resolve he didn't take notice of the muffled low thud of their signal gun at the lookout post. It wasn't until Bowden came down to report that all choices and options narrowed to one. The signal – black balls and a red flag – signified that an enemy fleet had been sighted. He had no need to hunt Dubourdieu down: he was coming to Kydd.

To fight or fly, this was now the only question left. And with the strategic stakes so high, there could be only one answer.

'Tysoe! My sword.'

As soon as he appeared on deck all motion ceased, the chat died away and a dozen pairs of eyes turned to him.

'Sir?' Bowden asked.

'We fight.'

A mighty storm of cheering rose as the news spread, full-throated and joyous, resounding and echoing around the anchorage. The nearby moored frigates needed no explanation and very quickly their rigging was full of men adding their roars to the whole in a ferocious shout of defiance.

The enemy were still hull down, sighted only from the lofty height of the lookouts. Some thirty or forty miles off, they would not be on the scene for five or six hours – plenty of time to prepare.

Chapter 65

Kydd needed some quiet time in his cabin ahead of the last frenetic hour before they joined battle, but when he opened the door his sister was waiting there. She got to her feet, her face set. 'So you're going to stand against the French,' she said, with a lift of her head.

In the intensity of his decision-making Kydd had forgotten about her. To have a lady of quality on board when the ship went into a full-blooded action was impossible: he had to make some kind of provision for her.

'I am, Cec, and I mean you to know that you will be made safe, never fear. You shall be taken ashore well before we sail and—'

'Thomas, I'm not going on the land. I'm staying on this ship with you.'

'Dear sister, you cannot do that.'

'Thomas. Have you not thought about it? A woman left alone on an island for any marauding Frenchman to distress while you're away?'

'I shall provide you with an escort, naturally.'

'Nonsense! And you know it, Thomas. You will need every man, and none to spare in idleness ashore.'

Kydd swore under his breath. She was right, but he had a duty to Renzi to keep her from harm, and *Tyger*, in the next few hours, would be about as hazardous a place as it was possible to be.

She gave a determined smile. 'I can be useful – the doctor will be very busy and I'm sure would welcome another pair of hands.' She saw his look of horror and hurried to add, 'I'm not squeamish, as we might say, and promise not to swoon or anything silly like that.'

The cockpit of a man-o'-war while the guns were blazing was the nearest definition Kydd could conceive to Hell on earth but it had one saving feature: it gave her something valuable to do instead of being banished for hours, unknowing, somewhere in the bowels of the ship. 'If this is what you desire . . .'

'It is,' she said simply.

'Then . . . then I'm rating up a helper for you. A young rapscallion, but willing if given a good steer.' Tomkin and she would be good for each other.

'So. If you'd report to Surgeon Scrope he'll show you the ropes.'

'Aye aye, Captain!' Cecilia said breathlessly, and hurried away.

It would be about the ship in no time that she was going to be aboard for the battle but as women were not officially permitted at sea by the Admiralty, unless particularly applied for, she would not appear in the ship's records as having served.

But now he had to deal with more immediate details, such as how to conduct a fleet consisting of frigates, something he'd never heard of being called for in the face of the enemy. And without a confidential secretary.

The dry and patient ship's clerk was to be relied on in the matter of copying out duplicate orders in a fine round hand but could not cope with petty decisions or awkward phrasing, which meant that Kydd must produce it all himself first. And, needless to say, the clerk had to be kept from secret information in any form, a constant drain on Kydd's time.

He had a routine. List the headers, amplify by paragraphs and get a master's mate to fill in the signal sequences. It varied with the order and—

'Captain? I'm truly sorry to disturb.' Craddock hung at the door, hesitating to enter.

'Oh, do come in,' Kydd said politely. Craddock never intruded if he could help it and obviously had something on his mind.

'Sir, this is by way of the eve of battle,' he said carefully, 'when, as Shakespeare so stirringly portrays it, things are said which a man might remember all his life.'

'Um, I expect you're in the right of it,' Kydd replied, not at all willing to engage in some long philosophical debate, however entertaining.

'This *rencontre* has come before I've had chance to make my farewells to this fine vessel and I find I shall be still within her when she meets her fate.'

'This is not your fight,' Kydd made haste to say. 'Your refuge will be the orlop deck, below the waterline. You need have no fear, sir.'

'On the contrary, it is my fight, sir! Am I not an Englishman? Captain, have you any conception how galling it is to stand back and watch others in mortal striving defend the right?'

'Mr Craddock. We've discussed this before – you're no seaman or gunner. There is no place for you in an action, certainly not of the order of violence we shall shortly see. There is no shame to bear.'

'No position, however humble?' he said, in a pitiable voice.

Kydd flinched, affected despite himself. 'It's not that, sir. You are a merchant of marked success, a gentleman of distinction, whose word commands more men than I can ever claim to. There is nothing here I can offer one of your reputation and, in truth, it has to be said that you should now be returning to a wider world more fitting to one of your undoubted talents. I'm sorry.'

'My talents? Captain, is this why you haven't asked me to follow on in Edward Dillon's footsteps?' Craddock asked incredulously.

'Um, yes.'

'And I believed you didn't ask me because I didn't have the argot of the mariner.'

'Not at all, Mr Craddock. If I wanted a salty sailor I'd have my pick of all aboard. I really needed . . . someone of quality and perspicacity . . . someone like you.'

'Ha! And because you didn't ask me, my conclusion was you didn't want me – so I didn't venture to offer myself for the position. Dear sir, I beg – is it too late to remedy that, do you think?'

Kydd swayed back in delighted astonishment, but needed to be certain of his man. 'Mr Craddock – you are willing to sacrifice your prospects as a merchant and banker ashore for a life at sea with no expectations at all, save a modicum of prize money?'

'Nothing could be more congenial to my soul.'

There was no need to pursue it any further. He and Dillon had been friends and he must have no illusions about what he was entering into.

'Then, Mr Craddock, I'm hereby appointing you to the post as of this hour.'

'Thank you, Captain. I do assure you that you'll never have cause to regret it.'

'Well, now,' Kydd said, unable to repress a wide grin, 'and we have a pile of work before us. Shall we start?'

Chapter 66

The orlop, HMS Tyger

'Surgeon Scrope? I'm told by Captain Kydd to be of what assistance I can to you.' Cecilia was dressed at her plainest, without ornament, her hair tied back. Nevertheless, in the flickering light of several Muscovy lanthorns, the appearance of a refined lady in the dark reek of the lowest deck of all was incongruous.

The surgeon turned to her, securing the last of his smock ties as he took her measure. 'I see.' He was middle-aged, soft-spoken and greying. 'I do thank you for your offer, my lady, but must point out that in a close-fought action this is not the place for a well-bred woman.'

'My brother has told me of it, sir, and that is principally why I'm come to volunteer my services.'

'I have my assistants.' He nodded in the direction of his surgeon's mate and three older seamen in the shadows, loblolly boys, swabbers of blood and feeders of gruel.

'Nevertheless I'm sanguine there is work to be found for a woman wherever there's distress or misery.'

Scrope regarded her for a moment, then said quietly, 'In some hours this space will be a charnel house. I shall be working to my elbows in gore and should you fall unwell no one can attend on you in any wise.'

'Sir, I'm the sister of the captain of a man-o'-war and might be trusted to know my duty. You shall not be inconvenienced.'

He hesitated, then said in a softer tone, 'Your good offices in steadying the men with grave wounds not expected to survive would be appreciated, else they must die alone. Can you do this?'

'I will do it,' she said firmly. 'And any other charge you may lay upon me.'

'Very well, my lady.' He called for another smock and without a word handed it to her. It was made of stout duck-cloth and she couldn't help a shiver of presentiment as she tied it over her dress.

'Croker, do show, er, the good lady about.'

The surgeon's mate, dark-jowled and sinister in the low light laid down what he was doing and looked at her suspiciously.

'While under your direction, Mr Scrope, I should be honoured to be called Miss Cecilia.'

She paid strict attention as he took her in hand for she knew that, once in the fury of battle, there would be no one to direct her to where things were stowed or remind her of the names of surgical instruments.

The operating table was made of a number of sea-chests covered with sailcloth, several lanthorns triced up above it. Close by the head, a chair held an open multi-layered chest of medical apparatus, and on the opposite side, another contained needles, tourniquets and swabs. Further out along the ship's side were racks of bottles, canisters of medicines, as well as casks of water with sponges and cloths. Forward, and discreetly out of sight behind massive vertical beams, were three empty mess-tubs.

The table was not far from the foot of the main hatchway, which led down from the seamen's mess-deck above and the gun-deck above that again. Further forward into a musty gloom was the platform over the hold where she was told the wounded would be laid about the pungent-smelling cable tiers.

Not sure whether to be fearful or reassured, she learned that the main reason for the surgeon setting up in the bowels of the ship was that here they were below the waterline and, while operating, would be spared the danger of a cannon shot bursting in.

She turned back to the monotonous *whit-whit* of the sharpening of instruments and the smell of newly lit lanthorns.

Standing by the hatchway was the remembered figure of the seaman Stirk. Next to him was a wide-eyed youngster, dressed almost as a complete replica.

'M' lady,' he said, awkwardly touching his forelock. 'Y'r mate – that's t' say, y'r assistant. Name o' Tomkin, Tomkin Toughknot.' He cuffed the lad playfully. 'Say an ahoy t' the lady, younker!'

'Miss Cecilia,' she prompted.

'Ahoy, Miss Sisi,' he whispered in awe.

'Now this is going t' be a tough beat to wind'd, young man. I wouldn't blame ye if y' sees enough to make ye pipe the eye, but while ye blubbers don't ever forget t' do y' duty to the lady. Compree, shipmate?'

'Aye, Uncle Toby.'

'And after, I'm comin' down again t' see how y' fares and

if I get a bad report on ye, why, I'll tan y'r hide.' He tousled the lad's hair and left suspiciously quickly.

'Well, Tomkin, and you're to be my, er, assistant's mate. Shall we make tour to see where everything is?'

Chapter 67

Craddock was relishing his new role. Captain Kydd was going to be a fine man to work with. He was quick-thinking, decisive, and had the knack of getting to the root of a problem without delay. Above all, he listened to any reasonable suggestion.

They had cleared the outstanding matters rapidly, and now turned to the task in hand – orders of battle for the Adriatic Squadron. The sailing master was called and Kydd gave his reasoning in terse, professional phrases, which as yet meant little to Craddock. Joyce seemed satisfied and left quickly to pass on to the signals crew to hang out an 'all captains' for the pre-engagement council.

'Just take down all that signifies,' Kydd told Craddock, 'objections, ideas, observations. We'll tidy it up afterwards.'

They went to the ship's side to greet the captains, and it felt strange, almost intimidating, to be part of the naval ritual of coming aboard with the wail of the boatswain's call sounding clear and pure above shipboard noises and barked orders. Kydd, at the head of the side-party, with sword and cocked hat, formally greeted his veteran captains as they came in. When all three were on board Kydd led the way to *Tyger's* great cabin, which Craddock had laid out in accordance with Kydd's instructions.

'Gentlemen. I won't waste time, we have little enough. I will tell you at the outset that this action is of crucial importance to the nation, requiring as it does that we exterminate Dubourdieu and his fleet. I won't hide it from you that we're grievously outnumbered – Mr Craddock, my secretary, will list out what opposes us from our latest intelligence.'

He was ready, paper at hand, feeling a peculiar mixture of nervousness and elation – he was now indisputably a part of the grand panoply of war. He delivered his summary strongly and with conviction and was rewarded with a respectful hearing.

The grave odds didn't need emphasising and Kydd went on immediately to his plan. It was to be a tight line-ahead formation of the kind that had been tested so often in the clash of fleets at sea, a wall of guns that the enemy had to get past to grapple with them and which would allow his squadron to stay together and concentrate its force.

The strategics were simple: the enemy were approaching the harbour entrance from directly downwind before a north-westerly. The Adriatic Squadron would put to sea to meet them, helm over to take up close-hauled on the starboard tack along the northerly coast of Lissa in tight line-ahead formation, its broadside aimed at the enemy squadron as it came for them. How Dubourdieu would deploy in reply to their line-ahead would dictate Kydd's next moves, which would be signalled from *Tyger*, leading the squadron.

And Commodore Kydd would not quit the field of battle until there was a conclusion . . . whatever it was.

Then, apart from the odd question about signal codes and

timings, it was done, and Kydd was seeing them over the side back to their ships.

Craddock stood in awe as the Adriatic Squadron weighed anchor and proceeded to sea. He had seen this before but now it was very different. He was on board *Tyger* by right, a member of her company going out to face the enemy, and therefore he could be called on to do his duty to the very extremity. And he knew he would, if only to join Kydd in a merciless grappling with an enemy that had done them both an incalculable injury.

The squadron slipped out of the harbour and rounded the humped islet that marked its mouth to take up close-hauled. The manoeuvre complete, the ships cleared for action – with the heart-stopping sight of the topsails of the enemy just over-topping the horizon, a cloud of tiny pale shapes making for them with malice in their hearts.

But there was Kydd, watching expressionless from the quarterdeck as the ship boiled with activity, his sword buckled on, his well-worn sea rig comfortable and cocked hat jammed pugnaciously down. The single mind that was controlling, directing, leading, the one whose hands held the destinies of friend and foe, whose very words would mean death to those unknowns whose eyes were on him even now.

Above him men were spread out along a yard, hanking and tying, stretching along extra ropes, some at mysterious work with chains where the yard crossed the mast, while whole teams laid lines along the deck and secured them doubly to massive pulley blocks. The gun captains were at their iron beasts, checking gun-locks, match-tubs and the implements of battle, while others were stretching fearnought screens at the hatchways and still more were, for some obscure reason, hoisting rolled-up hammocks up the mast.

Water casks had been placed amidships, well charged with vinegar. The arms chests were next to them, with the dull gleam of steel from the cutlasses and pistols, cases of neatly stacked paper cartridges to hand.

The activity died away and the ship took on a more deadly, committed air. *Tyger* was ready for the worst the enemy could contrive.

Kydd looked about him, once only at the distant image of enemy sail, and rapped, 'Quarters!'

Instantly a marine drummer at the main hatchway beat a long roll, which had all hands in a rush making for their stations. In the stillness that followed the long roll took on a beaten rhythm – 'Heart of Oak', with its unmistakable stirring thumps that couldn't fail to rouse.

'Quarters at three bells,' Kydd prompted quietly.

Red with embarrassment, Craddock duly made a note, trying to remember to bring several pencils next time as, in his haste, he broke the point and needed to resharpen it.

There was, however, no need for haste: the enemy were miles off to the northward and it was a light breeze carrying them.

'I believe a tot would not go amiss,' Kydd added. 'Make it a double, Mr Bowden.'

Craddock realised what Kydd was about. Not only was a tot a seaman's right before going into battle but he was showing he cared by making it a double, and the time it needed the team of master-at-arms, purser's steward and the officer at quarters to dispense it was going to occupy the men agreeably until they closed with the foe.

He stood by Kydd, who himself did not join them.

A jerking hoist caught his eye: a Union Flag was being raised at every masthead. 'A brave sight!' he said, taken by the wonderfully brazen, almost medieval display.

'Yes,' Kydd replied evenly. 'As they'll be seen above the gun-smoke.' And therefore not mistaken for the enemy.

Craddock reflected that, before the day was out, he'd be learning much more that would fit him for the illustrious post he now occupied.

Chapter 68

The hours passed. Kydd had decided to shorten sail to avoid the appearance of fleeing and now the enemy – Dubourdieu – was nearing. He studied the oncoming armada. Was it staying as a shapeless cloud or would it form up?

Beside him, Craddock paced equably, seemingly unperturbed by the martial displays. If he was able to keep composure in the hours to follow then it was confirmation that he'd chosen his new secretary wisely.

'That's *Favorite*, their flagship,' Brice volunteered, pointing to the left-hand leading vessel. A peek through his pocket glass had revealed a pennant.

As they watched, the French began to form up – and Kydd recognised what was going on. There would be two columns – divisions, one to windward and one to leeward. This was exactly what Nelson had planned at Trafalgar, designed to thrust like a lance into the enemy innards to bring about a mêlée that would see ship against ship in a one-to-one fight to the finish. What Dubourdieu was after was to place his ships alongside those of the enemy and board to take advantage of the immense French superiority in men.

Kydd knew that only the tightness of their formation could save them – and the ability of British seamen, long practised in the arts of maritime war, to respond to his orders on the instant and with skill and daring.

In a surge of pride he recalled the many actions he'd experienced since those unthinkably long-ago days as a young seaman when his sea values and attitudes had formed among the unlettered but straight-talking men, whose being – and those before them – had been shaped by their life before the mast. Now, as a commodore, he was carrying many of the same values into a contest to the finish against the odds. And he craved to reach out to them, to say something of what they were going on to achieve this day, their country and nation looking on – their shared warrior bonds, the exaltation of the moment.

Then he realised he had seen it done before. In the hour before the climactic encounter off Cape Trafalgar – Admiral Nelson, with his immortal signal: 'England expects every man to do his duty!'

'Mr Carew!' he called imperiously.

The signals master's mate hurried up, his face pale and set, ready for any complexity of signals demanded of him.

'Make to all sail.' Kydd's voice was thick with emotion. There was only one signal needed, which would say it all. 'Make . . ."Remember Nelson!"'

In a trice it was hoisted to the mizzen peak, the colourful flags gaily fluttering as they proclaimed to all the world that this tight little squadron was the inheritor of the legacy of the greatest seaman of the age.

Almost immediately, delirious cheers broke out from the ships of the Adriatic Squadron as it stretched out into the open sea, with the enemy now in full view bearing down from windward.

While the cheers redoubled Craddock finished his careful notebook entry, shaking his head in wonder. This was what it was like to be a leader at war, to carry the men forward as you threw them at the enemy horde.

'A ranging shot, if you please.' Kydd's calm order was followed by a pause as the gun captain of the first gun on the starboard side took his time laying it on the first ship of the French windward division, *Favorite*, the flagship.

In the time left to them, the oncoming warships were at their mercy, unable to fire ahead while at the same time Kydd's broadsides faced out to them.

But simple arithmetic told its story too. In this brisk breeze the rate of enemy advance would be more or less seven knots under battle sail, which, from a position at the maximum effective range of the British guns of a mile or so, would be covered in not much more than ten minutes. In that time the French need endure no more than, say, three aimed broadsides and, given the smaller target they offered end on, they would not suffer overmuch.

The gun went off with an iron crash, the smoke carried aft with its characteristic reek, all craning to see the result.

A first plume rose a good several hundred yards short, and to one side, before it skittered on over the cold grey seas.

'We'll give 'em a few more cables,' Kydd ordered. There was no use in throwing away good powder and shot before it could tell.

As they sped on he took in the baleful sight of two divisions of the enemy stretching back in line. He began his battle pace, a slow back and forth over the seventy-odd feet of the quarterdeck to the breast-rail, a pause to look down on the gun-deck and ahead to the shouldered seas creaming away from *Tyger*'s bow, then back towards the group about the conn. With him were Bowden, the first lieutenant, and the sailing master, Joyce, industriously thumping along on his wooden leg, with a midshipman messenger. And Craddock, his secretary, thoughtful and calm by his side.

The gunner's mate appeared up from the gun-deck, bare-footed, in his customary battle gear – a bandanna around his head, striped jersey over duck trousers, and all set off by the barbaric glitter of brass earrings.

'Mr Stirk?' Kydd enquired.

'I'm thinkin' the Frogs have only one thing in their sights. A boardin' – and, with their pack o' poxy mud-rats, they could give us a hard time of it.'

'Yes, I agree.'

Only one going back so far with Kydd as this seaman could expect to discuss tactics with the commodore on his own quarterdeck, but what he had to say was usually a model of practicality.

'An' I've just the medicine for 'em.'

'Which would be?'

'The lobsterbacks. Left it in the hold after they finishes, like. It's one o' they Coehorn howitzers, a nasty little brute. We set it up on the fo'c'sle but not loaded wi' mortar shells but as much canister as we can ram in the beast. Sir.'

The howitzer, more massive by far than their biggest carronade in that part of the ship, would be lethal if well handled. Canister, tightly packed musket balls, would spread out in a deadly hail to mow down massed boarders without pity.

'A grand idea, Mr Stirk. And you'll be the one—'

'I'll take care of it, Mr Kydd, never fear.'

Another *blang* from forward was number-three gun, and this time the first shot strike was well past the forefoot of the big oncoming frigate, if a little off line.

'That'll do,' Kydd said decisively. 'Signal – "engage the enemy".'

As if held back until now, the pent-up anger of the line of British frigates opened up in a blaze of sound and fury.

Battle was now joined and Craddock, flourishing his watch, entered the event in his notebook, deafened by the roar of guns up and down the line. In a way it was intoxicating, the martial thunder that was erupting all about him. But in minutes the enemy would be able to grapple, their guns seeking to end his life – and he had no idea how he would conduct himself.

The cadence of the guns fell away into irregular volleys as individual gun captains took care over their aim before they yanked back on their gun-lock lanyards and the gunfire blended into one long cannonade. The smoke was driven away downwind leaving the enemy in full view and, with taut, straining sails, they made for their prey.

Kydd glanced down the line of his squadron, then at the angle that Dubourdieu's weather division was approaching at and saw where it was headed. It was for *Tyger* – unmistakable as the British flagship with her commodore's pennant at the main and in the lead of the single line. But not directly. *Favorite* was tracking arrow-straight to cut off *Tyger* from her second in line, *Active*, and even as they watched, its fore-deck began crowding with boarders, eagerly brandishing their steel in their lust for close-quarters slaughter. Their howls and jeers came faintly over the water as it loomed close enough to cast a moving shadow.

Kydd observed impassively, his preparations made, but with leaping heart he'd noticed something that seemed to have escaped *Favorite*'s captain. As they themselves cut through the seas, *Active* was tucked in close astern in accordance with his orders. In effect, at speed there was no room for *Favorite* to slice her bowsprit between them without being run down by *Active*. The manoeuvre was going to fail.

Then, as if in realisation, *Favorite*'s jibboom tracked over until it trained on the open space ahead of *Tyger*. It was going to ram bow to bow – to bring their ships into bruising contact to allow their boarders to rush aboard in an unstoppable flood.

A shaft of primeval fear stabbed through Craddock at the awful sight of whole divisions of enemy ships coming on in their resolve to fall on them. Why didn't Kydd set the ship to repel boarders? He dared a glance: Kydd was slowly pacing, a slight frown showing as he seemed to be measuring distances, calculating angles.

And then everything changed. From forward in *Tyger* came a sheeting flash and ear-splitting crack and the fore-deck of *Favorite* was instantly transformed from a screeching, murderous host into a crumpled, beaten-down desolation of corpses. Blood began issuing in runnels down the side of the ship.

Kydd wheeled about and bawled at the signals crew, 'All ships – wear sixteen points!'

Tyger's bow fell off the wind as she obeyed her stout rudder and the squadron wheeled about, taking up on the opposite tack with a surge of speed – but now in precisely the reverse direction, going from first to last ship in line, with *Volage* suddenly in the lead eastwards. Caught in a double confusion, *Favorite* careered on, across what had been *Tyger*'s bow and in the process receiving another brutal hammering from her broadside.

It was masterly. A well-known doctrine taught never to attempt manoeuvres when in contact with enemy, still less put about while under attack but the Adriatic Squadron had done just that to preserve a line-of-battle that the enemy, breaking formation, had still to pierce.

Kydd spared Dubourdieu's flagship but a single glance. It

had passed and in a shambles of torn sail, ragged lines and pandemonium on deck was helplessly drifting before the wind towards the stone-fanged shoreline of Lissa. More to be concerned about was the second in the enemy line, *Flores*, visibly the bigger of the two and, from its rapid reaction to Kydd's move, it had a more intelligent commander.

Taking advantage of its upwind position it surged around until it took up a position on *Tyger*'s leeward quarter, its unused larboard broadside run out – but this was a clever ploy for, revealed behind her, was the third in the enemy line, *Bellone*. Now the two heavier ships had *Tyger* pinioned between them.

The first broadside from *Flores* was brutal and devastating. Unlike the usual French practice of firing into the rigging of an opponent to cripple her, this captain wanted a ship-smashing, man-killing fight.

Tyger suffered. Shot smashed and slammed in with visceral thuds and the sinister whirring of shards and fragments. The boatswain and his men hurried past with a hank of rope and swarmed up into the deathly heights of the fore-rigging to secure a wildly swinging yard.

Sudden groans and screams tore at Craddock's reason. Kydd seemed not to notice so Craddock resolved that neither would he.

They paced together in the hellish chaos, stepping around a writhing body as it was carried below, another sprawled still on the deck beside his shattered gun. Craddock knew *Tyger* was still short-handed, unable to fight both sides of guns together – and in this unequal contest, how long could she survive against one each side?

Chapter 69

The orlop, HMS Tyger

In the gloom there was no sign of the familiar bright outside world. Timber creaks and cracking were magnified by their confinement into a sinister racking that, for ears straining to make out the sounds of battle, were unnerving.

The little group stood together by the light of the operating table, the expressionless face of Scrope giving nothing away as he stropped blades, and Tolley, his mate, aimlessly passed a cloth over the table. For Cecilia, her arm protectively around young Tomkin, it was hard to bear, not knowing what the day would bring and what would be expected of her.

When a muffled thud was accompanied by a shock transmitted through the fabric of the hull she jumped involuntarily.

Tolley looked up in surprise. 'Ours. If you hears a gun and at the same time feels it, that's one of our smashers. If you only feels it, we've taken a hit somewheres.'

Another.

'Ours?'

'Yes, m' lady.'

'We're firing now, Tomkin. Isn't it exciting?' The wide-eyed lad said nothing.

Shortly afterwards there was a flurry of thumps but none she could detect without the deep *blam* of a gun accompanying it.

Tolley gave a pleased smile. 'The owner – beggin' your pardon, the cap'n – he's a right good hand and has seen us off to a good start, the Frenchies taking our shot without a one in return.'

There were more, and even Scrope allowed himself a small smile.

It went on but then, to her consternation, it ceased and she became aware that the deck was now taking on an increasing slope. 'Are we . . . are we . . . ?'

'No, m' lady. We's only turning, doing a manoeuvre. Does a lot o' this when it gets busy.' Tolley was clearly relishing his role as instructor in battles.

Just at that moment the deck levelled and there was an abrupt flurry of thumps and sharper-toned knocks.

'Our turn. Like as not we'll be collecting some customers now I shouldn't wonder.'

All eyes turned to the hatchway. Somewhere up there lay whatever chaos and ordeal *Tyger* was suffering, and pain, misery and death would soon make visitation on them. Cecilia's instinct was to shield Tomkin from the sights coming down the ladderway but realised she couldn't do so for long. Other youngsters, like the powder monkeys, would already have seen worse.

Judging from the pounding on *Tyger*'s hull, they were in the thick of it. A mental picture of the enemy's iron shot slamming in on those neat decks above, to tear limbs, gut and bowels so indiscriminately among her crew, numbed her.

When she heard the first sounds of a casualty arriving she tensed. It was three sailors bearing the writhing body of a fourth, who was piteously whimpering and sobbing. Blood dripped copiously, its ominous dark glittering on the rungs of the ladderway, then pooling at the bottom where they laid him to be inspected by the surgeon. Grotesque jagged black protrusions from his leg caused her gorge to rise.

It took seconds only before Scrope indicated with a gesture for them to place him on the table. Without being told the loblolly boys quickly had a stanchion line on each leg and arm, spread-eagling the unfortunate while his crew-mates looked on, their expression beseeching some kind of pronouncement from the doctor.

'Splinters. Only one side.' He ran his hand down from the neck to the leg, bringing howls of agony. 'Two large, rest small. I'll deal with it now.'

Under the dull gold of the lanthorn light Cecilia watched in horrified fascination as Scrope, with skilful rapid movements, cut the blood-steeped clothing away from the pale skin.

With a muffled gasp Tomkin twisted away, burying his face in her smock, spasmodic movements telling of his distress but bringing a frown from Scrope. She hugged him tightly and soothed his agitation but was herself held by the drama of the moment.

Scrope turned to the three men who'd brought the fourth. 'Get back to where you came from, you shabs. You'll find out how he does before the sun goes down.' They hesitated, then left with several backward glances.

He gave a rough nod to his mate, who took a bottle to a chewed-over black leather pad. A raw odour of rum temporarily overcame the foetid aroma of the orlop as the pad was passed to the surgeon, who eased it into the man's clenched jaw. The stanchion ropes were tightened and Scrope got to work to remove the foot-long splintered shards.

The muffled cries almost undid Cecilia, and then there was a scuffle at the companionway – another casualty. Ominously still, head flopping as he was lowered down on a blanket, he was laid in the same place, straightened with rough kindliness by the two smoke-grimed seamen who'd brought him. Scrope spared a quick glance but carried on with quick, dexterous movements. The two large splinters came out, dark, cavernous wounds where they'd been, the blood staunched by the loblolly boys while he looked carefully at the result. 'Compresses over both, John,' he muttered at Tolley. 'I'll attend to the rest later.'

As the contorting body was cut down and taken moaning to the unlit shadows of the cable tiers, there was a scrabble at the hatchway and a high-pitched scream and gurgle – a youngster was being fought down the steps, his unhinged shrieking wrenching at her sanity.

She forced her way past Scrope, who looked back venomously. 'Waits his turn!' he snapped savagely, and returned his attention to the still form being laid out tenderly on the operating table.

Cecilia ignored him and dropped to her knees beside the boy – it was not hard to see what was causing him such agony. The right side of his face and shoulder was burned horribly, the deep red and purple weal only just beginning to swell and exude matter.

She heroically squeezed back tears as she tore off part of her petticoat and tried to pat dry the wound but it only brought on an uncontrollable screech and demented flailing.

'He – he's only a boy, Mr Scrope. Isn't there something you can do for the mite?' she called out.

Scrope twisted his head and, against the increasing noise and chaos, barked back, 'No! If you can't take it, you're no use to me. Get out now and let me get on with my work!' The lanthorns were being moved closer, the loblollies assisting, and she knew he was beginning another operation. This child would get no help from anyone yet.

The two older seamen who'd brought him still held him down, the grey-haired one openly weeping. 'Powder monkey, eighteen-pounders forrard,' he choked. 'Took a spark fr'm wadding.' A sob, and then, 'Same age as m' own younker . . .' He couldn't continue.

Cecilia reached for calmness, control. Scrope was right – if she was of no use, what was she doing here?

She found a part of the boy's head not hideously touched by the blast of flame and stroked it, softly and gently, on and on, leaning close to murmur soft, motherly things to the pitiful creature. After a while he slowed writhing and, through swollen, puffed-up eyes, sought out the only thing in his universe of pain that made sense.

She wasn't ready for another tiny voice by her elbow. It was Tomkin. He'd crawled under the operating table to reach her, trembling, his face chalk-white and fearful. 'He wan' water, Miss Sisi.'

'Um, what?' Cecilia answered, distracted.

The lad tried to say something, then mimed ferocious barbs buried in the flesh.

'Yes. Well, you know what to do, Tomkin. Take the pannikin and dip it into the water over there and take it to him, but be careful not to spill it, mind. And tell him . . . tell him I'll be with him soon.'

Tomkin's simple loyalty to his ship and those who sailed in her moved her. She would do the same.

Hearing hesitant steps coming down she looked up to see

Halgren, the well-built Swede who, she remembered, was the captain's coxswain, making his way painfully.

'M' lady,' he recognised hoarsely. He was on his own and held his left arm across his chest as though carrying something precious. He looked about, seeing the various bodies, writhing forms, and the tense work on the table and quietly squatted behind the ladder.

Cecilia said nothing for this was the immutable way of the navy – take your turn with the surgeon, which even Nelson with his death-wound was obliged to obey.

Another two came down, placed together, one stifling groans and with a bloody face, the other quiet and composed but with a piteously mangled leg that a marine tried unsuccessfully to straighten.

'Gone. Lost too much blood. Couldn't save him.' Scrope's curt admission at the operating table was wrung out of him, she could see.

Without ceremony, various instruments were removed from the corpse and it was bundled forward to disappear.

Scrope turned without a pause to the burned young lad, and seeing the wound, traced its extent and grunted, 'Linseed dressings. Ceruse sparingly.'

Tolley gave a dismissive wave to the loblollies who dragged the youngster to the ship's side and told him to stay there or be flogged for disobedience to orders. Surprisingly, it worked: the boy held on to reason and settled back as he was treated.

Cecilia left them to it and went to Halgren. 'Is there something the surgeon can do for you?' she asked gently.

Without a word he took his right hand away and exposed his left. It was a pulp of blood and white bone. 'You're next,' she prompted, and helped him to Scrope.

'It's off,' he said, after one look. 'Comminuted, danger of the lockjaw. Now or later?'

'Now,' Halgren calmly answered.

He stood, shaking off the loblollies and took up position on the table, accepting the rum-soaked gag.

Scrope looked at the wound speculatively. 'Ball?'

'At the helm, took a six-pounder.'

'Ah, yes. Well, has to come off.'

He threw over his shoulder to Tolley, 'Saw, knife, catlin, um – forceps, ligatures, the rest.'

Two loblollies took up familiar positions about the body, the third at the left arm.

'Tourniquet on the brachial,' Scrope ordered Tolley.

The skin was drawn tight and a grubby tape wound around the lower arm as a guide. Scrope took a long double-bladed knife from his instrument chest and stood poised as he deliberated.

Halgren, with terrible intensity, turned to Cecilia and held her eyes as a scalpel fell to his lower arm above the mutilated mess that had been his left hand.

It bit and sliced, then flicked up a pale fibrous membrane, which was caught and drawn out of the way for the saw to do its work.

Handed it briskly, immediately Scrope set to, the sound of its cut a travesty of that in wood. Only a few choked mewlings escaped the big man, his eyes still locked on Cecilia's, and in the darkness beyond, the sound of a child's vomiting could be heard.

Quite suddenly the hand fell away lifelessly, landing with a meaty thud in the tub beneath. Halgren's eyes flickered once but never strayed as a flap of skin was folded back neatly over the stump and, with two or three quick sutures, the procedure was complete.

'Done!' Scrope declared, and straightened painfully. 'Anodyne tincture of opium, another tonight. You'll live.'

Halgren was assisted to his feet, swaying with reaction, and Cecilia helped him away.

In the shocked stillness the noises of battle continued without a pause. As did the pitiable groans and sobs of those who had just arrived into the now-crowded space.

'I'll let the captain know you're doing well,' Cecilia told Halgren, finding a blanket and, with Tomkin's help, tenderly wrapping it around him. 'And I'll be back soon to see how you are.'

She looked down on the little waif with inexpressible fondness. 'Come along, then, there's a good boy – we've many more as needs our help.'

Chapter 70

No sooner had *Bellone* taken position to windward of *Tyger* than it began a ferocious all-out pounding with *Flores* to leeward, near fifty guns bellowing out in a hurricane of flashes and towering grey smoke at one British frigate.

His senses numbed by their insane roar and the lethal menace of invisible missiles whipping past, Craddock stayed with Kydd. Now would be the time for *Tyger*'s captain to produce a battle-winning move that would even the odds, but with every ship of his squadron in mortal combat with an enemy there didn't seem to be much that could be done.

Yet minutes after *Bellone* had opened fire Kydd bellowed, 'Hands to set sail! Loose all courses!'

Looks of astonishment met this order, words normally heard when peacefully putting to sea at the outset of a voyage, not in the middle of a desperate fight when every gun was barely manned.

'Sail trimmers aloft!' Joyce followed on, urging those detailed at every gun for sail-handling to dare the storm of shot and take their place along the main yardarm of every mast to cast off the gaskets and shake the canvas free to drop and catch the wind.

All ships closed for battle under topsails, both for manoeuvrability and because a ship under full sail would fly past any opponent and only get away a shot or two from each gun. But Kydd had taken a gamble – and *Tyger* under the impetus of her big driving sails surged ahead, clear of her two tormentors who, confounded, fell away astern.

Kydd hadn't finished. 'Hard a' starb'd!' he rapped, after they'd cleared *Flores'* bow. Slewing across it, they hammered in a raking broadside that caused visible mayhem. His masterstroke followed immediately. With his well-disciplined crew he shivered his courses and took them in, causing *Tyger* to lose way and drop back – now to the leeward side of *Flores* where she was completely shielded from *Bellone*'s fire. From there she set about pounding the hapless Frenchman with every gun that could bear.

The abrupt change of sides to serve guns was more than *Flores* could do, and after the carnage of *Tyger*'s raking broadside, men were seen fleeing the guns.

'Take her in to half-pistol-shot, Mr Joyce.'

The sight of the vengeful British frigate closing to point-blank range was too much for the enemy ship and, with frantic movement on its quarterdeck, the French *tricolore* jerked down. As if this wasn't enough to indicate what was meant, the colours were bundled up, thrown bodily into the sea and all sail struck.

'Sir!' An urgent cry came from Brice pointing astern to where the gun-smoke was dispersing to reveal the headsails of *Bellone* emerging around the stern-quarters of *Flores*, too late to be of any use to her consort but bent on revenge.

In an instant, orders were given that had the big driver sail on the mizzen hauled across to send *Tyger*'s own stern downwind, training her broadside directly at *Bellone*'s bow. When it had fully come into view her guns thundered out an appalling devastation.

Bellone replied with all the venom of a wounded animal and its shots told on *Tyger*.

One heavy ball took a gun squarely, dismounting it and scattering its crew into a mix of writhing bodies and ominously still figures, while another smashed a section of bulwark between two gun-ports. With a sudden bright flare at one gun forward, despairing cries cut through the hoarse thunder of combat. And the grim tally mounted . . .

It was too hot an action to last.

One by one the enemy guns fell silent in *Bellone*, while *Tyger*'s guns delivered their wrath at the bigger frigate unchecked.

And then it was all over.

Bellone's colours came down and all guns fell silent. 'Mr Bowden, take possession,' Kydd repeated, his voice harsh and uneven.

'Aye aye, sir.'

Weary beyond belief, his sea rig smeared smoke-grey, Kydd tried to make sense of the battlefield.

Dubourdieu's windward division, led by *Favorite*, was no more. The flagship in its disorder or panic had careered on past *Tyger* and was hard and fast on the rocks, thin smoke now issuing from it. The remaining two had struck their colours to *Tyger*. The leeward division was scattered in all directions and, as far as he could tell, was being engaged and chased by the rest of his squadron. He had every reason to be hopeful.

Bowden came and stood before him apologetically. 'Sir, I can't do it.'

'Er, what can you not do, Edward?'

'Take possession of *Bellone*, sir.'

'Pray why not, sir?'

'We haven't a boat that will swim, sir. All are shattered.'

'Find anything but get across there before they get up to mischief.'

Bowden left him to consult the boatswain who told him, 'There's aught else, Mr Bowden. Unless y' wants t' take a frigate's capitulation wi' a painting punt? There's our larb'd one under the pinnace . . .'

'Get it out, and I'll need a midshipman and four to man it.'

It was, to say the least, undignified but as he went down the ship's side to board it, *Tyger*'s pock-marked and battered hull was thrust into his vision and he could feel nothing but a dull resentment at what the enemy had done to his gallant ship.

The narrow, flat-bottomed craft only just accommodated the boarding party but he assumed the stern-quarters as if an officer were taking to his boat.

A cry of alarm drew his attention. Suddenly the punt was filling, and quite fast.

'All hands – bale!' He snatched off his cocked hat and furiously started the water over the side in bright sheets, the others following his example.

'Go!' he rasped to the midshipman. 'Harder!'

The lad's 'paddle' was the shattered remains of an oar, which he plied manfully and with four on the baling and the fifth on the paddle the punt crept across in the lee of the frigate to its side-steps.

Even as he mounted, the air was filled with cries and groans and from the scuppers threads of scarlet ran down the ship's side. At the top a dazed officer introduced himself as the first lieutenant and indicated that the captain was lying fatally wounded in his cabin.

Bowden pulled himself together. There were duties to be observed when boarding a captured ship and one was the security of the magazines. The gunner was summoned and confessed that the captain had previously ordered him to hide kegs of powder in the cable tier with fuses and await his order to sink the ship. It had not come.

Bowden then went with the lieutenant down to the dying captain, who lay in stupefying agony from a stomach wound but in his last moments grasped Bowden's hand and held his eyes until the life left him.

Shaken to the core by the encounter, he left through the gun-deck and saw the breath-taking carnage *Tyger*'s gunners had wrought. Corpses piled one on another, smashed and shattered guns, debris, splinters, body parts – it was a charnel house that conveyed no feelings of triumph to him.

When he reached the upper deck he was stopped by the midshipman, who pointed eastward. 'The scurvy shicers!'

It was *Flores*, sailing headlong through the rest of the fighting, on its way to the open sea. 'Sir, the beggars, they've gone and un-surrendered!'

Unbelievably, the capitulated frigate, which had been drifting aimlessly while *Bellone* was being subdued, had seen *Tyger*'s shortage of boats to take possession and had stolen the chance to flee. This was against the traditions and unwritten law of the sea that if a vanquished vessel hauled down its colours it would be spared further cannonading.

'Tell that Frenchy lieutenant to get a boat in the water. I'm not going back in the punt,' he snarled.

The remaining fights had died to one or two pursuits, with *Tyger* in possession of the field.

At that moment, as if in acknowledgement that the battle was lost, the fire in *Favorite* reached her magazine and the ship disappeared in a blast of smoke and flame.

It was over. Commodore Kydd and the Adriatic Squadron had prevailed.

Kydd interrupted work on the fore topsail. 'Stoppers and beckets is all, Mr Herne,' he told the boatswain, who, with his exhausted party, was doing his best to re-reeve lines high in the rigging. 'We've only to make Port St George and we'll then have time for a good job.'

He summoned his first lieutenant. 'Mr Bowden – I'll take a look around the barky, I believe. Do stay within hail.'

In a daze, he began his tour through scenes of ruin and desolation, havoc and wreckage, where an hour or so before men had fought and died under his flag. That they had triumphed was one thing, the cost another – he would find out the butcher's bill soon enough.

Everywhere were the harsh reminders of striving and death: sails scarred, punctured and torn; stranded rope streaming to leeward; bright wounds in shot-struck timber; dark marks of blood-daubed decking. Boats were shattered and drooping on their skid-beams – even the ship's bell had a glittering weal of a bullet-strike across it – and he passed more than one dismounted gun.

Below decks, veiled in half-light and with untidy heaps of debris and gore-splashed fitments, was even bleaker and sadder.

When he reached the after hatchway he hesitated to go further, to whatever awaited in the cockpit.

The discordant sound of cries and groans, the reek of wounds and bile should have warned him, but it was like a physical blow to enter the domain of the surgeon. There, in a lanthorn-flickering hell, was Scrope, with his mate, bent over a heaving bloody hulk on the table, sawing free a mutilated leg. Kydd held still until the last flourish of needle and suture, saw the man taken down and dragged away to one side, where his sister took tender charge of him.

'Cec,' he blurted, making to go to her.

'No, Thomas, I'm much too busy to attend to you,' she said, expertly plying bandage and compress and taking a tow pledget from Tomkin. 'Later.'

He stopped. She was right – her work was more important than his at the moment and instead, when he was free, he turned to the surgeon. 'Mr Scrope, I'd be obliged for a casualty report, if you please.'

'No time, no time, sir. I'll do it when my patients allow.'

Kydd hesitated but knew he would not get a reliable figure if he pressed him, and moved on to the men, who lay thickly about.

A word here, some advice there, always cheerful, respectful by turns. Some he knew well, inwardly weeping at what they'd become. Others were newer to the ship but he did his best to reach out to them all and their hurts.

On deck, matters were now well in hand, and impulsively, he ordered, 'I believe we to be most fortunate this day, Mr Bowden. When we've safely anchored back in Port St George do you clear lower deck and we shall offer up our thanks.'

Over an improvised lectern at the break of the quarterdeck, Kydd watched as the ship's company of *Tyger* massed on the gun-deck below, some with hair blowing in the chill breeze, all with features solemn and earnest as they waited to hear his words.

He kept it brief and to the point: the Good Lord had seen

fit to send them a victory, but it was not Christian to triumph over a vanquished enemy. A well-known hymn, a short prayer, then words to catch the mood – how *Tyger* and her consorts had taken on twice their weight and emerged from battle with not one but two frigate prizes larger than *Tyger*. That this was due to gunners serving their iron beasts with the utmost skill and dedication in the face of brutal enemy ferocity was certain, and their escape from fire from two sides could only have been possible by the daring and prowess of the topmen.

And that His Majesty's arms had once again been victorious was not to be overlooked in the article of celebration. When the boatswain agreed that the ship had been made seaworthy, there would be a double tot to drink the King's health and a good hot supper to follow.

And, given the magnitude of their achievement, the squadron would be leaving the Adriatic to others and departing soon to Malta for temporary repairs and to leave their prizes. *Tyger* would call at Palermo on their way to returning to the commander-in-chief, who might very well be relied on to send *Tyger* home with dispatches, her task done.

Cheers thundered out and were echoed from the other frigates, who'd also given thanks for their deliverance in similar fashion.

Kydd turned to Bowden. 'And get word to our valiant three over there that I'd be honoured to see them at dinner tonight.'

Chapter 71

'So few of us to punish the enemy as we did,' pronounced Whitby of *Cerberus*, as the captains sat down together at Kydd's table. Each was studiously ignoring the disfigurements and blemishes of battle – the cabin spaces had suffered cruelly from *Bellone*'s first broadside.

Kydd murmured something, but his mind was reeling from two pieces of information he'd just received.

One: that his arch foe Dubourdieu and every one of his officers had been killed in the merciless mortar blast at the outset of the battle, the reason why, leaderless, the flagship had gone on to end piled up on the rocks.

Two: he'd received a report from the surgeon, and he now had to face that the cost of the battle for *Tyger* was more than in any engagement he'd ever been in, a fearful price. Among the casualties, his third lieutenant, Maynard, had been taken by a ball early in the action, Teague, the quieter of the three midshipmen, had died under Scrope's knife, and the dry and painstaking ship's clerk, Hambly, had been struck by a fragment of iron from a shattered gun – and there were so many others.

'Sir – you're not, as who should say, joyous at your victory?' Gordon of *Active* asked.

Kydd raised his eyes to the younger man. 'At such a penalty?'

Tysoe and the stewards had distributed wine but the glasses remained untouched.

'I ask you – before us all – to tell of your butcher's bill. *Active*?' Kydd then said sombrely.

'Twenty-eight. Four killed, twenty-four wounded.'

'*Volage*?'

'Forty-six. Thirteen killed, thirty-three wounded.'

'*Cerberus*?'

'Fifty-four. Thirteen killed, forty-one wounded.'

'And *Tyger*, I must tell you, has sixty-two, fifteen killed and forty-seven wounded.' The heaviest toll of all.

'I then ask you, gentlemen, that we raise a glass between ourselves in token of our grievous loss. To the fallen . . .'

To make up numbers, Kydd had invited Bowden and Brice, his two remaining officers, with Joyce, the sailing master, and Craddock who sat by him.

Without prompting, the entire table rose with glass in hand and made the toast, holding wordlessly for a moment before taking their seats again.

The conversation resumed awkwardly until there was a tinkle of a spoon on a glass for attention.

It was Hornby of the tiny *Volage*. 'Gentlemen, I've a boon to ask of you. Do please raise your glasses with mine to Captain Gordon of *Active* to whom I truly declare I owe my life and that of my ship.'

They did as bade, but Gordon held up his hand. 'As it would not be fit to leave it at that, for the true hero sits among us as I will tell.'

It was a thrilling tale. At Kydd's order to wear ship and reverse course, *Tyger* had ceased being lead ship and the previous rear, *Volage*, had assumed the van. With *Tyger* taking the attention of Dubourdieu and the windward division, the French leeward division had turned its whole attention on the little ship, the smallest rate in the entire Royal Navy. Three heavy frigates in furious cannonade on a ship armed only with carronades, useful in close-quarter fighting among equals but sadly wanting to defend against such odds.

Volage had fought furiously but had found her carronades easily outmatched by the long-range carriage guns of her opponents. To try to reach the enemy Hornby had ordered his gunners to double the powder charge. The resulting violent recoil had burst guns and parted breechings until *Volage* was left with only a single six-pounder gun to defend herself. It was then that *Active*, seeing the one-sided match, had clapped on sail to come to her rescue. The French division had then, as one, broken off and fled for the open sea.

There were admiring murmurs of professional appreciation and Kydd reached across with his glass to touch Hornby's. 'As will be heard in wardrooms around the Fleet for an age to come.'

The young man blushed and took refuge in his wine.

In a lull in the talk Craddock stirred and made to speak. His quiet, refined manner commanded respect and they turned to him.

'I'm to be rated as a cove unaccustomed to great sea battles, but I must, I vow, learn why this one is to be accounted much above your usual affray.'

Whitby gave a chuckle. 'Why, our much-honoured commodore did change his mind of avoiding an encounter when he saw them actual topsails over on the horizon.'

'Not so,' Kydd said, with feeling. 'And I can prove it.'

'Sir?'

'One who can give to us the deeper reason for today's moil.'

It stopped conversation and all eyes were on Kydd when he asked Tysoe, 'Please enquire of the countess if she is at leisure to visit us.'

Well into the night, the surgeon would have secured his operating table and was probably fast asleep – but what of Cecilia, hours without counting at her work, looking after Tomkin, the wounded, the dying. What if—

'Captain?'

Cecilia was dressed as she had been in the cockpit, with a hastily snatched shawl covering her stained clothing. Her eyes were sunken pits, her movements slow and considered. But she was his sister and his heart went out to her, the child of his younger days, the one who had advanced so much in society and proved a matchless wife for his closest friend.

'Cec – that is to say, my noble sister, the Countess of Farndon. These gallant officers desire to know if there was any particular reason for we giving a drubbing to Bonaparte's finest, apart from the usual?'

She looked at him dully, then at the silent faces racked with battle fatigue, and knew she must say something. 'Gentlemen, I believe you are owed an explanation,' she said, in a husky, moving voice. 'Concede if you will that this is not for common knowledge and it would particularly disoblige should my presence aboard be made public.'

Understanding nods came from around the table so she carried on and told of the glittering court of Kaiser Franz of Austria, the marriage of his elder daughter to Napoleon Bonaparte and the thunderbolt of the Austrian Alliance, with its strategic complications and betrayal, that had seen a chancellor reduced to helplessness.

In the sturdy naval warmth of the cabin, it all sounded so

like a fairy-tale until she gave the real reason for Dubourdieu to be tasked with extirpating the Sea Devil from the 'French Lake'. Once clear of the hostile presence of the Royal Navy, an army of a quarter-millions would be set a-march around the Balkan shore to erupt on the world and grant Bonaparte his coveted outer empire.

Flying from Vienna over the Alps to Trieste and on still, she had brought her message of urgency and despair to Kydd, who saw the stakes and knew his men would fight the French to a finish.

In a shocked silence she gave a shy smile. 'As it seems, therefore, you should know that, by your actions this day, you must surely be accounted as having delivered the world from the scourge of the tyrant – nothing less.'

The men remained locked in mute astonishment at what had been divulged.

It was broken by Craddock murmuring something to Tysoe, who quickly returned with an old and dusty bottle of uncertain shape. 'A right vintage Haut-Armagnac of my hoarding,' he said brightly, 'as I believe should grace our lips this evening.'

Glasses were charged, and acknowledging first Cecilia, then Kydd, Craddock's outstretched hand swept the gathering from left to right. 'I ask you to make toast,' he declared, in ringing tones. 'To *Tyger* – and Balkan glory!'

Glossary

à sabrage	a technique for opening a champagne bottle with a sabre
Almack's	London high society mixed-sex assembly rooms
Almanach de Gotha	directory of European royalty and higher nobility
Alps	mountain range across the north of Italy that separates southern Europe from the northern
Außenminister	Austrian foreign minister
Austerlitz	decisive battle in 1805 putting Austria out of the war
bights	untidy loops of hanging ropes
bold-to	steep, close to sea, therefore deep water
Bora	hurricane strength northerly wind in the Adriatic
burra peg	big measure (Hindi)
cafone	a rustic, peasant
canard	false rumour
cannon (billiards)	to strike and rebound a ball to score
Carpathians	an arc of mountains extending across eastern Europe
cartel	a ship by agreement on a humanitarian passage able to pass between two belligerents
casa semplice	a simple dwelling
ceruse	white lead ointment used for burns
cobbs	money, coin
Continental System	attempt to reply to the blockade of France and its empire by denying its countries trade relations with Britain
dimber	smart, good-looking
dogwatches	the half watches of two hours each from four to six and six to eight in the evening
Fifth Coalition	between Britain and Austria; ended in battle of Wagram that left Austria subject to a punitive treaty

footpads	robbers on foot
Forralt Bor	a favourite Hungarian mulled wine
Freiherr	baron
furfante	villain, rogue
Full and bye	sailing as close as comfortable to the wind
Geheime Hofkanzlei	secret chancellery within the Court chancellery
Gehenna	where the kings of Judah sacrificed their children by fire
genau richtig	'precisely'
hances	the point along the bulwark where the fife-rail descends
Hofmeister	senior palace servant
Hofkanzler	Chancellor
houri	voluptuous dancing female
humpen	local Viennese term for German beer stein
Il sindaco	head man of a minor village
larbowlines	members of the larboard watch
Magyar	nation and ethnic group of the Hungarians
moschettiere	Italian musketeer
nicht wahr?	'isn't it?'
obstler	Austrian country schnapps
oversway	projection of quarterdeck at its forward end to give slight shelter
palinka	fruit brandy popular in Hungary
petard	small bomb placed against gate or door to make a breach
pfennig	Austrian penny
planksheer	horizontal planking to extend smooth surface over the timber heads
podere	a farm taking paying guests
ponente	a fine westerly breeze
pranzo	mid-day meal
prigger	petty thief
rapscallion	mischievous child
roband	plaited lines that secure the head of the sail to the yard
scunnered	take a dislike to
tare and tret	legal term for overhead or wastage in a transaction
toper	an habitual drinker
tow pledget	twisted blood-staunching fibres of hemp or jute
trabàccolo	common lug-rigged Mediterranean trading vessel
trow	believe, trust
verdammt	damned
Walcheren fever	either typhus or malaria endemic at the mouth of the Scheldt
Werbunkosch	a village dance held to aid in the Hungarian army's recruiting
xebec	three-masted fast vessel, narrow and able to carry much sail

Author's Note

The battle of Lissa was an extraordinary affair: in one sense a rousing naval battle of the old tradition, in another a modern engagement reminiscent of the fierce destroyer flotilla actions of the Second World War. But one thing that characterises it is the extraordinary battle-craft and seamanship of the Royal Navy, displayed here at its highest flowering.

Yet it was more than that. In researching this book I was struck many times by the sheer depth and variety of the elements involved – the continent-spanning intrigues, conspiracies and great unfolding events within which it's set, a striving of empires that left no room for mercy or compromise.

I first entered the story-formation process with the notion that this was a trade war, with Britain desperate to find a way in through the Continental System and Bonaparte determined to keep her out. It was such, but fairly soon I found myself, as well, deep into Sicilian grand betrayals, Machiavellian chancellors, Napoleon's wedding plans and an Alpine traverse.

Sicily is a deeply fascinating island with history on every side. From the still-existing Fountains of Arethusa in Syracuse, which the ancients knew and which Nelson regularly visited to water his fleet, to the vast apartment in Palermo we stayed in with its polished-brass open lifts and wondrous view of the Tyrrhenian Sea towards Stromboli – courtesy one Benito Mussolini.

The grand palaces still exist, and Kathy was able to hoist in a few tips on cooking *panelle*, delicious chick-pea fritters, in noble kitchens at the hand of the Duchess of Palma herself.

Naturally I made a pilgrimage to the seat of the Duke of Bronte, unfortunately closed as a result of some legal dispute. It lies on the inner side of Mount Etna near the pleasant town of Bronte, set in a sea of picturesque vineyards. It was poignant to recall that Nelson himself never once had the joy of striding over his holdings.

At the other end of the island is Messina and the Strait of Scylla and Charybdis. It is startlingly atmospheric, many of the British defensive works still existing including the Telegraph Redoubt and the Heights of Curcuraci, known locally as 'Campo Inglese'.

Further down the coast the immensity of Etna dominates, allowing the curious to be in the same morning baking in south Mediterranean heat and, not much later, throwing snow-balls.

Vienna is as different as it's possible to be but, thankfully, has been largely spared Hitler's century. Virtually all of the Habsburg monuments are intact, the great Hofburg complex as Renzi would have known it, Metternich's chancellery standing handily by the Kaiser's apartments and still in use for its original purpose. I had no difficulty in tracing where Renzi had his adventures and Kathy and I spent happy hours wandering the old walled medieval city.

These walls incidentally were partly demolished by Napoleon in bombardment, but were originally paid for by the English long before in ransom for Richard the Lionheart.

Furthering my location research, I explored the old trade route between Vienna and Trieste over the Alps to solve the conundrum of how a great Central European power could have such nautical connections. In fact Trieste has a surprising number of reminders of its Austrian past, not least of which is its hearty local cuisine.

I found the Adriatic itself a unique place of the sea. Tideless, the Balkan shore has marine ways of life not seen in other parts – the high-stemmed boats, the lateen rig, the huge number of tiny sea-ports.

Some of the sea hazards were a personal eye-opener. Travelling down the coast road we came upon the Margate-esque seaside town of Senj, with some curiously bleached offshore islands in the blue distance. And there we experienced one of nature's more awesome phenomena – the Bora. Under a warm, cloudless sky the wind within minutes mounted in fury, whipping the seas to strange vertical waves, their crests smoking as if drawn upwards by a giant vacuum-cleaner. Our driver told us that it's not unusual for big fish to be sucked out of the sea and thrown inland, and occasionally for vehicles to be carried helplessly into the sea. In 2003 Senj set a wind-speed record of 304 kilometres per hour, and in winter it experiences wind-blown ice-drifts of twenty to thirty feet high. The Admiralty Pilot for the Ionian and Adriatic, not known for its prolixity, goes to some length to warn mariners of these remarkable and intimidating conditions.

Lissa itself is a charming place, the harbour now one big promenade and marina, but relics of the British temporary occupation are still to be seen, as are the forts built after the French had been swept from the seas. The most permanent of these is marked on my chart – at the strategic entrance to the harbour is a small, rounded island where certain midshipmen once set up their lookout post and later a brace of cannon. To this day the Croats call the island Host, after Commodore Hoste, upon whom this book is based.

Murat, who had married Napoleon's sister and was made King of Naples, realised how things were shaping for Bonaparte and deserted him for fear he would lose his throne. Ironically he returned to Napoleon's side at the Hundred Days when he saw how the allies were planning to restore all conquests to their original owners and lost it anyway.

The Sicilian queen, Maria Carolina, who harangued the King from the balconies of his own palace, did not long survive her intrigues. Exiled at British insistence, she was made to return to her birthplace, Vienna, there to die before she saw her Bourbon husband restored to the throne of her beloved Naples.

The colourful Sir Sidney Smith would achieve no further distinction at sea. Eventually he became second-in-command to Pellew off Toulon, consoled with the huge 110-gun *Hibernia* as flagship and there saw out the war.

The Balkans have passed through many hands since Kydd's day, the last as Yugoslavia under Tito, and it has to be said are still recovering. Trieste is no longer Austrian (which once again is completely land-locked), and belongs to the municipality of Venice, a reversion to earlier times when the Doge ruled as a super-power.

The convergence of all these historical threads into a single contest at sea might seem a step too far but several historians have written of how the victory at Lissa robbed Bonaparte of an open road to India, and the world had a devastating sequel. Maddened by frustration, he turned on a friend: he set an army of half a million marching against the Tsar. But they were equipped for the Adriatic, not a Russian winter, and from that point on the end was in sight for Bonaparte. The heroism at Lissa had saved the world.

To all those who assisted in the research for this book, my

deep thanks. My appreciation also goes to my agent, Isobel Dixon; my editor, Oliver Johnson; designer Larry Rostant, for another outstanding cover; and copy editor, Hazel Orme. And, as always, I must acknowledge the role of Kathy, my wife and literary partner, in a collaboration that for nearly twenty years has been bringing Thomas Kydd's great journey from pressed man to admiral to the printed page.

DON'T MISS THE NEXT THOMAS
KYDD ADVENTURE!

THUNDERER

AVAILABLE TO ORDER NOW

HODDER &
STOUGHTON